DOC

DOC

by

Robin Peterson

DIADEM BOOKS

DOC

Published by Diadem Books
An imprint of Spiderwize

For information, please contact:

Diadem Books
Mews Cottage
The Causeway
KENNOWAY
Kingdom of Fife
KY8 5JU
Scotland UK

www.diadembooks.com

ISBN: 978-1-907294-65-5

This book is dedicated to my colleagues and my patients who, over the years, have taught me more than you or I will ever know. And, of course, to Maddy. Thank you. I could not have written it without you.

Alas, have I not pain enough, my friend
Upon whose breast a fiercer gripe doth tire

Sir Philip Sydney

Chapter 1

JOHNNY decided that Monday the 23rd of December 2013 was the day he was going to die. He had been troubled—badly troubled—for a while now and his troubles had multiplied to a point that they were never going to go away. Never. They were going to get worse and worse and the chances of him ever living any sort of a normal life were disappearing.

He stumbled out of the pub. It was just after eleven o'clock at night and a fine cold drizzle was falling slowly from the dark Manchester sky. It was 23rd of December and Christmas for everybody else was just over 24-hours away.

Johnny walked about 50 yards to the junction where Great Western Street came out on to Oxford Road and straightaway he could see a taxi with its orange light switched on heading towards him. He flagged it down.

"Where to mate?" asked the driver.

"Railway Road, please. Just near the crossing."

"Sure mate."

The journey took about five minutes.

"That's five quid please mate," said the taxi driver.

"Here's twenty, my friend," said Johnny. "You can keep the change."

"I can't mate; it's too much."

"Go on. It's nearly Christmas."

"Are you sure?"

"Buy your wife a drink or some chocolates."

"Cheers mate—have a good one."

"And the same to you, my friend."

The taxi pulled away. Johnny looked round. The railway crossing on this suburban street was about a hundred yards away. He knew that there was a train every twenty minutes in each direction till about midnight. That would mean an average wait of about ten minutes. He reckoned that there was about an even chance that in ten or eleven minutes or so his many problems would be over. The pleasures of life had retreated so far into the background of his consciousness that all he could see ahead was disgrace, humiliation and ruin. He had drunk a lot of beer that evening but, at the same time, he was sober enough to realise that his career would end tomorrow. Everything he had worked hard for would come crashing to an end. Everything. He had done the sums and he had worked out that carrying on was not a worthwhile option.

Johnny walked in the direction of the crossing. He could see that the station was just down a short path to the left. At this point the gates came down and the red lights flashed, stopping traffic. On both sides were modern houses built in the nineteen seventies. Inside them people would be watching late night TV, wrapping presents or going to bed. Some of the houses shone bright with Christmas lights.

A train left the station and picked up speed travelling from left to right. As it went over the crossing, Johnny could see that there were about 20 passengers on board. It looked warm and inviting.

The gates went up and Johnny walked towards the track. No one could see him. The next train would, no doubt, be travelling from right to left. He looked down the track to the right. The two lines each divided, making four lines altogether, about twenty yards down the track. He wanted to die out of sight of the road. It would not be fair on people driving or walking past it; it would cause them terrible undeserved distress which would be even worse for them so close to Christmas.

Kind and considerate to the end, Johnny therefore walked about thirty yards down the track. There was just enough light from the streetlights to see that, of the two inbound lines, one was clean and shiny and polished and the other was slightly rusty and not so frequently used.

He checked his watch. The inbound train would be along within eight minutes.

Johnny then did a final calculation. The future problems in his life outweighed the good bits by a ratio of about a hundred to one and there was no chance of it ever getting any better. Ever.

He checked his pockets, simply to remind himself as to what they would find. Wallet containing about eighty pounds; one debit card; two credit cards; one Boots Advantage card; one Tesco club card; West Yorkshire library card; Driver's Licence. Loose change in trouser pocket. Hotel room key in other pocket. Hair a bit damp. Nothing more to check really. Bladder a bit full.

Dr Daniel John Cash, middle-aged family doctor with a previously unblemished record and highly popular with his patients, chose his spot and lay down across the brighter of the two railway lines. It was difficult.

The line was a continuously welded steel rail with a gauge of four feet and eight and a half inches resting on timber sleepers on a crushed stone ballast bed. Johnny got down and lay on his side with his back to the direction the train would come from. One rail made a perfect fit with the right side of his neck; he wished that he had brought a small pillow from the hotel room just for his head. The other rail came just above his ankles. They would find his body in four distinct sections after the train stopped. Two feet (with ankles), one torso with shortened legs attached. Etc.

Vehicles kept driving over the level crossing and he could see three people standing on the inbound platform waiting for the next train. He felt like running over and telling them to phone home to say that they would be late home that night or maybe to club together and get a taxi.

Johnny waited and, at first, nothing happened. Then, all of a sudden, with that feeling that you can only get after a night in the pub, he went from having a comfortable bladder to bursting for a pee in about ten seconds. For a minute he thought that he could hang on as the train would surely be along shortly but after a minute was up, he was so desperate to go that he thought, well fuck it I'd better do what nature intended.

He got up slowly from the railway track, turned his cold and stiff body towards the bushes at the side, lowered his zip and poured forth in the direction of the back garden of a house. Inside there was a lady clearly visible (about seventy) in the kitchen. She reached into a cupboard and removed a large packet of cornflakes followed by a bowl from the next cupboard.

It seemed to take an eternity to empty his bladder. The steam from his warm urine rose and then disappeared into the night air, mingling with the light rain. At last he was finished. Johnny pulled his zip back up, wiped his hands on the wet grass beside the track, dried them on his jacket and, for the second time that night, lay down on the railway line. God, it felt uncomfortable.

He tried to remember if he had any referral letters that he hadn't had time to do after he finished seeing patients the previous evening. He then recalled the first CD he had ever bought ('Brothers in Arms' by Dire Straits, a bit overblown but not bad, to be honest) and the last one he had played ('Red Headed Stranger' by Willie Nelson) and then he recalled the first girl he had ever gone out with (Julie Fletcher, seventeen and gorgeous, when he himself was eighteen) and the last girl (Kate Williams, just as irresistible, and American to boot, but you couldn't really call it going out properly like other people go out and have a lot of sex, because she had been his patient once, with her blood pressure, except of course, for that one night on the rug when it did feel that they were going out properly).

And then it started. You could feel it before you could hear it. The cold hard railway line started to vibrate. At first, it was almost imperceptible but then it became more forceful and then you could hear the low-pitched sound of the train. The red lights flashed and the crossing gates went down. The noise of the train gradually got louder and louder. The line shook more and more and the noise was deafening. Johnny thought that this must surely be what it is like entering hell.

The train got closer and closer and finally Johnny knew that his life would soon be over. For the first time in weeks he actually felt calm and relaxed.

Chapter 2

FAR AND AWAY the biggest part of this story takes place just over ten years into the twenty-first century, in the early part of the second decade, somewhere about the year twenty-twelve. Looking back from then, it was much easier to reflect upon the times when the decades had names like the sixties or the seventies, periods clearly defined in their own distinctive way. In the present time, the decades of the first part of the twenty-first century don't even have a name that people can agree on. Anyway, that's enough about those times for now.

The very first part of this story, however, happens more or less exactly thirty-seven years before the main part; in 1975, or thereabouts. On reflection, when you look back at different periods in your life, you ponder and think and you decide whether you had fond memories of that time or not. For many people they judged it by the quality of the music scene at the time or by the fashions or by whether they were happy with the person they were with or whether they thought the people across the street were having better sex than they were or maybe the fortunes of their football team. For everyone it was different. Maybe not better or worse. Just different.

The 1975 bit of this story revolves around two families, the Cashs and the Bradfords. Later on we will have more families whose lives will be intertwined and whose problems will occupy their every waking hour for months and months. Problems of the most enduring overwhelming sort. Anyway, this part of the story is for later.

The Cashs and the Bradfords lived next door to each other in an ordinary road in an ordinary town, a town called Valley Mills. No one is sure where the town's name came from but maybe some of it came as a consequence of its setting deep in a valley in the hills of Yorkshire, in England. In the springtime and summer the whole place looked fabulous, but in the autumn and winter it had a bit of a sad and grey appearance, with low clouds and endless spells of rain.

The story started something like this. The Bradfords owned a caravan on a static site on Anglesey, a lovely large island off the coast of North Wales. In the summer it is beautiful and one of the nicest places on earth. To the east, across the Menai Strait, are the mountains of Snowdonia. The strait of water itself has two big bridges taking, respectively, the main road and the railway line to Holyhead and to the busy ferry port where ships leave for Dublin sixty miles away across the Irish Sea.

The family in the caravan next to the Bradfords (no one can remember their name after all this time; he did something managing air freight at Manchester airport and she worked in a bank) were decent people and they let it be known to the Bradfords that if they wanted to ask any of their friends to stay when they were not there themselves then all they had to do was ask them to pay for the bottled gas for the cooking stove and to leave the place tidy. The Bradfords were staying a full week in their own caravan and they told the Cashs that they had first refusal on the neighbouring caravan for that week. They were delighted to be asked. The Cash family had a week's holiday lined up and didn't want to spend too much money as they were saving for a newer car than the one they had and they were delighted to have an inexpensive holiday and see the beaches of North Wales. They could just about afford it, and with great thanks, they told the Bradfords that they would arrive on the Sunday and stay till the end of the week.

It was just over one hundred and fifty miles from Valley Mills to Anglesey and in the seventies the drive took the best part of four hours. The road from Yorkshire through Lancashire was slow and winding and the road along North Wales' spectacular coast had yet to be widened. The Cash family, Mum and Dad and five-year-old Johnny set off in their old car just after eleven on the Sunday morning. Johnny had been christened Daniel John but his grandma, long since departed, just adored his namesake country singer and used to tease (in a nice sort of way) her young grandson and say that if he could write songs and sing and play guitar then he might be famous one day, just like her hero, the man in black. So he was Daniel Cash on the school register and Johnny all the rest of the time. He wasn't sure which name he liked the best. The family looked forward, very much, to playing on the beach and paddling in the Irish Sea that July. The weather forecast for the week was for high pressure and warm and sunny days, but with the chance of a shower.

Two hours into the journey provided the first sight of the sea and it looked beautiful.

"Dad, can I go with Joe and play on the magic island one day?" asked Johnny.

Joe was fourteen and he was the Bradford's only son.

"We will see, Johnny," said Dad. "We'll have to ask his Mum and Dad if it's okay with them and then we'll see."

"I hope so, Dad," said Johnny.

The magic island was half a mile off the shore. It wasn't quite an island because for nine hours out of every twelve you could walk to it down the sloping wet beach, then up again to the island. It was about as big as four football pitches and it was hilly and there was an old ruined cottage on it. For ninety minutes either side of high tide you were cut off; the water in the deepest part of the gully gradually became about six feet deep.

"I'm really excited about it!" Johnny exclaimed.

"We'll ask Joe and we'll ask his Mum and Dad and see what they say," said Dad.

"I think that island is really magic," Johnny went on, "and it can be my secret favourite place, with just Joe and me there."

And so the car journey continued. The sun shone and at two thirty they crossed the big bridge over to Anglesey. The road was busy with cars and trucks heading for the ferry to Ireland.

"I can tell which trucks have come from Ireland, Dad," Johnny noted.

"How can you tell, son?"

"They have red number plates, Dad."

"You're a smart little boy, Johnny," said his Mum.

Half an hour later they arrived at the caravan site. The Bradfords were pleased to see them.

"Can we go to the magic island tomorrow, Joe?" asked Johnny.

"I hope so Johnny, but we'll have to check the tides and if it's a nice day then maybe we can go."

Mrs Cash unloaded some groceries from the car. The Bradfords made a cup of tea for the grownups and the two boys drank some lemonade. This was, of course, well before the time when every adult in Britain who wasn't at work or driving a vehicle marked every social interaction by opening a bottle of wine. Times were different then. There wasn't as much money and pubs even closed by law in the afternoon from three until five thirty. Quite how Britain's traditional habit of beer drinking became displaced by wine nobody is quite sure. It just seemed to happen. But this was the time when real men drank beer and, therefore, the two dads planned to walk to the pub in the village to arrive about six o'clock (it was a fifteen minute walk) and stay for two drinks; then both families would have a meal together, cooked, of course, by the two wives. Before that, the families had a joint planning meeting about the magic island. High tide would be at twelve thirty the next day. The two boys would have to walk the ten-minute walk across the beach at ten thirty. They must be on the island before eleven o'clock, and they could not leave before two o'clock. For three hours they had to stay put and they could not make contact with anyone. Joe Bradford had a wristwatch and was a bright boy and, at fourteen, he understood all of this. He would delight in showing his little friend all the secret places on this little island. There would probably be no one else there. They would take some sandwiches and a bottle of lemonade. Joe knew every inch of the island from previous holidays there. Everything was planned and every eventuality was catered for, or so they thought.

The two dads went off to the pub for an hour and, on walking back to the caravan site, thought that the world had never looked as beautiful as it did that summer's evening.

Monday morning the sun shone after breakfast and the plans for the island trip were gone over again. The parents would stay on the beach nearest to the little island. The two boys would walk across the sands at ten thirty and would leave the island at two o'clock and be safely back on the beach at two fifteen.

"Is the magic island really magic, Joe?" asked Johnny.

"It's the most magical place in the world," replied Joe. "There are secret places where people say that pirates once buried some treasure, and there's an old cottage where an old sea captain used to live, and there's a dog that no one alive has ever seen."

"How do you know?" asked Johnny.

"Well, I'll tell you what it does. It swims across at night and finds houses where bad people live and it sits outside their houses and barks. Then, if the bad person wakes up and looks out of the window and sees the dog, then their heart just stops beating."

"What happens then, Joe?"

"Well, if your heart stops beating then, well, that's the end of you."

"Will we see the dog, Joe?"

"No, it sleeps all day in a special hiding place and no one can find it. That's why no one has ever stayed on the island at night, Johnny."

"What would happen if we stayed on the island at night, Joe?" said Johnny.

"I don't think we'll try it, my little friend," said Joe.

And so, full of excitement, just after ten thirty that Monday morning, with a bag containing cheese sandwiches and a big bottle of lemonade, fourteen-year-old Joe and five-year-old Johnny set off across the sands. Their parents watched them go and the sea was still safely away on the other side of the island.

"Don't forget boys," said Joe's dad, "you walk straight to the island and you don't talk to any strangers and you stay till exactly two o'clock. Is that clear?"

"Sure is, Mr Bradford," said Johnny.

"Have a good time boys."

And so the boys walked the ten-minute walk across the sands to the rocky and grassy outcrop that would soon become an island. A few minutes later, the water started, slowly at first but then more quickly, to encircle it. The two boys were alone in their own magical world.

Chapter 3

"I LOVE the magic island," said Johnny. "Is it really magic?"
"I'll show you Johnny," said Joe.

They walked round the perimeter of the island and then played hide and seek amongst the low hills. You could just see the beach where both sets of parents were sitting but it was too far away to identify who was who. There seemed to be about twenty people on the beach, identifiable as tiny dots in the distance. There was no one else on the island. In the next half hour while they were playing, a big thunderhead cloud grew in the heat and then the sky turned dark and a breeze started up. It was eleven thirty and high tide was in an hour. The water looked deep on all sides.

"Johnny, shall we have a sandwich?" asked Joe.

"I'm okay, Joe. I'm not hungry and my tummy hurts."

"Are you sure, Johnny?"

"Yeah, Joe, my tummy is really sore," said Johnny.

They sat next to the ruined cottage and Joe ate his sandwich. The sky got darker.

Five minutes later Johnny said, "My tummy is so sore, Joe, and I want to go back to the beach to see Mum and Dad." He started crying and looked pale.

"I'll look after you Johnny and we'll be able to go back as soon as the water goes down," said Joe.

"Okay, Joe. Thank you. I know that you are my friend."

"I will always be your friend, Johnny. You know that!"

"You're great, Joe."

"Shall we go and look at the lighthouse?"

"That'll be great, Joe," said Johnny.

They tried to walk the 100 yards to the lighthouse but halfway there Johnny collapsed and fell to the ground.

"What's the matter, Johnny?" said Joe, looking worried.

"It's the pain, Joe. I can't move with it."

"Do you think you can wait an hour, Johnny? Then I'll get you back to the beach and see what your Mum and Dad say."

Johnny burst into tears again. "I can't wait that long, Joe. The pain is so bad. I want my Mum and Dad."

Joe looked at his wristwatch. It was half an hour before high tide. If they set off straightaway, then they could hopefully make it back. The water could be about four feet deep and the currents around the island were not very strong. He could carry Johnny if the water was too deep. If they didn't set off now there would be no way they could make it for over an hour. It was now or never, more or less.

"Okay, Johnny. We're gonna set off now. We'll walk through the water and if it gets too deep then I'll carry you."

"Thank you, Joe."

Joe knew that this would be a risky venture but that if they didn't set off now then Johnny could be really, really ill.

And so they set off paddling through the cool water towards the beach. The sky got darker and it started to rain. After about 100 yards, the water came above Joe's knees and at this point young Johnny collapsed into the water. Joe was still holding his hand.

"I can't go on, Joe," said Johnny.

"I'll carry you then, Johnny. I'll get you back to safety and back to your Mum and Dad."

So, at this point Joe cradled Johnny in his arms and carried him through the ever-deepening water. After another minute it was up to Joe's chest and he had to lift Johnny higher. Joe's legs and arms were tiring rapidly.

"How's the pain, Johnny?" asked Joe again.

"It's bad, Joe. It's really bad."

"Okay, Johnny. Another five minutes and we'll be back at the beach."

It looked a long way away. They pressed on through the cold water and the rain. The figures on the beach had all disappeared. Another minute passed and the water was up to Joe's neck. It crossed his mind that he might have to swim and pull Johnny behind him.

"Joe, will it get any deeper? Thank you for carrying me, Joe."

"Anytime, Johnny. You are my friend and I will do anything for you. Anything Johnny. You know that."

"Thank you, Joe. You are great. Thank you, Joe."

The beach looked a bit closer and the rain shower stopped and people started returning from their cars in the car park back to the beach. Joe could feel that the seabed was starting, ever so gently, to slope upwards. The water level started to go down and a minute later it was down to his waist.

"Do you think you can walk now, Johnny?"

"I don't think so, Joe. My tummy is too sore."

"Okay, Johnny, I'll keep carrying you. Don't you worry, Johnny."

Joe felt that he was on the point of collapse but nonetheless he kept going.

"We'll be there in a couple of minutes, Johnny," said Joe.

They were three quarters of the way back. All of a sudden Joe could see the two dads running into the water towards them. Both mums were standing on the beach at the water's edge. A minute later they met up.

"What's happened, Joe?" asked Johnny's dad.

"I don't know, Mr Cash. Johnny started with a pain in his tummy when we got to the island. Then it got worse and worse and he couldn't walk so I've had to carry him back, lifting him all the way over the water."

"Thank you Joe, you're a good lad. You know that."

"Anytime Mr Cash. Anytime."

"How's your tummy now, Johnny?" his Dad asked.

"It's really sore, Dad. It's really sore. Joe saved my life Dad. He really did, Dad, he saved my life." He cried more and more.

"Joe, we can't thank you enough. Honestly."

A minute later they were back on the beach. The two dads and the two lads were soaking wet and both lads were cold. Both mums gathered round.

"What's happened?" his Mum asked.

"Johnny got a pain in his tummy as soon as they got to the island. Joe's been terrific with him. Thank you again, Joe," Johnny's dad said.

Johnny lay on the beach and the other five huddled round him. He looked very unwell. He was pale. The pain was bad. They looked at him for a minute.

"I think we'll take you to the hospital, Johnny, and we'll find a nice nurse and a nice doctor to make your tummy better," said Johnny's dad.

And so they set off, three of them in each car, for the half hour drive which took them back over the big bridge over the beautiful Menai Strait. They found the hospital in Bangor and went into the Emergency Room. There were a handful of people sitting on the seats in the waiting area but no one else was waiting at the reception desk. The nice lady looked up and asked a couple of questions.

"We've got a little boy with a bad pain in his tummy," Johnny's mum answered. "He's five and he's called Daniel John Cash."

"He doesn't look well. I'll get the doctor to see him soon. Just have a seat."

"Thank you," Johnny's dad said.

And so the six of them sat in the waiting area. Johnny looked worse. Five minutes later they were called through. A friendly nurse and doctor said to Johnny:

"Let's pop you on to this bed, Johnny, and then we can make your poorly tummy better."

They asked a couple of questions and then asked Johnny to show them where the pain was. He pointed to his lower abdomen on the right.

"I'm going to ask the on-call surgeon to come and see him, Mr Cash."

"What do you think it could be, Doctor?" asked Mr Cash.

"I'm not totally sure because tummy pains in children can be complicated, but he might have appendicitis. I think we need an expert in the field."

"Thank you, Doctor," Johnny's dad said.

"He should be with you in a few minutes."

"Thank you, again."

"You're welcome. Are you on holiday here?"

"Yes Doctor. On Anglesey."

"You've picked a beautiful place, Mr Cash."

And so, about ten minutes later, the surgeon-on-call, Dr Mohamed Khan, appeared. He looked reassuringly capable and had a natural friendly manner.

"Where are you from, Johnny?" he asked.

"I'm from Valley Mills in England, Sir. Where are you from, Sir?"

"I'm from a long way away from here, Johnny. A long way away. Now where is your pain, Johnny?"

Dr Khan asked a few more questions directed at both Johnny and at his mum and dad. He then asked Johnny if he could press gently on his tummy asking Johnny how it felt. He then listened to Johnny's tummy with his stethoscope, listening for intestinal movements (there were none: it was silent) and he inspected Johnny's tongue and counted his pulse rate at his wrist. Johnny looked poorly.

Dr Khan asked Johnny's dad to pop out from the cubicle.

"What do you think it could be, Doctor?" asked Mr Cash.

"One can never be totally certain but I'm ninety per cent sure that Johnny has a burst appendix."

Johnny's dad started to look pale himself.

"If you are in agreement then we'll take Johnny to theatre in the next hour or so and then we'll be able to tell you more later on."

"Thank you, Doctor. We are very grateful."

"Anytime, Mr Cash. Let's go and have a word with the others."

They went back inside the cubicle. Johnny looked worse. The pain was awful.

"Johnny, you are going to be all right but we need to have a closer look at your tummy."

Johnny nodded with difficulty. Dr Khan explained to Mr and Mrs Cash that Johnny would maybe be in the operating theatre for an hour and then, if it was a burst appendix, he would have to stay in hospital for a few days.

"I will have a word with you later," said Dr Khan.

And so, with the consent form signed, and the reassurance that Johnny had not eaten anything since eight o'clock that morning, Johnny was wheeled away for his operation. His parents, and the Bradford family, went for a cup of tea in the hospital cafeteria and then waited in the waiting area on the surgical ward. Ninety minutes later, Dr Khan reappeared dressed in theatre scrubs.

"Johnny's appendix was black and it was leaking pus and it was on the point of bursting. Everything else looked okay. If you're staying in Wales till next Saturday then I think that Johnny is likely to have to stay here till at least Friday. Sorry about that. But he should have no long term consequences from his illness."

"Dr Khan, we are so grateful to you," said Johnny's mum. "We can't thank you enough."

"It's what we are here for, Mrs Cash."

He smiled and patted her reassuringly on the shoulder and then he was gone, back into theatre, to deal with the next emergency patient.

The next day, Tuesday, Johnny felt frail but he looked a little better. An IV drip was running into his left arm. Wednesday he started eating and drinking and the drip was removed from his arm. Thursday he looked better again. The nurses continued to make a fuss of him and he asked Sister Jones if she knew whether or not Dr Khan ever ate any chocolate.

"I think he might do, Johnny."

And so when Dr Khan visited later and told Johnny that he could leave hospital on Friday, Johnny asked his dad if he could give Dr Khan a ten pence piece so that he could buy some chocolate.

"Sister Jones says that you like chocolate, Dr Khan," said Johnny smiling.

"I do, Johnny. Thank you so much."

Johnny got dressed in a slow and laborious way as his tummy was still a bit sore. Walking was a bit different for the same reason, but the whole world could see that he was getting better.

The following day they made the four-hours drive back to Valley Mills in a short convoy of two cars. Johnny felt every bump in the road. A couple of hours after getting home the Bradfords called round to see their neighbours and to see how Johnny was feeling. He was sitting quietly watching 'Doctor Who' on the TV. It was Saturday teatime.

"I'm feeling better, thank you. Two people saved my life, you Joe and Dr Khan."

The other five left him watching 'Doctor Who' quietly and had a chat in the kitchen.

"Joe, what can we say to you? You were great. Just great," said Mrs Cash.

"I was worried, Mrs Cash, I was really worried. I thought should we wait till the tide goes down or leave the island there and then. And then Johnny looked so much worse so we had to get going. The water was pretty cold and I thought, at one point, that we'd have to swim and me sort of pull Johnny behind me. But the water never went deeper than just under my chin. Then I thought that my legs and my arms carrying Johnny couldn't keep going, but I knew that I just had to do it. And then it felt that someone was helping us. It was all a bit scary till that point."

"Joe, we can't say any more than we've said already. Thank you. I know it's your birthday next week, Joe, and we know that you like records, Joe, and we just want to get you one—just as a small way of saying thank you. Who do you like best, Joe?"

"I like the Bay City Rollers, Mr Cash."

"Okay Joe."

On the Tuesday, Johnny went to his own Health Centre and the nurse removed his stitches and by the following week he was back to normal. On the Saturday, the Cash family went shopping and bought the latest Bay City Rollers album for Joe. And then a sort of calm descended on the town of Valley Mills. After near drownings and near burst appendixes things settled down to relative normality. People kept being born and other people kept dying and summer went and winter came and it rained and rained. It was a typical north of England town.

Chapter 4

MARKET RESEARCH organisations and various statisticians loved Valley Mills precisely because, as towns go, it was so ordinary. What Valley Mills did then, so did much of the U.K. If there ever was such a thing it was a microcosm of English life.

A researcher for the British TV station Chanel 55 commissioned a survey of the lifetime habits of the people of Valley Mills. They concluded that, over a lifetime, the residents of the town did the following: in their two and a half billion seconds on earth Valley Mills people took 7,237 baths; drank 72,197 cups of tea; ate 1,188 chickens; 10,217 bars of chocolate; drank 10,727 pints of beer; 1,482 bottles of wine and went on 59 vacations. They had sex, on average, 4318 times with eight different partners. The researchers had to point out that the 4318 was a total lifetime score, not the total per partner. It wasn't *that* good! The number of sexual partners per resident ranged from 0 to 285. For the vast majority, however, the number was in single figures but often nearer the top end of the single figure range. Seven or eight seemed to be a very frequent answer.

Another way of doing surveys is, instead of counting how many times people do certain activities in their lifetime, to ask them what they are doing at a particular moment chosen by the researcher's computer at random. This gives you a fairly clear snapshot of a typical day.

The North of England Development Guild attempted to do this as part of an effort to plan leisure facilities. They sent a form to every household in Valley Mills and got a 53% response rate. The age range of the respondents was 14-96. The replies were predictable and included the following: working overtime; attending high school; micro-waving a pizza; ironing clothes; looking at websites on the internet (nature of websites not specified); tiling the bathroom; changing car engine oil (on domestic premises); feeding a baby; watching sports on TV; participating in a pub quiz; mowing the lawn; visiting a funeral director (whilst alive); visiting a religious establishment; downloading tracks onto an MP3 player; reporting a lost or stolen MP3 player to household insurance company; complaining about the food in a restaurant, and sending a text message to a friend. No one in this survey admitted to any intimacy; then the researcher for the Guild realised that she had forgotten to include it in the list of possible activities. She then recalled that someone once admitted that it has been estimated that 18.95733% of official government statistics could possibly be inaccurate.

Valley Mills has a population of 17,186 people, slightly higher from Easter to Christmas and slightly lower from Christmas to Easter. People tended to be born evenly throughout the year (192 births) and to die in larger numbers in winter (190 deaths). Just a couple more bits about the town and then we'll get back to the story. It's a busy place with two main shopping streets which include Boots, WH Smith, a travel agency, a shop which repairs shoes and cuts keys, four banks, a market on a Wednesday and a Saturday, a grocery superstore with its own parking lot half a mile out of town, nine eating establishments and twelve pubs. It is located in a deep valley with both main roads and railways linking the town to the county of Lancashire to the west, and the towns of Rochdale to the south and Halifax and Leeds to the east. People are always coming and going and it is only ever quiet between midnight and six in the morning. None of the roads or railway lines were ever straight for more than 200 yards because of the terrain.

The town started to grow with the arrival of the Lancashire and Yorkshire Railway in 1841. Notable past residents included Diggory Arkwright, the uncle of the Minister for Telecommunication Development in Harold Wilson's government (born in 1899) and Gregory Taylor (born in 1945), the keyboard player in the late 1960s prog rock band Aldebaran. The town was thought to be the setting of the fictional romance novel *Beauty of the Valley* written in 1962 by the best selling local author, Joan Clegg.

The good people of Valley Mills speak with a variant of the Yorkshire dialect studied by linguists from Boston to Yokohama. The word 'the' is often shortened by townspeople to 't' and in one or two older residents, the word disappears altogether. Its intended use can be inferred from a brief pause in the conversation which goes something like this: "Harry, are you going to… quiz tonight?" You get the picture?

Anyway, that is enough about the town. The real purpose of this short chapter is to update you about what happened to Johnny and to Joe.

Johnny did well at school and, one night when he was lying in bed at the age of fourteen before drifting off to sleep, he recalled clearly how he owed his life to two separate people, people whose paths crossed only for a few minutes. There was Joe, who carried him to safety from the island (without him this book could not have been written) and there was Dr Khan, who accurately diagnosed and removed his nearly burst appendix. He had two chances of dying that day in 1975, from drowning and from illness and he was grateful that he avoided both of them, entirely due to the kindness, strength and extreme skill of others. He could not forget it. So he decided after a bit of thought that he wanted to apply to go to medical school and train to be a doctor. He fancied the intellectual challenge and reckoned he was up to it and he thought from watching TV medical dramas that if you could cut the mustard then at the end of a seventy-hour week there would be girls and, maybe even, a sports car. And so he focused himself and at the age of eighteen, in 1988, he started at university. He worked hard (very hard, in fact) and, in 1993, he qualified as a doctor. Whilst doing a surgical rotation at Brampton District Hospital in 1995, he fell madly in love with Sarah Tweedale, one of the operating theatre nurses. She was gorgeous, intelligent and amusing; he felt at times that she was out of his class a bit. Her dad was a barrister and his dad was a manager on the Railway. They married in 1997. Things were perfect for a year but then she fell in love with Rodney Chamberlain, the senior neuro surgeon at the hospital. In 2000, Johnny and Sarah divorced. There were no children. After a year, she cut her hours of work to two days a week and on a whim one day, traded in her three-year-old Volkswagen Golf GTI for a one-year-old Range Rover Sport. It had previously been bought for fifty-five thousand pounds (new) by a charmer and fantasist to impress his girlfriend. He could not keep up the payments and so the bank employed an agency to repossess the car on their behalf. The agency sold the car to the local dealership. Sarah smiled at the salesman and got the price down from forty thousand five hundred pounds to thirty-six nine fifty. She wrote a cheque for two thousand pounds and got seven for her Golf GTI on the trade in, whilst borrowing £27,950 from the same bank that lent the original loan to the charmer. Most parties were reasonably content with the arrangement with the possible slight exception of Rodney. Sarah was ecstatic. Later that month they did it once (but only once) on the back seat in a lay-by off a country lane one night on the way home from a dinner party. It was one o'clock on a Sunday morning. Rodney had been on call for neuro surgical emergencies at the Hospital and had drunk mineral water all evening. They were somewhere between twenty-five per cent and ninety per cent of the way through having sex (despite being a doctor he found it very difficult to decide when the halfway point had been reached) when his pager went off.

Johnny worked hard and then trained for another three years to become a GP. A vacancy in a nice practice in a Health Centre came up in his hometown. The post attracted thirty-two applicants. Johnny's CV was impressive and he was shortlisted. At the interview, he displayed intelligence, stamina, warmth, good humour, a love of the job, and Northern common sense and decency; after fifteen minutes deliberation, he was offered the job. And so, in 1998, he moved one hundred and ten miles back to his hometown and, full of hope, excitement and trepidation, started work amongst the people he had grown up with. He remembered some of them from years earlier.

Now let's find out what happened to Joe.

Joe Bradford stayed put in the town where he was born. He got a job in Halfords' and became a local legend with his knowledge of auto parts and accessories. He did some taxi driving on a Friday night (a private hire company where you drove your own car and made an arrangement about splitting the takings). He enjoyed driving. In his mid-twenties he trained as a truck driver and got a job driving for Taylors (Halifax) Ltd. He drove fifty-thousand miles a year and after a couple of years, he knew every main road in England and some in Wales and Scotland also. He became one of their most popular drivers because he was always punctual, never sick, never got lost, and never got a speeding ticket. Taylors loved him! In 1988, the day before his twenty-seventh birthday, he was shopping in Robinson's superstore on the edge of town. His mum and dad were away and he planned to have about a dozen lads and girls back home after the pub closed on the Saturday evening. He reckoned that about forty-eight cans of beer would be sufficient (four for each of them—they would have four or five in the pub first and mum and dad weren't back till Monday so he had Sunday to tidy up). He bought twenty-four lagers and twenty-four bitter (half Tetley's and half Yorkshire Devil Olde Fashioned Ale) and they presented twenty quid to the beautiful young woman on the checkout. Whilst fumbling with his change and the receipt, he put too many cans of lager in one of the carrier bags and whilst transferring it to the trolley one of the handles split and twelve cans of Norseman Norwegian lager rolled all over the shop. On four of the tins, the plastic strip holding them together tore completely and one of the cans rolled about twenty yards. An old lady walking past with her basket tripped over it. By the time her husband caught her, her feet were about six inches above the ground and she, momentarily, was at a very funny angle. She was rescued by her husband and miraculously landed the correct way round on her feet. Joe ran over to help and then he, himself, fell over a can of Norseman and he went flying. The beautiful young woman on the checkout ran out to help.

When all the excitement had died down and after the briefest conversation with Joe, she established that the 24 lager and 24 bitter were for a party he was having at his mum and dad's after the pub closed the following evening. They would be in the Railway (pub) first. He would be delighted if she came and she would feel welcome and safe; there would be other girls present.

And so Joe had his first date with Jenny McBride. He had been anxious all day on the Saturday wondering if she would turn up. She arrived at the Railway exactly at nine o'clock with her friend Rosemary.

Joe and Jenny got on just fine. The party back at the house went on till about half past one and Joe got one of his taxi colleagues to take her home safely. They met again the following Saturday. The following year, Joe Bradford and Jenny McBride got married and they settled in Valley Mills.

Over the next three and a half years they bore two children. In 2005, Joe's dad passed away and they moved in with his mum, back to the house in which he had been born in 1961. Two years later, Joe's mum fell and fractured her femur. She had it pinned in hospital but contracted pneumonia and died seven days later. There were now just four of them in the house. Joe became depot manager at Taylor's, in charge of twenty-eight wagons and Jenny worked three days a week at Robinson's.

Johnny enjoyed the single life and seemed to spend every waking hour either working or studying to keep up to date, or, a couple of evenings a week, in the pub.

Joe (and Jenny) and Johnny lived less than a mile apart. Their paths seldom crossed; however, one evening in 2007 at a James Taylor concert in Manchester, Johnny and his girlfriend took their seats in the Arena. Two seats immediately in front were empty. A minute later Joe and Jenny Bradford arrived. The concert was excellent. 'You've Got a Friend' was well applauded and, Johnny thought, very apt. Joe and Johnny agreed to meet in the Railway the following Friday at eight thirty. They had a pleasant evening. Whilst they were drinking their fourth pint Johnny became emotional and reminded Joe that he was one of the two people he could thank for his being able to come to the pub that evening. He was very, very grateful to his old friend.

In Valley Mills the years rolled by. Joe and Johnny bumped into each other now and again and they liked each other and enjoyed each other's company. Their lives would continue in a busy but unremarkable way until events would overtake both of them five years later—different events, but events which would devastate both men. The year 2012 would affect both Joe and Johnny profoundly.

Chapter 5

JOHNNY felt rough. It was half past six on a Friday morning and, to make matters worse, it was midwinter—February, in fact. The only consolation is that February is slightly better than January. It's not as dark and spring feels a little closer. January 2012 had been terrible at work. Twelve hours in a day was not long enough to get the work done. As January rolled into February, it was a miserable time.

Johnny opened his bedroom curtains a little. It was dark outside and it was raining. It was an all embracing darkness and wetness and it looked as though it would take over the whole world. He hoped he could avoid the epidemic of winter gloominess and hang on in there until Spring arrived.

Being a GP in the UK's National Health Service was emotionally rewarding for doctors with intelligence, compassion and, above all, stamina. He had a lively brain, an amiable manner and an uncanny ability to work long hours. Johnny decided years earlier that what people want from a GP is someone who will be friendly, listen to them, diagnose their illnesses and organise some treatment and do it with a slight dose of humility.

The reason Johnny felt rough is that it had been his birthday the night before. He was between girlfriends. That's what he used to tell folks. He wasn't sure that he was really between girlfriends because there was no one else in sight at that time. He had dated a teacher from Halloween until Christmas but with that particular lady things didn't really seem to get going. So, instead of going to a restaurant to celebrate the pub instead and Thursday night was Quiz the Railway Arms or the Railway Tavern, just uilt in 1856 and was less than a hundred yards quiz was advertised to start at nine o'clock but, only ever really started at twenty five past nine. It gave to get two drinks in before it started. He would usually have thre nts of beer (Olde Sheep Rustlers Dark Bitter or, if it had run out, Tetley's) but it had somehow become five on this particular evening. Birthdays and all that. Friday morning he regretted it. His pub quiz team (a conglomeration of three men and the then girlfriend of one of the other two) had come joint first but lost it on the tie break to a crowd of teachers on the next table. They were two men and two girls. One of the girls was stunning; no one quite knew who she was as no one could recall seeing her in the Railway before that night.

Johnny again wondered why the quiz always started twenty-five minutes late. The answer to that is that it always had started at that time. Being English can mean being a little bit disorganised at times, but we usually get the important bits right. Twenty-five minutes late for a pub quiz was neither here nor there. Natural English characteristics include humour, inventiveness, tolerance and kindness towards strangers, but the main feature underlying much of what being English means is that we are never quite sure of what we are or where we are going. We muddle along. Whilst we enjoy visiting our continental neighbours in Europe for holidays, at the same time we, more often than not, enjoy American culture, American music and many American values. Maybe we are just spoiled for choice. We don't celebrate a national day or feel the need to put the name of our country on our postage stamps. Add all of this up and maybe we can work out why the quiz always started late.

Johnny closed the curtains again. He took some paracetamol for his headache and drank a large cup of coffee. The paracetamol came from a carrier bag in the corner of his bedroom which was otherwise full of returned, half consumed courses of penicillin which patients had brought back if they felt they had become allergic to them. There were some asthma inhalers and some out of date suppositories.

Shortly after seven thirty he felt better and he set off to drive to work, a drive lasting less than five minutes. It started to get light.

Two ladies were at work inside the building already. Susan, one of the reception staff, was switching on the computer on the front desk. In the waiting room, Judy, the young cleaning lady, was vacuuming and tidying the magazines. Johnny also employed her at home, just for two hours once every couple of weeks, to make his apartment look ever so slightly respectable. Judy was 28, was bordering on being beautiful and was reputed to be getting a good reputation as a country singer with a local band. She saw Johnny and switched the hoover off.

"How were your birthday celebrations, Johnny?" she asked.

"They were okay but I shouldn't really go out for three hours on a Thursday night."

"Another year older and, by Jesus, you look it this morning."

"And you just look younger and younger, Judy."

"You are a real charmer, Dr Cash."

"You know me better than that, Judy," he replied.

"If I could get both you and your flat looking really polished and tidy then maybe your love life would improve a bit."

"When would I have time, Judy?" he asked.

"Johnny, the way I see it is, if you don't have a girlfriend then someone somewhere is being just a little bit deprived. And you know that yourself, don't you?"

"Jesus Judy, it's not even eight o'clock in the morning," he replied.

With that thought he went to his consulting room to switch his own computer on. In another twelve hours he would be at home. However much he loved his job (and he did, very much so, in fact) he hoped not to have a late night.

Valley Mills Health Centre had been there since the nineteen eighties and Johnny had worked there for nearly fourteen years. He could not accurately count how many people worked in the building but he thought it must number about twenty.

In England, on every weekday, about three quarters of a million people go to see their GP. That is about one person out of every 68. Valley Health Centre (VHC) had nearly 7000 patients on the books and about a hundred of them would be asking for an appointment on this particular Friday. Why a hundred? It's just the way it was, about a hundred a people a day, rain or shine. Sometimes more in winter but never far from a hundred. You may think that you don't go to the doctors yourself very often but I bet that your grandma or your neighbour across the street might. That's where TV medical dramas like 'A Moorland Practice' get it so completely and utterly wrong. They see one patient a day between all three doctors and then go jogging at lunchtime and take their patients to the hospital outpatients and call round to discuss blood test results. It ain't like that at all. By quarter to nine in the morning they have done more than these TV soap docs do in a day. Wave after wave after wave of patients appear, many with multiple complex medical problems and the receptionists liken it to a much safer version of being shelled on the Somme. It just never stops.

The VHC had three very full-time doctors and a young doctor who was in the advanced stage of being trained to be a GP, and it was mostly Johnny's job to do the training. They had nurses and reception staff and ladies in the back office, who understood things that only ladies in the back office can understand, plus Judy and, another lady, Mary, who cleaned in a morning. Nobody knew how old Mary was because she was registered as a patient at Aubrey Kendall's practice down the road and you couldn't accidentally look her up on the computer. The consensus figure was that she was 67. She had a son who was amazingly bright; he had been an Assistant Professor of Genetics in Southampton and was spending a year at the Mayo Clinic in Minnesota. They also had District Nurses and that made about twenty people in total.

So there you have it. A hundred patients a day plus home visits plus repeat prescriptions (more than you could count). Right, you are wondering what it is that GPs actually *do*? You'll get a flavour of some of it in the next two or three hundred pages and you won't be disappointed.

The front door at VHC was unlocked at eight o'clock and by eight thirty it was like Piccadilly Circus. It would be like that till after six that evening.

Johnny's computer was warming up and Susan brought him a cup of strong coffee.

"How was last night?" Susan asked. "Did you go to the Railway?"

"I did and stayed out too late, Susan."

"What about the quiz?" she asked.

"We did okay and came joint first and then we lost it on the tie break. Some school teachers beat us."

"Another year older, eh?" said Susan.

"And deeper in debt," said Johnny. "To the tune of about eighteen quid last night. The beer was fifteen quid and two pounds for the quiz and then two packets of peanuts."

"You tight arsed so-and-so," smiled Susan.

"I'm a Yorkshireman," said Johnny. "And we're meant to be tight with our money. It doesn't seem right spending eighteen quid on a Thursday night."

"Well Johnny," Susan replied, "it's a leap year this year, so next year your birthday will be on a Saturday. And if you have a girlfriend you'll be spending eighty pounds if you take her out for a meal. No two-for-one offers on a Saturday night."

And so, thinking briefly about money (not quite enough) and then for the next ten and a half hours about his patients (lovely people but slightly too many), Johnny started his four thousandth day in General Practice.

Chapter 6

JOHNNY kept very busy throughout February. His clinical work seemed to grow every year. What seemed like a long day a couple of years ago was now commonplace. He kept his sanity in the pub two nights a week. Occasionally bands played in the Railway on a Friday night. Johnny was a capable guitar player but only a handful of people knew that.

This particular Friday a local rock band called Methuselah were scheduled to play at the Railway, aiming to start their first set at nine o'clock. (It would, of course, be twenty-five past.) They arrived at the pub at seven thirty and set up their stuff on the small stage. Johnny had seen them play before. He was talking to Rob, the guitarist, at the bar (the guitar player was a mechanic who, occasionally, used to see Johnny about his painful attack of gout) when Rob's mobile rang. It was his mum. His dad was on his way to hospital with a probable heart attack and she, naturally, wanted Rob to drive to the hospital in Rochdale. He had only managed a third of his first pint of beer.

"Fuck me!" said Rob. "I love my dad to bits but I'm not sure about his sense of timing. It means we'll have to cancel the show."

Johnny was on to his second pint.

"I'll stand in for you," he offered.

"How many of our songs do you know, Dr Cash?" asked Rob.

"All of them! You always play the same two sets of ten and you always finish with 'Bohemian Rhapsody'."

"What about rehearsing?"

"Don't need to. Just introduce me to the other three lads and then you can fuck off to Rochdale."

And so, as a result of a conversation lasting less than two minutes, the band had a new guitarist for the night. The show went surprisingly well. Johnny got lost a bit in the middle of 'Hotel California' but it was half way through the second set at ten to eleven and not many people seemed to notice. He got fifty quid from the band, spent twelve quid on beer and went home with thirty-eight pounds more than he set off with. By anybody's reckoning it was a good night. Even Rob's dad did well; it was only a small heart attack and he was home again by Monday evening.

On Saturday, rumours began to circulate about Johnny being the stand-in guitarist and on Monday morning both Susan and Judy stopped him at quarter to eight and asked him, "When are you going on England's Got Talent then, Johnny? We heard you were all right."

"I got lost in the middle of 'Hotel California' but apart from that I thought I sounded all right. How many people know?"

"Well, in Robinson's on Saturday, the bloke on the meat counter knew and Jenny Bradford on the checkout said she had heard that Eric Clapton was working at the Health Centre."

"Oh, right then?" That made him ponder for a short while.

And so another week began. Johnny's new-found fame kept him momentarily distracted from the rigours of his work. Then he remembered that the following week his new young doctor, Fiona Graham, was coming to work with him for twelve months. Fiona had worked in different hospital specialities for three years since qualifying and now she wanted to finish her training to become a GP. She was a bright young woman from Glasgow and had followed Celtic since she was ten years old. Her most upsetting day working in hospital in Glasgow was when a seventy-five-year-old man was brought in straight from Ibrox Park vomiting blood in copious quantities. She got a drip up in each arm within two minutes and transfused him vigorously with O-negative blood. Sadly he expired on the way to theatre. It was a bleeding ulcer and he could not be saved. On the Monday, her consultant thanked her for doing her best and said it could have been even worse. He could have been a Celtic supporter.

Fiona would be taught mostly by Johnny. Two hours on a Tuesday afternoon from four till six were set aside exclusively for teaching. Johnny's partners in the practice, the other two GPs, Patrick and Angela, would stand in when required.

Fiona arrived and sat in with Johnny on the Monday and on the Tuesday morning. Whilst Johnny introduced Fiona to the staff on the reception desk she witnessed her first general practice altercation. A businessman called Clive Hillman parked his Mercedes in the disabled parking bay (well, it was three quarters inside the bay and one quarter on the bit where you're not meant to park at all) and strutted into reception to demand his prescription for his blood pressure pills.

"I'm sorry, Mr Hillman, but I think you only ordered it at nine o'clock this morning. We process five hundred prescription requests a day and we usually like 24 hours to have it ready."

"I could be dead by nine o'clock tomorrow. Can I have my prescription now please?"

His six foot four frame and his 400-guinea suit suggested that he meant it.

"Give me a minute then, Mr Hillman."

She printed off a prescription for 56 days of his Atenolol tablets and asked Johnny if he would check it and sign it, and gave it to Mr Hillman.

"For what I pay towards the National Health from my taxes, I could get better and cheaper treatment by going private."

"I am sorry that you are not happy, Mr Hillman, but always remember that we try our best."

"Don't you be funny with me, young lady," he retorted.

"Mr Hillman, I'm sorry but we have seven thousand patients and we do get busy," she replied.

Johnny and Fiona were quietly impressed. Clive Hillman reversed his Mercedes S430 (registration number CAH 1) at a dangerous speed out of the handicapped parking spot and the girls on reception concluded that his middle name must really be Attila, not Arthur.

At four o'clock the practice would be visited by Dr Al Hussein, the regional co-ordinator for Post Graduate General Practice in Calderdale. In this story containing many smart characters, Al Hussein is the smartest. He had been born in relatively humble circumstances in Leeds in 1962 and was a GP for three days a week and supervised training for another three days. He knew the strengths of each training practice in the area and questioned and helped and suggested things to, and asked questions of, the young doctors and helped them, along with their individual trainers, to become capable young GPs. He turned up at five to four and inspected the practice library and had a half hour chat with Johnny and Fiona.

"Johnny will give you tremendous help, Fiona, although I daresay from what we've heard about you, that you're pretty capable already."

"Thank you Dr Hussein. I'm going to ask Dr Cash if he'll go through the theory of different diagnostic models in General practice."

Johnny suddenly woke up. "Well Fiona, there is Inductive Reasoning, which they teach you in hospital, which can be too rigid for general practice purposes, and there is the Hypothetic-deductive method, where, in response to patients' symptoms, we form a diagnostic hypothesis, and then test this hypothesis by asking further questions; or there is Pattern Recognition where we make diagnoses based on previous experiences, and in fact we use all of these and we use them twenty, thirty, forty, fifty times a day."

Goodness! Johnny didn't know which of the three of them in the room were the most impressed.

"Johnny, you're doing great. Keep up the good work and go practice your guitar, and go get yourself a girlfriend and take her out for a drink on a weekend. Apart from that you're doing fine. Fiona, you're in safe hands and you're much too young for him!"

"Jesus, Al, I thought you were a good Muslim," said Johnny.

"I am, Johnny. The drink is purely medicinal in your case. You need it or you'll be fucked in a couple of years. If I'm in town I'll have an orange juice with you. Best of luck, Fiona. Johnny will help you to synthesise your vast hospital experience so that you can use it in proper frontline medicine. You'll enjoy your time here."

"Thank you, Dr Hussein. I'm sure I will."

And with that he was gone.

"Christ, they swear a lot round here," said Fiona.

Johnny showed Fiona the sequence to get the computer going. They started from scratch.

"First you switch it on; then you enter your first password for the computer; then you enter your second password to book patients' hospital appointments; then your user name; then your third password for Docman so that you can read letters from the hospital; then you click on Vision; then you click on Consultation Manager; then you click on appointments; then you click on your first patient. It is only a nine-stage process. With each patient we have all their details going back 20 years, diagnoses, drugs, operations, allergies, whether or not they are *Guardian* readers. All that sort of thing."

"Why the bit about *Guardian* readers?"

"Well, they have all sorts of allergies and can't get here before ten in the morning or if it's raining."

"Christ, what a place," said Fiona.

"There is also a bit you can go on to get blood test results, a bit for emails and the internet. So if you're here late and you want to see how Blackburn Rovers are doing against Arsenal, or Celtic against St Mirren, you can go onto livescores.com between patients and you're away."

With that the phone rang.

"Johnny, one of your acquaintances is at the desk and he says he needs to see you urgently," said Susan.

"Who is it, Susan?" said Johnny.

"Martin Roberts."

"Jesus, he always says it's urgent."

"Shall I ask him to have a seat?"

"Two minutes, Susan. I've got Fiona in and we'll see him together."

"Fine. Thanks, Johnny."

"He's a funny fellow, is this man, Fiona. He's 43 and lectures at the University and feels he can't work due to stress. To be honest, I'm not sure that he's totally genuine but, of course, I just have to give him the benefit of the doubt."

Johnny buzzed and Martin Roberts came in. A rolled up copy of the *Guardian* was under his arm.

"Martin, this is Dr Graham. She is working with us for 12 months. What can we do for you?"

"I need some more Diazepam and I think I might want you to refer me to see the Psychologist about my anxiety. And I will come back next month for you to do my bloods and repeat my ECG and then maybe you could help me to lose weight. I've heard that there's some capsules that make you shit. Oh, most importantly, I need another sickness certificate. And I need some more Betnovate and some Ramipril and some Lansoprazole and that pink stuff."

"Fine, Martin. But your sick note's not due till next week," said Johnny.

"I know but I'm going away at seven in the morning. That's why I need it early. There's a bargain cruise on offer. I only booked it yesterday. You fly to Madeira and then sail to Rio. I got it half price."

"Sounds impressive. I'll check your blood pressure first."

He did that and it was normal.

"If I write to the Clinical Psychologist, what do you want me to tell him you can't do, Martin?"

There was a silence for a second.

"Well, I can't do my work, I suppose."

Johnny sighed. He mentally thanked God that most of his patients were humble, hardworking, genuine folks with illnesses you could read about in a textbook.

"Have a nice time, Martin," he said.

"Thanks, Doc," he replied and he left carrying a sickness certificate, a prescription for five items and the knowledge that the Psychology appointment would be on his doormat when he returned in 24-days time.

"I fell out with him a few years ago. Over a girl," said Johnny.

"Goodness me, Dr Cash. This is some place."

It was getting late.

"You get going, Fiona. You can see some patients by yourself tomorrow."

"Thank you, Dr Cash," said Fiona.

She went home with her head spinning. Her perception that general practice was complex, multi-layered and unpredictable was proving to be true. Johnny stayed for another 90 minutes during which he did some reports and planned the next teaching session. He looked outside. It was dark and it was raining. He went home and watched TV. Fiona got a

Chinese takeaway and a bottle of wine. Martin put his pills in his suitcase. Clive Hillman, who lived in a large barn conversion up the valley, watched football on his 42" TV whilst his wife made supper. Joe Bradford changed the oil in his Toyota (at home). Jenny Bradford was working till nine at Robinson's and Judy Carter was getting ready to sing with her band, Nashville Express, at the Trades Club. All was well with the world. It was a typical Tuesday evening in the Valley.

Chapter 7

IT WAS EASTER SUNDAY. The sun was shining. There was a gentle north-westerly breeze. The air was as clear as crystal but spring had not properly arrived. It would be another month before the sun brought any real warmth.

Clive Hillman was 47 and he owned and ran a car dealership. He was not affiliated to any particular manufacturer; he could buy and sell any vehicle. His customers in the past had tended to be people who wanted an eighty thousand pound car for seventy five thousand pounds, often dealing in cash. From where his customers obtained their vast cash fortunes he was meticulous in not asking. When discussing deals and prices in the private office of his gleaming showroom he was keen to let the customer know that he was happy to produce an artificially low price on the invoice (taking the difference between the stated price and the real, higher price in cash) if the customer wished to hide earnings from the taxman. Similarly he would, on request, provide an invoice for a higher price, if asked, so that, when the customer eventually sold the car, he or she could save tax by claiming that the car had depreciated more than it really had done, if they used the car for business purposes and if they could claim its use as a legitimate expense. He was flexible and it helped him get sales. Both Clive and the customer tended to view the whole business as a victimless crime, as the only victims were schools, hospitals or poor people. The fact that it was fraudulent was, of course, never discussed. Clive's male customers all seemed to share the same two characteristics; their hair was swept back and severely flattened as though they used invisible Brylcreem and they never, ever looked you straight in the eye. Very few of them were doctors or teachers or people who got their hands dirty working for an employer.

Clive was in his office at home looking at his bank statements both for his business and his personal bank account. He also inspected his credit card statements. He was not happy, because, between the two bank accounts and five credit cards, he owed approximately five hundred thousand pounds. His garage premises were leased and the cars in it were worth about four hundred thousand pounds. He also owed the Valley Car Auctions one hundred and sixty four thousand pounds for the last three cars that he had bought—a Merc, a BMW and a large Lexus saloon. Their terms were thirty days. He was poorer than anyone knew him to be and was aware his business success partly depended on him appearing to be affluent. Nobody wanted to buy an expensive car from a man who appeared not to be affluent himself. He also knew that the people he hung around with had very few criteria for deciding who they wanted for a friend. As long as the person looked wealthy then most of the boxes were ticked. Certainly neither morality nor culture seemed to be important. This did not bother him at all (he had never actually thought about it). What did bother him was that he was skint and that he did not know how to extricate himself. The recession and the credit crunch had even adversely affected the buying habits of his normally financially well-endowed clientele. Things were bad and no-one outside the family seemed to know.

Clive had two teenage children who lived in London with his first wife. She had been unable to tolerate his regular beatings and found the big city to be a safer environment. London was 200 miles away. She was a nurse and she had remarried. Her new husband was a police sergeant in the Met.

Clive had been married to Karen for three years. She was twelve years younger than he was and they had one child, a daughter of two called Orla. To anyone not aware of their perilous finances (and Karen said afterwards that she herself wasn't aware of how stretched they were although many of their friends subsequently didn't believe that she didn't know) the Hillman's family life looked pretty serene. They were good looking and successful.

Dinner was ready at seven. Karen had made paella. As well as the Arborio rice, she had included chicken, chorizo, king prawns, red peppers and sun-dried tomato paste. She had opened a bottle of Chateauneuf-du-Pape 2007 from Caves-du-Fournalet. A second bottle lay unopened in the kitchen. She had paid fifteen pounds each for the two bottles and thought that thirty pounds to start off the evening's drinking was reasonable enough for a successful family. She wasn't sure that Orla would like paella so she had cooked her some fish fingers. After the meal Clive would probably drink a couple of cans of Norseman Special Brew lager and then a couple of whiskies before bedtime.

After two glasses of Chateauneuf-du-Pape Karen summoned up the courage to raise the topic of the possibility of changing her car.

"When are we likely to be going to Leeds next, Clive?" she asked.

"Why do you ask? What are you thinking of?" he replied.

"Well, you know…," she began hesitantly, "my Celica has its MOT test coming up next month and I think it might not get through without spending a lot on it."

"Fuck me, Karen," Clive said, "you've only had it for about a year. You have obviously got another car in mind. Am I allowed to ask what it is?"

He didn't sound pleased, not by a long way.

"Oh, don't bother then," Karen replied in a surly manner.

"Don't you fucking well tell me not to fucking bother. I fucking asked you what fucking car you want. And now you fucking say not to fucking bother."

He was angry and Karen felt that the neighbours would be able to hear if he raised his voice any further. Then Orla stopped eating her fish fingers and started crying.

"Now look what you've done," Karen said.

"I'm sorry Orla, I'm sorry."

He got up and dried Orla's tears. He then bent down to whisper in Karen's ear hoping that Orla would not be able to hear. Her young brain deciphered the whisper as something like this: "I will deal with you later. You mark my words, lady. I will deal with you later."

Things settled down a little. Karen put Orla to bed at nine o'clock. She poured another drink each for Clive and herself, and then they went to bed. Clive seemed to have settled down a little.

"I'm sorry I blew up at you earlier," he said as he switched the light out.

He stroked her upper thigh a couple of times but there was no immediate response of any sort. He kept doing it and Karen then sensed that he would get mad again so she yawned and turned towards him in the dark. He knew, even without being able to see her, that there was a large degree of reluctance to join in on Karen's part. She herself could sense that she would just have to tolerate the next one to five minutes and just sort of get on with life.

"Okay then Clive. It's Easter Monday tomorrow and you'll not have to open the garage till nearly ten o'clock. There is no hurry."

He tried and tried but could not get an erection, even with her help. She waited but nothing happened.

"For fuck's sake Clive, you let me know that you want to shag me, then you can't fucking do it. Either that or if you can it's over in a fucking minute."

"If you fucking wanted me then it would be fucking different, wouldn't it?" he said.

"Oh go fuck yourself, you fucking wanker."

With that she turned away from him and they went to sleep. They did not speak at all the next day. Over the next two days Karen managed to learn about their perilous finances—she had found his hidden bank statements. They were breaching their agreed overdraft limits and the likely salvation (of sorts) would be that their gorgeous house would be repossessed and sold. She became less confrontational in her dealings with Clive but he himself became worse. Every week, either once or twice, there was either a beating or a threat of one.

She related the story of the beatings to her sixty-year-old mother in Rochdale. Her mother said that she would not take sides. She reminded Karen that she used to be a lovely little girl but then that she became obsessed by money (she didn't know where she got that from because they didn't have much when she was growing up, and neither did any of her friends). Karen then told her that Clive was a monster and that she was only staying with him because of Orla and because of the thought of an open-topped Lexus. Her mother told her firmly that if the marriage dissolved (and it would, of course, she predicted) then she would attach sixty per cent of the blame to Mr high and mighty Clive Arthur Hillman and forty per cent to her daughter Karen, for marrying him when she knew what he was like. To finish off she said to Karen:

"Are you sure that his middle name isn't Attila rather than Arthur?"

She didn't know that they were bordering upon bankruptcy.

Chapter 8

SPRING ARRIVED in the valley and Fiona settled in well. Learning to become a GP was a period of adjustment. The near certainties of hospital work contrasted with the equally busy but more unexpected and less predictable nature of working in general practice. She soon found out that anybody could attend at anytime, more or less, with anything. The day could start with an eighty-eight-year-old grandmother with diabetes, arthritis, asthma, high blood pressure, depression and dermatitis and finish thirty-six patients later with a girl of sixteen requesting the contraceptive pill. In between there would be patients with every permutation and combination of medical conditions. On top of this would be home visits, audits, preparation for the membership examination, tutorials with Johnny on a Tuesday afternoon, and socialising and team building with the other doctors, nurses and reception staff in the pub for an evening, once every couple of weeks. Fiona learned that to be a GP in the same community meant that not only every success in terms of making a brilliant diagnosis, etc., would be remembered vividly by the families of the patients concerned, but also every slight error or every inappropriate delay in solving a problem would be remembered even more. At times she felt vulnerable but she then was reassured by the knowledge that Johnny and his colleagues were good teachers. The breadth and depth of knowledge required for every working hour of every working day seemed wide and bottomless, yet she felt, at the same time, that her work was producing worthwhile results.

The overwhelming problems which Johnny and Joe and a few other people would face, problems which would take over their whole lives and gnaw away at them and gradually try to seem to threaten their very existence, would not manifest themselves until the later part of the year. Spring and summer were a period of relative calm, although they were blissfully unaware of this at the time.

Johnny explained to Fiona that whilst every patient was equally important, there were some patients where you didn't get a second chance of getting things right. Patients in this category included things like people with heart attacks and asthma attacks, but also things like terminal care.

One Tuesday afternoon Fiona asked Johnny, "Why is terminal care, in particular, in this group of conditions?"

"It's because you don't get a second crack at it, Fiona. If the guitarist from Methuselah comes to see me with his gout, well, if the first combination of drugs doesn't work, then he can come back a couple of days later. But if someone's got cancer and they're in pain, well, you can't say well try this and we'll see you in a few days. You have to get the pain relief right. If you prescribe too small a dose then the patient suffers unnecessary pain. And then you have to involve the families. Keep them informed of what's going on. Then you have to follow the strict legal requirements of the law regarding prescribing and storing controlled drugs."

"Just remind me what controlled drugs are, Johnny," said Fiona.

"Well, they are a special category where there are special restrictions on their use. They usually include the stronger painkillers and in particular morphine and such like," said Johnny.

"What about storing them?" asked Fiona.

"They have to be logged and counted and stored in a locked container inside another locked container. And if a patient doesn't require any of these drugs which have been prescribed and they have in their possession, well, they have to be destroyed in controlled circumstances, and the destruction and disposal have to be recorded."

"Do you keep them on the premises?" asked Fiona.

"We have a small supply locked in the Controlled Drug Cupboard."

They inspected the cupboard and the register, kept with meticulous care.

"Tomorrow on home visits I'll take you to see a man called Percy Potts," said Johnny. "He's 72 and he's got terminal lung cancer. His pain is now controlled with a syringe driver."

"How comfortable is he?"

"He is pretty content, I think. We have to adjust the dosage every day or two and we work in conjunction with the District Nurses and the Nurse from the Hospice."

"How long has he been ill?" asked Fiona.

"Well, he presented in January coughing up blood. We had him thoroughly investigated, chest X-ray, CT scans, and all that, but the tumour on his lung had spread before he had any symptoms. He accepted it with good grace. And now I visit him every couple of days. The only thing you can say against him is, well, you remember Martin Roberts who needed his sick note early because he's booked a last minute cruise? Well, Martin is his nephew. But Percy can't help that. Poor old bugger."

Johnny and Fiona went to visit Percy every couple of days. Fiona learned a lot from Percy and his family and from the Nurse Specialist from the Hospice. Percy appreciated the good attention he was getting. Martin called at the house one day. Fiona arrived when he was there. He had enjoyed his cruise. He had been reading about morphine and such like on the internet and suggested some dose modifications to Fiona. Fiona was polite and listened to him, said thank you and said that she would take his suggestions into account. Percy's wife advised Fiona to ignore Martin, and told her that he feels that he knows everything about everything, but he doesn't, and it's time he went back to work and stopped interfering. Fiona winked at Mrs Potts when she said this. Martin didn't see this happen as he was sitting in a chair in the corner engrossed in the *Guardian*.

Spring became warmer and as May progressed Percy Potts became weaker. He remained comfortable with his precisely calculated dosage of drugs in his syringe driver and one Friday evening at the end of May, during the commercial break at quarter to eight, half way through Coronation Street (an episode which revolved mostly around a funeral supper in the Rovers Return, with lots of beer and sausage rolls) Percy Potts died peacefully.

After the funeral Mrs Potts wrote two nice short letters, one addressed to Dr Daniel John Cash and the other addressed to Dr Fiona Graham. She thanked them both for the expert care and attention received and she wrote also to the District Nurses and to the Specialist Nurse from the Hospice.

As an exercise Johnny asked Fiona to list eight things she had learned from dealing with Percy during his final illness. She wrote the following:

1. Terminal care is difficult to get right.
2. You only get one go at it.
3. It demonstrates (and tests) multidisciplinary working within the extended primary health care team
4. The rules are complex but you have to adhere to them on pain of severe sanctions.
5. Patients are very grateful for the attention received.
6. They often (but not always) want to talk about the implications of their condition.
7. Relatives appreciate full and frank discussion at all times.
8. Martin Roberts (the nephew) is a bit of a complete wanker, but I can't prove it scientifically!

Johnny felt that he could not have done any better himself. Al Hussein later asked Fiona about the patients she had learned the most from and she said that Percy came near to the top of the list because, in hospital, however good you were, you never fully understood terminal care because you weren't fully geared up for it. You would stop at the patient's bedside on a ward round but feel somewhat embarrassed because you knew that you couldn't cure them, and you didn't want your embarrassment to show so you hurried on to the patient in the next bed who had just had a hemi-colectomy for Crohn's disease because you knew that they could be made better. Hospitals were often unimaginably brilliant places for people with serious but curable illnesses, but dying from cancer was better done at home. He agreed completely.

Chapter 9

SPRING IN THE VALLEY turned into early summer with the arrival of June. The previously dark and possibly previously satanic mills in the town looked bright in the sunshine. Few of these old mills were currently engaged in any type of industrial productivity these days. Some had been demolished, just one had been divided into small factory units, one was split into small shops and one had been converted into apartments, pitched at the higher end of the market. All around the trees were green and Valley Mills had a buzz about it. The more enlightened and travelled townspeople realised that maybe they were more fortunate than at least ninety per cent of the world's population. The hills above the town looked magnificent. Most people (though not everyone, of course) had a job. Nobody went hungry and the restaurants and pubs were full, at least at weekends.

Johnny was busy seeing forty or fifty patients a day as well as finding time to teach Fiona. He watched her turn gradually from a brilliant young hospital doctor into a seasoned young GP. She learned to manage multiple problems in the same consultation and to retain her dry Glaswegian humour. The patients liked her and one or two of them asked if she would be staying in the practice permanently.

A meeting was held early in June at which Al Hussein witnessed Fiona's progress. Her teaching and learning programme was discussed with Fiona herself and Johnny. District Nurse Kirsty joined them for an hour and they discussed pathways of care and team working. Kirsty promised to take Fiona on a full day of home visits to show her how elderly housebound patients are cared for in the community. Fiona was impressed. Also present were Johnny's two partners at the Valley Health Centre, Patrick Moore and Angela Townsend, both doctors in their late thirties.

Teaching rotas were drawn up (Johnny did about two thirds and was always grateful for the wisdom and understanding of his two colleagues). Al had an unpublished league table in his head which listed the training practices under his supervision in order of effectiveness. The Valley always came near the top. Their mixture of intelligence, stamina and flexibility impressed him. The place had a vibrancy which he did not find in every practice he visited. He noted that if ever he moved from Halifax to Valley Mills, then he was pretty certain where he would want to register himself and his family as patients. Doctors treating doctors; he recalled very early in his career that if you have a doctor as a patient facing you across the desk then if you treat them exactly the same as if they were a teacher or a barman or a motor mechanic then you never ever go far wrong. They breathe, eat, drink and visit the bathroom in a similar fashion to a beggar on the streets of Naples, a Tibetan monk or the President of the United States. He felt that basic bodily functions were one of the great equalising forces in life; he wondered how, as a result of this, anyone could possibly not believe in egalitarianism. The meeting, which had started at six o'clock, went on for longer than planned, and when it curtailed Al asked if anyone would care to join him for a meal at the Koh-i-Noor Palace, half a mile away from the town centre, as a small compensation for keeping them all for longer than he intended. He was paying. All five hands went up and ten minutes later they were seated round a table for six. District Nurse Kirsty's mum and dad owned the Railway pub just round the corner and as a result of dealing with customers since her teens she knew good service when she saw it. She couldn't help wonder why a bowl of rice cost three quid in a recession but apart from that the meal was lovely. Johnny noticed Joe and Jenny Bradford sitting at another table about thirty feet away. He had not seen them for some time and after the meal went over to say hello.

"Good to see you, Johnny," said Joe. "I've just met Jenny outside Robinson's and we thought we'd sort of give the kitchen a rest tonight."

Jenny smiled.

"How are you, Johnny?" Joe asked. "Any girls on the go?"

"A couple since I last saw you but then I think, well, maybe I haven't the time to pursue such ventures," said Johnny, smiling also.

"You've got to make time, Johnny, you got to make time," said Joe.

Johnny nodded in agreement. He knew that Joe was absolutely right when he saw two more people enter the restaurant. They were Judy Carter, the delightful young cleaning lady and her boyfriend, Tony Smith.

Judy saw Johnny, excused herself from Tony for a minute, and came over and started whispering something in his ear. Johnny quickly nodded again, and returned to his seat with the other five. Judy followed him over and asked Kirsty if she would ask her mum and dad if they could use the Railway for a fundraising night for the local Hospice. She told the assembled gathering that she was going to organise a small variety show with a supper and a raffle and that, yes, she was going to sing, and that it would not be night to be missed and that it would be in July if Kirsty's mum and dad were in agreement. What she didn't say was that she and Johnny were going to do half an hour of Country Duets. She would sing and Johnny would sing and play guitar. Sort of unplugged. Something like 'All I Want To Do Is Dream' and 'Return Of The Grievous Angel' and stuff like that. For four minutes and nineteen seconds (at least) they would become Emmylou Harris and Gram Parsons.

Johnny (and everyone in fact) agreed that it had been both a pleasant and a productive evening. He had another bottle of Kerala Finest Indian Ale (in big bottles and at least five and a half percent alcohol unlike some you could name) and after shaking hands with the other five and saying goodnight to Joe and Jenny and Judy and Tony on their respective tables, he set off for the short walk home, watched one of the heats of England's Got Talent (a TV show featuring loads of amazing amateur singers, musicians, dance acts and such like) and went off to bed and slept very soundly.

Next day was uneventful from eight until six. The hour from six in the evening till seven in the evening was uneventful in the extreme. He would not realise how uneventful until October, some four months later, and he would not for many months after that realise how much the events of that late afternoon early evening surgery in June would unfold from twenty twelve well into the following year and possibly for ever. There was no way that he could anticipate what was coming and no way that he would ever know how much that evening would affect both himself and many others and many of the people in the restaurant the previous night before. He had, for a long time, realised the interconnectedness of much human activity, but even with this knowledge and also a doctor's awareness of the many possibilities which can arise from a combination of circumstances, he would still be shocked. Very shocked indeed, and the shock would hang over him for a long, long time into the future. It would be the type which, if inflicted upon other people, could send them into a state from which they might never recover. He had read articles in the medical press. Some of these were reports of inquests but not just inquests relating to the deaths of patients (although God knows these were bad enough) but inquests about doctors who had simply not been to work one day and the rest of the story usually involved stout ropes, or railway lines or train drivers saying that they had only just time to apply the brakes but that it didn't make any difference to the speed of the train in fifty yards and then when they had seen the terrified look in the eyes of the person standing on the track looking directly at them (they always looked straight at the driver) they would look away and then, half a second later there would be a bang, a bang that the train driver would never ever quite forget. Sometimes in these inquests there would be drugs mentioned, but not as often as you would expect when you consider that doctors are surrounded by them all day. Drugs were not mentioned half as often as you would expect in circumstances like these.

Chapter 10

SO, SIX O'CLOCK the next day arrived. Johnny had three patients left to see but three became four as the last hour unravelled. It went something like this.

The first of these last three (which soon became four) patients was Clive Hillman. Johnny called him in from the waiting room. He seemed to be unusually modest or humble or however you want to describe it. They exchanged pleasantries.

"Now then, Mr Hillman, what can we do for you?"

"Thank you, Dr Cash. To be honest I'm a little bit embarrassed coming with what I've come about today, Doc."

"Don't be embarrassed, Mr Hillman. Whatever it is, I promise you I will have heard the same story before from someone else. When it's men in their forties who say they are embarrassed, nine times out of ten it's about erections," Johnny said, trying to minimise Clive Hillman's obvious embarrassment.

Clive Hillman breathed a sigh of relief. "How did you guess, Dr Cash?"

"I just sort of knew, Clive,' said Johnny. "I've sat behind this desk for fourteen years and with nearly two hundred patients every week, it's a story I hear lots and lots."

And so, at great length, they discussed the problem that Clive Hillman was having down below.

"When I'm in bed with Karen, not forgetting that she's 12 years younger than I am, I can't seem to get a proper hard on. And when I do, on the rare occasions that it actually happens, then it's all over too quickly, much too quickly, to be honest."

"Ladies who are lateral thinkers sometimes view that as a compliment," joked Johnny.

"I can see that but Karen doesn't," replied Mr Hillman.

"I'm going to be really nosy here, Clive. You don't have to answer this next one if you don't want to, honestly. But I was just wondering how the two of you well, sort of, get on?" asked Johnny.

"Most of the time we're okay. But, well, you know, sort of, we're both strong characters and we have our rows and such like."

"I'm going to be really, really bold now, Clive. Have you any other worries?" Johnny then smiled. "The sorts of things I hear about from time to time include money troubles, physical violence, latent forced transvestitism, bookies shops, online gambling, alcohol, unfaithfulness. You know the typical things that could go on in and around Valley Mills. Even the people who live in the posh part like you," he joked.

"Nothing comes to mind, Dr Cash. We have a couple of drinks in an evening, but I think that's normal round here."

"I'm sure you're right," Johnny replied.

So they went on, after a couple of questions about Mr Hillman's general health, to discuss what could be done.

"I can make you harder or I can make you softer, or I can make you faster, or I can slow you down so that you can do it all night, so much that Karen will fall asleep frying your bacon on a Sunday morning. But what I can't do is make her love you if she doesn't. You know what I mean?"

Clive appeared interested. "Tell me more about harder and longer and stuff like that," he said.

"Well," said Johnny, "there are drugs like Dykohard that give you erections. You take it about an hour before intended sexual activity; then, when you get sexual stimulation, you're away. And the benefit can last for up to 36 hours."

"Do you mean the erection can *last* for 36 hours?" asked Clive Hillman, almost incredulously.

"No. But the potential for an erection lasts for up to 36 hours. So, let's say, if you sleep with Karen on Friday night then if her mother is taken ill on Saturday and gets taken into Rochdale Infirmary and kept in and you offer to go and visit but Karen then says that you don't need to go, honestly, and there's 101 reasons why she doesn't want you there and Karen says she's staying in Rochdale till Monday and she's taken Orla with her and you suddenly find you're free on Saturday night, well, you know what I mean," joked Johnny. "You don't need to take a second tablet."

Mr Hillman smiled. "You're not condoning adultery, are you, Dr Cash?"

"No, I'm simply stating medical facts, that's all," replied Johnny.

Clive nodded and smiled again.

"You've got me thinking now, Dr Cash. Now tell me about longer and shorter and all that sort of thing."

"Well, there are drugs like Prozac, and like St John's Wort that, although that is not the reason they were invented, they do delay ejaculation. It is a very useful side effect which can be, sort of, exploited in situations like this."

"Sounds all right by me," said Clive. "Tell me more."

"Well, you could have Dykohard when you need to take it. And you could take one of the others on a daily basis. And with perfect titration we could have 7 inches and 25 minutes or 5 inches and 40 minutes or, indeed, 6 inches and 3 minutes, if your favourite TV programme is about to start. Unless you have Sky Plus. So there you have it. Any permutation you want. The only uncertainty, of course, is working out when you have reached half time. Even as a doctor I have trouble working that one out."

"Do you mean professionally or personally, Dr Cash?" asked Clive Hillman, smiling.

"These days it's just professionally. And I'm only 42."

"I could give you some phone numbers," joked Clive.

And so both men were happy with the outcome of the consultation. Johnny was happy because he thought it had gone well and Clive was happy because, for once in his life, he had been bordering on being nervous for a short while, and Johnny had managed to sort him out. Johnny wrote on the computer under Clive Hillman's name: Erectile

Dysfunction. Possible marital difficulties. Seems healthy. Dykohard 8 tablets and Prozac (Fluoxetine) 30 capsules.

"You have been brilliant, Dr Cash," Clive said. "Thank you. I appreciate it."

He shook Johnny's hand and, slightly sheepishly, picked up his prescription and left. Johnny wondered what had got into him to make him so nice, but, at the same time, he felt that it wouldn't last.

Johnny usually called his next patient in while he was finishing off writing the notes for the patient he had just seen. This was in case the next patient was elderly and took a long time to come in. His next patient was Martin Roberts, *Guardian* reader, University lecturer and probable malingerer (although he wasn't totally sure about the malingering. Only ninety per cent sure). Johnny called him. Martin Roberts was half way through the door when Susan on reception buzzed him.

"Johnny, can you come straightaway? A lady has collapsed in reception."

"I'll be straight there," said Johnny.

He said to Martin Roberts, "Have a seat, Martin. Someone's been taken ill at reception. I won't be too long, hopefully."

Martin sat down in Johnny's consulting room and Johnny ran out to reception. An old lady who had come in to collect a repeat prescription had collapsed but it was hopefully just a bad faint. He stayed with her for a few minutes. Her daughter who had been grocery shopping in Robinson's just happened to turn up for her own prescription five minutes later and the situation settled down. No serious harm was done. Johnny excused himself and went back to his consulting room. Martin Roberts was reading his *Guardian.*

"Sorry to keep you waiting, Martin. An old lady was quite unwell but she seems to be okay now, thank God. I'll be ten seconds writing these notes on the computer, then I'll be with you."

He finished Clive Hillman's notes and then asked, "What can we do for you, Martin?"

And then there was a long, animated discussion about why Martin felt that he was not yet fit for work. Johnny became mildly confrontational at one point as he felt that Martin was trying it on, but then he backed down. He remained mildly envious though, feeling that the most fortunate people on the planet are the ten per cent of the people who are on the sick who have nothing much wrong. Johnny believed that out of two million people in the UK like this, one point eight million were genuine and deserved every penny of sick pay, and two hundred thousand were trying it on, just like Martin. But he couldn't prove it. So, with slight reluctance, he wrote him another sick note. Martin would be able to spend his time looking things up on his computer and feeling that he was an expert on everything in the universe. He would get paid and he would get paid for doing precisely nothing. Johnny felt uneasy.

His last patient of the day was a new patient he had not met before. She was Kate Williams and she was 36. She had no previous medical notes. Johnny called her in.

Kate came in and sat down.

"Sorry if I'm not sure how things work here, Doctor, but I've never used your National Health Service before."

Johnny thought she sounded North American but couldn't immediately say which part.

"Where are you from, Kate?" he asked.

"From Washington State, the United States, Dr Cash. From Seattle, in fact."

"Famous for Kurt Cobain, Frazier, Boeing, Starbucks and an English type of climate, or so I've heard, Kate."

"You're right, Dr Cash."

They were both impressed. Very impressed, in fact.

"It's a part of your country that I have never visited, Kate. The closest I've been to Seattle is San Francisco, I think."

She smiled, "I love it here and the climate makes me feel at home. I like your rain. And the valley is beautiful when the sun shines. The strangest thing about England is how close together your towns are. It's only ever ten miles from one to the next. I love it. And your countryside is so, well, so nice and so English."

"Glad you like it, Ms Williams. Now, what can I do for you? And before you ask, you don't have to pay me a nickel or a dime so long as you are staying in England for a while."

"I'm an Assistant Professor at UMIST in Manchester," Kate said. "Aeronautical Engineering,"

"Sounds like rocket science to me, Kate," said Johnny.

"It is, Doctor."

"And how come you're living in the valley and not in the fleshpots of Manchester?" Johnny asked.

"I just love being nearly out in the country. It is so pretty and I can get into Manchester by train very easily."

She had come to the doctor's office to hopefully get some prescriptions for her asthma inhalers and blood pressure pills and to have her peak flow and blood pressure measured.

"Do you know many people in the valley, Kate?" Johnny asked.

"One of my colleagues lives in Rochdale and I sometimes talk to him on the train, but that's about it. I've only lived here for three weeks."

"Do you ever visit pubs, Kate?"

"It's hard for a single woman to go by herself into a pub, Dr Cash, as much as I would like to."

"Call me Johnny, please."

"Gee, Johnny Cash! My grandma loved him. Used to see him whenever he did a show in Seattle in the sixties and seventies."

"I play guitar and sing a bit but I'm not in his league. Nowhere near, in fact."

"Well, you can't be a physician and a world famous singer as well."

"It does no harm to dream though, Kate. No harm at all. Now one more question. In America, do you have pub quizzes?"

"What are those?" asked Kate. "I've never heard of them."

"Well, it's a general knowledge quiz and it takes place in a pub, so you can have a drink and get a tiny bit exuberant. They're always good fun. Can get a bit competitive though, sometimes."

"Sounds like good fun," said Kate.

"Okay. If you're free Thursday (and every Thursday in fact) get yourself into the Railway. It's the pub just near to the station."

"What time?"

"Well, it says that it starts at nine but it only usually starts at twenty five past."

"Why is that?" asked Kate.

"It's a long story," Johnny smiled. "I'll explain it to you one day." "How many people are there in a team?" wondered Kate. She looked interested.

"Usually four—me and two men and one lady who is a friend of one of the men, but the numbers can be flexible."

"Thank you for that," said Kate. "I hope to see you there."

"So do I," said Johnny.

Kate picked up her prescriptions, smiled and left.

Thursday night came and Johnny arrived at the Railway at five to nine. It was raining. 'Smells like Teen Spirit' was playing on the jukebox. Ninety seconds later Kate arrived, soaking wet.

"Feels just like home. Raining and Nirvana playing on the jukebox."

Johnny introduced Kate to the others and went to the bar for a drink. Kate wanted a pint of Guinness. Johnny ordered a pint of Norseman. One of the others from the team came up to the bar.

"Who is your lovely North American friend, Johnny?" he asked.

"She's a patient and she's just moved here from Seattle and doesn't know anyone in the valley yet," said Johnny. "And she's called Kate. I just thought I'd invite her along."

"A good choice, if you ask me," said Johnny's teammate.

The evening went well. There were 30 general knowledge questions, plus 10 questions identifying the artist and the name of the song when 20 second bursts of songs were played, then a numbers round where you don't have to get each number right but the total of the five numbers has to be closest to the right number. For example: how many years ago was the 'Boston Tea Party' and how many episodes of 'Fawlty Towers' were there—and then you add them up and the nearest wins that particular bit for a separate prize. The first question in the main part was a technical question about Concorde and the second tune on the music bit was 'Rearviewmirror' (all one word, of course) by Pearl Jam. Kate impressed in all departments and the team won by a margin of five points above the teachers on the next table who came second. At eleven thirty Kate got a taxi home and promised to return the following Thursday. She did, and they won again and they were all glad.

Chapter 11

HIGH SUMMER produced more work at Valley Health Centre. Johnny and the others saw their usual one hundred patients per day with the usual diabetes, depression, high blood pressure, infections, sciatica, arthritis, eczema, migraine and bowel problems, to name but a few. Most of these patients had complex medical problems, problems which seemed to grow more complex year on year. If they started at eight in the morning, they would still be lucky to get home for eight at night.

One Thursday evening in the Railway, Johnny arrived at five to nine and found Martin Roberts and Clive Hillman talking at the bar. They looked serious and kept nodding in agreement with each other. They saw Johnny and promptly finished their pints and hurriedly left. Johnny had not been aware in the past that the two of them knew each other; he wondered whether or not this was a chance meeting but he dismissed this idea when he saw them drink up quickly and leave together.

Over the following two weeks Johnny and Judy rehearsed for the Hospice Fundraiser at the Railway. Theirs was going to be a half hour show, opening up the evening's entertainment, to be followed by a comedian and then a one-hour set by Yorkshire band Steeltown Blues. The pub got very busy and the Hospice raised over one thousand pounds of voluntary donations. The chief fundraiser was present and he gave out leaflets to advertise the annual hospice garden fête. The beer flowed. The community outreach nurse for the hospice, Sally O'Donnell, advised people of her services to patients in the community and then introduced the acts before they came on stage. She introduced them as Judy Carter and Johnny Cash and the country duets then flowed. After they finished their set with 'Return of the Grievous Angel' an elderly lady asked them what the song meant and asked where you could buy a calico bonnet. Johnny said he wasn't sure. Several of the health centre team were in the pub and they appeared to be having a great time. Susan Adams and her husband were sitting with Emma Foster, the new recently appointed receptionist, along with Emma's boyfriend. Emma seemed to be fine for most of the evening but suddenly she burst into tears. Susan took her outside and she confided in her that she found about one patient in ten to be rude and unpleasant and that she tried her best to help them but some people you just couldn't please however hard you tried. Susan said that she would try to sort things out as she thought that Emma would make a very good medical receptionist indeed. Emma cheered up and they went back inside to find Judy and Johnny going back on stage to do an encore of 'Grievous Angel'.

After the show Johnny introduced Sally from the hospice to Fiona and Sally invited Fiona to look round the hospice the following week. Then Percy Potts' widow whom they had not seen before, during the course of the evening, came to say hello and to thank Sally for the excellent work that she and her colleagues did. She gave Sally a twenty-pound donation for the hospice and then she took Fiona aside and apologised to her for what her nephew Martin Roberts had said about the dose of morphine. She said that he prided himself on knowing everything about everything and said that the thing that would do him the most good than anything would be to do a day's work and to use his brains for what God had intended and not to meddle and interfere with everybody and everything.

Monday morning at the Health Centre started out well but by eight thirty things were going badly. There were not quite enough appointments to meet demand. Emma was talking to Mr Norman Cameron, a seventy-eight-year-old man with a bad chest and a mild dependence on sleeping tablets. He was leaning right over the reception desk asking for an appointment with Dr Cash and when Emma told him that all appointments with Dr Cash were fully booked he replied, "You're bloody useless, you lot. You're overpaid for what you do and you never seem to help people. You just sit on your side of the desk and you're just obstructive."

"We're just trying to help, Mr Cameron," Emma said.

"But you're not helping, you're just hindering."

"But there are appointments with other doctors, Mr Cameron," said Emma.

She was only eighteen and was starting to buckle under the pressure.

"I'm not interested in other bleeding doctors, young lady. I just want an appointment with Dr Cash."

"The other doctors have over thirty years of doctoring experience between them, Mr Cameron," said Emma.

"Don't you speak to me like that, you little upstart. I will speak to your practice manager later and by this time next week you'll be looking for another job. Mark my words. I'm taking this much further. Much further. And don't you believe that I won't, because I will. Mark my words, young lady, I will. Mark my words." He started pointing his finger at her. "You will be looking for another job, young lady, another job by next Monday."

If Adolf Hitler had dressed from top to toe in beige, then you would have had real trouble working out who was who.

"Excuse me, Mr Cameron, I just have to leave the desk for a minute."

Susan saw what had happened and took over. Emma went to the little sitting room at the back and burst into tears. Susan ran round and comforted her.

"He was awful with you, Emma. I heard most of it."

"I can't take any more of it, Susan," Emma said.

She dried her eyes. Susan organised a short meeting with the doctors at lunchtime the following day. They got sandwiches from the local bakery. Johnny and Susan asked Emma to outline the problems that she was encountering.

"I don't know whether I can keep going, Dr Cash," Emma recounted. "The phones never stop and the front desk is always queued out to the front door. It never stops for a minute. And then, while most of the patients are very nice, about one in ten are terrible. They are rude and aggressive and arrogant, and they belittle you all the time. As though it's my fault. After a while, I start to believe that it is my fault. I can't believe how abusive some people can be." She started crying again. "We are so busy and not many people see it from our point of view."

"If it makes you feel any better, Emma, I agree with nearly everything you say," said Dr Cash.

"Maybe if we put up a big sign saying that verbal abuse will not be tolerated then that might help," Susan suggested. "And what would you say if we write a stiff letter to some of them? As you say, ninety per cent are fine. It's just the others."

"Go and buy some extra stamps, Susan, and we'll do it," said Johnny.

And so the summer progressed. As far as this story at the centre of this novel is concerned, there were no enormous developments till September. However, as you now might have come to expect, these would be developments that would leave many of the participants in this story reeling. For the time being things ticked along.

Johnny and Fiona had an interesting teaching and learning session about how it really felt to be a GP. What do your head and your heart tell you at the same time? That sort of thing. Fiona felt that sessions like this were even better than pure clinical teaching: for instance, if you wanted to know about the optimum detection and management of high blood pressure in people with maturity onset diabetes, then there were loads of learning resources out there. Instead of that she was looking forward to discussing with Johnny how it *felt* to be a GP and she wondered if he felt it in exactly the same way.

Johnny believed that this was the sort of tutorial which would go even better in the pub on a Thursday night before the quiz rather than at four o'clock on a Tuesday afternoon. People's *real* perceptions would come out then.

Johnny said that he noted over the years that being a GP could well be the best job in the world, at least for much of the time. "Doctors are fascinating, set apart, part-observers, part-actors in people's saddest, strangest and most exhilarating experiences," he said. "The price we pay for this amazing privilege is that as a group we are the Chelsea, if not the Manchester United of the alcoholics league table, up there with the public house landlords and sailors. And we harm ourselves with great regularity. And the drugs—well, what can I say?"

"How come we are so well represented in these league tables?" asked Fiona.

"Well, it's something to do with being as good after 14 hours as you are at eight in the morning. And we never like to lose face. And we keep going and if we're feeling shit with bronchitis or flu you never call in sick, you just take some Orange Sip Powerful Extra Strength Decongestant and keep going dosed up to the eyeballs with Ephedrine. It's great. You'll know all that from working in hospital."

"All too true," said Fiona. "You just keep going. One other question has crossed my mind, Johnny. You read about the doctor-patient relationship and you and I know that it helps patients to get better, if it's done well, but is there any *proof* that it works—scientific, cast-iron proof?"

"A doctor in London called Michael Balint started the ball rolling back in the nineteen fifties. He said that if you were a good listener, tuning into what the patient said, both in words and in unspoken body language, you could reflect back to the patient by means of what he called 'counter-transference' and use your own feelings and encouragement to the patients' advantage."

"Wow!" said Fiona. "Go on."

"You could say that if the job is done well, then patients can get a health gain over and above what you'd expect from applying pure science, like simply prescribing penicillin for a child with tonsillitis. Beyond that, we also are there to interpret the patients' story and, at times, to witness their suffering."

The discussion went on and on and when Johnny asked her to later list some learning points from the tutorial, her written list went something like this:

1. The better the doctor-patient relationship, the more quickly the patient is likely to get better.
2. We are usually not that far away from events at the best and at the worst parts of peoples' lives.
3. Being a GP is not an ordinary job.

4. We are expected to break society's taboos by handling people's intimate places. If we don't do it when we should, as part of a thorough examination, then we could be held to be negligent.
5. We must be able to carry the responsibility of making numerous complex decisions, every day, often on the scantiest of available evidence, and if we get it wrong then the consequences can be serious.
6. We must show empathy and we must help people to face tragedy, loss and death.
7. We must be able to do all of the above on over 150 occasions every working week with minimal support.
8. Governments can't measure any of the above and therefore they give the impression, rightly or wrongly, that they are not interested in that aspect of the job.

Instead of just the eight topics she listed after the terminal care and peaceful demise of Percy Potts some weeks previously in the middle of Coronation Street, she listed three more:

1. No wonder that some of us turn to drink!
2. I still can't get it out of my head that Martin Roberts could be a bit of a wanker, although there is no scientific evidence to support my theory.
3. To keep me sane, I hope to watch Celtic play at least one match during the 2012-2013 season and I pray that they again come top of the Scottish Premier League. Please God.

Chapter 12

SUMMER ROLLED ON, and as August rolled over into September, the valley was bathed in unseasonable late summer sunshine. It stayed pleasantly warm despite the nights closing in. It was dark by eight thirty and Johnny felt that this was usually the first sign that winter would be here sooner rather than later, and with that the extra workload that the change of the seasons would bring.

The quiz team did well and seemed to win on at least one Thursday night in three, more often if Kate Williams was able to join them. Johnny bumped into Joe and Jenny Bradford one Saturday in Travelaway.com's branch on the High Street. The railway regulars were having a 'cultural' two-night weekend break in Barcelona which would mostly revolve around visiting the football stadium, the cathedral and a lot of tapas bars. Johnny and twenty-three others were listed to go. They had got it for one hundred and seventy quid each including flights and two nights in a three-star hotel including Catalonian hot buffet breakfast. Johnny was buying some Euros from the money exchange desk at the back behind the brochures. Joe and Jenny had just booked a last minute week in Cyprus and they were collecting their tickets and currency. While Joe was collecting his money, Jenny took Johnny aside out of Joe's line of vision and told him quietly that she was worried about Joe: for the past ten days he had been leaving food on his plate (he had never done that before, ever) and he had, she thought, lost a couple of pounds in weight. Johnny advised Jenny that she should bring Joe in either before Cyprus or shortly after they came back. She said that she had tried to do that just last week but that he simply kept saying he didn't want to trouble you and that he was sure he would be all right.

"Okay then, Jenny," said Johnny. "See how he gets on in Cyprus and maybe get some over the counter Ranitidine at the Pharmacy at the airport, but if he's not right then I want to see him the day after you get back."

Jenny nodded and out of the corner of her eye saw Joe returning from the currency counter with his Cypriot money.

The weekend after the Barcelona trip (it was a great success) Judy Carter invited as many people as were able to come from the Health Centre to the Trades Club. Her band, Nashville Express, were the warm up act for the legendary Canadian country band Waylon Hamilton and the Forty Niners who were playing at the Trades Club as part of a ball breaking forty two night UK and Ireland tour. It was fifteen pounds on the door and both bands were brilliant. Kate came along; she had planned to go to the Manchester Arena with three of her rocket scientist friends to see popular up-and-coming comedians, Ball and Sockett (thirty-two pounds fifty plus four pounds booking fee) but the show had been cancelled due to Adrian Sockett getting laryngitis. They would get the thirty-two and a half quid back but not the booking fee.

"Fucking daylight robbery if you ask me," said Frank Gilsenan, the pre-eminent world expert on how, if we ever sent a manned flight to Mars, you would slow it down prior to landing. "I mean, if you went to a brothel and paid an agreed price of say, seventy quid on the door, would they then say, 'Well sir, on top of that I am afraid there is a nine pounds twenty five pence shagging fee'—I ask you!"

They couldn't agree on that one. Anyway, Kate enjoyed the night thoroughly. She thought that both bands were brilliant. She had never heard the Canadian band before and it reminded her of when, as a child, she had been on vacation in Orlando with her parents. They were in Burgers International, on Route 192 in Kissimee, eating a seven-dollar special including side salad and were sharing a table with a family from West Virginia who, when they told them they were from Seattle, said sure, they'd heard of it and wasn't it a suburb of Vancouver.

The third Monday in September arrived and Johnny's last patient of the day, booked in for six fifteen, was Orla Hillman, brought in by her mum, Karen.

"Hello, Orla," Johnny said cheerfully. "Now then Karen, what can we do for Orla?"

"Well Dr Cash, she has been fine until bedtime last night, but since then, you can't really put your finger on it, she's just not herself. I don't know what it is, to be honest."

"Tell me a bit more," said Johnny.

"Well, you know, she's just a bit off, a bit, sort of, lethargic. I can't say any more than that. But she certainly doesn't look right."

Johnny asked a few more questions and then said to Orla, "Orla, I'm going to shine my little light into your ears, Pet, and I promise not to hurt you. I promise."

Orla was very good and Johnny felt her brow, looked into her ears and her throat, felt for her neck glands, counted her pulse rate at her wrist, and produced his stethoscope and listened to her heart sounds at the front and her lung sounds at the back. He took his time with her and thanked her for being so good.

"Well Karen, all I can find is that the bottom half of Orla's left ear drum, say, if it were a clock face, the part below the line from nine to three o'clock, well that bottom half is a bit red. Everything else looks fine. She is a borderline case for an antibiotic; having said that, they will usually mend without the help of penicillin or what have you, so I'll write you a prescription and then leave it to you as to whether or not you get it tonight. Certainly if she seems worse tomorrow then start her on it."

Karen nodded.

"The other thing that's worth saying, Karen, is that, as you know, children's conditions can change rapidly, in either direction, so if you are at all worried, in any shape or form, then bring her back, and we will look at her again. Any time at all. You know that. Any questions then, Karen?"

"No. Thank you Dr Cash. I think you've covered everything. What about eating, did you say?"

"As long as she gets liquids down, that will be okay. She should start eating properly tomorrow. With these ear infections it can knock them a little bit sideways. I certainly can't find anything else, Karen, but if you are in any way concerned tomorrow then I'll look at her again."

"Thank you Dr Cash. Thank you for seeing her." Karen took Orla's hand and they left. Orla smiled at Johnny as they went out of the door and for a second, and for the thousandth time in his career, he knew that he would never, ever, want to make a living doing anything else. He made a rough calculation in his head that there was, maybe, a two in one hundred chance that they would be back tomorrow. With children you could never be totally certain.

Johnny got home, for once, in time for Coronation Street, followed by Hartlepool Blues, a new post nine o'clock watershed police drama series in which the custody sergeant played in an Eric Clapton and Muddy Waters tribute band on his weekends off; it was filmed around all the famous landmarks of the North East. Johnny secretly wished that he played guitar just as well as Sgt Alasdair Durham did. And then he thought, just for a second, about WPC Jane Bellingham and her lovely handcuffs. He then watched News at Ten and went off to bed, his head full of nice thoughts. At about five thirty (he reckoned it must have been about five thirty) he had a lovely dream. In it his doorbell rang and there was WPC Jane Bellingham standing there, smiling, not in Police uniform but wearing jeans and a T-shirt, holding in one hand a pair of handcuffs and with the other hand beckoning to him to come with her. He did not have to say anything. Then all of a sudden it was six thirty and he woke up.

Tuesday morning his first patient was booked in for ten past eight. The computer was fully switched on and by five past eight Johnny was all ready. He had a couple of minutes to see if any of Monday's blood test results had come through online overnight.

All of a sudden he heard loud voices outside his door. There was obviously some sort of commotion at the front desk. He put his head round his consulting room door. It was Clive and Karen Hillman. Karen was holding Orla. She looked worse. Clive was shouting at Emma and Susan: "I want to see Dr Cash NOW! Half past eight is not good enough. This is what I pay my taxes for."

Johnny went back into his room and called the front desk.

"Send them right in if you want," he said to Emma.

"Thank you Dr Cash," she replied.

They came in. Orla looked worse.

"Tell me how Orla has been overnight," Johnny asked.

"Well," said Clive, "she looked a bit off at bedtime but this morning she is so much worse. She's gone very floppy. I don't know what to make of her."

"Let me have a look," Johnny said.

As he examined her he noticed, very faintly at first, a tiny spot appear over her right shoulder, followed by another tiny one nearby. He got a glass from his shelf and pressed it over the area. The spots did not disappear and Johnny felt sick in his stomach. Whatever happened the next few hours and days would be hell, absolute hell on earth, whatever the outcome, however good it would be. He prayed hard for a second, asking God for a good outcome. Orla deserved at least that.

"What do you think is the matter?" asked Clive Hillman politely but with a slight air of irritation.

"It looks as though Orla has some potentially very serious septicaemia type of condition, I'm afraid," said Johnny, showing that he was nervous.

"How come you didn't diagnose it last night?" demanded Mr Hillman.

"Well, how can I explain it? With every medical condition you care to name, there is a time when, if you see the patient right at the very start, there are no signs or symptoms. None at all. I examined her very thoroughly and I promise you that there was nothing like this at all, I promise. Absolutely nothing."

"Fuck me," said Mr Hillman. "Jesus, how can this happen?"

His wife said nothing.

"What I am going to do now," said Johnny calmly, "Is to give Orla some Penicillin and then we are going to get a blue light ambulance and take her straight to Rochdale Infirmary and I will come with you in the ambulance."

He lifted the phone and spoke to Susan. "Susan, I need the key to the drug cupboard here now immediately and dial 999 and get a blue light ambulance here straightaway. No delays."

There was a short pause while Susan asked him a question.

"Tell them it's a child with meningitis."

Ten seconds later Susan was in the room with the key.

"They're on to the ambulance people now," she said.

"I'm going to go in the ambulance," Johnny replied. "I might not be back for two or three hours. You'll have to cancel my morning surgery. If any patients complain just tell them that we have a very serious situation here. Tell them anything, in fact."

Johnny unlocked the cupboard and calculated the correct dose of Penicillin for a two-year-old child. Within 60 seconds (and within four minutes of them actually arriving in the building) he had given Orla an injection of 600mg of Benzylpenicillin into her muscle. She was too ill to cry. One or two more spots appeared and Johnny said a silent prayer again.

Within eight minutes of receiving the call the ambulance arrived. Johnny said to the paramedics that he would come in the ambulance and just to set off straightaway through the morning traffic. They switched on the siren and the blue light and the ambulance, containing the two paramedics, Orla and her mum and dad and Johnny set off as fast as they could. The journey was to take 28 minutes. Johnny rang the hospital on his mobile from the ambulance and asked to speak to the Emergency Room. They put him through straightaway.

"Accident and Emergency. Sister O'Hanlon speaking. How can we help?"

"It's Dr Cash, GP from Valley Mills, Sister. I've got a child called Orla Hillman, date of birth 10th of January 2010 with me. She looks like she's got meningococcal septicaemia. She's poorly and I'm in the ambulance with her. We should be there in twenty minutes. I gave her 600mg of Benzylpenicillin intramuscularly at nine minutes past eight. Can you speak to Paediatrics and maybe brief the Crash Team? I'm not normally very dictatorial, Sister, honestly, but I want everybody ready for when we arrive."

"Okay Doctor, leave it with me. I'll sort it all out."

"Thank you Sister O'Hanlon," said Johnny with a large note of gratitude in his voice.

The paramedic who wasn't driving erected an intravenous drip into Orla's weak little arm. They arrived at the Emergency Room after a breathless journey through the morning traffic and everybody was ready. Everybody Johnny had asked for was there.

He recounted the story to the Consultant and the system swung into gear straightaway. She took Johnny to one side and said, "You're on the ball, Dr Cash. You only saw her just after eight, didn't you?"

"You're right," Johnny replied, "but in actual fact I saw her at quarter past six last night and there was nothing to find. Nothing."

"I know. It's scary. It can appear to come from nowhere in hours, or, so it seems, in minutes, on occasions. See them too soon and there's nothing to find at all. It's terrifying. And you can't admit every unwell child to hospital, or where would we be then?"

Johnny nodded. For the second time since that day in Wales in 1975 (not counting being a medical student or a junior hospital doctor years ago) he was in a hospital emergency room. Orla had a lumber puncture, where they stick in a needle between two vertebrae in the lower back and take off cerebrospinal fluid and race it off to the lab to check for infection. They said that Dr Cash's diagnosis was correct. The consultant talked to Orla's parents and told them that the situation was very serious but that Dr Cash had done all the right things.

"Notwithstanding that, I have to inform you that the mortality rate for this illness is somewhere between one in ten and two in ten," Dr Dawood told them, "but your doctor has been very good," she said, "and Orla will get the best treatment available anywhere and, more than that, she is in our prayers and we pray that she will do well. We will be able to make a much firmer prediction by this time tomorrow, God willing. Thank you, Mr and Mrs Hillman."

For once, Clive Hillman didn't know what to say. Johnny got a taxi back to Valley Mills at his own expense and arrived back at quarter to eleven.

"How did you get on with Orla?" Susan asked.

"It was scary, really scary," said Johnny, "but hopefully she'll do well. We will know more after 24 hours with a bit of luck. How has it been here? Have they all been complaining?"

"No, only most of them," Susan said.

"You save someone's life and everybody complains."

"I know," said Susan. "Don't you believe it."

Johnny's last patient that night was Mr Cameron, squeezed in on the end.

"I am disgusted by you lot, Dr Cash. You can never get an appointment when you want one. And all that money they pay you."

"What have you come about, Mr Cameron?" Johnny asked.

"It's my haemorrhoids, Doctor."

"I want you to kneel down here on the floor in front of me, Mr Cameron."

"Do you want me to undress, Doctor?"

"No I just want you to kneel on the floor," said Johnny.

Mr Cameron, beige from top to toe, kneeled on the floor in the middle of the consulting room. Johnny picked up a scalpel from his operation tray.

"Are you a religious man, Mr Cameron?" he asked.

"Not really, Doctor, not really."

"Well, you are now, Mr Cameron. This morning I saw a little girl. Two years old. She had meningitis. Two years old. I did my best for her, Mr Cameron, but she might die, Mr Cameron, she might die. I want you to say the biggest prayer of your life for her, Mr Cameron. I'm not a particularly religious man, Mr Cameron, but this morning, in the ambulance with her, I said a prayer for her, Mr Cameron. Now will you pray for her?"

"If you say so, Doctor."

"We do our best," he replied, "and all that you and people like you can do is complain. Mr Cameron, if you were seriously ill, you would get all the attention you need, I promise you that. Now will you pray for that little girl, Mr Cameron?"

"I will, Doctor."

"Thank you Mr Cameron. You can get up now."

He sat in the chair again.

"You had one of our girls, young Emma, in tears recently, Mr Cameron, and she was only trying to help you. And all you could do was belittle her. You can sit in the nineteenth hole of your golf club and complain about us, Mr Cameron, but there are only 33,000 of us in the whole of the UK. If someone has real needs, Mr Cameron, then we will never turn them away. I promise you. All the GPs in the country would not even fill half of the seats at Old Trafford Football Ground. But we are there for you, Mr Cameron, and we always will be. I'm writing you a prescription now, Mr Cameron, and then you can go."

Johnny couldn't believe what he was saying. He had never spoken to a patient in that fashion before. He went home stressed and tired.

The following afternoon Johnny phoned the hospital. Orla was still in intensive care. She was stable and that was all that they could say at that stage. He phoned again the day after and was told that Orla was improving. She went on to have intravenous penicillin for a week and then, twenty-four hours after the drip came down, she was allowed home. She made a full recovery.

Johnny wrote a short but apologetic note to Mr Cameron saying that he had acted out of character because he had been worried about the little girl and he hoped that they would remain on good terms.

Mr Cameron visited the health centre again the following week and asked Emma for an appointment with that nice Dr Moore. He was really pleasant and thanked her profusely. She wondered what had got into him and she didn't ever find out about the altercation between him and Dr Cash or about the letter of apology.

Chapter 13

SUMMER TURNED INTO AUTUMN in the valley. The days remained mild but the season became increasingly wet. On the farmers' weather prediction for the coming week on BBC1 shown every Sunday evening (before Partridge and Pugh, a new family drama series about a grocer and a Methodist minister in Skipton in the Yorkshire Dales who join together to become amateur sleuths and help out their local police force to solve their most difficult cases) Senior Forecaster Bob Haddock vividly showed the storm systems and rain fronts on a mild south-westerly airflow, with menacing looking lines on the weather map, stretching as far back as Cape Cod, some 3,100 miles away. They would then drench Newfoundland, then soak North Atlantic shipping and finally make landfall in Dingle in County Kerry. Johnny said a silent prayer and thanked God that the mountains of Ireland and of Wales would soak up some of this watery advance before it hit Valley Mills. He remembered, fondly, a weekend in Galway with five of his friends when he had been a student, sometime around 1990. They had a fabulous time. They asked a man in a pub just off Eyre Square what the forecast would be for the next couple of days: he said that both days would be different—on Saturday it would rain vertically and on Sunday it would rain horizontally. The weekend was a great success.

On the first Thursday morning in October, Johnny's sixteenth patient (there had been fifteen before and there would be one after before the house calls) was Joe Bradford, date of birth 31st July 1961, of number 44 Moorside Crescent, Valley Mills. Johnny himself had grown up next door at number 42, from 1970 until he went away to University in 1988. They had been happy days. Johnny called him in. There was a gentle knock on the door and Joe and then Jenny came in and sat down. Johnny greeted them warmly.

"Come in. have a seat. It's been a long time since you were in this place, Joe," he said.

Jenny looked nervous.

"I think the last time was about five or six years ago," Joe said. "I came to see Dr Townsend about my dermatitis. A tube of Betnovate lasted me two years and then it went away. She cured me!"

"We're a smart bunch here, Joe," smiled Johnny. "We're definitely the smartest doctors for at least a quarter of a mile radius. Now tell me what's troubling you."

Jenny took up the conversation.

"Joe has had trouble eating recently and, to me, he has lost a bit of weight."

"Tell me a bit more," said Johnny.

"Well, he takes ages to get through a meal and he leaves stuff on the plate. It's not like him at all."

Johnny nodded and turned towards Joe.

"Thank you Jenny," he said. "Now Joe. Tell me exactly how it feels. Talk me through what happens at mealtimes."

"Well, it seems to me that certain foods get stuck on the way down. Usually meat, but some days it can be anything."

"What about liquids?" asked Johnny.

"Usually they go down okay but now and again it seems to be a bit slow."

"Anything you would describe as pain?"

"Not really, Johnny," replied Joe.

"Any indigestion or acid burning or anything like that?" asked Johnny.

"Just now and again, maybe after a hot curry or something like that."

"How much weight have you lost, would you say?"

Jenny butted in, "I'd say about half a stone, Doctor. Something like that."

Johnny thanked her for the information and after a few more questions about how he felt in himself, any allergies, had he had his blood pressure checked recently, and that sort of thing, he said to Joe that he was going to examine him. Joe slipped off his jacket and shirt. Johnny asked Joe to point to where he felt that the food stuck and Joe pointed towards the lower end of his breastbone.

"Just behind there," Joe said.

Johnny checked Joe's blood pressure and asked him to lie on the couch so that he could examine his tummy. He felt around and he could not feel anything unusual. Joe got dressed again.

"What do you think it could be?" asked Jenny.

"Well," he replied, "I think there are four possibilities; one is that it could be gastritis, which is inflammation of the stomach lining; two, is that it could be an ulcer. Number three, could be gall stones and, number four, could be something in the gullet, either acid refluxing up from the stomach, or it could be a swelling in the lining of the gullet."

Johnny knew which of them it would be.

"What should we do?" asked Joe.

"Well, I think that we need to do two things. Firstly, in case it is acid, I'm going to prescribe some Lansoprazole capsules. Secondly, I'm going to organise an endoscopy where they get you in for half a day and have a look down. I will do the referral letter today. And thirdly, if these show nothing, then I'll organise an ultrasound of your gall bladder."

Johnny printed the prescription for 28 days of Lansoprazole and told Joe that he would hear about the endoscopy in about a week. He shook both their hands and said to Joe that he wanted to see him in 28 days anyway. Mr and Mrs Bradford then left. Jenny, in particular, looked nervous.

Johnny dictated a referral letter straightaway. An abbreviated version of it would go something like this:

Dear Doctor,

I would value consideration of an urgent upper gastrointestinal endoscopy on this delightful 51-year-old truck driver and haulage depot manager whom I have known since both our childhoods. Mr Bradford is usually in good health. He attended recently with a short history of food sticking during mealtimes and he has lost about half a stone in weight. Physical examination is totally unremarkable. I have a very strong suspicion that Joe has a cancer approximately 60% of the way down his gullet and I would be grateful if you would see him, if possible, in the next few days. Thank you in anticipation.

Yours sincerely
Dr Daniel John Cash MRCGP

The letter was faxed to Rochdale Hospital and Joe received an appointment card inviting him to see Dr Alasdair Donaldson at 8.30 the following Tuesday. He should have nothing to eat or drink for 18 hours prior to the endoscopy and he would be given mild sedation and he should, therefore, not drive himself home after the procedure. Car parking would cost £2.50 for up to 6 hours. The directions were enclosed. Joe and Jenny both phoned their employers and told them that they would be having at least half a day away from work for medical reasons on the Tuesday.

While all this was going on on the Thursday morning, Judy Carter was doing her two-hours-every-two-weeks cleaning up and tidying at Johnny's apartment. She spent most of the time tidying his impressive CD collection (947 at the latest count, ranging from his namesake Johnny Cash to the Beatles to Mississippi Fred MacDowell) and putting away medical journals and his newly ironed shirts—she did them at home, twelve every two weeks—and leaving a note if he was down to less than 12 cans or bottles of beer. He did not drink at home as a rule. There were also bottles of malt whisky, gifts from grateful patients the previous Christmas, patients who didn't realise that he was not a regular whisky drinker. Judy charged him £15 for the cleaning and £12 for the shirts, making £27 every two weeks, paid in cash. Both were pretty sure (but neither of them totally sure) that the other person would be more than happy for the debt to be settled in kind. Then maybe it would be weekly rather than every fourteen days.

Whilst Judy was making Johnny's bed there was, all of a sudden, a ferocious rapid knocking at the front door. Judy instinctively opened it. Standing there were Martin Roberts (whom she knew a little bit; they had lived within 200 yards of each other for over ten years) and an elderly man she had never seen before. Martin asked if Dr Cash was at home.

"No," Judy replied. "He's at work. Can I pass on a message or anything?"

"I've just found this gentleman outside and he said he was feeling very unwell and I just knocked on the off chance," said Martin.

"No, he'll be out till about seven or eight tonight," said Judy.

"Can I bring Mr Smithies in just to sit down for a minute and maybe give him a glass of water?" asked Martin.

"Sure," said Judy. "Have a seat in the sitting room."

Judy went through the kitchen. She waited for the water to run cold. She had been playing her R.E.M. 'Automatic For The People' album in the kitchen (and had just got up to track eleven 'Nightswimming') loudly and she thought she'd better just turn the volume down a little. Less than a minute later she handed Mr Smithies a glass of water and sat down with them both. After a couple of minutes Mr Smithies said that he was feeling better thank you and that he felt okay to carry on to the bus stop.

Martin thanked Judy and said, "You'd better not tell Dr Cash that we've been: I know how hard he works and I'm sure he wouldn't be too pleased if he knew that we'd been calling at his home."

Judy nodded and the two men left. Judy went to finish her work. REM had just finished playing so she took them out of the CD player and thought, 'I wonder where he keeps "Gas Station Hero—the Greatest Hits of Hank Turner 1962-2001."' Hank was, of course, a legendary country singer from Fayetteville in Arkansas. He had been born into a poor family in 1939, received a small inheritance from an uncle in 1960 and used it for the down payment on a gasoline station. Around the same time he was becoming popular playing Marty Robbins and Jimmy Driftwood songs in local bars and he than discovered a talent for song writing and from that point on the rest was history. Fame did not prevent him from remembering his roots and he delighted in serving gas on his forecourt for his loyal customers, rain or shine, in between world tours. He died suddenly in a hotel room in London, England in 2001 at the age of 62, in the company of one of his fans, a 57-year-old lady called Martha Brodie from Newcastle. She subsequently told the Coroner that they were just sitting drinking tea in the hotel room when Hank suddenly felt unwell so he went to lie down on the bed and then he suddenly stopped breathing and that that's all that really happened.

By the time track fourteen, 'Back Seat of a Chevy,' had finished playing she was ready to leave. The place looked spotless. Judy collected the £30, left £3 change and went on her way. Pocketing the £27, she let her mind wander, just for a minute.

Every Monday Karen Hillman employed a gardener, Tony Kirkbride, to tidy up the half-acre garden around their splendid rural home. Tony was 27 and had replaced George Nelson in August. George was 71 and had had a minor stroke and had been advised to slow down.

Orla had recovered fully and every Monday attended Play Group from 9 until 3. This was her first week back after her illness.

Tony usually arrived on his motorbike at ten o'clock and stayed until 2. Karen usually made him a sandwich at 12.30. Over the last seven weeks Karen had fantasised more and more about Tony and she decided that this was the week that she would make her move.

It was unseasonably mild but very showery. Karen shouted for Tony at half past twelve to say that his sandwich was ready. He appeared at the back door and was soaking from the rain.

"You remind me of Mr Darcy in *Pride and Prejudice*, Tony," she said.

He took a bite of his cheese sandwich.

"Maybe you'd better take your top off and I'll dry it on the stove. In fact, if there is anything else I can do for you, then I'm sure you'll tell me, Tony," added Karen.

Their eyes met. She took him by the hand and, without a word, within ninety seconds, they were fucking in the marital bed. They lay down. He kissed her on the nipples and his rough hands grabbed her by the buttocks and they made love for a good thirty minutes. She came twice.

After a while she asked him, "How do you keep it going for so long?"

"Thirty minutes isn't long, Karen. It's not long at all," he replied.

They kept banging away for another five minutes and he then thought, "Well, this must be it" and he, too, thought of WPC Jane Bellingham with her handcuffs, and then, conscious of the time, he held his breath for ten seconds and, in spectacular fashion, came, pumping away for what seemed an eternity.

They lay still for a few minutes. It was wonderful. He withdrew and wiped himself.

"When the garden doesn't need doing in the winter, Tony, I am sure that we can find you some indoor jobs," Karen said.

On the Tuesday evening, Karen told Clive that she had to go and see her old school friend, Julie, who had come up from London to Rochdale to see her mother for a couple of nights. Karen, in fact, as you can guess, went to Tony's flat and there, in his scruffy bed, they had their second (out of seventeen) fuck. It lasted for an hour. For the first time in nineteen years, Karen felt sixteen again and she loved it.

The next Saturday morning, some nine days after Joe had come to see Johnny at the Health Centre, and some five days after Karen and the gardener had had their first session of lovemaking, Johnny was sitting at home around nine thirty. He had been to the Railway the night before, had three and a half pints of beer, slept well, woke up, had a large cup of coffee and was reading his many medical journals. He felt good about himself.

There was a brisk knock at the door. Johnny answered it. Outside were three people. One was a pleasant, smart looking man in his early forties, around Johnny's age. The other two were uniformed police officers, men in their twenties. There was no Jane Bellingham and no handcuffs.

"Dr Cash," the pleasant plain clothed man asked.

Johnny wondered what was going on.

"Sure. Yes. Dr Daniel John Cash. What can I do for you gentlemen?"

The plain-clothes man remained friendly.

"Dr Cash. We have received certain information about you and we would like to look around your residence, if you don't mind. Is this your main residence, Dr Cash?"

"Yes," Johnny replied. "I only own one house."

"I'll just tell you a bit more, Dr Cash." He remained pleasant and open. "I am Detective Inspector Richard Lees from West Yorkshire Police. We have received information which would suggest it would be appropriate to have a look around your house, Dr Cash. We are not in possession of a warrant but, with your co-operation, I am sure that we can wind this whole thing up in less than an hour. I can tell you now that I don't expect that we will find anything, Dr Cash. We are just following up a line of enquiry."

"Sure, come in lads," Johnny said. "Come into the sitting room."

All four of them sat down.

"Do you have anywhere in the house where you may have any drugs, Dr Cash?" asked Inspector Lees.

"Certainly, Inspector, every GP does," Johnny said. "There are two lots. Sometimes I bring my medical bag home. It contains emergency drugs. I don't think I brought it home last night as I'm not on call this weekend. And then there is a carrier bag in my bedroom, just by my bed. It contains my own blood pressure and cholesterol pills, some Gaviscon for Christmas, and some leftovers that patients return when they haven't taken a full course. That sort of thing."

"Any morphine or controlled drugs, Dr Cash?" asked Inspector Lees.

"No. Never. Ever. It wouldn't be right. We have a small quantity at the Health Centre locked away officially and logged in and recorded. But there is none here," said Johnny.

"Okay then, Doctor. Do you mind if we look around? I'm sure it won't take long," asked the Inspector.

"No lads, carry on. I'll stay in here with my journals then I'll not get in the way, if you see what I mean."

"Fine Doctor, thank you."

They started their search. Sixty seconds later the three officers returned into the sitting room. One of the constables was holding a Robinson's carrier bag from the supermarket.

"Is this the bag you mentioned, Dr Cash?" asked the Inspector.

"Sure, have a look through it. I don't mind," said Johnny.

The three officers examined the contents of the bag, removing each item one by one.

"First we have some Amoxicillin 500 capsules, 21 prescribed for a Mrs Elsie Blanchflower on 29th May 2009. There are 20 left in the pack," said Constable O'Neill.

"She thought that they gave her a bad stomach and she wouldn't take any more," said Johnny.

And so they went through them. Some Cefalexin capsules for a Helen Cartwright, some Bisacodyl suppositories for a Jane Hull, some anti dandruff shampoo (unopened), some Co-codamol effervescent painkillers for a Hubert Rigby, some Atenolol 50mg tablets for Dr Daniel Cash dated 5th October 2012 and some Simvastatin 80mg tablets for Dr Daniel Cash also dated 5th October 2012.

"It's reassuring to know that you doctors are made of the same stuff as the rest of us, isn't it, Doctor?" joked the Inspector. "I take Simvastatin but I only take 10mg."

"Next time you see your GP, ask him to look again at the evidence," said Johnny, smiling.

"I go to Aubrey Kendall down the road from you and you have to be dead before you can get an appointment there."

"Marginally safer than Harold Shipman," replied Johnny.

They both nodded. It was going well until Constable O'Neill interrupted the proceedings.

"I think we may have something here, Richard," he said.

"Let me have a look."

There were some ampoules of clear liquid. It was a packet of five and one was missing. There was no outer packet and no patient's name anywhere.

"Can you tell me what these are, Doctor?" asked the Inspector.

He held them for Johnny to look at. Johnny examined them closely. He looked baffled.

"They are ampoules of diamorphine. 10mg in each ampoule," said Johnny.

"What would they normally be used for, Doctor?" asked Inspector Lees. His tone changed almost imperceptibly.

"They are normally used for terminal patients, Inspector," said Johnny. "I have to say though that I had no idea that they were here, no idea at all and I can't offer any explanation as to why they would be there. Not the slightest idea, in fact."

"Well Doctor, to save me phoning the Chief Inspector, can you remind me what the rules are about storing controlled drugs like morphine and diamorphine? I am sure that you know them better than I do and probably better than her ladyship does."

"Sure. They have to be logged in in a special book, and they have to be stored in a locked container inside another locked container. It's that that makes it all the more baffling."

"Why is that, Doctor?"

"Well, I have never had any facility in the house to store morphine and what have you, and for that reason I have never done it. Never."

"And so you have no explanation?"

"None at all, Inspector. It's a mystery," said Johnny.

Johnny paused for a second and then he asked, "Can I ask you what has led to you coming here this morning, Inspector?"

"No problem at all, Doctor. We are just following up a line of enquiry, that's all. I can't tell you any more than that at this stage. What I can tell you though, Doctor, is that you are obviously as surprised by all this as myself and my two colleagues here. Furthermore you have been totally cooperative. I will obviously have to make a report on all this; then my superiors will decide whether or not to take it any further. Personally, I will recommend to them that no further action is taken because it is obvious to me that you didn't know that the drugs were there and you look as honest as the day is long and that you have no intention to use them for any nefarious or illegal purpose. Hopefully that will be that, to be honest."

"What could they do with me, if they wanted?" asked Johnny.

"Probably not so very much. But these days, if they follow the letter of the law, they may report the circumstances to the General Medical Council. As you probably know, if any doctor is convicted of a criminal offence, then there is a statutory duty to report him or her to the General Medical Council. Even stuff that has no immediate bearing on the practice of medicine. It's usually drunken driving, drug addiction, common assault at football matches, bar room brawls, that sort of thing. To be honest, we don't like reporting doctors to the General Medical Council because they've been trying to get it right for 154 years and to me, you'd get a more sensible opinion from the regulars at the Railway at half ten on a Friday evening. But that's a personal opinion, of course. For fuck's sake, don't quote me."

"I won't Inspector. Anyway, I appreciate your advice, honestly," said Johnny.

"What I want you to do is to come down to the Nick at two o'clock today, just to make a statement. Who you are, where you live and what happened this morning. And then, by half three, you'll be in Robinson's buying your groceries and then you can go home and forget all about this, watch England's Got Talent, then there's a good band playing in the Railway tonight, Methuselah. They're well worth listening to," said Inspector Lees. "Get yourself into there and forget about all this."

"I played guitar for them one night, at two minutes' notice, when the guitarist's dad had a heart attack," said Johnny.

"I know. I heard. They told me that you got a bit lost in the middle of 'Hotel California' but, apart from that, you were even better than the usual bloke. If his dad has another heart attack then you can stand in for him again, I'd say."

"I can't, I'm afraid," replied Johnny.

"Why not?" asked the Inspector.

"His dad's dead," replied Johnny. "Choked on a piece of meat in a restaurant in Benidorm a couple of weeks ago. No one there to do the Heimlich Manoeuvre."

"He sort of left without checking out," replied the Inspector.

All four men smiled. The three officers left, leaving Johnny alone. He reported to the Police Station at two o'clock. The WPC on the desk was lovely. She had been in to see Johnny the previous day for a prescription for the contraceptive pill and her eczema cream and you could see her wondering what the bloody hell Dr Cash was doing there on a Saturday afternoon.

Inspector Lees thanked Johnny for cooperating fully. They wrote down everything that had happened that morning and Johnny signed the bottom of the statement, Dr Daniel John Cash.

"Have a nice time in the Railway tonight, Doctor," he said.

"I sure will," said Johnny. "Thank you."

"Any time Doctor. I'll not be in the Railway myself tonight though, I'm afraid."

"How come, Inspector?" asked Johnny. "Something better on?"

"Lodge. Yates's," he replied.

Chapter 14

EARLY NOVEMBER 2012 saw the busy workload at the Valley Health Centre increase to something bordering on breaking point for some of the time. To lighten people's spirits, and to act as an antidote to the darkening days and the hectic pace of work, there was the expectation and the anticipation of the annual Valley Health Centre Christmas Eve party. This year it was to be held at the Steamer, a pub with a large function room situated on what is almost an island between the river and the canal, about a mile out of town. The function room held about 120 people and there were usually parties of people from four or five different workplaces. The menu included traditional Christmas fayre plus a vegetarian option. The booze would flow in what looked like unlimited quantities. People paid a small deposit in September; the numbers would always be approximate because with a workforce of about twenty people, someone was bound to have a significant change in their personal arrangements and relationships in the intervening three months. The entertainment included Ricky and Razzle (a local comedy act), Kev and Bev (a singing duo; not the most popular choice but the *really* good bands were booked up at Christmas for 2 or 3 years ahead), followed by Steve Slade, (a DJ specialising in glam rock and Christmas number ones). People were planning baby sitters and the womenfolk were choosing party outfits. There were rumours that Judy and Johnny had a secret pact to sing 'Lonely This Christmas', borrowing Kev and Bev's microphones. As in many things in life, nobody was totally sure. The Christmas Eve party would always produce a surprise or two; you could bet your life on it.

The first Sunday evening in November, the Hillmans were having supper. Things had been relatively peaceful in the household; no sex (or so Clive Hillman thought) and no recent beatings. Orla was keeping well and they were both grateful for the fact that she was back to full health and strength.

The topic of Tony Kirkbride came up. Clive asked Karen why he needed to come every Monday.

"There are always inside jobs to do. Small jobs inside the house," she told Clive.

He thought of their deteriorating financial situation.

"Maybe when the jobs are finished then we can let him go until Easter, then, Karen," he said. "What do you think?"

"Fair enough," she replied.

She deduced two things from the last sixty seconds of conversation—one, Clive probably didn't suspect anything (if he did he would probably have been more forceful in the discussion) and two, she could carry on fucking Tony in his flat (all she needed would be a steady stream of lies and excuses; nothing she couldn't come up with with a little forethought).

The following morning, Monday, Joe Bradford came to see Johnny at the Health Centre. He brought Jenny with him. She was working the 12 till 9 shift at Robinson's and didn't have to be at work for another three hours.

Johnny called them. They came in nervously and sat down opposite Johnny.

"We were just wondering what the hospital said, Dr Cash," said Jenny.

Johnny got the hospital letter up on the computer. He sighed almost imperceptibly. He knew that, despite all the skill and expertise available, skill which would match the best available anywhere on earth, Joe's situation was not good. He had decided to tell him most of the bad news on this occasion. There was only so much that a person could take in in one sitting. He would have to go over it again in the next couple of weeks anyway and he knew that he would be seeing lots of them over the next few weeks and, hopefully, months. Johnny took a deep breath. He recalled, as clearly as if it were yesterday, the day in July 1975 when Joe had carried him to safety through the sea in Wales. He would be grateful to him forever.

"Joe, you've got a partial blockage sixty per cent of the way down your oesophagus, your gullet. You know where I mean? I am pretty sure that that's what's been causing your symptoms."

"What do you think could be causing it?" asked Joe.

Johnny took another deep breath.

"It could be just scarring from acid reflux from your stomach, when acid burns the lining and causes scarring."

"What else could it be?" asked Joe.

The three of them became more and more nervous.

"There's no easy way to say this, I'm afraid. At your age, Joe, there is always the distinct possibility that it could be some sort of cancer that is the cause of the trouble," said Johnny.

"To be honest, Doctor, we had both sort of wondered if it could be something like that. You sort of start thinking," said Jenny.

"What do we do next, Johnny?" asked Joe.

"Well, I will get you a very urgent appointment with an oncologist. That's another name for someone who deals mostly with patients with different types of cancers. They are pretty expert at what they do. When the oncologist has seen you, I would imagine that they will organise an urgent CT scan of your chest and abdomen and that will tell us if the cancer, if indeed it is cancer, has remained localised or alternatively if it has spread."

He paused momentarily.

"I can see that this is likely to be a terrible, worrying time for you both. I can't begin to picture what it must be like. What I can promise is that firstly, I will move the situation on as quickly as humanly possible so that we know absolutely what is going on; secondly, I will answer any questions that you may have either now or in the future about your condition or about anything; thirdly, I will be available whenever you need anything, and lastly I promise that I will never, ever let you down. If there is anything that you need that either I or my colleagues here at the Health Centre can provide then I will obtain it for you, whether it be oncologists, radiotherapists, specialist nurses, any drugs you may need whether for treatment or symptom relief, anything at all. That is an absolute promise, Joe. Some people in your situation have said on occasions that they feel that they have been left high and dry, as though nothing is happening and no one is looking after them. I will never let that happen. Never. You understand? Joe, as you can imagine, I would do this for anyone in a situation anything like yours. But with you, you know, it's hard to say, but it's like… it's like I owe you one. I can't describe it any better than that."

Johnny himself was becoming emotional.

"You don't owe me a thing, Johnny. Don't be daft," said Joe.

"I do, Joe. I would do what I just described for any of my patients who would need the kind of help that you may need, Joe, but this is different. If it weren't for you then I wouldn't be sitting in this chair now. And I will never forget that, and I will never, ever let you down Joe, never."

Johnny's eyes became red and watered a little. He wiped them and smiled gently.

"I'd better shut up now, hadn't I? I'd better shut up, I think."

He stopped talking. Johnny shook both their hands and Joe and Jenny left the room silently and went home to digest the news.

Joe and Jenny arrived home. Jenny switched on the kettle and they sat down.

"How are you feeling, Joe?"

"I'm a bit stunned, to be honest."

"Same here," said Jenny.

"It makes everything sort of… sort of different. Things that seemed important yesterday are now less of a worry. It's like it is hanging over everything. Everything we do from now on will revolve around the cancer in my gullet."

"We'll fight it together, Joe. You know that."

"I'm nervous, Jenny. Very nervous."

Johnny decided to base the following Tuesday's teaching largely around issues of talking to patients who have a diagnosis of a life threatening or terminal illness. It would also be the time when, once a month, Al Hussein would call in to review Fiona's progress. Al's remit included many things but he excelled in particular in monitoring the progress of his younger doctors, watching them turn from highly capable junior doctors into intelligent, resilient, pleasant and industrious young GPs. General Practice training in his part of the Deanery was safe in his hands.

Many tutorials revolved around hard clinical topics such as Rheumatoid Arthritis, Diabetes and Childhood Infections, but Fiona found the more interesting ones revolved around practical, ethical and attitudinal subjects, not forgetting the principles behind how you run a medical practice. By the end of her year with Johnny, Fiona would know about Community Dependency Index, the Mental Health Act, Pill Ladders, Disability Benefits and also how to consume enough caffeine by day and wine by night to work for twelve hours and sleep for eight. On top of this she was trying to maintain a long term relationship with a young man called Christy McManus who was a Royal Air Force navigator currently based at Lossiemouth far away in the north of Scotland, some 400 miles away. It would take her eight hours to drive to see him, whereas his Nimrod reconnaissance plane could be overhead in 55 minutes. Their meetings bordered on being infrequent.

Al was pleased with Fiona's progress. He asked her if she had any questions or comments about how her year was going. She volunteered that general practice was very different from hospital work and that the sheer volume of illness being treated in the community left her with her head spinning some days.

Al told them he was writing a book entitled *Becoming a GP in Nine Years: what they don't teach you at Undergraduate Medical School* and he asked Johnny to write a chapter entitled "Facilitating Your Young Doctor" and he wondered if Fiona would write one entitled "The Longest Year—from Hospital Doctor to GP". They were both pleased to be asked.

When Al had gone, Johnny asked Fiona what she would say to a man in Joe Bradford's position with a probable diagnosis of inoperable cancer of the gullet.

"When you reach the stage where the diagnosis becomes certain, Fiona, how would you explain it?" he asked.

"That's a difficult one, Johnny," she replied. "As a group, doctors tend to skirt around the issue. It seems that we are not sure that there is a correct way to do it."

"Go on," said Johnny.

"Well, we tend to become anxious and fumble about and mess it up, I think. On the one hand, you could say to Joe Bradford that he has a two in one hundred chance of living for five years and a forty in one hundred chance of living for a year and be precise. But then, of course, you are aware of the fact that you can't be precise. Everyone is different. Or you could beat about the bush and say that this or that may help when you know in your heart that they won't. Not really."

"I think you've got it in one there, Fiona," said Johnny.

It was six o'clock and both of them were feeling a bit tired.

"Before we finish for today, Fiona, I love asking young doctors this question. Tell me what changes might occur in the practice of medicine in your professional lifetime. Say, roughly, the next 35 years," he asked.

"Jesus Johnny, You've put me on the spot there. Well, I don't know really," she paused. "I suppose you could have legislation for end of life decisions, or a cubicle type of thing where you walk in and you get instant blood test results, instant CT scanning and a diagnosis, all within five minutes, followed by an algorithm to help you decide what to do next with the patient."

"A bit like what we do now, only quicker," said Johnny.

"You're right," Fiona replied. "Oh, and there's one thing I nearly forgot—the male contraceptive pill. Now that *would* be interesting."

"You're telling me," replied Johnny. "Now I've got a totally non-medical question for you. Last year I was on a conference in Glasgow, and the year before I was visiting friends in Derry, and there's one word in the Celtic vocabulary that I don't understand. People kept going on about doing their messages. What the bloody hell does that mean?"

"Well, let's say on Saturday you went to fill your car up, then went to Robinson's to buy some lager and food and then went to WH Smith for a *Lead Guitarist Quarterly* magazine and then went to the bookies to put a bet on a horse, then that's doing your messages."

"You mean errands."

"No, they're not errands, they're messages."

And so, yet again, Johnny and Fiona learned a lot from each other and Johnny started thinking about the male contraceptive pill. He knew that it would probably be a good idea but he knew, at the same time, that he would probably never ever need it.

Chapter 15

TWO DAYS LATER, on the Thursday evening, during the part of the quiz where there is a hiatus between the papers being handed in and the answers and the winning teams being announced, Kate Williams asked Johnny if he would like to come round to her house the following week for a meal. Wednesday would suit her best, if it was okay for Johnny. Johnny checked his diary. Kate said that she would expect him around eight o'clock and as it was only two miles then maybe he should come by taxi. Johnny nodded and was secretly very pleased.

At the Hillman household, the domestic arrangements remained strained. Tony Kirkbride visited the house every Monday. It always seemed to be a Monday and Clive Hillman noted that this coincided with the day that Orla attended a playgroup. He was troubled by the fact that he had difficulty fucking Karen and he then concluded that maybe there were too many coincidences going on here and that on Monday he would do a bit of research.

He deliberately left his wallet in the pocket of a suit he did not usually wear for work in the back of his wardrobe so that, if nothing was going on when he got home, then at least he would have a legitimate excuse for arriving home at midday instead of after six o'clock.

Tony Kirkbride was late. He had had to get some petrol from a garage on foot as his motorbike had run dry. He arrived at eleven thirty and apologised to Karen profusely. They went straight upstairs and Karen was ready for anything that Tony could offer. He stripped off and kneeled at the bottom of the enormous bed and, slowly and methodically, with his tongue, worked slowly, very slowly, upwards from the inside of her right ankle all the way up to the inside of her knee and then onwards and upwards to within an inch of her labium. He then did the same on her left leg and then he gently rolled her over and applied his tongue to the crack between her buttocks and then he would proceed ever so slowly up her back to the nape of her beautiful neck. He would then roll her back over and they would then, he thought, fuck away for half an hour and then they would go downstairs and look into each other's eyes across the kitchen table. This would be their seventeenth time and there was no sign whatever for either of them that they were losing interest; on the contrary, each one seemed even better than the last, if such a thing could be possible.

Clive parked his Mercedes about 100 yards away from home and quietly walked the remaining distance on foot. He would pretend to Karen that a large wagon had been blocking the narrow road, if indeed nothing untoward was going on. The motorbike was parked on the drive. Clive quietly unlocked the back door, tiptoed through the kitchen and silently crept up the carpeted stairs. There were no sounds coming from anywhere in the house. Clive then imperceptibly opened the bedroom door and saw Tony Kirkbride's hairy back and his hairy head bent over Karen's buttocks. Both of them were totally naked and Karen was lying on her front quietly groaning with pleasure. He watched Tony Kirkbride slowly, ever so slowly, move his tongue upwards from her buttocks to her waistline. Clive calculated that this must have taken at least a minute.

At this point, at the top of his voice, Clive shouted out, "What the fuck is going on here?"

He had never seen two people move so quickly in his entire life. Never. They both turned over and both of them, at exactly the same time, saw Clive Hillman standing there holding a large pointed kitchen knife in his right hand. The knife was at least fourteen inches from tip to handle. Clive just stood there.

"Don't do anything Mr Hillman, please!" cried Tony.

“I’m going to cut your fucking cock off, take it down to Hadfield’s Chippy, make them dip it in batter, deep fry it, bring it back here and watch you eat it, you worthless little piece of shit.”

“No, Clive, No!” cried Karen.

“As for you, young lady, I’m going to make you watch.”

“Clive, no. Clive, please,” Karen pleaded.

Clive put the tip of the knife to Tony Kirkbride’s throat.

“You have two minutes to fuck off out of here. And don’t think that that’s the end of it, ’cos it’s not. It’s nowhere near the end of it. I know where you live and I have some powerful friends in this town. There are some of them that I wouldn’t want to get on the wrong side of myself. You will have to be very, very lucky to avoid them, you little prick but, you know, looking at it from their point of view, they will only have to be lucky once. Do you understand me? You will never know when they are coming for you. You will not see them until they are ready to deal with you, and deal with you they will. They will leave you alive, but in the sort of state where you will probably wish that you weren’t. Now fuck off out of here. If it’s me that ever, ever sees you again then you will be dead. And believe you me, you will prefer it that way.”

He stood and watched while Tony Kirkbride hurriedly dressed and then raced off on his motorbike. Neither of them would ever see him again.

“How many times?” he asked Karen.

“Two,” she replied.

“You lying little cunt!” he shouted. “How many? Don’t fuck me about.”

“Seventeen, I think.”

“You *think*? You don’t give me any but that little fucking shit gets seventeen!”

“I did try, Clive, you know that. I did try but then nothing seemed to happen. You remember surely?”

She wondered what to say next as he was still holding the knife.

“I tried Clive, I did try honestly. You know that I tried.”

For thirty terrifying seconds, long after the disappearing sound of the motorbike going down the drive had faded away, Clive Hillman held the tip of the knife to Karen’s throat.

"Please Clive, please don't do it. Please," she cried.

Then, as in the best gangster films, he stuck the tip of the knife into the skin on her neck but only by a millimetre, enough to draw, he hoped, just one tiny drop of blood. He withdrew the knife and hurled it on to the bedroom carpet.

"You fucking disgust me, you know that, you fucking well disgust me, you little whore," Clive said with bitter contempt. "It's all you're good for and, to be honest, I'm not even very sure about that."

Still in a state, Clive went back to work. He forgot his wallet again for the second time. Karen got dressed and went to collect Orla.

After work he went to the Railway and had two drinks with Martin Roberts and arrived home at seven thirty. Karen had made a beautiful meal for the three of them. Clive gave Orla a little kiss on the cheek but for the entire forty minutes there was no actual verbal communication between any of them.

Kate started planning dinner for Johnny's visit on Wednesday evening. She was not totally sure what the outcome of the evening was likely to be but she was equally sure that both of them felt that it was an excellent idea. The likely course of events would be that she would demonstrate her culinary skills and that she would talk about Seattle and that it would be a simple reciprocation of friendship. Johnny had made her very welcome when she first arrived in Valley Mills and she would always remember his kindness.

They would have asparagus for the first course. She would simmer the fresh asparagus for seven minutes and drain it and serve it hot with melted butter and lemon juice. For the main course she would make prawn jambalaya. She found her *Favorite American Recipes for All Occasions* book (a culinary travelogue, 25 dollars on special offer from Barnes and Noble in Seattle) and looked up Shrimp Jambalaya under the 'Flavors of the Deep South' chapter. She got unsalted butter, 1 medium onion, 2 cloves of garlic, 1 cup of celery, 3 red bell peppers (fairly mild), 5 yellow peppers (medium hot), 3 medium tomatoes, 700 gms of prawns, fish stock and Uncle Ben's rice. From Robinson's Fine Wines aisle (£9 per bottle and above) she chose a bottle of Daniel-Etienne Defaix Chablis (£11.99) and a bottle of Faustino VII Rioja (£9.59 on offer) and then got some Wensleydale cheese and crackers. She then bought a six-pack of Norseman.

Before leaving for work she checked that the ingredients were all present and correct and she made a point of being home for six. She changed into black jeans from Next and a red long sleeved silky top and she looked lovely. Johnny would arrive at the end of 'Coronation Street'.

At exactly eight o'clock, just as 'Based on an idea by Tony Warren' was disappearing off the top of the TV screen, her doorbell rang. She let Johnny in. He looked relaxed and gave her a tiny peck on her left cheek and then he gave her an identical bottle of Faustino VII Rioja and a box of After Eight Mints. She glanced at the bottle.

"Robinson's?" she asked, smiling.

"You know me well, Kate."

He then grabbed her gently round the waist and gave her another kiss on the cheek, a slightly more meaningful one this time.

"Did Steve McDonald get out of the police Station?" Johnny asked.

"Yes," Kate replied. "Liz collected him and he is due to be before the magistrates in the morning. Nine o'clock sharp."

Johnny reflected on the fact that courtrooms the world over must be a bit like what goes on many times per day in his consulting room. You could equate, say, a drink driving charge with, say, passing blood and losing weight. You would know instinctively that *something* was bound to happen but you wouldn't be sure of exactly what. For all the participants it would be an exhilarating mix of drama, excitement, disappointment and loss.

Johnny thought that Kate looked lovely. He took a seat in the sitting room. She brought him a pint of Norseman and twenty minutes later they sat at the dining table to tackle the asparagus. She told him about growing up in the Pacific North West. The rest of America felt, at times, to be a long way away. She then recounted how she sometimes missed America but, then again, Valley Mills and Manchester were good places to be.

"And your television, Johnny, well, what can I say? There are lots of programmes that intelligent people like us actually want to sit down and watch."

"And plenty that nobody in their right mind would want to watch, ever. Apparently, there was a programme on channel 121 about Eastern European Folklore in the nineteen eighties, shown last year and it only had one viewer—one viewer out of 61 million people. He was a Slovakian truck driver who had a small TV in his cab. He was stuck for five hours in a jam on the M62 near Leeds when a trailer load of battery acid overturned and burned six lanes of the road surface—three in either direction."

"I wonder if it made him homesick," said Kate, smiling.

They got on to the Jambalaya and it was beautiful. The wine was flowing and they were getting on really well.

"One thing I have to ask you Johnny is, well, why do they speak differently in every town and village over here? Someone told me that a librarian, say, in East Manchester, say Gorton, would have a different accent from a librarian in West Manchester, say, Flixton. It amazes me. It's great. But how come?"

"Well," said Johnny. "I'm no expert on Manchester accents but I know a bit about Yorkshire accents and dialect."

"But they're only 30 miles apart," interjected Kate.

"In England, 30 miles is a long way, Kate. Just try driving it. It's a major adventure. Anyway, to get back to speech," he went on. "In Leeds and Harrogate, two cities with only 14 miles between them, they speak differently from each other. And then you get bits of words that go missing altogether."

Kate was loving this and she listened intently, smiling and taking it all in.

"We have what they call Definite Article Reduction, one example being where the word *the* all but disappears," Johnny went on.

"What do you mean?" asked Kate.

"Well, the word *the* can be reduced simply to the letter 't' or, indeed, around the village of Wath-upon-Dearne in South Yorkshire, the word *the* goes missing altogether."

"Why is that?" asked Kate again.

"Well, there is a recession on, so people have to be economical with words as well as food and petrol and what have you," he joked.

She smiled.

"So, tell me if I'm wrong. There is a rock band called 'The The'. So, if someone from Wath-upon-Dearne told a friend in t'pub that they were going on the train to the arena to see The The, it would be something like this: I'm going on train to arena to see."

"You've nearly got it, Kate," said Johnny. "But there is, in fact, a quarter of a second pause where the *the* should be. Don't ask me why. It goes something like this: I'm going on… train to… arena to see …"

"Right," said Kate. "I understand. But why do they have the short pause?"

"Two reasons, firstly to give the listener an indication that the word ..*the*.. should be there, and secondly so that if somebody goes to the bar to buy a round of drinks then they haven't missed any of the conversation. Something like that."

Kate took the hint and opened the second bottle of Rioja. They finished the meal and then went to the soft seats and sat closely together on the small sofa. The CD player was playing Joni Mitchell's 'Blue.' Kate slipped her arm round Johnny's waist and pulled him gently towards her and, ever so softly, started kissing him. Johnny just melted and they kissed and kissed and Johnny put the flat of his hand on the front of her red blouse and could feel her erect nipples beneath. This was wonderful.

All of a sudden Johnny sat bolt upright.

"I can't, Kate. I'm sorry. I'd love to but I can't. I'm so sorry. I just can't."

"How come, Johnny, what's the matter?" she said, softly, without a hint of annoyance in her voice.

"I am your doctor, Kate. That's the only reason. It would go against every rule in the book. The rule is there to protect vulnerable patients from doctors who might exploit them. That's all."

"But I've only been to see you once, for my blood pressure pills. And I don't think I'm what could be classed as vulnerable, do you?"

"Not really," Johnny agreed.

With a lovely home cooked meal inside him and a pint of Norseman and four glasses of wine, Johnny agreed that the lovely Kate Williams, rocket scientist from Seattle, five feet six inches tall, with shoulder-length blonde hair and a beautiful face and who reminded him exactly of what the ideal girl-next-door should look like, didn't look vulnerable at all.

And so they rolled on to the rug on the floor and, in front of an open fire, he unfastened her black Next jeans, clumsily at first as the button at the top wouldn't undo. He then slid the zip down as far as it would go. Following this he slipped his hand around inside the top of the waistline of her jeans and, with his hand around the back, gently slid them down a centimetre at a time. He remembered from twenty-five years previously that if a girl lifted her beautiful buttocks off the floor/rug/bed/ sand/grass or hay at this point, then that could be interpreted as consent of some sort. In a choreographed fashion, beautiful Kate Williams used the strength of her beautiful legs and with her feet flat on the rug, lifted her gorgeous shapely backside about two inches into the air, or it could have been about three inches. Johnny couldn't tell but it was definitely far enough to be going on with.

Chapter 16

IT WAS THE END OF NOVEMBER. The valley was drenched by day after day of rain. People were busy getting ready for Christmas but, beneath the surface, there were families with problems and some of these problems were of the most overwhelming nature.

Joe and Jenny Bradford attended the hospital to enable Joe to have a CT scan of his chest and abdomen.

The expert Radiographer greeted him.

"Mr Bradford. Can you pop into the cubicle and strip everything off and slip into the gown, please? Then I'll come back for you in five minutes."

A short while later she showed him into the scanning room. The CT scanner seemed to nearly fill it. The machine was large and white and it had a round hole at one end.

"Mr Bradford, the doctor who performed your endoscopy believes that you could have a swelling on your oesophagus which may be cancerous. What this machine does is to take pictures of your gullet and your chest from different angles and it will be able to tell us the nature, size, shape and extent of this swelling. What I want you to do, Mr Bradford, is to lie absolutely still in there for me."

Joe thanked her. After his half hour in the tunnel, Joe asked about the follow up arrangements.

"We will send you an appointment for about seven days, Mr Bradford, when everything will be discussed with you. We will be able to go through all the aspects of your future treatment then. I know that this must be a very very anxious time for you but we will move things along as quickly as we can."

Joe and Jenny went home dreading what next week would bring. They were driving home when they noticed that the local garden centre was advertising a large selection of Christmas goods and decorations for sale. It would be a magical display, as usual, and had been a popular feature of Christmas in the valley for as many years as they could remember.

"Should we have a look inside?" asked Joe whilst they were waiting at a red light.

They both instinctively looked at each other and at that exact point they both suddenly realised and they both *knew*. Nothing was said but they both knew. They had heard of people who could earnestly and philosophically discuss death and dying over a nice Claret. They were probably lovely people of the *Guardian* reading classes and the conversation would probably go something like this—

"Clarissa, I have just been wondering how I can dovetail my terminal illness and all the implications of it with my responsibilities to you, the family and the bridge team."

But Joe and Jenny Bradford were not like that. They just took what life threw at them and took it on the chin and got on with it. They didn't ask for much and they certainly didn't ask for any more than they believed they were entitled to. They worked hard, paid their taxes, never cheated anybody, never broke the law and never got as much as a speeding ticket. Joe once found a wallet in the street. There was a driving licence in it so he returned it to the rightful owner. The address was a large detached house in the country near to the head of the valley. He rang the doorbell. The owner kept him waiting for twenty minutes while he spoke to his lawyer by telephone about getting off a speeding ticket. He could hear the conversation from the hallway—122 mph in his Jaguar on the M62, previous drink driving, previous speeding offence, all that sort of thing. When the Jaguar man finally elected to speak to Joe in the hallway, he thanked him half-heartedly and said, "Hold on, my good man, I have something for you," and gave him a pound coin out of his pocket and said, "You can see yourself out, old chap. Okay?" There had been one thousand and fifty pounds in the wallet along with ten credit cards.

They drove into the Garden Centre car park, parked the car and had a virtually silent look around the beautifully decorated shop. They bought a few Christmas decorations and paid at the checkout. The nice lady on the till wished them a happy Christmas.

"It will be lovely, won't it, love? I always look forward to Christmas. Best time of year."

The nice lady smiled and they smiled back and thanked her and wished her a very merry Christmas to her and her family.

The same day that Joe Bradford went for his CT scan, Johnny was doing his morning surgery. He saw his twentieth and final patient of the morning and she left his consulting room, with advice to lose half a stone in weight and carrying a bunch of prescriptions totalling fourteen items. She had asthma, diabetes, high blood pressure, high cholesterol and polyposis of the colon. Her prescriptions cost the NHS £2,700 per year.

As Mrs Jackson left the room, Emma came in carrying a large envelope.

"Sorry to bother you Dr Cash but the postman has just brought this envelope. I had to sign for it. I thought I'd better bring it in. It looks as though it could be important."

"Thank you, Emma," Johnny said. "It's good of you."

Emma left.

Johnny looked at the large envelope and for a minute could not believe his eyes. It was postmarked Manchester and on the outside in big letters said, "General Medical Council." He started trembling. It was the sort of correspondence that most doctors would never see in an entire professional career. It was bound to be bad news. With his shaking hands, Johnny opened the envelope. The contents ran to several pages of A4, beautifully typed. It read:

Dear Dr Cash,

I am writing to let you know that we have received two separate complaints or statutory notifications about you. The complaint is from Mr Clive Hillman and Mrs Karen Hillman. The statutory notification is from West Yorkshire Police.

We need to review the information provided by both these parties and look at the concerns raised. I have enclosed a leaflet that provides some information about our procedures which I hope you will find helpful.

At this stage you may provide any comments you may wish to make. However, you are under no obligation to do so. If you do wish to comment then it would be helpful if you could do so within the next four weeks.

We need you to complete the enclosed form about your Registration Status and your employment details as a Doctor.

We do understand that this type of enquiry can be stressful but your co-operation would be extremely helpful to enable us to reach a decision as quickly as possible.

I look forward to hearing from you.

Yours sincerely
Ms Alexandra Smith
Investigation Officer
Fitness to Practice Directorate
General Medical Council
Enc: Correspondence from Mr and Mrs Hillman
Correspondence from Chief Inspector George Dalgleish, West Yorkshire Police
A guide for Doctors referred to the GMC
Booklet outlining Good Medical Practice.

Johnny was shaking. He read on. The letter from Mr and Mrs Hillman was on their domestic notepaper. It looked corporate in nature with the address in the middle of the front page at the top:

HIGHER WARBLE HEY FARM
DOLLIPOTTS LANE
THWATT
VALLEY MILLS
HX99 5CU

We wish to complain about our GP, Dr Daniel John Cash. [It went on and on and lots of words were written in type heavy enough to sink through the page.]

Our GP, Dr Daniel Cash, recently saw our daughter, Orla Hillman. We write to accuse him of WILFUL NEGLECT of our daughter when he saw her recently on a Monday evening. He CURSORILY EXAMINED HER and FAILED TO DIAGNOSE THAT SHE WAS SUFFERING FROM A LIFE THREATENING ILLNESS. The examination (if you can call it an examination) lasted LESS THAN A MINUTE and he SENT OUR DAUGHTER HOME TO DIE.

In our opinion, and that of many of our friends, THIS MAN IS NOT FIT TO BE A DOCTOR and should be STRUCK OFF IMMEDIATELY and we also firmly believe that a CRIME has been committed. He should NEVER be allowed to treat a patient again and he is an ABSOLUTE DISGRACE TO HIS PROFESSION.

Yours sincerely
Clive and Karen Hillman

The letter from West Yorkshire Police went something like this:

We wish to report to the GMC the following facts. As a result of a definite line of enquiry we searched the home of Dr Daniel John cash recently. The search revealed evidence of various legal prescription-only medicines including partly consumed packets of antibiotics and suppositories. Notwithstanding this we also found, in a carrier bag in his bedroom, the quantity of four ampoules of Diamorphine, of 10mg strength.

Dr Cash was completely unable to account for the presence of these Controlled Drugs in an unlocked container (the aforementioned carrier bag) in his house.

I have to say that Dr Cash co-operated fully with the search of his house and appeared to have nothing to hide throughout the proceedings. He was helpful and open but could not, on specific questioning, give an explanation for the presence of this Drug. The Inspector who supervised the search was firmly of the opinion that Dr Cash had no sinister or ulterior motive with regard to the possession of the diamorphine.

He voluntarily attended Valley Mills Police Station by appointment and made a statement, copies of which can be made available on written request. The four ampoules of diamorphine were retained in safe storage at Valley Mills Police Station and can be released as evidence as required, subject to the requirements of the Controlled Drug Regulations.

Yours sincerely
George Dalgleish
Chief Inspector

Johnny was heartbroken. He felt that, at best, his career would be on hold for the next twelve or eighteen months. At worst, he may be struck off and could, in complete disgrace, be looking for another job by Easter. He thought of taxi driving or working at Robinson's on the next checkout to Jenny Bradford. Worst of all, and even worse than losing his job in a humiliating fashion, he would let down his friend Joe and he would have to break the promise that he had made to him to look after him over the coming months. Johnny had never before made a promise that he did not subsequently honour and it would break his own heart to do so.

Johnny made a phone call to his professional malpractice mutual insurance company, the Medical Indemnity Union, at their northern office in Sheffield. He had always paid them roughly five thousand pounds every year for discretionary insurance against malpractice claims. They were, by all accounts, a very professionally run, efficient and lean outfit. He had an appointment to see their Senior Solicitor the following week. December would be busy.

Johnny did not feel particularly religious but that night, at bedtime, he knelt down and prayed for two people, firstly for Joe Bradford, and secondly, for the first ever time in his life, he prayed for himself.

Chapter 17

JOE BRADFORD received his hospital appointment. The purpose of this was to discuss what would happen next with regard to his problem with his gullet. Johnny had previously given him the strongest hint that the swelling was likely to be a cancer of some sort. It was just more than half of the way down from his throat to his stomach and the CT scan the previous week would give an indication of how big it was, how far it had grown into his chest and whether there were any obvious signs of spread.

Joe and Jenny arrived ten minutes before their appointment time.

"Come in, Mr and Mrs Bradford," said a voice from inside the consulting room.

The voice belonged to Dr Adrian Jones, an affable Welshman in his late thirties. He reminded them of that Welsh newsreader on the BBC, both in appearance and manner. He put them completely at ease. Jenny expected him to start the discussion by saying, "In the House of Commons today…"

"Good morning Mr and Mrs Bradford," he said. "Before we start, how are you feeling, Mr Bradford?"

"I'm feeling nervous, Doctor. And I have a bit of an ache inside my chest. Otherwise I'm not feeling too bad, all things considered," said Joe.

"I can understand you being nervous, Mr Bradford. Everybody who comes here feels nervous. I even feel nervous myself even though, so far as I am aware, I am in pretty good health. The trouble with us doctors is that we become worriers. We do if we do our job properly. Anyway, that is enough about me."

Joe shuffled in his seat. He knew that bad news was coming his way. It was just a matter of finding out how bad. He knew that it must be somewhere between very bad and very very bad but he just wanted to know where. Jenny leaned over slightly and held his hand. Dr Jones continued. His voice took on a slightly grave tone.

"Mr Bradford, a significant percentage of the patients who come to our unit here have a type of cancer which can be put right, but the other side of the coin means that there are other patients who cannot be helped quite as much."

Joe knew what was coming and, nice as Dr Jones was, he just wished that he would get on with it.

"I have had a look at the films from your CT scan last week, along with the expert Radiologist, and we both feel that the CT scan shows a very large tumour around the middle part of your oesophagus, from the middle bit down towards your stomach." Dr Jones went on, "There is more of the tumour on the outside of your gullet than there is inside it. There are various ways of treating these things, Mr Bradford. Ways that include very major surgery, chemotherapy or radiotherapy."

"Which of these would be most appropriate in my case, do you think, Doctor?" asked Joe.

"Well, I think that the size of the tumour suggests that it is too big to remove surgically. I think that the best way of treating this would be a course of radiotherapy treatment, in which the radiation is directed directly at the tumour. What we would hope for would be for the radiotherapy to shrink the tumour down. This would give you a better quality of life and would, for the time being, make eating and drinking more straightforward. I am afraid that we are not looking at a cure here though, Mr Bradford. I am very, very sorry about that. Very sorry indeed."

Dr Jones fell silent. There was a lot of information being exchanged and he wanted to give Joe time to take it all in and ask any questions he wanted to. Jenny grabbed Joe's hand more tightly.

"Thank you for explaining it to us, Doctor Jones," she said. "I think it's in line with what we were expecting. Can you tell us, Doctor? What causes these things to start up and then to grow?"

"The honest answer, Mrs Bradford, is that, in most instances, there is no obvious cause behind it all," Dr Jones said. "I know that that may not sound like a satisfactory answer to you but it is the scientific truth. In some people it can be linked to drinking spirits and what have you, but the honest answer is that, in most instances, it just happens."

"How long do you think I have got, Dr Jones?" asked Joe.

"It is hard to generalise, Mr Bradford, I am afraid. It is sometimes possible for a person with what you have to live for a couple of years; sometimes, however, it is often only months though. Beyond that, we can only speculate."

"Thank you for being so honest with me, Dr Jones. I appreciate your openness," Joe Bradford said.

"How well do you get on with your GP, Mr Bradford?" asked Dr Jones.

"Well, Doctor, I actually grew up next door to him many years ago and then there was a time for a few years when our paths hardly ever crossed, but now I know him quite well again these days. He's a nice bloke."

"That's good, Mr Bradford, because Dr Cash will be the main co-ordinator and provider of your treatment as time goes on. I will write to him this week. In the meantime, I will book you in to start your course of radiotherapy. We can have the first session on Christmas Eve. And you will be home in time to take your lovely wife out for a Christmas Eve drink."

"Thank you, Doctor."

"What will happen on the first session, Mr Bradford, is that the expert radiation therapist will plan exactly on your body where the radiation beam needs to be directed. The process is called simulation and the therapist will mark your skin with tiny dots to mark where the radiation will go. The machine itself is called a linear accelerator. The whole process is, at the time of the course, totally painless. And then we will see how you get on in the New Year. I promise you, Mr Bradford, that the session on the 24th won't, of itself, spoil your Christmas."

At that point exactly the same thought went through the mind of all three of them but none of them revealed their thoughts to the other two.

"Thank you Doctor," said Jenny. "You have explained things very thoroughly."

"I never know how much people want to hear, to be honest. If you tell them too little then you worry that you have not told them as much as they would want to know. Then, if you bombard the person with information then you think that they might forget half of it. And some people don't want to know anything."

Doctor Jones was very nice but he was obviously a worrier, thought Jenny. They received their appointment card for 24th December and called again at the garden centre on the way to buy some more decorations.

Johnny had an appointment to keep in Sheffield. He was due to see solicitor Mr Charles Taylor, at the Northern office of the Medical Indemnity Union. They were a type of insurance company but not strictly an insurance company, in that their help was discretionary. They were a non-profit making mutual organisation. Basically they were there to defend doctors who are in difficulty; the help was restricted to medical things and did not cover the tiny number of cases where doctors got involved in murky activities such as theft, defamation and that sort of thing. Johnny, along with thousands of other doctors both in the UK and abroad, paid the medical Indemnity Union out of their own pockets. His premium was about a hundred pounds a week, week in, week out. An obstetrician or a neurosurgeon in Beverley Hills may find that they were paying a quarter of a million dollars insurance premiums in a year. Johnny was glad that his own insurance cover cost him a considerably more modest percentage of his income.

The meeting took nearly two hours. Charles Taylor went through the General Medical Council's letter. He was friendly, professional and he took his time going through the GMC correspondence line by line. After an hour his secretary brought in some coffee and some ginger biscuits. He had been too nervous to eat his breakfast before the journey.

"The GMC are a nervous beast, Dr Cash," said Mr Taylor. "And nervous beasts react in strange ways, as we all know."

Johnny nodded.

"We'll look at the two halves of this case separately. Now tell me first about Orla Hillman."

Johnny went through what happened, speaking slowly, in meticulous detail. He said that Orla had not looked too bad on the Monday evening. He had examined her thoroughly. But on the Tuesday morning things were very different.

"Is it true that if you see someone with meningitis at a very early stage then it can be very hard to detect?"

"Absolutely," said Johnny. "There are no symptoms or signs at all."

"And then what happens next?"

"Well, the usual course with this sort of thing is that a pin prick rash appears. It can be hard to detect but I spotted it straightaway."

"Well done," said Charles Taylor. "How is Orla doing now?"

"I am pleased to say that she is fine. She has made a full recovery," said Johnny.

"Excellent, and entirely due to the hard work of the good people in our beloved National Health Service."

Johnny had to agree with him. Without the expert treatment that she had received, Orla would have died in a matter of hours.

"Why do you think that the Hillmans have complained? I'm not completely sure that I understand it."

"I don't know either, Mr Taylor," said Johnny. He liked him and felt that he was in safe hands. He hoped so.

"He is, shall we say, a bit of a forceful character. Arrogant, big Merc, parks in disabled parking spaces, expensive suits. And he's got a difficult side, I'd say. The ladies on reception dread him coming through the door."

"Well, I think that the line we should take is to not give an inch. Despite his version of events, tell them that she got excellent care and made a full complete recovery. And you made thorough notes?"

"Yes, I've brought a copy."

"Good." Charles Taylor paused. "Now, on to the second and final bit. Where did this diamorphine come from?"

"I've honestly no idea. I'm fully aware of the regulations about storing controlled drugs and there is no way that I would break the rules or whatever. And why would I want to?"

"Could anyone have planted them in your house?"

"Nobody I'm aware of."

"Does anyone have access to your property? You live alone, don't you?"

"No. Yes. The only person who comes in is a young woman called Judy Carter. She cleans at the Health Centre and she does two hours at my place once every fortnight. Pay her cash. She's a lovely girl. Twenty-eight, a bit scatterbrained but she's honest as the day is long. And she's a hell of a good singer. Fronts a band called Nashville Express."

"God, she's beautiful," said Charles Taylor.

"I know."

"Saw her picture in the local paper last month. They played at the Hallam Arena. Didn't go myself, mind you. I only have one country album in my collection. Hank Turner, the Gas Station Hero. Died in a hotel room in London. A shame. He was with my Auntie Martha, Martha Brodie from Newcastle, at the time. She said he felt unwell, went to lie down on the bed and his heart just stopped beating. Something like that. Anyway, before he died, she got his autograph. One of his biggest fans, I think. Martha Brodie. On my dad's side." He paused, "Most of my CDs are the Stones. Seen them fourteen times. How they keep going I'll never know."

"A bit like lawyers and doctors."

"You're right," smiled Charles Taylor. He had gone up even further in Johnny's estimation. "Now where were we? Just go over the facts about the Morphine again."

Johnny went over the story again, including the voluntary visit to the police Station.

"You say you said the Police were pursuing a definite line of enquiry."

"Yes," said Johnny.

"Did they say what line of enquiry?"

"No. They were very nice but they told me they couldn't tell me anything more."

"Right. A bit of a puzzle."

"They certainly gave me the impression that they didn't think that I was up to anything."

"Good. Not that that will make a jot of difference to our learned friends."

They looked at the GMC letter again. After a couple of minutes Johnny asked Charles Taylor what might happen.

"The General Medical Council were brought about by an Act of Parliament in the year 1858. Parliament believed that the public needed protection from rogue doctors. And now each and every doctor in the land has to pay them over £400 per year for the privilege of the public being protected. You pay for them, not the taxpayer. Now what are they likely to do with you?" He went on. "They will consider my reply when I write to them on your behalf. And then, after that, there are various options. Firstly they could decide that there is no case to answer. Secondly they could, if they think that you have been a bad lad but only a bit of a bad lad, give you a written warning. Thirdly, they could have a Fitness to Practice hearing at their Star Chamber in Manchester. The newspapers would be there, the public galleries would be packed, with ice cream vans outside, burger vans, entertainers, TV cameras, Uncle Tom Cobley and All. Everybody would be there. The best cases are the ones where the doctor is screwing somebody. There was a GP from Lincoln who booked a last minute cruise, sharing a cabin with one of his patients. She was a country singer, also. Twenty years younger than him. He told the GMC that he'd only booked it because it was a half price offer online. Wouldn't have done so otherwise. They flew to Majorca then had two weeks around the Mediterranean. One of these P&O ships. Banging the arse off her morning, noon and night, by all accounts. Anyway, to cut a long story short, he stood in front of the GMC, in the dock for five days, with the world's press there and recounted the entire story. He was totally honest with them."

"Who grassed him up?"

"His ex-wife was in the next cabin. Pure coincidence. All alone. Outside cabin with a small balcony."

"What happened to him? What did the GMC decide?"

"They listened to the evidence and then they struck him off the medical register. Completely. Would never work as a doctor again."

"How old was he?"

"Seventy two."

Johnny returned to Valley Mills feeling a little easier. He phoned Al Hussein to put him in the picture about the complaint, phoned Judy to arrange a rehearsal (they were expected to sing a song together at the Christmas Eve party) and on the way home, bought 55 Christmas cards and 60 stamps. Three of the cards were for friends in Ireland (two stamps) and one for the United States (three stamps).

A few days before Christmas, Joe was feeling under the weather. He wasn't sure whether this was due to his illness or due to his anxiety about his illness. He booked an appointment to see Johnny. Jenny came along with him. The Health Centre looked busy. There were decorations and cards all over the place and a fantastic eight-feet high Christmas tree in the waiting room.

They sat opposite Johnny. Jenny herself thought that Johnny looked tired. Joe opened the conversation. Johnny was running nearly an hour late (he had seen twenty-three patients already that morning) but he didn't appear to look hurried. He let Joe go on.

"Morning Johnny. I went to see Dr Jones last week. We had a discussion about my condition and what he thought would be the most appropriate treatment. He reckoned that radiotherapy would shrink the tumour and then he said, to cut a long story short, that it's over to you, more or less. That you would be in charge."

Johnny smiled gently.

"The jobs I get, Joe, the jobs I get. At least no two days are the same. Adrian Jones has written to me. He wants you to have five radiotherapy sessions about ten days apart, starting Christmas Eve. That will shrink the tumour. And then I will be in charge, for my sins." He smiled again. "How do you feel about what you've been told so far, Joe?"

"Okay. It's a bit of an ordeal but you just get on with it. That's the way I do things. Same as you, I'd say. We were brought up that way."

Jenny nodded in agreement.

"What side effects could I get?" asked Joe.

"You could get a dry, sore mouth and throat, a bit of trouble swallowing, swelling of your gums, tiredness and a feeling of sunburn in your chest where the radiation enters. And tiredness. Overwhelming tiredness."

The room fell silent. Nobody quite knew what to say next.

After a few seconds, Johnny broached the next subject.

"There will come a time, Joe, when you will need what we call palliative treatment, treatment for pain or for any other symptoms you may or may not get. I will invite Sally O'Donnell, the specialist nurse from the Hospice, to come and see you, and between us and the District Nurses, we will provide any care and any support that you need, Joe, both for you and for your family. I promised you that much last month and well, at times, I can be a bit of an idiot but I never, ever go back on my promises. Ever. You are being very brave, both of you, and it is my job to do the rest. Joe, if it's six months or six years I will be there for you. I can't say any more than that."

"Thank you Johnny. Thank you so much," said Jenny. "Can we take this opportunity to wish you a happy Christmas, Johnny? And also Johnny, you look after yourself. Try and get a couple of days off. Get out to the pub more. It's Christmas. Just have a bit of rest."

"Thanks Johnny," said Joe. "Thanks for everything."

He shook his hand warmly and they left. All three of them knew that it would be Joe Bradford's last Christmas and, of course, at this point, they all developed a state of automatic collusion. They colluded with each other silently. Everybody knew but nobody said anything. They drove home and then Jenny drove off to Robinson's to start her eight hours shift on the checkout. It started to snow, ever so gently. Robinson's would be busy. Trolleys full of food, drink, wrapping paper and cranberry sauce. Always cranberry sauce. Joe's appetite was slowly getting less and less and Jenny continued to wonder where everybody else put all this food. She loved her job and she loved the company. The chief executive from Leeds turned up one morning at seven o'clock, put on an apron and told the ladies on the delicatessen counter that he was the new trainee. They liked him and he didn't divulge his real job title till six o'clock that night. He thanked them for being so nice, gave them £50 from his wallet to spend in the pub that weekend along with some stamped addressed envelopes, marked Private and Confidential: destination—Neil Robinson, Chief Executive etc etc saying to send any ideas for improving the company to him and the winner with the best idea would get a cheque for twenty thousand pounds.

Chapter 18

THE FOLLOWING THURSDAY at the pub quiz, Kate invited the whole quiz team and a couple of regulars from the Railway to have a light pre-Christmas supper at her house. It would be just for an hour and a half on the Thursday night closest to Christmas. She told Johnny and the team that a few of her University colleagues would be present but that they knew that they had to leave for quarter to nine; that was no problem because they were meeting some more folks from UMIST about 9.45 in a pub near to Victoria Station in Manchester.

Johnny didn't know quite what to make of the invitation. The atmosphere between him and Kate had been ever so slightly strained since the night of the dinner party. He reckoned that both of them were taken aback by what happened on the rug in front of the open fire that night. Not a word about it was exchanged between them, but Johnny thought he could detect that a very slight distance between them had opened up since that night. They were, above all, friends and also quiz team buddies and also there was a doctor-patient relationship to think of. Doctors were not supposed to do that sort of thing, ever, with a patient. There were rules about behaviour like that and Johnny had to agree that the rulebook was right. The relationship between patient and doctor was complex and was based on mutual trust and understanding and it was therapeutic. Academics could actually prove scientifically that a positive doctor-patient relationship helped people to get better more quickly. Furthermore, in the United Kingdom, it was not even based on money. He felt that he had let the side down ever so slightly; it would never ever happen again and he hoped that Kate would not tell a living soul. He did not want any more threats to his career than the ones that were already hanging over him.

He went to Robinson's on the way home to buy some wine and had a short natter with Jenny on till number 16. She wished him a merry Christmas. Johnny said that he hoped Joe was feeling reasonable enough and that he was taking the wine to a friend's house before the quiz. He got to Kate's by ten past seven. A few of the aerospace people were there, talking respectfully about the 1986 space shuttle disaster.

Johnny was idly looking at Kate's Christmas cards on the mantelpiece. There were loads. In the middle of this conglomeration of pictures of Santa and open fires and sheep in snowy fields at dusk was a Christmas card of the type he had never seen before. It was a large card. The picture on the front showed a large Christmas tree on a large lawn but behind the Christmas tree was the White House. A Christmas tree on the White House lawn! Johnny felt that he had to look inside. Johnny's eyes were nearly on stalks at this point. The printed text read something like this (he had to read it twice):

WITH WARMEST WISHES FOR
CHRISTMAS AND THE NEW YEAR
FROM PRESIDENT MACDONALD AND FAMILY

It was signed underneath. Jesus. A Christmas card from the President of the United States! Johnny went to find Kate in the kitchen. He waited until she had finished speaking to Angus from the quiz team. He wasn't totally sure how friendly she would be after the rug incident. He whispered fairly softly, about two inches from her right ear.

"I've been peeping at your Christmas cards and you have a lovely Christmas card from President MacDonald," he smiled. "It reads: *With love to Kate... hope you are enjoying England... maybe you will find that special relationship*!! Would you like to explain?"

Johnny could not get over this bit of excitement. Kate was friendly enough when she answered.

"I am President MacDonald's niece."

"Jesus, Kate."

"No, just the President, not Jesus."

"How long have you been President MacDonald's niece?"

"Thirty-six years and eleven months, I suppose. President MacDonald is exactly fourteen years to the day older than I am."

"Well, I'll be damned."

"Whatever you do, don't tell anyone Johnny. I meant to put that card away. Please don't tell anybody. My life is busy enough."

"Okay Kate, I'll not tell a soul. But just answer me one question and I promise that I'll never mention the subject again. What is President MacDonald like?"

"President MacDonald is lovely. Warm, intelligent, hard working. Now, no more discussion about the President, please, Johnny. Not in this context anyway."

She smiled beautifully with that girl-next-door smile that he could not resist.

"That's a deal, Kate, now go and hide that Christmas card as soon as you're able."

"Okay, Johnny."

The evening went very well. At the quiz he whispered again, this time in her left ear, "Did you hide the Christmas card?"

"No, I brought it here. It's in my bag. You have to take it home and put it up in your house."

"What will Judy think?"

"She'll think that at long last you've made good. Local boy made good. She'll be impressed."

"But she'll see that it's addressed to Kate, not to me."

"I have a friend high up in the CIA. I'll get him to post you some magic stuff that makes things invisible. You just paint it over what the President has written. And then you write your caption in. Something like...*To Johnny, from your old friend.*"

"Kate, you're too smart for me sometimes."

He loved her when she teased him like this.

The quiz went well and, yet again, they were joint first and yet again they were in a tiebreak with that same team of teachers on the next table. The question was a numbers question and the closest won the quiz.

The whole pub went quiet. Sean, the quizmaster, read the tiebreak question out: "How many years ago was the General Medical Council established by an Act of Parliament?"

Everybody laughed. A medical question and a doctor in the team! Not exactly fair. (Mind you, he was known to get them wrong now and again.) Everybody looked at Johnny. Little did they know. Not even Kate knew. The teachers conferred and they answered first.

"131 years, Sean."

It was Johnny's turn. Every single person in the pub was watching him. There was total silence.

"154 years."

There was silence again.

"Yes, it was 154 years exactly. Established by Act of Parliament in 1858. How did you know the exact answer, Johnny? You're not in any sort of trouble are you? Screwing patients or that sort of thing?" said Sean, in fun.

Everybody laughed again.

A red-faced man at the bar shouted, "I bet he hasn't got it in him."

The laughter was now wall-to-wall and uncontrollable.

"And you can piss off mate, for a start," joked Johnny.

"My sister wants to screw you, Johnny, and she's only sixty-six," the red faced man replied.

"Tell her to make an appointment at the Health Centre and I'll show her my mettle. And tell her there's a discount for pensioners," Johnny retorted.

And so the evening finished off in a hilarious fashion. Kate had blushed a bit when the screwing patients bit came up in the banter but, thankfully, everybody was too caught up in the fun to notice. She slipped Johnny the Presidential Christmas card and they all went home their separate ways. It had been an excellent night and they had £30 to spend on beer and peanuts at the next quiz night at the beginning of January.

There was at least one more night of revelry before Christmas and it was the Health Centre Christmas Party. Johnny had wondered about asking Kate to go along with him but thought it better not to, in view of what had happened on the rug that night in November. The party was always on Christmas Eve. Johnny and Judy had been asked to do a song together with the band accompanying them.

At the Health Centre at ten to eight one morning they agreed to do 'Return of the Grievous Angel' as planned. Everything was set for the night.

Johnny was shocked to see that Clive Hillman had booked an appointment to see him later that morning. When he came into Johnny's consulting room he sat down and came straight to the point.

"Dr Cash, I have come about my eczema. I've been somewhat stressed lately and it has flared up."

He didn't mention the GMC. Johnny was baffled.

"What has caused it to flare up, Mr Hillman? What is stressing you out? And how, may I ask, is Orla?"

"Orla is fine, Dr Cash." He paused briefly. "I found my wife with another man, Dr Cash. I think it's that that's started it off," said Mr Hillman.

"I'm sorry to hear that, Mr Hillman. I'll get you a prescription for some good cream."

Mr Hillman nodded.

"As far as the General Medical Council is concerned, Dr Cash, I have no doubt that the medical establishment will close ranks and exonerate you. I have no doubt at all. What do you think, Dr Cash? You are all well known for looking after your own kind."

Johnny stood up. He felt that he could get his point over if he was standing up whilst Mr Hillman was seated. He remembered that Clive Hillman was taller than he was. Clive Hillman then stood up at this point, presumably to use his height to his advantage.

"Sit down Mr Hillman. Sit down, please."

Clive Hillman sat down again in the same chair.

"Mr Hillman, we have no medical establishment in this country, Mr Hillman. None at all. We are not like a golf club or Freemasonry or the Catenians. There is no 'you scratch my back I'll scratch yours' mentality. None at all, Mr Hillman. We are a loose conglomeration of individuals or dare I say, individualists and we are too busy treating the sick to have time to club together in smoke-filled back rooms and collude and hatch plans. I have no doubt, Mr Hillman, that the General

Medical Council will give you a fair hearing and listen to your complaint and adjudicate in a reasoned and a professional fashion. What is more, I pay over £400 per year out of my own pocket for the privilege of having them as my lord and master, judge, jury and, very often, Mr Hillman, executioner."

Johnny did not mention the ampoules of Diamorphine as he felt that Mr Hillman would use that particular piece of information to his own advantage.

"Is there anything else, Mr Hillman?" asked Johnny.

"No thank you, Doctor; nothing at all."

He got up and left. If there was any Christmas spirit in Clive Hillman then it certainly didn't show.

Joe and Jenny went to the hospital and Joe was measured up for his course of radiotherapy. He felt a bit unwell with everything that was going on so Jenny phoned the Health Centre and asked the girls to ask Johnny to do a sickness certificate for Joe.

After the hospital they went out into town for two drinks and then they had a curry on the way home. Joe struggled with it. There had been a light snowfall and Joe slipped coming out of the pub. Jenny caught him and they laughed about it. They were home for ten o'clock and finished wrapping presents and put them under the Christmas tree. They both felt tired and they decided to have an early night.

The Steamer looked beautiful for the Christmas Eve party. Three groups of people were booked in for the evening. First there was a crowd from Robinson's, about forty employees in total. Then there was a party from Calder Automotive, a factory where they manufactured catalytic converters. And then there were the 35 people from the Valley Health Centre, made up of twenty staff, fifteen of them with partners. Johnny went alone. Two of the others had no partners and two people were ill at home with influenza or bronchitis. The least enjoyable part of the evening was when 110 people all turn up within 15 minutes of each other and the bar staff were run off their feet. Johnny remembered one Christmas Eve party. He was standing at the bar having bought a drink for the first four people to arrive. He had pocketed his change and was just about to sit down, very relieved that he had only had to buy a small round of drinks, when one of the girls came back to the bar and asked Johnny if she could have more ice.

"Of course," he said, painfully aware of the fact that this could add another 20 seconds to the proceedings and that in those 20 seconds more people from his party could arrive.

At exactly the same second that he said "Thank you" to the barman for the extra ice, fourteen more of the party arrived. This went on and on and he ended up standing at the bar for twenty-eight minutes and in that time bought 25 drinks, costing well over £50.

There were two rounds of drinks before the meal and they had paid in advance for 14 bottles of wine between the tables. Fiona and Judy sat next to each other. Fiona was wearing a little black dress with sequins and Judy was sporting a long ethnic skirt and a long sleeved top. The booze flowed and, by the time the main course was over, people's life stories, things which they have always kept to themselves and not divulged to others, started to appear, firstly in small morsels of information and then in larger, even tastier portions.

"I grew up in Glasgow," said Fiona to Judy. "Brilliant city. Friendly people. Weather is just the same as round here. At least one good football team and a strong sense of community."

Judy was listening intently and the wine kept flowing.

"And then, when I was nineteen, my life fell apart." Fiona started sobbing. "I was in my second year at Med School and I was dating a lad called Callum. Lovely, he was. Studying Civil Engineering. From Aberdeen. A brilliant singer. Traditional Scottish ballads and all that. No Bay City Rollers. We had a great time and I loved him, really loved him. And then I fell pregnant. Ten weeks on and I was wondering should I give up my studies and keep the baby and never become a doctor, or should I have a termination. I was racked with grief and guilt. A good Roman Catholic girl and me wanting a termination."

Fiona started sobbing more and more. Judy moved closer to listen as the band were playing quite loudly by now.

"And then it happened," said Fiona.

"What happened, love? Tell me what happened, Fiona."

She put her arm around her shoulder.

"I was standing at the bus stop waiting for the bus to go to lectures. Twenty to nine on a Thursday morning in January. It was raining. A steady rain, with a bit of sleet. It was snowing up in the Highlands. And then I looked down and the pavement was red. Bright red blood, just going drip, drip, drip without stopping. Drip, drip, drip. A lady waiting at the bus stop lived close by and she took me home and comforted me; asked me how I felt and then made me a big mug of hot tea. Hot tea. It was like nectar, that cold wet morning. And then she phoned for an ambulance and she came with me to the hospital. I'd never met her before. She stayed with me. The doctor said I'd lost the baby and I just cried and cried, and that lady stayed with me. I still don't know who she was, but if I could find her, and if I won a million on the lottery, I'd take half of it round to her house, knock on the door and say, 'Here you are love, it's from me. You didn't know me that Thursday morning but you helped me without hesitation. You didn't ask for anything in return. And I want you to have this.' And that experience helped me to be a slightly better doctor. I thought I'd always give slightly more than they'd expect. And so on. The experience helped me, Judy, it helped me. And you have helped me too, by listening."

Fiona slowly stopped sobbing. She felt just a tiny bit better by now.

"And what about Callum?" asked Judy.

"He finished Uni and then got a job offer in Toronto. We both felt that the relationship had run its course after two years. I saw him off to catch the Air Canada flight at Prestwick. The last thing he said to me was, well, he asked how things would have been if I'd not lost the baby."

Fiona started sobbing again.

Judy held her hand and said, "Now it's my turn, Fiona. I'll just top up our glasses first."

She filled their wine glasses. The band played on.

"In about twenty minutes they'll want me on stage with Johnny to sing a duet. We checked with the band and they know it."

"What are you going to sing, Judy?" Fiona asked.

"That's a secret till we get on stage." Judy smiled and paused for a while. "It'll be good though. You can bet your bottom dollar on that."

"I'm sure. Now tell me your story, Judy," said Fiona.

"I had a baby when I was fifteen," said Judy.

Fiona looked astonished.

"Where is he or she now?"

"He lives near New York. Somewhere on Long Island."

"What?"

"He lives near New York."

"How come?" asked Fiona.

"It's a long story. One night, just two weeks before my fourteenth birthday—we lived in Leeds at the time—my brother had been to the pub with some of his friends. They were all eighteen or nineteen. They came back at ten o'clock, about six of them. Mum and dad were out and I was lying in bed. I'd just finished my homework."

"Go on," said Fiona.

"They said they were going to the 24-hour corner shop to buy some more beer. But only five of them went and one of the lads, Keith Saville, he slipped back into the house and he came into my bedroom and raped me. He threatened to kill me if I screamed."

Judy's eyes reddened.

"What happened then, Judy?" asked Fiona.

"I didn't tell anyone. I was afraid of what he would do. Then, five months later, Mum took me to the doctor because my tummy was swelling. The doctor got her sonic aid machine out, put the probe on my swollen bit, listened intently for a minute and said, 'Mrs Carter. Judy. I can hear two different sounds here. One is from the aorta, at 96 beats per minute, and one is at 140 beats per minute and it can only mean one thing, Mrs Carter. Mrs Carter, I don't know how to put this but I think that Judy is expecting a baby." That set my mum off. She turned on the doctor. She said it couldn't be. The doctor said that there could be no other explanation and then my mum turned on me and said horrible things in front of the doctor, like calling me a dirty little bitch. It's only then that I told her what happened."

"In the name of Christ, Judy, what happened next?" asked Fiona.

"Keith Saville was arrested. He denied everything. And then it came to court. The Police believed me rather than him. His barrister cross-examined me for two hours. A tall elegant man called Morton Gould. Elegant, but not very nice with it. He tried to tear me to shreds, to make mincemeat of me. Said that I led Keith Saville on. He said, 'I put it to you Miss Carter, that you invited him into your bed and that you loved every minute of it, Miss Carter.' Then I said that I would not answer any more of his questions until he promised to let me speak without interruption. Tall, posh and elegant but not a nice man."

"What happened then?" asked Fiona as she held Judy's hand.

"The judge was really nice and told me to go on so I continued. I said that it was my job in court to tell the truth and it was Morton Gould's job to twist and lie and suggest things and plant ideas into the minds of the jury, things that hadn't happened. I pointed my finger at Mr Gould and said, 'You are like a bunch of whores, with your fancy wigs on.' Mr Gould then appealed to the judge. He said, 'Your Honour, this is completely out of order' and the judge said, he said, 'Mr Gould, you promised to let Miss Carter speak and let her speak you will.' And then he told me to go on. So I said again, 'You lot are like a bunch of whores. You do anything for anybody if the money is right. You would strip yourself bollock naked in this courtroom in front of this jury if I gave you a thousand pounds in cash to do it.' The jury's eyes lit up. The judge told me to stick to the point or he would place me in contempt of court. I apologised and then I paused for a few seconds and the judge said, 'Please continue, Miss Carter,' so, very, slowly I told the courtroom what happened."

"What did you say?" asked Fiona.

"I told them. I said, 'Ladies and gentlemen of the Jury, I will tell you exactly what happened that night.' The courtroom was silent. You could hear a pin drop. I went on. I said, 'On that night, the night I was raped, I had finished my homework and I had gone to bed. It was just after ten o'clock. I heard my brother's friends downstairs. They were laughing and playing music. Then I heard the front door slam and I thought they'd gone back out again. I was just dozing off to sleep when my bedroom door opened. I looked up and Keith Saville was standing there. I asked him what he wanted and he said he just wanted to talk to me. Then he slid his hand under the bedclothes and started stroking my tummy. Then his hand went further down, further and further.'"

"What happened then, Judy?" asked Fiona.

"I said, 'I leapt out of bed as quickly as I could, knocking him back against the wall. With that he threw me down on the bed and pinned my shoulders down and then he rammed his erect penis right inside me. And I was a virgin at the time. I tried fighting him but he was too strong. And then, in about thirty seconds, it was all over. He threatened to kill me if I said anything.' I, then, pointed at Keith Saville in the dock and said that if that man was innocent of rape then I am the Queen of Sheba. He just kept looking at the floor. The judge summed up then the jury went out and then the judge said that I could go with my mum and dad for a cup of tea. I was shaking. Shaking. Then after three quarters of an hour, they called us back in. A court official then asked the foreman of the jury if they had reached a verdict and he said, 'Yes.' He asked what verdict they had reached on the charge of rape against Judith Carter and he said, 'Guilty.' A few people in the gallery cheered. The judge asked them to keep quiet and then he addressed Keith Saville. He said, 'Keith Saville, you have been found guilty of the charge of rape against this young girl here. You have lied in court and you appear to have little or no remorse about your actions. She is carrying your baby and her life will never be the same after this. Never. When you lie in your prison cell at night then I would like you to contemplate the results of your terrible deeds against this young girl, Mr Saville. I sentence you to eight years in prison. Take him down.'"

"What happened then?" asked Fiona.

"I told the Social Worker that I wanted to give the baby up for adoption. And that's what happened. When he was born, weighing eight pounds, I felt an overwhelming rush of love and I held him and then I thought, I thought, am I doing the right or wrong thing here? I held him for five minutes and then they took him and I just cried. Those moments remain etched on my memory and they will remain there forever."

She was crying a little at this point.

"What happened to him, Judy?" asked Fiona.

"He was adopted by a lovely family. Couldn't have children. She was a stewardess and he was an airline pilot. First officer. He's now a captain, I think," said Judy.

"And when did they move to America?" said Fiona.

"About eleven years ago. The young lad's called Dean. Dean Lovell. Speaks with an American accent apparently. Fourteen years old. Same age as I was when I had him. And then you think, well, should I have done things differently? Should I have kept him? I have lain awake night after night wondering. I dream about him. I think about him all the time. But then you think, you think well, really you just get on with life. You just get on with it. You just keep going. And you look around and you see people who feel sorry for themselves the whole time and you don't know whether you should help them or give them a kick up the backside and say to them, 'Just get on with it' but I think you just keep going and you fight it and you keep smiling and you fight back and show a brave face to the world and dry your tears and try to look okay. Us plain folks, that's what we do, we dry our tears and we smile and we just keep going."

"Did you ever get to…?"

Fiona was speaking that last bit but when she had come out with the first five words of that sentence, the "Did you ever get to…?" they were suddenly interrupted by Susan who was tapping Judy on the shoulder.

"Johnny wants you on stage, Judy. The band is ready."

Judy nodded, smiled, had another sip of her red wine, dried her eyes, straightened her clothes, said "Thank you" to Fiona, stopped, and stood up straight, walked round to the side of the stage, up the five steps and into the spotlight. Johnny was on stage already. There was rapturous applause. Even the people from Calder Automotive, who probably didn't know them, joined in.

Johnny spoke first.

"The band have kindly said that they will accompany Judy and myself whilst we sing a little duet."

There was more applause and people banging tabletops with their hands.

"Judy is a much better singer than I am, folks, and, what is more, she gets paid to do it. But not tonight, I am afraid, Judy."

He paused for a brief peal of laughter.

"It is an honour to be on stage with her."

Judy took over.

"For four minutes and nineteen seconds folks, tonight, we are going to be Emmylou Harris and Gram Parsons, and we're going to sing one of my favourite songs ever, and it's called 'Return of the Grievous Angel'."

And the song started with, "Won't you scratch my itch, sweet Annie Rich and welcome me back to town…"

The audience loved it and on the stroke of midnight everybody hugged and wished each other a very merry Christmas.

Chapter 19

THE DAY AFTER BOXING DAY (or St Stephen's Day as it is called in Ireland) the Health Centre got back to work. The period between Christmas and New Year was always horrendously busy and the festive cheer of Christmas had a habit of undergoing a metamorphosis into a period of resigned determination and an unspoken feeling that things would get worse before they got better. They always did.

Fiona had a week's holiday. She drove up to see her boyfriend at RAF Lossiemouth in the far north of Scotland, stopping for a night in Glasgow with her mum and dad on the way there and the way back. They exchanged presents and family news. Trips to Glasgow always reminded Fiona of losing blood at the bus stop and made her think about the alternative that could have happened. Her child would have been eight years old by now. She had heard from Callum for a few months when he had gone to live in Ontario but his emails had become fewer in number and then, after the best part of a year, they dried up altogether. She had heard nothing since.

Johnny spent New Year's Eve at the Railway, slept in on 1st January (a national holiday) and went back to work on 2nd January 2013. It was grim.

Six days later Johnny received a letter dated 7th January 2013 from the General Medical Council in Manchester. It read something like this:

Dear Dr Cash

Following our letter to you several weeks ago, we write to acknowledge the reply received recently from your solicitor, Mr Charles Taylor of the Medical Indemnity Union in Sheffield.

We appreciate the comprehensiveness of the reply which pertains to the two complaints against you.

The information provided will be considered by the Case Examiners and you will hear from us in due course.

The resolution of this complaint may involve any of the following (or any combination of the following)

- No action being taken
- A written warning which will stay on your file for five years
- A Fitness to Practice Hearing
- Suspension for a period of months or years
- Erasure of your name from the Medical Register which would irrevocably terminate your career as a doctor.

We will write to you again when further consideration has been given and we may contact your employer and/or other witnesses to make statements. Furthermore, we will seek sworn statements from Mr Clive Hillman and from Mrs Karen Hillman and we may, again, contact West Yorkshire Police.

Yours sincerely
Alexandra Smith
Case Screener
General Medical Council

This letter was more or less what Johnny expected. His emotions concerning the issue involved a mixture of sadness, anxiety and not a small measure of anger: someone was stitching him up and, so far as he could ever tell, he felt that he did not really deserve it. There were other people out there who caused sadness, misery and mayhem to others almost on a daily basis and nothing ever seemed to happen to them.

Fiona was back from Lossiemouth and her year with Johnny would be finishing at the end of February. She was getting plenty of experience managing patients with multiple complex problems and Johnny knew that in her she had the makings of an excellent family doctor. She never seemed to tire and she always remained cheerful and the patients liked her and some asked for her by name.

The Tuesday afternoon tutorials still lasted for a full two hours and they each chose the main topics on alternate weeks. It was Johnny's turn the following week so he emailed Fiona with the list of suggested topics.

1. What does the local hospice actually do?
2. Over regulation of the profession
3. Learning from mistakes
4. Your next job
5. Your leaving do!?

He wondered how it could be fitted into two hours and reflected on the fact that it was a microcosm of life in general. You could do four hours work in two hours if you got a move on.

Tuesday afternoon came round and at four o'clock Fiona and Johnny met in the Tutorial Room. Fiona enjoyed these sessions as they cemented into place the new learning experiences of the past ten months and she found Johnny to be an inspiring teacher and mentor.

"I want to talk about Joe Bradford first, Fiona. He is having radiotherapy for an inoperable cancer just more than halfway down his gullet. When the time is right, what do you think that our local hospice could offer to Joe and Jenny?"

"Well," replied Fiona. "I had an excellent afternoon there. Sally O'Donnell, the outreach nurse, showed me what they can offer. They have in-patient facilities, community care, specialist nurses, family support and chaplaincy services for people of all beliefs and cultures, training facilities for other health professionals and so on."

"You've a good memory," said Johnny. "When do you think would be the best time to let Joe and Jenny see what the hospice can provide?"

"Well," said Fiona, "I think there are two ways of looking at it. One is to wait until Joe's condition dictates that he would benefit. The other is to introduce them at an earlier stage, to give the Bradfords time to think. How long would you say that Joe Bradford has got left? I know it's hard to estimate accurately."

"I don't know, Fiona. Hopefully the radiotherapy will shrink the tumour and give him a fairly long period of remission but beyond that you can't say. It could be weeks, or if he's more fortunate, then he might have another 12 months or so, but, to be honest, I doubt it. I'd say that we are talking about somewhere between August and Christmas."

"What do you base that estimate on?"

"Well, he is otherwise in good health, so far as I know. And at 51 he is only in middle age. The five-year survival rate is ten per cent with cancer of the oesophagus, but with other cancers—lots of other cancers—you can live to a ripe old age and die of something completely unrelated. Breast cancer, prostrate cancer, to name but two."

"When do you think you will mention it?" asked Fiona.

"Maybe the next time I see him. We'll see."

"What would you actually say to him?" asked Fiona.

"I think that he will be expecting it. He's a bright bloke. I'll tell him that the hospice is full of positive ideas and will be able to provide any need that it is humanly possible to provide. Right, Fiona, put the kettle on and then I'm going to change the subject to the part of the job that gives me the biggest worries. I'll have tea, please."

They carried on again after a couple of minutes.

"Okay, Johnny, what is it about our job that really causes you anxiety? To me, some days, it is everything that goes on that worries me. Everything."

"Well Fiona, where do we start? The way I see it is that if you are conscientious then you can never really relax. You have to doubt yourself all the time. And to make sure that we get it right, we have twenty organisations whose rules we have to adhere to every time we draw breath, look at a patient or write a prescription."

"Twenty?"

"Yes, twenty not including the criminal or the civil law. They would make twenty-two. We have the General Medical Council, the Joint Committee on Postgraduate Training, Clinical Governance, Primary Care Trusts, National Institute of Clinical Excellence, Beacon

Programme, Commission for Health Improvement, Caldicott Guardians, National Service Frameworks, Professional Revalidation, National Health Service Executive, Ethical Committees, Prescribing Analysis and Cost, Patient Advocacy and Liaison Service, Mandatory Participation in Clinical Audit, Modernisation Agency, Audit Commissioner, Health and Safety Executive, Health Service Ombudsman and the National Clinical Assessment Authority. If I see a patient at half past six tonight before I go home and they ask me about a strange rash or about pains in their chest, then I have to satisfy all those twenty sets of rules. I honestly don't know how we do it. I don't, Fiona."

"Neither do I when you look at it that way. What happens then if you make a mistake? A bit of a balls up, shall we say?"

"I'll tell you about a patient I once had, Fiona," said Johnny. "I was a junior doctor working on a kidney ward. A very good unit, they were. Surgical. Kidneys, bladders, prostrates. Well, I had a patient who had a proven stone in his right kidney. A proven stone. He was awaiting surgical removal and he was down for eight o'clock the following morning. Six o'clock the afternoon before, this poor man got an awful pain. I examined him. He had a proven kidney stone so I assumed that this pain was from his stone, so I gave him an injection of morphine for severe pain. This time though, the pain didn't go. I wasn't sure what to do next so I called the consultant in. She had a good look at this man and she was brilliant. She was always brilliant. Nine o'clock that evening she said to him, 'Mr O'Reilly, show me where this pain is centred.' He pointed to the lower part of his abdomen on his right so she said, 'Where was the pain from the stone, Mr O'Reilly?' and he pointed to an area about two inches higher up. Two inches. She said to him, 'Mr O'Reilly, can I press again?' and he said, 'Sure Doctor, press away.' So she pressed and he nearly jumped off the bed. She then said to him, 'Mr O'Reilly, Dr Cash has been spot on here. You have got appendicitis and we'll take out your appendix and also do your kidney stone tonight.' She turned round to me and gave me a look that said it all and then she said, 'Thank you for calling me in, Dr Cash.' So Mr O'Reilly went to theatre and he did very well. I had ballsed it up. What got me was that the pains were only two inches apart."

Johnny went on.

"I learned a lot that night. The hardest thing about being a doctor is that very often you learn best from your mistakes. And most mistakes that doctors make are mistakes made on living people."

"So that is why we have to watch and listen intently the whole time? Taking it all in?"

"You're spot on, Fiona," said Johnny. "With twenty or twenty-two organisations looking over our shoulders the whole time. I envisage a time when they all try to out-compete each other. Put the kettle on again. We'll have a final brew for the day, then you can tell me about where you're going after you finish here and then you can tell me where you want to have your leaving do. Susan told me that I've got to go and see a young baby before I go home and I'll tickle the little baby under the chin and I'll say 'Hello little baby, I'm going to cure you and I'm going to satisfy twenty-two regulatory authorities at the same time.'"

Fiona made two more cups of tea and then she told Johnny about an exciting vacancy in a practice in Glasgow near to where she had grown up. And, of course, she wanted her leaving party to be in the Railway, but not on quiz night.

Joe came to see Johnny during the third week in January. He had nearly finished his course of radiotherapy and he hoped that the tumour in his gullet was shrinking. Johnny greeted them both.

"I would imagine that you will feel better again when the tiring effects of the radiotherapy wear off. How are you doing so far?"

Joe updated Johnny about how he felt. "How do you think I'll feel in the spring, Johnny?" he asked.

"Go on, tell me why you are asking?" asked Johnny, smiling.

Jenny answered. "We are thinking of having a holiday, Doctor. How do you think Joe would go on?"

"Well, hopefully, if the tumour shrinks, you will not feel too bad for a while. With a bit of luck, anyway." Johnny sounded hopeful. "Where are you thinking of going to, may I ask?"

"Well, we've never been to America. Ever. For a long time I've had a dream of driving on Route 66 in an open topped car. See the open country. Somewhere I've always wanted to visit. We wouldn't want to do the full distance. Too far. What we've thought of is of flying to somewhere like Tulsa, Oklahoma and doing the western half. Drive from Tulsa to L.A.—1288 miles. We could do it easily in ten or twelve days. An experience of a lifetime if you ask me." Joe smiled at the thought.

"You could be in Tulsa by this time tomorrow," joked Johnny.

"Twenty-four hours from Tulsa!" replied Jenny.

"As soon as you are feeling better then get cracking," said Johnny. "Get on the internet. You could fly from Manchester to Newark, then Newark to Tulsa, then after twelve days, fly back from Los Angeles to Manchester overnight. About eleven hours."

"Jesus, Johnny," smiled Joe, "you're a travel agent as well."

"I know everything about everything," joked Johnny. "Leave it till May. Weather should be perfect by then."

Johnny guessed that May might be the best compromise. The weather would be warm, the side effects from the radiotherapy should have worn off and the tumour should hopefully not have had a chance to start growing again. It was a delicate calculation but Johnny guessed that May should be about right.

"But don't book it till you're feeling a little better," he said.

He didn't mention the hospice.

They thanked him and picked up a prescription for antacids and another sickness certificate and went to the pharmacy. Joe would then spend the next eight hours on the internet looking at Route 66 from every angle. As well as his lovely wife, children and grandchildren, the thought of driving into the sunset on Route 66 with lovely Jenny in a convertible Mustang gave him yet another reason to carry on living. And they would plan to go in May. They had known Johnny on and off for a long time and, so far as they knew, Johnny was always right. To the best of their knowledge, Johnny didn't make mistakes. Ever. Never.

Chapter 20

FEBRUARY BROUGHT FIONA'S LAST MONTH at Valley Health Centre. She had loved her time being taught by Johnny and the team and, even more than this, had enjoyed seeing many patients herself. She found the experience of sitting opposite a patient in a consulting room to be an exhilarating and sometimes a scary experience. She told Johnny that the stress of the challenge of being just as alert after eleven hours on the job was more than equalled by the job satisfaction gained from being able to really help many of her patients to get better.

Fiona's last appointment that Friday was Martin Roberts. Her heart sunk when she saw that he was the thirty-first and final patient for her that day. She called him in at ten past six. Outside it had been dark for hours.

"Come in, Mr Roberts," she said. "What can we do for you, Sir?"

It riled her to call him 'Sir' but this was a more palatable alternative to what would have been her first choice of address.

"There are two things I need, Dr Graham, if you don't mind. First is renewal of my sick note. Secondly, I think I've got prostatitis and I need something for that," he said.

Fiona thought that since she was leaving the Practice soon that she would try to be mildly controversial.

"Need is a bit of an absolute term, I think, Mr Roberts. People *need* to breathe and eventually *need* to eat and drink and what have you, but nobody *needs* a sick note. A better way of putting it would have been maybe to say, 'I would like you to use your professional judgement to decide whether or not I am able to have another sick note, depending upon my condition and your assessment of it," said Fiona.

She wasn't quite sure where the courage had come from.

"I am sorry that you see it that way, Doctor," he replied, fidgeting with his rolled up copy of the *Guardian*.

"I am simply doing my job in a fair and balanced manner, Mr Roberts."

"Fair and balanced, my arse, if you ask me."

"Let me put it another way, Mr Roberts," said Fiona. "If you got no sick pay and you had no food in the house and no money and the choice was between starving and going back to work, then which would you choose?"

"I would go back to work, I think, Dr Graham."

"Well, why can't you go back to work now, Mr Roberts? You can read the *Guardian*, go on cruises, make crazy suggestions about your late uncle's dose of morphine before he died, spend all day on the internet trying to find things out so that you feel that you are smarter than the rest of us. I have a brother, Mr Roberts, a younger brother, twenty-five he is, and he can't do most of the things that you take for granted, Mr Roberts."

She paused, with the intention of seeing what he would say next.

"Why is that, Doctor?"

"Well, Mr Roberts, he works for a living. He's an electrician. Works for one of the bigger electrical firms in Glasgow. Not the biggest but they're a fairly big outfit nonetheless. They do lots of work in hotels, new office buildings, leisure complexes, all over central Scotland and the north of England. Loch Lomond in the north to Chester and Lincoln in the south. He drives 25,000 miles a year and stays in B&Bs and he's often on the road at five o'clock on a Monday morning and home nine o'clock Friday night, just in time for a drink with his mates; then they follow Celtic on a Saturday, then come Sunday he's preparing for the next week's work. Not the best of lives is it, Mr Roberts? Not bad, but not the best, I don't think. And you're just as fit as my brother is, Mr Roberts."

"But I have anxiety," he retorted.

"Are you saying that my brother doesn't have anxiety? Let's say he's driving over Shap at six o'clock on a Monday morning in winter, pitch dark, with the van headlights shining their beams through rain with bits of sleet and snow, with ten hours work to do that day crawling around in the roof space of some hotel. Would you not say that he's not a bit anxious?"

She thought that she might have said too much.

"Dr Graham," he replied. "I have heard about doctors like you. Doctors who don't listen to the patient."

"I'm straining every sinew listening to you, Mr Roberts, every sinew in my body and I've still not worked out why it is that you can't go to work; why you need a sick note from me. I can't see that anything that you say you've got is bad enough to stop you going to work."

"Dr Graham," he replied. "What if I reported you to the General Medical Council for insolent behaviour? What would you think then? Eh?"

"I think that you would win, Mr Roberts, and the reason that you would win is that you could sit down from now until Christmas writing letters and essays about yourself. And there are hard working people out there toiling away so that people like you can laze about all day. You're a disgrace to genuine sick people; people housebound with multiple sclerosis and that sort of thing."

The consultation finished icily. Martin Roberts got exactly what he wanted in the end and Fiona tidied her consulting room that night whilst thinking that life favoured the cunning more than the industrious. Thank God that ninety-nine per cent of people are honest and decent, she thought to herself.

Before she left she knocked on Johnny's door and told him what had happened. She was mildly surprised when he praised her and told her that he'd been meaning to take that particular stance with him for months but that, as always, he was busy sorting even more important things out and that he would have got round to it sooner or later.

"Also between now and tomorrow, Fiona," he said, "what I want you to do is to write on a piece of paper the ten most important things that you know now that you might not have known a year ago. If it looks good then I'll copy it and give a copy to your probable successor. He's coming to look round at half past five tomorrow. A lad called Mark Greenall. He's a Liverpool graduate. Al Hussein will be here at that time also. Before they come I want to talk about Joe Bradford."

"Brilliant, Johnny. Thank you. Looking forward to it."

She drove home. After supper, Fiona opened a bottle of wine and started composing her list of ten significant learning experiences. It was a mildly drunken list and it went like this:

1. General Practice is a brilliant career for doctors with intelligence and stamina.
2. It's not for the fainthearted. Johnny is never fainthearted.
3. Ninety per cent of illnesses are sorted out at GP level.
4. Valley Health Centre demonstrates excellent productive teamwork which can also be great fun.
5. Most patients are grateful people who strive to get better.
6. Most patients are also decent people but they come with multiple complex problems. Many will have tried to cure themselves first.
7. The knowledge base required to work in GP is immense.
8. Everyday GP work is hard but rewarding.
9. I will miss absolutely everybody, except—
10. Martin Roberts, who is a wanker.

Next morning, about ten minutes past seven, she hurriedly wrote the list out again, making it a bit tidier and a little bit less controversial.

Tuesday at four o'clock Fiona and Johnny talked about Joe Bradford.

"What do you think," Johnny asked, "will be going through his mind, with the diagnosis of cancer dropped on him like a ton of bricks before Christmas?"

"Well, I'd say his first reaction would be one of extreme shock and disbelief, followed by inner helplessness and then some folks would retreat into themselves."

"You're right. Twenty per cent of cancer patients can show depression, grief, anxiety, even anger. And I'd be the first to say that you can't honestly blame them. And then people fight back in different ways. Somebody studied a group of women who had recently been diagnosed with breast cancer. They found that most of them responded in three ways; first they looked for a meaning, wondering why they'd got cancer in the first place; secondly, they tried to get a sense of mastery of the condition, trying things like positive thinking; and thirdly, they tried self-enhancement. The women who fought back did best of all."

"Does that mean that in any situation like that, whether it be a serious illness or any other difficult situation, that it's better to stay positive and keep fighting back?" asked Fiona.

"What do you think?" said Johnny.

"That's what I would do and that's what you would do and that's what Joe Bradford would do," Johnny nodded in agreement.

Al Hussein and Mark Greenall arrived at five thirty. All four of them met together. Al Hussein told Mark that it would be an enjoyable, stimulating year.

Johnny butted in gently: "Last night, I asked Fiona, partly for a bit of fun, to write down ten things about General Practice that she didn't know this time last year. Have you had time to do it, Fiona?"

She rooted in her case and produced what she thought was the revised version of the list and gave it straight to Mark. He looked down it slowly and meticulously, smiling and nodding gently.

"This looks interesting. Looks like I'm in for a busy year."

He kept reading down the list till he got to item number 10. He looked puzzled.

"I understand the first nine but I'm not sure about the last one. Who's Martin Roberts?"

"Oh, he's just a wanker!" said Fiona.

"I'll try and avoid him then," said Mark.

"No chance," said Fiona smiling.

"I think that this is my sort of place," said Mark.

A couple of days later Joe Bradford came to see Johnny. This visit was different because for the first time since he became ill, he came to the Health Centre alone.

"This is different," said Johnny. "Where's Jenny?"

"She doesn't know I'm here. I haven't told her. She thinks I've gone shopping," said Joe.

"Is it something you want to discuss without Jenny?" asked Johnny with concern.

"It is a bit, Johnny. There are two things I want to ask you about, to be honest."

"Go ahead. Take as long as you want."

"Well, it's difficult." He paused. "It's just that I find it hard to talk about my illness at home. I don't know what to say to Jenny. I know that she must be thinking the same as what I'm thinking but we just seem to skirt round it."

"It's difficult, Joe," said Johnny. "All couples are different. Some people prefer not to talk about what is going on because they don't want to get the other person worried. It's like a vicious circle."

He, too, paused for a few seconds.

"Is there anything else that you want to ask about? Anything at all?"

"Firstly, I think you can sign me back to work next week. Also, well, we're almost certainly going to go to America in May, just as we discussed. I've never been and well, you know, it will be what you might call a special holiday."

"I'm sure," said Johnny.

Joe started talking again, in a quiet voice.

"Well, you know, in a motel at night…."

He stopped again and this time Johnny kept completely silent.

"Well, since I started radiotherapy, I've not felt like making love to Jenny at all. Must be the radiation. Jenny's great. She's never said a thing. But, I can just feel it starting to come back and at the same time I'm starting to feel better in myself. I feel that the cancer must have shrunk a bit, you know. I was just wondering, if Jenny and I have sex whilst we are on holiday, could it be harmful either to Jenny or even harmful to myself? Could I pass any cancer cells on to Jenny and could the activity start the cancer growing again? I'm sorry to ask you what must sound like a daft question but I just thought I'd better check with you. I'm sorry."

Joe stopped talking

"I'm glad you asked, Joe," said Johnny. "I'm glad you asked. You should have no particular problems in that department. None at all. If you are starting to feel it coming back, then that in itself is a good sign. You can count on that. In fact, there is only one thing you need to warn Jenny about."

"What's that?" asked Joe.

"Tell her that you'll be fast asleep within two minutes."

Johnny kept in touch with Kate but only through the quiz nights. She made it to the Railway nearly every Thursday, only missing one week when she was unwell with a virus. The slight distance that had come between them after the rug incident seemed to be getting smaller.

One Thursday, Johnny noticed Martin Roberts and Clive Hillman standing together. He recalled having seen them together some weeks previously. Johnny was buying a round of drinks when Martin Roberts wandered over to speak to him.

"Your young Scottish lady doctor was a bit over-the-top with me recently. I just thought that you'd want to know, in view of the fact that you are training her to be a proper GP."

"She told me," said Johnny.

"What do you mean, she told you?" asked Martin with a hint of annoyance in his voice.

"We were running through a list of patients whom we feel might possibly be able to work. People who are on long term sick. Your name came up, that's all. You only got ten seconds. We are busy people, you know," said Johnny.

"I was going to report her, on account of her attitude."

"She was going to report you, Martin. She told me. There's a new body with powers of enforcement. They're starting up next week. They're called P.E.S.T.— Professional Equalising Squad regarding Troublemakers. They can make you pay back sick pay if they find that people have claimed fraudulently. They have the power to walk people to a cash point wearing an orange coloured boiler suit with the initials PEST on the back in big letters and get them to draw out £200 every Saturday afternoon, in front of all the other shoppers. Oh, and if the person writes a letter of appeal they charge them £1 per word in advance before they agree to read it. Then they add it all up and if the person has consulted a health professional in the previous month then they send them an extra bill, charged at £1 for every ten words that the health professional has uttered."

"You're kidding me?" said Martin.

"No I'm not and, by the way, you owe me twenty quid."

Johnny left him to it.

Fiona's leaving party at the Railway the following week went well. Everybody clubbed together to buy her a nice leaving present and a card. The present was a hundred-pound voucher from a local jewellery shop and the card was signed by all the team. Judy thanked her for being such a good listener at the Christmas party when she had poured her heart out to her.

The leaving do was on the Wednesday night and Fiona had two more days to work before leaving to take up the appointment in Glasgow. Her last patient booked in on the Friday afternoon was Daniel John Cash. Johnny did it properly and waited properly outside her room before she called him in.

"Jesus Johnny, sit yourself down. I didn't know that you were ill. What can I do for you?"

"Two things, Fiona. Firstly, you've been brilliant this past twelve months. Thank you. Secondly, I've got a rash on my abdomen."

"When did it start?" asked Fiona, looking surprised.

"Two nights ago," said Johnny.

"How does it feel?"

"There's a bit of discomfort in the area. Nothing much."

"Can I have a look?" asked Fiona.

Johnny lifted his shirt up.

"It's shingles."

"Just as I thought," said Johnny.

"Are you under any stress?" asked Fiona.

"Nothing much really. Nothing you'd write home about."

"I'll write you a prescription then. And take it easy doctor. Slow down a bit. That's what you should do, slow down a bit."

Ten minutes later, Fiona put her medical bag into her car, kissed everyone goodbye and set off for Glasgow. She was sorely missed.

Chapter 21

JOE AND JENNY BRADFORD were busy packing. The following day they were to fly to Tulsa, Oklahoma. They had been to see Johnny earlier in the week and he was happy for them to travel. Joe was feeling better and he had regained a couple of pounds of weight he had lost over Christmas and the New Year. The tiring effect of the radiotherapy had worn off and he was eating well. His vitality had returned. Johnny explained carefully to them both that hopefully Joe would stay well for a few weeks at least. It was accepted by all three of them that Joe's cancer, which was encircling his gullet, would start to grow again by the autumn.

Neither of them had ever been to America and it had been a long-term ambition of Joe's to rent a convertible and head west along Route 66 into the sunset. They felt that the full length of the road from Chicago to L.A. would be too much both for Joe's health and also for their finances. The insurance alone had cost almost as much as the flights and they all agreed that two weeks would be perfect. They would have to forego the pleasures of Illinois and Missouri but would have the great pleasure of driving through the wide-open spaces of Oklahoma, Texas, New Mexico, Arizona and California. Joe had been a great Blues Brothers fan but he was resigned to the fact that he would never, ever get to visit Chicago in this life. Maybe heaven would have its own version, with Belushi and Dan Ackroyd sporting pork pie hats and sunglasses. He certainly hoped so and if Cab Calloway provided the music then it would be nearly as good as the real thing. He was feeling not too bad at all and 1288 miles in a Ford Mustang with the girl that he had loved for over thirty years would be pretty darn good compensation. Chicago could wait.

They had finished their packing by seven in the evening, leaving out only the clothes they needed to travel in plus their passports, money and tickets. Their daughter, Catherine, had offered to take them to Manchester Airport at five in the morning. The flight to Newark was at eight thirty and then they would have nearly four hours in Newark followed by the shorter flight to Tulsa. They would arrive early evening the following day, Oklahoma time.

Joe fastened the zipper on his suitcase and turned round and unbeknown to him, Jenny had been standing behind him in the hallway.

"I was just watching you there, Joe. You reminded me of 29 years ago. I called round to see you the night before the wedding if you remember and you had just fastened your suitcase for the honeymoon. Scarborough, it was lovely. And you look just as good now, Joe, as you did back in eighty-four. Just as good. Maybe better, even."

"So do you, Jenny," said Joe. "So do you."

"Is all the packing done?" asked Jenny.

"Sure. I don't think we've forgotten anything. Nothing I can think of, anyway."

"I think that maybe we both deserve a little lie down, Joe, after all that packing of suitcases. I think we could do with an hour in bed. Tomorrow will be a long day. By the way, did you leave the money out where we will remember to pick it up, Joe?"

"Sure, it's on the hall table. You're not going to charge me, are you?" he joked.

"Fifty pounds and I accept credit cards."

"American Express?"

"You can go as quick or as slow as you like, Joe Bradford, as quick or as slow as you like. You can hang on in there all evening, if you wish to. But don't forget we're up at four thirty in the morning."

"How could I ever forget it? The land of opportunity with the girl of my dreams. Just imagine!"

"And we're off to America as well," replied Jenny.

They got into bed.

"Which land of opportunity do you want to explore first, Joe Bradford? You can start in the North and work Southwards, or you can try East to West first. What do you think?"

"Don't mind honestly," he replied. "Don't mind at all."

"Well, you can try East West first, then North and then you can head South, ever so slowly, Joe Bradford. My waist is like that narrower bit, Mexico, and then it broadens out a bit and then there's the Amazon rain forest. Can get a bit sticky at times but it's well worth finding, Joe Bradford, well worth finding. Warm and humid, I'd say."

"Do I need a visa stamp in my passport?" he asked.

"No."

"How warm and how humid would you say?"

"Thirty seven degrees all year round. That's ninety-eight point six in America. And it's getting more humid by the minute."

They caressed and then he penetrated her ever so gently and slowly and it was wonderful for them both. For the first time since Joe had become ill six months earlier they made love again. And for both of them it was as good as their first ever time. They both knew that they were going to have a brilliant vacation.

They both slept soundly and the alarm went off at four thirty. They got dressed. The cases and hand luggage were ready in the hall.

"Did you water the pot plants, Joe?" asked Jenny.

"Would I forget to do that, Jenny Bradford?" he replied.

Catherine arrived at five to take them the one-hour drive to Manchester Airport and there was a lovely surprise for them when they got to the check in. Their son David was waiting for them. They were delighted.

"I thought you were away on business," said Jenny.

"I am, but it's only in Chester and it's only a forty minute drive to come here and see you both off," said David.

Catherine then took over.

"We have clubbed together and we've paid for an upgrade for you both on all three flights. You're now going to be sitting in Executive Class. Here are your new tickets for all three flights."

"You shouldn't have! We appreciate it very much but you shouldn't have. You are much too kind."

"The two of you mean the world to David and to me and it's just a very small way of showing our appreciation," said Catherine.

"All we want you to promise to do is to have a good time and keep safe and if you're tired then break the journey. Oh, and don't forget, they drive on the right in North America," said David.

"I'm glad you told us that, and I've just had an interesting thought," said Joe.

"What's that?" asked Catherine.

"Well, the car is a two seater, so if your mother is going to do any back seat driving then I think that she'll be sitting on my right," said Joe. "Or something like that."

"Now take it steady and have a good time, the pair of you. And we'll be here when you get back in two weeks. What time does the LA flight get in?"

"Seven thirty I think," said Jenny.

So the two of them checked in for the flight from Manchester, England to Newark, New Jersey in the United States of America. The time for their big adventure had arrived. They kissed the children and waved goodbye before they went through the security bit. All four of them were, by now, a bit tearful.

"Time for a cup of coffee and a newspaper," said Joe drying his eyes. "We're going to have a great time."

Jenny held his hand for a minute.

"It will be lovely, Joe," she said.

Their flight was called and they got away from the departure gate two minutes early. They were thrilled by it all. After the safety announcements, the Captain's voice came over the intercom.

"Ladies and gentlemen, this is Captain Farrell speaking."

He sounded Irish.

"Welcome on board our flight today to Newark. Our flight time today is seven hours and fifty-five minutes and our route will take us via the westerly runway up over Preston and Glasgow and then we turn left slightly and head out to sea past the Hebrides and then we make landfall over Newfoundland and then Nova Scotia and cross the American border into Maine, and then we will slowly descend and the last part of our flight will take us over New York city before landing in Newark. The weather forecast for there is for a light westerly breeze, sunny and a temperature of twenty-two degrees, or, for any American passengers on board, seventy-two degrees Fahrenheit. Now relax and have a good flight and I will talk to you again in a while. Thank you, ladies and gentlemen."

Joe nudged Jenny.

"Do you think he is related to that other Captain Farrell?"

"Who's that?" asked Jenny.

"That bloke in that song. Whisky in the Jar."

"Probably. I can guess what his first name might be."

"Likewise," said Joe.

They landed bang on time in Newark. The US immigration man was professional but friendly at the same time.

"What is the purpose of your visit, Mr and Mrs Bradford?" he asked.

"Vacation, sir," said Joe.

"A bit like a second honeymoon," added Jenny.

The immigration man looked them right in the eye and for a couple of seconds there was silence. They wondered what was coming next.

"Mr Bradford, there is one thing that you must do on this vacation. Do you know what that is, Mr Bradford?"

"I'm not sure," said Joe.

"Well, at least one night during your vacation you have to order some champagne and get that bottle of champagne on ice and then think back to your wedding day. How many years ago was that, if you don't mind me asking?"

"Nearly twenty nine," said Jenny.

"It's thirty six for my wife and me," said the immigration man. "Now where are you folks heading from Newark?"

"We're flying to Tulsa and then we're driving to Los Angeles in a convertible Mustang," said Joe.

"Always wanted to do that myself. Always," said the immigration man. He paused. "Now folks, when you're driving, have a good look at the country and at the people. Things are pretty wild out west, you know."

He stamped their passports.

"Have a nice day, folks."

"Thank you," Jenny said.

They had walked a couple of paces when the immigration man called them back. He looked them both in the eyes again and then a broad smile broke out on his face.

"Second honeymoon eh? Don't forget that bottle of champagne, Mr Bradford."

The flight to Tulsa departed fifteen minutes behind schedule and they were tired by the time they landed in Oklahoma. It had been a long day. They had booked a room for the first night in one of the airport hotels. They set their watches back six hours and got into bed just after nine o'clock Tulsa time.

"I bet you we're awake by six," said Joe.

"How do you work that one out?" said Jenny.

"Well, six o'clock here will be midday in England and we didn't stay in bed that long even on our honeymoon," said Joe.

"Do you want to bet?" replied Jenny.

Two minutes later they were both sound asleep. It was the best sleep of their lives and Joe woke up at precisely two minutes to six.

They found the Sunset Car Hire depot on the airport perimeter road.

"One shiny red convertible Ford Mustang, one way rental to LA international airport. Sign here, here, here, here and here please," said the Sunset lady. "This car is travelling some distance. In four weeks and four days time this red Mustang will be in Chicago, Illinois. Day after you leave it back in LA it's booked out to a couple from New Zealand. Driving LA to Chicago. Second honeymoon or something. Now just four more signatures please. Also, for an extra eight dollars and ninety cents a day, plus sales tax, you can insure against alien attacks and that also includes them big rattlesnakes jumping in the car when you're stopped at a red light. Strange things happen out west, you know."

Joe and Jenny looked at each other.

"Only joking folks. Just kidding you. You don't need that extra insurance."

"Are you sure?" asked Joe.

"Yeah I'm sure. You're covered for that sort of thing already; it's in the main policy. Now have a nice trip folks. And don't forget there are some wild places and strange people out there. Did you ever see Butch Cassidy and the Sundance Kid?" asked the car rental lady.

"Yes, loads of times," said Jenny.

"Well, if you see that place where they jump over that cliff into the river to escape, well don't do it." She paused. "Long way down to the bottom and there's only three inches of water in that river this time of year. Now have a good trip, why don't you."

They loaded up the Mustang, got used to driving on the right and promptly got lost in the Tulsa traffic within ten minutes of leaving the Car Rental Depot. It was going to be a lively two weeks.

The first night they were going to stop somewhere around Oklahoma City until Jenny had a serious read of the Route 66 Guidebook for Families. It recommended having a look at the smaller town of Guthrie, Oklahoma. They had a look at the National Four-String Banjo Museum.

After an enjoyable hour looking at banjos of all descriptions, Joe said to Jenny, "I feel that we should stop here in Guthrie for the night. Get over the jet lag, then we should be okay for a longer day tomorrow."

"Whatever you say, my gorgeous," replied Jenny.

They liked the look of the Western Highway Motel and Restaurant so they pulled in and got a room, unloaded the Mustang, made love in the late afternoon heat and enjoyed a steak dinner in the cosy restaurant.

"Joe Bradford, this time last year, did you think that today we'd be somewhere slap bang in the middle of America? Just the two of us and no one else to worry about," said Jenny.

"I didn't guess that we'd be doing anything like this at all. I thought I'd be managing a truck depot and you'd be on the checkout at Robinson's," replied Joe.

They had an early night and made love for the second time that day before falling happily into an exhausted sleep.

They woke refreshed and the sun was shining. A high in the upper eighties was forecast. By late morning they had crossed the border into Texas for the 178-mile drive across the panhandle. This was more wide-open country with big skies with occasional thunderhead clouds that seemed to reach into the heavens themselves. They passed mile after mile of cattle ranches and windmills. By five o'clock they were getting tired. Amarillo was only 37 miles away, straight ahead, due west. They felt that this was real cowboy country.

"What would you say if we stop in Amarillo? Tony Christie liked it and Peter Kay liked it. So, if it's good enough for them then it'll be okay for us," said Jenny.

They found the Big Texan Steak Ranch and Motel and got a room for the night. After supper there was an old-time Opry show. A group of five men in check shirts and cowboy hats sang country songs. It had an old fashioned feel about it, which they loved. And so the holiday continued. Next day they pressed on through the sunshine and crossed the border into New Mexico.

Route 66 was the road that had first connected California to the eastern parts of the United States about eighty years earlier.

Mile after mile of semi-desert stretched out in front of them and there were mountains in the distance. The land looked as though it had never seen rain. Joe and Jenny stopped the next night of their western pilgrimage in Santa Fe, an arty town situated high in the mountains at 7,000 feet above sea level. It was fabulous. New Mexico's state capital looked wonderful in the glorious sunshine.

They slept well and next morning visited the Museum of Indian Arts and Culture. In the afternoon they headed west again and made Albuquerque before nightfall. This large city in the mountains, according to the research they had done prior to leaving England, was a magnet for Route 66 aficionados. The old road wound its way into the city through the suburbs and into the downtown area. Old Town Plaza looked beautiful. It was the hub of the city's tourist area, reflecting 300 years of history.

That night, after dinner, they enjoyed a couple of cocktails before bedtime. They snuggled down in bed with a warm glow inside them.

"How are you enjoying the vacation?" asked Jenny.

"It's great. It's wonderful, and I'm just so glad to have you here with me, Jenny. What more can I say? I'm overcome by the beauty of the desert and the mountains. I knew that it would be good but I didn't think it would be *this* good."

"Glad you're enjoying it," said Jenny.

"In that Native American Museum in Santa Fe," Joe went on, "There was a section about North American Indian beliefs about death and dying. They believe that death is not the end but a journey into some other world."

All of a sudden Joe Bradford broke down in tears. Jenny comforted him. She had wondered for months when this might happen. Joe had more or less kept it all to himself and now it was coming to the surface.

"I guess it kind of made you think, Joe?"

"All this beauty. Look at it. Mountains, deserts and the sun shining. And in twelve months I'm not going to be alive to see it again, ever."

He started crying again.

"Joe, just think of how your life has touched the lives of others. And one day we'll be reunited, Joe. Just think of that."

She wiped his eyes and comforted him.

They dozed off to sleep for eight hours and woke refreshed.

"How is my gorgeous husband this morning?" asked Jenny.

"I feel okay. And thank you for listening last night. I don't talk much about it, and maybe I should but, you know, we all have different ways of handling things and it's just as though people retreat into caves of their own making when they're upset. Caves. Just to gather our thoughts. Trouble is, you sometimes feel that you don't want to come out of the cave. You just want to sit in it and think and wonder what's coming next. Sometimes I get afraid, Jenny, real afraid, but then I remember that you and Catherine and David are there and I know that you will all look after me when the time comes. And Johnny will. I know that the four best people on earth will look after me. And that means so much. So much to me. It's when I remember that, that the fear leaves me. And when I look at you, Jenny Bradford, my eyes light up and then I feel a lot better again."

He stopped talking. Jenny had never known him to be so sentimental, ever, in all the years she had known him.

And so the westerly journey continued, past the middle part of the United States, getting ever closer to California and the sight of the Pacific Ocean. They stayed the next night in a ranch style motel just outside of Gallop and the next morning made it to the Arizona state line. Big country and even bigger skies stretched out ahead of them. By nightfall they made Flagstaff and the next day visited the Southern Rim of the Grand Canyon. The beauty of it was beyond description.

They stayed one more night in Arizona and the next day crossed the border into California. This was the final part of their wonderful journey, the land of forests, mountains, deserts, vineyards, the summer of love, Hollywood and then the endless Pacific Ocean, an area of ocean a thousand times bigger than your wildest estimation.

Joe checked the Mustang over that night. Oil, water, tyres. The next day they were to drive across the Mojave desert, one of the last places on earth that you would ever want to break down. Joe and Jenny Bradford were now nearly at the end of their vacation. They spent the last night of their trip in Santa Monica. After checking in at the last, most westerly motel on their voyage of discovery, Joe suggested that they should walk on the pier and have a look at the beach.

The sun was shining out to sea but in the distance Joe noticed a band of clouds forming and just for a second or two he likened the approach of the clouds with his own situation.

He turned to Jenny, embraced her, pointed out to sea and said, "There's a change coming, Jenny."

She nodded and knew exactly what he meant.

"Let's go and dip our toes in the Pacific Ocean. We've come a long way to do this."

And so, as the sun dipped down into the approaching clouds, with the water up to their ankles and the waves breaking gently, Joe Bradford kissed Jenny Bradford on the cheek. She tasted lovely.

"We made it, Jenny, we made it," he said.

He then stopped talking for what seemed like a long time. The water still lapped at their feet and ankles.

He spoke up again, "There's one thing I have forgotten to do."

"What's that? Surprise me," said Jenny.

"The immigration man in Newark. Champagne. In a bucket of ice."

She smiled.

Room service knocked on their door. Joe opened it and standing there was a young Hispanic lady, with a bottle of champagne on ice and two champagne flutes.

"Are you two on your honeymoon?" she asked.

"It's a bit like that," replied Joe, smiling.

He slipped her a couple of dollars and she was gone.

"Gotta do what the immigration man said," said Joe.

And so they drank the champagne and it tasted gorgeous and Joe thought that really this is a good world after all. A glow came over him and it crossed his mind that the beauty of his surroundings must be very much like what his late Dad had seen in Anglesey thirty-eight years earlier. They had a steak dinner that night and then another cocktail and then they got into the lovely soft king-size bed for their last night in California.

Joe put his arm round Jenny.

"I couldn't have had a better wife than you, Jenny, you know. If there is such a person as a better wife than you then I cannot for a minute picture what she is like. Thank you and thank you for all the good years we have had, Jenny."

"You're welcome, Joe."

And so they made love again, the last time they would do it in America, and it was wonderful. They slept soundly.

Next morning they checked out, returned the Mustang to the car rental depot, got a cab to the airport and checked in for the overnight flight back to Manchester. The flight was on time. At the other end Catherine and David were waiting for them in the arrivals lounge.

"How did you get on?" Catherine asked. "You look great, both of you."

"Fantastic. Great," said Jenny. "It was simply wonderful. Thank you."

Chapter 22

JUNE 2013 brought early summer to the valley. The Health Centre enrolled fifty-five new patients; a new housing development on the edge of town had recently been completed and fifteen new families had registered. The pace of work for the reception staff, nurses and doctors showed no sign of easing. Mark Greenall was busy finding his feet and the Tuesday afternoon teaching sessions with Johnny were proving to be useful and thought provoking. Al Hussein called in to see Mark when his first three months were finished and both men were happy with his work and his amazing ability to learn new facts. Al told Mark that Fiona had been a hard act to follow but that he was impressed with his progress so far.

Johnny kept busy at work and still attended the quiz every Thursday and remained on good terms with Kate. He enrolled on a learn-the-bass-guitar-in-a-month course, which was for established guitar players who wanted to learn more about the wonderful four-stringed instrument. Everyday he looked in the post for sight of a big brown envelope from the General Medical Council which he expected would advise him of their decision making about the two complaints against him. It had been five months since he had heard anything at all from them. He felt that the waiting was possibly as bad as whatever sanction they would impose against him and he secretly wished that they would get a move on; any outcome would surely be better than not knowing.

Things at the Hillmans appeared to be stable, a view held by everyone who knew them except for two other people. The world's perception of their family unit was that they lived in a state of permanent readiness for war but that it was a war that never quite broke out. The national security services would have a classification for something similar that is the scenario in which trouble of some sort was about to take place but no one could decide when and where it might happen and what the end result would be. Acquaintances felt that Clive could be a bit of a gangster if he wanted to but that he must have a good side to him, somewhere, although no one could ever recall having seen much of it. At least they were financially sound, or so everyone thought. Karen was held to be the more decent of the two of them although everyone felt that she had a mercenary side which involved bartering an ample suburban lifestyle (better than she had grown up with, even if only from a monetary point of view, people believed) for enforced sex with a man whom she couldn't possibly love, trading three quick ones a week for an overflowing larder and wine cellar and a house with a garden big enough to need a paid gardener. There were rumours as to why Tony Kirkbride left so quickly but most of them were slightly wide of the mark.

The two people outside of the family unit who knew that something secret was going on were Lorraine Mercer, Karen's friend since high school days, and Jim Cowley, her latest lover, a man she had met online. She told Lorraine that the website was called www.naughtyshags.com and that for forty pounds every three months you could specify man or woman, age group, unusual preferences and how many miles from Valley Mills you were prepared to travel. There was a bloke of 66 in Inverness who would travel up to 350 miles for one; Karen couldn't help but wonder why, whoever he was, he didn't move to somewhere like Birmingham where he would have a potential target population of 48 million people within a 3-hour drive.

The deal was that Lorraine Mercer provided an alibi for Karen every Wednesday evening. Karen told Clive that she had caught up again with Lorraine after not seeing much of her for a few years. She told Clive that Lorraine expected her on Wednesday evening at eight and that they would either have a bottle of wine between them or go for a curry or a pizza. The reason that Lorraine Mercer was chosen (and she received a bottle of wine every week for keeping quiet—wine she could drink all by herself if she wished) was that she lived seven doors away from a young man called Jim Cowley. Jim Cowley, a Londoner by birth who had moved north two years previously, was a Food Safety Inspector for the local council in the daytime and an occasional nightclub doorman at night, on a Friday and Saturday in Rochdale. Wednesdays suited him fine.

The website rules were that meetings were for any lawful purpose but that it was implied that anyone arranging to meet a person through the website was expected to have sex. There was the usual safety advice about meeting first in a public place with lots of other people around such as a restaurant or a public library, etc., and that no responsibility whatever could be placed at the door of the website if things did not turn out as expected.

Karen wondered what to wear for the first meeting with Jim Cowley, wondering whether he would expect suspenders and stockings or whatever, but then remembered that really she should dress as though she were going to Lorraine Mercer's so, looking at the rain outside, she put on her blue jeans and pvc winter rain jacket, kissed Clive on the cheek, kissed Orla on the top of her head, told her she would not be late home and set off to Jim Cowley's house, number 44 Hilltop Road, Valley Mills. She parked outside Lorraine's at number 30, rang Lorraine's doorbell, had a short chat with Lorraine in the hallway, gave Lorraine a bottle of Shiraz (on offer at Robinson's) and set off to walk up the road to number 44. Quite what Lorraine would say to Clive if ever he came looking for her hadn't been worked out. Thankfully it never happened.

Karen rang Jim Cowley's doorbell at exactly eight o'clock, on the dot. Jim answered the front door and then the conversation went something like this:

"Karen Hillman?"

"Yes. Jim Cowley?"

"Yes. Come in Karen. You look lovely. It's a wet night, isn't it?"

"Thank you."

He was tall and muscular with a shaved head and was wearing jeans and a Pogues Christmas Tour 2008 T-shirt.

"Do you want a cup of tea or a drink, Karen, or anything like that?"

"No it's okay, Jim, honestly," she replied.

The formalities over with, he led her upstairs, showed her where the bathroom was, led her into the bedroom and within sixty seconds of walking into the bedroom he had penetrated her. She was sure that she could feel him pushing her cervix up towards the middle of her abdomen. Within two minutes she had the best orgasm she had ever had (better even than with Tony Kirkbride). Jim Cowley kept on going and by the time he came, after about half an hour, she had orgasmed for the second time. For an idle moment she wondered what all these Valley men were taking, enabling them to keep going for so long.

Afterwards they got dressed and went downstairs and Jim Cowley made them both a cup of tea.

"Do you like Kojak?" asked Karen.

"Yes. Put anything you want on to watch," replied Jim.

"I'd better stay till ten if that's okay with you because it would look strange if I'm home after an hour and a half. I told my husband that I was visiting my friend Lorraine at number 30."

"No, that's fine," said Jim.

And so they watched TV until one minute to ten when the detective show finished.

"Same time next week?"

They both spoke the same words at exactly the same time. This must be some sort of telepathy, they both thought. They kissed each other in the hallway and then Karen was gone, arriving home at ten minutes past ten.

"How was Lorraine?" asked Clive.

"Fine, thanks," she said as she shook her wet coat in the hallway. "We covered a lot of ground and she wants to see me again next week. Probably Wednesday."

"Fine," said Clive. "Glad you had a good time. Orla's been asleep for about an hour."

He carried on watching News at Ten; the next item was about a deadly tornado in Arkansas, with shots of people in shorts standing outside of wrecked suburban homes.

The following day Karen started with tonsillitis. Friday she was worse so she went to see Johnny. They both agreed that it was tonsillitis so he prescribed her a seven-day course of Penicillin.

"Be sure to take the full course, Karen," Johnny said.

"I will surely, Doctor. Thank you," replied Karen.

The consultation had been friendly and relaxed and despite all the previous trouble they parted on good terms.

"If you're not right Karen, then do come back," said Johnny.

"I will, Doctor, thank you again," and she was gone.

Nobody mentioned the GMC.

Over the following few Wednesdays Karen and Jim managed to get the interval from the ringing of the front door bell to full penetration down to 59 seconds on one occasion and so they went on: every Wednesday for the next five weeks they screwed in the bed for an hour and then they sat and watched repeats of Kojak until ten o'clock and then she went home. One week she orgasmed three times; it was always at least once. They both loved it and they knew not to contact each other in between visits. It was a perfect arrangement.

Chapter 23

THE FIRST QUIZ NIGHT of July found the Railway to be bustling as usual. There were about a dozen teams getting ready to take part and a few non-quiz regulars were drinking quietly at the bar. Johnny kept wondering where we would be without regulars in a pub. They were surely one of the most undervalued groups of people in the country in that they always make a pub look fairly busy. They contribute to the exchequer, never ever cause an ounce of trouble, give their wives a break for an hour or two and always get up for work the next day without any problems. Johnny wondered if they should form a political party: the Regulars, a middle-aged conglomeration of mostly men with much experience of life, with political views slightly but not too far to the right, and a generous kindly nature, and an imaginative approach to taxing alcohol. Johnny felt that they could easily be as good as the present lot and that he could easily find himself voting for them one day.

For the first time ever, Kate turned up late; she usually demonstrated unfailing American punctuality but on this particular Thursday she arrived just as the first question was being asked and she looked a bit anxious.

Johnny collared her during the 15-minute break between question 30 and question 31. She explained that she had to go back to Seattle in nine days' time but hopefully only for two weeks but that it may be longer.

"My Mom has just been to the doctor today and I have been on the phone for twenty minutes. Sorry I was late. She has gallstones. She's 62 and the surgeon wants to take her in and remove her gall bladder, probably a week Monday and probably keyhole surgery. So I'm going to fly over to Seattle in nine or ten days and book an open return and hopefully, if Mom's okay then I'll be back two weeks later."

"I hope that she's going to be okay," said Johnny. "You know that I will miss you, just like the rest of the team will, but I'll miss you a teeny weeny bit more than they will."

"How do you know?"

"I'm just guessing," said Johnny. "But I guess that I've guessed right."

The evening went well but, for once, they did not win, losing by a point by saying that Newmarket racecourse was in Cambridgeshire when it was really in Suffolk.

"We'll put in a shit performance the next two weeks without you, Kate," said Johnny. "Tell your Mom to get well very soon 'cos we need you here just as much as your mom needs you there."

She wasn't sure what he meant and, with hindsight, neither was Johnny.

The following morning Joe and Jenny booked an appointment to see Johnny. They had been back from Route 66 for about seven weeks and Johnny hadn't seen them at all during that time.

"Come in," Johnny said. "How are you all doing?"

Jenny spoke up.

"Joe was fine when we were away and we are so glad that you said we could go. It was wonderful. The wide-open spaces. A trip of a lifetime."

She suddenly realised what she'd said and after a short awkward pause, kept going.

"Joe has not been so good for about ten days now, Doctor."

"Jesus, Jenny, call me Johnny for goodness sake. You've known me long enough."

"Sorry Doctor," she continued, looking nervous. "He has got a pain around where we imagine his gullet is and the swallowing difficulty is returning. Sometimes a meal is a real struggle."

Johnny addressed Joe directly.

"Thank you, Jenny. How bad is the pain?"

"Bad enough at times."

"What about at night?"

"It sometimes wakes me; not every night but some nights it does. For an hour or so."

"What about your weight?" Johnny thought that he looked thin.

"I've lost about half a stone, I think."

"What about the hospital?" asked Johnny.

"I saw them ten days ago and they organised a further CT scan. I had that yesterday. They said that you'd have the report by the middle of next week."

So Johnny examined Joe on the couch, looking for signs of an enlarged liver which can often occur with this sort of cancer. There was no sign of any enlargement and Johnny could find nothing except for the obvious sign that Joe was looking thin and unwell. They all sat down again. Johnny addressed them both.

"What we should do here with all this lot is as follows. First I will get the scan report. Have you had any chance to think about what it might show?"

He stopped talking.

"Well," said Joe. "I sometimes think that it is going to be bad news, with the tumour growing and all that, but then I think well maybe there is just a bit of inflammation and that it all might settle down for a while. I don't know, to be honest."

He looked understandably worried. Johnny took over.

"What I think I will do is to speak to Sally O'Donnell from the Hospice and ask her, if possible, to come to your house around midday next Friday and I'll come along as well and we can meet up and talk about things. Will you be able to come, Jenny?" he asked.

"I'll try to organise my shifts at work. Hopefully it shouldn't be a problem. I'll phone them this afternoon and see."

"Anything else you want to ask, either of you?" Johnny said.

"No, I think we're looking at it from all angles. I'm worried, understandably so, but we'll just have to see what comes up. I think I'd better ask you for a sickness certificate. I'm thinking of telling them at work that I'll not be going back. And thank you for recommending that we go away in May. It was fantastic. Places you can't imagine till you've seen them. You should go one day, Johnny. You'd love it."

Johnny thought for a split second about taking Kate one day.

"If you don't hear from me before then, then we'll all meet at your house next Friday at twelve."

"Thank you, Doctor," said Jenny.

The first patient booked in to see Johnny in the afternoon was Karen Hillman. Johnny called her in. She had come alone and, like Joe and Jenny had been in the morning, she looked nervous.

"Come in, Karen. What can we do for you?" he said.

She shuffled uncomfortably in her seat.

"I'm pregnant, Doctor, and I don't think I can go ahead with it. Do you remember prescribing me the penicillin when I had tonsillitis? Well I think it must have stopped the pill from working."

"Sorry to hear that, Karen," Johnny said. "It's none of my business, of course, but have you discussed it with Clive?"

"I don't think it's his, Doctor. In fact it can't be his because we've not slept together for months now."

"Right," said Johnny. "Obviously there are two directions you can go in, Karen, and it's not for me to point you in either direction because again it's none of my business at all. But whatever you decide then I will sort it out for you. Maybe you want to go away and think about it and let me know on Monday. Either way, I'll be guided by you, of course."

"I'll phone you on Monday, Dr Cash, if that's okay."

So Karen went home and thought again, realising all the time that she was not going to change her mind. She phoned Johnny at the end of morning surgery on Monday, having barely thought about it over the weekend.

"I'll go ahead with the termination, Doctor, if you don't mind," said Karen.

The phone call lasted less than ninety seconds. Johnny subsequently thought that he *did* mind, to be honest, but doctors are there to adhere to the wishes of the patient for much of the time, so long as the wish is a reasonable one and so long as it was legal. He found it difficult to come up with a precise definition of reasonable.

One evening that week Judy was having a quiet drink with the other members of the band in the Railway, prior to rehearsing some new songs. She went up to the bar and whilst she was waiting to be served she felt a tap on the shoulder. She looked round and standing there was Martin Roberts, looking very intoxicated.

"Sorry to trouble you, Judy," he said in a drunken manner.

"What can I do for you, Martin?" she asked politely.

"I want to know what Johnny drinks, Judy. I want to get him something for looking after my Uncle Percy. And something for you Judy for the day you let me into Johnny's flat."

He had clearly had a few too many.

"Give me your mobile number, Martin and I'll ask him what sort of bottle he would like, and I'll text you. Is that okay, Martin?" she asked.

"That will be lovely Judy, thank you. Can you see that I'm celebrating, Judy? I feel great Judy."

"What are you celebrating, Martin?" she asked.

"There's a girl I've been chasing for years, Judy. Lives in London. I heard that she may be coming to visit her family up here, Judy. Sometime in the next few weeks. Been after her for years. She's fucking gorgeous."

"What's this fucking gorgeous girl called, Martin?"

She was getting exasperated with him by now.

"Belinda Blackburn. Known her from University. Not seen her for years, Judy."

"I hope you get to meet her soon, Martin. I'll text you with Johnny's preference for a bottle."

Martin left her alone and she returned from the bar to sit with the band. The rehearsal went very well and they were pleased that they had added six new songs to their repertoire. Judy had written three of them herself. The band's long ambition was to release a CD featuring largely their own material.

The following Friday lunchtime Johnny met with Sally O'Donnell at Joe and Jenny Bradford's house. They arrived within 30 seconds of each other and had a short chat on the pavement before going inside.

"It's not good news for Mr Bradford, Sally, I'm afraid," said Johnny.

"Have you got the latest scan report through?" she asked.

"Yes. It's shown that the tumour is actively growing and that he also has some secondary tumour deposits in his liver. It's not good at all, Sally, not good at all."

"Sorry indeed to hear that. Maybe we'd better go in."

"You're right," said Johnny. "I know this house well."

"How come?" asked Sally.

"Joe lived here as a child and I grew up slap bang next door, Sally. Five yards from where we stand now. Joe moved away when he got married but he moved back here after his mum passed away. His family and my family had a holiday in adjacent caravans in Anglesey in 1975. It was lovely. He was fourteen and I was five years old."

He didn't trouble Sally with the details of Joe rescuing him from the island, even though the memory was imprinted into a small part of his brain and would remain there forever.

They knocked and went in.

"Joe, this is Sally O'Donnell from the Hospice. She is one of the specialised nurses who visit patients in the community. She is a veritable encyclopaedia. Sally, can I introduce Joe and Jenny Bradford. I was telling Sally how I had many happy childhood years living next door to here. They were good days," said Johnny.

They all shook hands.

"Have you heard anything about the scan?" asked Joe.

"Joe, I got the report through yesterday and I'm afraid that the news isn't good, I'm sorry to say. What it suggests is that the tumour is growing and that there may be some cancerous deposits in your liver, Joe. I'm so sorry about that and I wish that I could be able to sit here and tell you differently but I can't, Joe. I think that it's more or less in line with what we were all expecting. However, between Sally and the district nurses and myself we can provide any sort of palliative treatment that is physically possible to provide."

"How long would you say I've got, Doctor?" Joe asked quietly.

Johnny thought it strange that Joe had used his professional title but then he realised that since the subject matter was so serious, it would suit Joe to think of him as a doctor as well as a friend.

"That's a hard one, Joe. That's a real hard one." Johnny went on: "If you want a timescale, then as much as I hate to do it, particularly since it is such an imprecise science, I have to think along the lines of three months to six months. I'm so sorry about that, Joe, but three months to six months wouldn't be so far out."

"I appreciate your honesty, Johnny, I do."

He used first name terms again. Jenny clutched Joe's hand.

"Sally is now going to have a chat with all of us to tell us what sort of help is available," said Johnny.

They all then made silent calculations of their own. Three to six months would be roughly somewhere between Halloween and St Valentine's Day. Roughly.

Sally O'Donnell spent over two hours with Joe and Jenny Bradford that Friday lunchtime. Johnny had had to leave after half an hour as he had other house calls to do as well as getting back for three o'clock to start another long afternoon surgery. Sally said that she would speak to Johnny the following week so that Joe's care could be seamless and coordinated. Sally had witnessed the death of her own mother at the age of 61 about two years earlier; she had died of lung cancer having been ill for twelve months. From this particular tragedy in her own family she had witnessed how the care of the dying can be done in a professional, friendly and enlightened manner.

She started initially by going through Joe's symptoms, asking about pain, sickness, eating difficulties; all sorts of things which can afflict someone with Joe's condition. After a few minutes Jenny butted in.

"You are brilliant, Sally, if you don't mind me saying. It's as though the care that Joe is going to receive is personal and individual. Not just what the textbook says, I would imagine," she said.

"I agree," said Joe.

"At Nursing School and Medical School twenty years ago they sometimes used to teach clinical topics by saying something like, 'The case in the fourteenth bed is a duodenal ulcer' and I used to think to myself that it's not a case, it's a person, a real person with a real illness," said Sally. "And if you got someone who had an incurable condition, well, sometimes nobody would quite know what to say, but now we do things much better."

Joe and Jenny were inclined to agree. Sally, at great length, went through everything that the Hospice could offer, including community care, in-patient care, day care, family support, complementary therapy and so on.

"Brilliant," said Joe. "It's as though you don't find much out about all this sort of thing until you think that you might need it. It's wonderful to know that it's all there when you do. Just a thought, Sally—who pays for it all?"

"Well, it's complicated," she went on. "Some funding comes from the National Health Service and the rest comes from fund-raising and from voluntary donations. Also, to keep costs down, we have what you might describe as an army of unpaid volunteers who give their time free, for no reward apart from that of feeling that they have done a little bit to help others. We have all types of people: a multimillionaire owner of a telecom company, a school cleaner, the boss of a Bangladeshi restaurant, two taxi drivers—about fifty volunteers in total. What you find is that every person who is involved at the Hospice contributes in some way to make sure that patients, carers and families may receive the best possible specialist care, and to be treated as individuals."

"You know," said Jenny, "I didn't know about any of this at all. I've seen the occasional advert for fundraising events in the local paper but beyond that it's all new to me, all of it."

Joe nodded in agreement.

"What I might suggest," said Sally "is that I arrange to show you round one day just so that you can see it all for yourselves."

"Lovely," said Joe. "How likely is it that I'll need to come in as a resident or whatever you might call it?"

He knew that it was not the right word but it would do for now.

"It depends on your condition, Joe. All I can say is that the good news is that our community support from GPs and district nurses is so good that most patients on our books never ever need to come in apart from to have a look round. On the other hand, if someone can't be looked after at home, say for instance if their carer is unwell, then there are places for them if and when they are needed."

"Sounds fair enough to me," said Joe. "Can I just ask you about relief of symptoms? What if I am ever in real pain?"

"What is the pain like now?" enquired Sally.

"It's just there. It reminds me that it's there but then I find that I can forget about it at other times."

"Well, what we do," Sally went on, "is to start a person on a low gentle dose of the tablet form of morphine."

"Morphine?" Jenny interrupted.

"Yes, it's a very safe drug so long as it is only prescribed for people with a definite medical need and so long as the dose is right. We always start on a safe, low dose to begin with."

"Sounds sensible to me," said Joe. "What about the later stage, if for instance the tablets aren't enough?"

"Well, we can gradually increase the dosage and then sometimes we use a thing called a syringe driver, which is a battery powered device which delivers a steady dose of painkiller all day and all night. It never stops working and only needs topping up every 24 hours. By doing it like this we always reckon that it is always possible to keep one step ahead of the pain. Always. Our patients never suffer in pain, Joe, because pain is not necessary and pain is preventable."

Sally went on to arrange a ninety-minute tour of the Hospice for Mr and Mrs Bradford the following week. They were very grateful to her.

Before she left she asked them, "How well do you get on with Dr Cash?"

"Great," replied Jenny. "Joe has known him since childhood and I've known him for twenty-five years. He's a bit of a, shall we say, loose cannon but he's a bloody good doctor. Doesn't make many mistakes and always pleasant with it."

"Loose cannon?" enquired Sally.

"Well," Joe went on, "he spends a lot of time in the pub and he stood in for the lead guitarist for Methuselah one night in the Railway at two minutes' notice and he was brilliant—only got lost in the middle of 'Hotel California'. The lead guitarist's dad had had a heart attack and was being rushed to hospital in Rochdale. Apparently what Dr Cash said was, 'You lend me your guitar for the night and then you can fuck off to Rochdale'."

"Fuck off?" said Sally, wishing immediately that she had not said it.

"Yes, he uses swear words as terms of endearment. And he has imported a word from Ireland—a word he heard in western County Donegal. It's only used in three small villages, in a five-mile radius of each other."

"What is it?" enquired Sally.

"Yacunchya."

"Eh?" Sally went on.

"Yacunchya," Joe repeated.

"Explain," said Sally.

"Well, he was in this pub overlooking the Atlantic Ocean and he said that this farmer came in, wellies and all, and said to the barman, 'How are you, Yacunchya?"

"I can just picture it," said Sally

Sally shook hands with both of them and left and whilst she was driving away she wished that Dr Cash were her doctor. The GP for her and her family worked eight miles away down the Valley. He was brilliant but not friendly and wore a bow tie summer and winter and you were in and out in no time and what is worse, he never, ever wavered from what the protocol said. Never.

On the Monday, Johnny and Sally had a discussion about Joe and Jenny Bradford. And he prescribed Joe a 30-day prescription for the lowest dose of morphine in tablet form, one to be taken twice daily, and within 24 hours Joe felt better than he had felt for weeks.

The following Sunday afternoon at one o'clock, Kate arrived back safely from Seattle. Her mom had had her gall bladder removed by keyhole surgery, without any complications and she was getting better. On the Thursday Kate arrived early for the quiz and for the first time in three weeks the team won by a margin of four points above the next team, who joked that it was a fix because one question was about Boeing, one was about Starbucks and one was about Kelsey Grammar. The team who came last thought that Kelsey Grammar was a high school in Leeds. It was business as usual at the Railway and Johnny was pleased to see Kate back, safe and sound.

Chapter 24

LATE SUMMER ROLLED INTO SEPTEMBER and for weeks the valley was bathed in warm sunshine. Kate said one Thursday that the term Indian Summer had come from the early settlers in Massachusetts who were able to store up more food for the winter if the weather held, following in the same tradition of the native American people.

Johnny received a letter from the Wanted Child Trust saying that Karen Hillman had had her pregnancy terminated without incident and that she had been asked to see her GP after two weeks. In the same envelope was some promotional literature from Sheila Rubin, Marketing Manager UK Operations, saying that if a woman had had a previous termination with them then the Local NHS Care Commissioner would get a 12.5% discount for the organisation on the cost of the second termination.

Also in that day's post for Johnny were one prestigious journal, one less prestigious journal (the *European Blood Pressure Monthly*), thirty-eight clinical letters about patients, two details of GP Education courses, a letter from Al Hussein about training, a letter of complaint from a patient about repeat prescriptions taking too long to organise, the quarterly prescribing data for the Practice from Gateshead, the monthly prescribing data from the PCT (different data), the National Institute of Clinical Excellence guidelines for Maturity Onset Diabetes, a mailshot about Dykohard, another mailshot about a new rival preparation to Dykohard; this new one was a drug in the form of a nasal spray with the name of 'Puff you up', reputed to work within 60 seconds, and a postcard from two of his patients, an elderly couple called Mr and Mrs Malcolm who had visited Malta every September since 1970 and who wrote the same message on the postcard every year, and a CD from Amazon (Hank Turner—the 'Gas Station Hero: the Lost Tapes' [referring to an old reel to reel tape of an unplugged session taped in the bedroom of a fan in Dublin in 1976 and just unearthed]). That night, at home, Johnny found that he had received through the post a holiday brochure, his Barclaycard bill, a special offer mailshot from Guinness, a charity appeal letter and an advertising leaflet for a newly opened Bangladeshi takeaway, the Sylhet Palace: it looked wonderful and for September, only there was the bonus offer of free onion bhajis with every main course costing more than five pounds. Johnny wondered how he ever managed to read this same volume of mail when it came more than 300 times a year. He calculated that his job could be full time even if he didn't have to see any patients. Simply reading all this stuff would fill the day very happily, thank you.

Judy Carter got a lovely letter from her adopted son, Dean. He was now fourteen and he liked living on Long Island and he hoped very much to meet her whenever Judy had saved up enough money to visit New York. Dean had enclosed a recent photograph showing a nice looking boy standing in the back yard of a lovely suburban house on what looked like a hot summer's day. She wrote back to him promising to visit as soon as she could. She was excited.

A couple of days later Karen Hillman booked an appointment to see Johnny, as requested by the Wanted Child Trust. She told him that she was feeling fine. Johnny took her blood pressure and asked her if she wanted a further prescription for the contraceptive pill.

"Yes please, Doctor," she said.

She had nobody on the go at that particular time and she knew (even though Johnny didn't know) that Clive wasn't able to fuck her but she was simply planning ahead. She felt that she was bound to get fixed up within a week.

"While I'm here, Doctor Cash, I'd just like to say that I'm sorry about this General Medical Council business. I really am. It's all Clive's doing, to be honest. I know that you were brilliant with Orla that morning but Clive just seems to have got it in for you for some reason. And he's a convincing liar when he starts. Lying is second nature to him, to be honest."

"It's caused me a lot of anxiety, Karen, I have to say. These things drag on for months and years and then you can never predict the outcome."

"I'm sorry," said Karen.

"I appreciate that Karen, thank you for saying it. From my point of view, Karen, I'm not too bad and I am fairly sure that I will get through it, God willing. But I have to say that there are doctors in a similar situation who have killed themselves due to the worry."

"How come?" asked Karen.

"Well, as a group of people we tend to just work through our difficulties. You can't tell any patients because nine times out of ten it would reduce that person's confidence in you."

"But why do doctors kill themselves sometimes?"

"Well, there are no support systems in place. It's a terrible feeling that, unless you confide in your colleagues then you're on your own with it. Absolutely on your own. And, to some doctors, the worry that the complaint might terminate their career for ever is more worry than they can stand. Then, when they feel that there is no way out, it's usually either drugs or, if you want a really bloody ending, you get the train timetable up on the internet, pick your train, pick your spot and bingo, they take you home in four different bags."

"You would never do something like that, surely?" asked Karen.

"I don't think so, Karen, but I've heard of doctors who have done. They feel that all the cards are stacked against them and then they think that if the complaint results in a suspension then they feel that is the only thing that patients will remember. The patients forget the small miracles and they just remember the crap, the bad bits. That's what happens, Karen, believe you me."

She thanked Johnny for the prescription and left. Johnny wondered what, if anything, she would say to Clive. He did not know that she would certainly hide the packets of the contraceptive pill from him.

Johnny received another item in his morning mail later in September. Amongst the six hundred pages a week he had to read to keep up to date was another large envelope again posted by recorded delivery. It was from the GMC and it read something like this:

21st September 2013

Dear Dr Cash
Re: Two complaints against you

Following our letter of 8th January 2013 we have sought further evidence related to the complaint and this evidence has been painstakingly reviewed by our case Examiners, along with the evidence provided by yourself and by Mr Charles Taylor of the Medical Indemnity Union in Sheffield, in December 2012.

Our Case Examiners consist of one medical and one lay person and their role is to provide a balanced opinion with regard to what may be the next step required.

The opinion of the Case Examiners is that the charges against you are of such magnitude that it is necessary to hold a Fitness to Practise Hearing. You will be advised as to the date of the Hearing in due course. You are further advised that it is in your own interests to continue to seek legal advice with regard to these matters.

The possible outcomes range from, on the one hand, no sanction against you whatever and, on the other hand, complete erasure from the medical register, meaning of course that your career as a doctor will be finished.

You will hear from us again in due course.

Yours sincerely
Alexandra Smith

Case Screener
General Medical Council

This letter of less than two sides of A4 contained enough of a threat to make Johnny think that sometime in the next few months, his career as a doctor could be over forever. That night at home, he read it again and, for a minute or so, tears ran slowly down his cheeks. He had never done much else apart from being a GP. Going back a long time, whilst at university, he had done various holiday jobs—bar work which he loved; kitchen portering in a large hotel in Scarborough; that sort of stuff and all sorts of visions crossed his mind. He felt that a fairly exemplary career could be ended 20 years too soon by two silly complaints, the second of which he could not even provide an explanation for, and the first of which was, he felt, malicious in the extreme. He knew that Clive Hillman could be an unpleasant bully but he could not work out what had got him angry enough to want to terminate another person's career.

The next day Johnny got a letter from Charles Taylor confirming receipt of a copy of the GMC's letter to him, and saying that as soon as the date of the hearing was known then, at that point, he would appoint a barrister to represent him at the hearing and that he would invite Johnny to come to Sheffield to meet him or her.

Later that day Johnny went to see Joe Bradford at home. The slip of paper tagged to the front of his medical notes read as follows:

Date	25th September 2013
Time	8.02am
Visit requested by	Wife
Nature of problem	Not so good. More pain. Nauseous.

Johnny called to see them after morning surgery. Joe looked distinctly unwell.

"He's not so good, Doctor," said Jenny. "The pains have got worse and he doesn't feel like eating much at all, do you love?" she said, turning towards Joe, who was sitting on the settee looking pale and looking as though he had lost more weight.

"Tell me how you feel, Joe," said Johnny, who himself was also looking anxious.

"Well," said Joe, "the pain became more noticeable yesterday and I've only slept a couple of hours: the pain keeps me awake."

"And how much are you managing to eat and drink?" Johnny asked.

"Well," Joe replied. "Clear liquids and soups are going down okay but anything with meat in it is taking much longer than before and I'm not so hungry also, to be honest."

Johnny asked him a few other questions and then he examined him, in particular his heart, lungs, blood pressure and abdomen, with Joe stretched out flat on the settee. Johnny sat down again and then, somewhat nervously, started to speak.

"It probably means that the tumour is growing again. What we should do is to put the dose of the morphine tablets up from 30mg twice a day to 50mg twice a day and I'll add in some anti-nausea tablets called metoclopramide, 15mg twice a day to be taken around the same time and they should help you to eat something. And I'll have a word with Sally O'Donnell just to check that we don't need to do anything else at this stage and then I'll come to see you tomorrow."

Jenny thought that Johnny looked nervous but she couldn't work out why. Doctors didn't usually look visibly upset when they were talking to patients, and she felt that by this time she knew Johnny well enough to know that something was troubling him.

Johnny wrote the prescriptions and closed his medical bag and stood up to leave. Jenny followed him to the front door and, out of earshot, said quietly to Johnny, "Are you all right, Dr Cash? You look worried about something."

"I've just had what you might call a minor professional setback. Nothing much to be honest."

He tried to force a smile but found it difficult, a point which Jenny noticed all too easily.

"What has happened?" she said. "I won't tell a living soul, I promise. Not a living soul."

"I'm in trouble with the General Medical Council and I might lose my job over it. You mustn't tell Joe, under any circumstances, ever. You have to promise me, Jenny. You mustn't breathe a word of this to him."

"I won't. I promise. Now tell me what's happened."

So Johnny went on to give Jenny a condensed version of the story of the two complaints.

"They can't fire you for that, surely," she said.

"You don't know them," said Johnny. "Anyway, thank you for asking, Jenny. It's nice to have somebody to talk to about it. It is, honestly. I'll see you tomorrow, as planned."

He got into his car and drove off.

"What did Johnny want?" asked Joe when she went back into the house.

"I was just asking him about what Sally O'Donnell might say."

"What did he say?" Joe asked.

"He said that she would probably say that the tablets are all right for now."

She was making this up as she went along.

"Fine," said Joe. He paused. "Go and make us a brew Jenny. I'm parched."

So that evening Joe increased his dose of morphine tablets and started on the anti-sickness pills and he felt a bit better, only lying awake for an hour in the middle of the night.

They had started sleeping in separate bedrooms, at Joe's insistence, because he felt that if he was restless then he would disturb Jenny and that she was the one who needed to get up for work in the morning, whereas he could sleep in the daytime if he needed to.

So, in separate bedrooms, and at roughly the same time, Joe Bradford and Jenny Bradford (nee McBride) lay awake thinking that night. Joe wondered how long he might live. It was late September and back in the summer Johnny had predicted that Joe would die sometime between Halloween and St Valentine's Day. Halloween was, of course, only five weeks away. He recalled last Christmas Eve. He had had his first dose of radiotherapy, and in the evening had gone out for a Christmas Eve drink with Jenny. It had snowed a little that day and he remembered nearly falling over on the way home from the pub: Jenny had grabbed him and saved him as he fell, and they went on to have a pleasant, if nervous, Christmas; the children had visited and they had opened their presents around the tree.

Jenny lay awake, no more than eighteen inches away from Joe who was on the other side of the bedroom wall, and all sorts of thoughts went through her mind, also. She worried about Joe, and she reckoned that if she could possibly do it, then she would sell everything they had ever possessed if it meant that Joe's life could be extended by a couple of months. And then she worried about Johnny with his own problems. She had a short silent prayer for both of them. She knew that Johnny would do anything at all within his power to help Joe, as he would for any of his patients and she found that comforting. Finally, before going back to sleep, she wondered for how many years she would be a widow. At 52 she knew that it would be twenty, thirty or maybe even forty years, and she knew that however long she lived after Joe died, that she would miss him terribly, and that it would be a long and unhappy twenty, thirty or forty years. She just wished that she and Johnny and Sally could do more, but she knew that, whatever any of them could do, with all their expertise, that Joe would eventually die sometime in the next few weeks or months. With that terrible thought she then drifted off into a restless and uneasy sleep. Joe's leaving party from work was being held at the Beefeater at eight o'clock the following evening, and she wanted to feel rested enough to be able to help Joe to enjoy it.

That evening Joe and Jenny arrived at the Beefeater at five minutes to eight. A table for six had been booked for eight o'clock. Joe's boss and his wife, and the company secretary and her husband welcomed them warmly.

Joe ordered pâté followed by a small fillet steak with the trimmings but he struggled to finish it, leaving half of it on his plate.

By ten o'clock he was looking tired and he felt a bit embarrassed about being unable to polish off his meal.

It was left to Tom Armstrong, Joe's boss, to say a few words before they all went home. He stood up at the table to make his short speech.

"Joe." His kind eyes looked red with emotion. "You've worked for us for as long as I can remember and Joe, you really piss me off at times. You piss me off because you've never ever, to the best of my knowledge, made a mistake or a cock-up. Never. The firm has done well largely thanks to you, Joe. As a driver and a manager you have kept our trucks rolling nearly 365 days a year. Joe, we all love you and we would do anything…"

Tom Armstrong stopped talking and he then walked round Joe's side of the table and gave Joe, and then Jenny, a big hug. Everyone knew what he meant by his speech and these gestures, and they appreciated it. He was a good boss and he went on to keep visiting Joe at home every week, often asking his advice about the finer points of keeping his fleet of wagons on the move up and down the highways of Britain. Tom knew that he would miss Joe not just as a work colleague but also as a good friend.

Chapter 25

AUTUMN IN THE VALLEY turned into a mild damp affair. There was hardly ever a day that did not produce either rain or, at the very least, a steady drizzle. The mood of the people was seen to correlate closely with the state of the sky and folks, when going about their business, seemed to adopt a look of resignation. It would be wet, cold and dark for the next few months and there was precious little that could be done about it.

To add to the infectious damp misery and the stress caused by more and more (if that were possible) people becoming ill, Johnny received yet another large envelope from Manchester and yet again the postman produced a form on a clipboard which required a signature from one of the girls on the front desk, to confirm safe receipt of the said item.

The letter from the General Medical Council went something like this:

11th November 2013

Dear Dr Cash

Following our letter dated 23rd September 2013 we write further to confirm that your Fitness to Practise Hearing will be held at our offices in Manchester on 23rd December 2013. You should set aside two full days for the hearing which will start promptly at 9.00am. On arrival you will be asked to confirm your identity and to produce your GMC reference number.

The case against you will be presented on behalf of the General Medical Council by Morton Gould QC. You are, of course, encouraged to bring your own legal representative to the hearing.

We regret that we are unable to pay for travelling expenses, accommodation expenses or locum fees for the time spent away from your practice.

You are encouraged to discuss with your partners and possibly your patients, the possibility that your name could be removed from the Medical Register either for a specified length of time or possibly permanently, thereby terminating your career as a doctor.

Yours sincerely
Alexandra Smith
Case Screener
General Medical Council.

Johnny started shaking. The realisation that in a little over six weeks he could be looking for another job suddenly dawned on him as though a ton of bricks, falling from a great height, had landed on him.

He got the letter out again at the end of afternoon surgery, before he went home. Johnny read it again and became angry. They couldn't even use the word 'confirm' in its correct context. To confirm meant to repeat something that the person knew about already. He had, until that day, had no idea that the hearing would be in the week leading up to Christmas. As if they weren't busy enough at that time of year without the terrifying prospect of a GMC court hearing, which may end with the prospect of disgrace and ruin. Johnny felt that things couldn't really become any worse; if they could get worse then he could not even picture what that might be like, not even remotely.

Two days later he received a letter from Charles Taylor in Sheffield inviting him to come to the offices of the Medical Indemnity Union to meet his barrister, a Mr Andrew Henriques. Mr Taylor appreciated that the proceedings could be stressful and that he would also be present at the meeting. He promised that he would use his best endeavours to secure a satisfactory outcome. The letter said that Johnny would be expected in Sheffield on 2nd December at 9.00am prompt.

Johnny visited Joe at home with increasing frequency. As the life slowly drained out of him and as the pain levels gradually built up, Joe's condition required greater monitoring. His dose of morphine in tablet form had had to be slowly increased and the weight seemed to be falling off him more and more rapidly.

One day over supper (and Joe was hardly eating anything by this time) Joe asked if Jenny would take him Christmas shopping, sometime in the next few days.

"It's hard, Jenny," he said. "It's hard. I know that this will be my last ever Christmas and I feel that I have to, you know, make an effort."

"What do you mean?" asked Jenny.

"Well, it's as though I have to get things right this Christmas. I won't get another chance."

"Another chance to do what, Joe?"

"To buy folks presents and send them cards and all that sort of stuff."

"That's not what Christmas is meant to be about, Joe. It's not about cards and presents. They don't matter. It's about goodwill and family. That's what it means to me, Joe Bradford. So when do you want to go Christmas shopping?"

Sally O'Donnell visited him the following day and they all agreed that Joe would be fit enough to go to the Trafford Centre for, maybe, two hours maximum and so, the following day they set off and had lunch out and then shopped for ninety minutes and Jenny managed to get Joe back home. He was tired that night and had an early night.

Jenny, without telling Joe, booked an appointment to see Sally at the Hospice. She was getting anxious about how things were going and she wanted to know that she was doing all the right things and that she was helping Joe as much as humanly possible.

Sally was very welcoming.

"How will I know if Joe is on the right dose of painkiller?" she asked. "It's as though the whole thing is so unpredictable."

"What we do is to check on the person every day and then we will know by seeing how he is. The right dose of morphine is the smallest dose that works. So, if someone is having morphine and if they are still in pain then it means that they need more."

"Is that safe?" asked Jenny.

"As long as the dose is only increased gradually then it's safe. Honestly," Sally said.

"Are there any side effects?"

"Well, it can make a person slightly drowsy but there are no serious complications, as long as it's monitored."

Jenny didn't speak for a few seconds and then she became tearful.

"I feel gutted asking this one, Sally, but," she paused again and wiped a tear away, and as she did this her whole married life passed in front of her eyes in an instant. "But how do you, how do you know," she paused again, "when someone is about to die? How can you tell?"

"Jenny, you're doing great," said Sally. "And I think that I can maybe feel, maybe, one thousandth of the pain that you're feeling. I am sorry to have to talk in an almost mechanical fashion and if it sounds mechanical then I apologise in advance, but what you find is that you see more and more deterioration in a patient's condition. They can become quiet and maybe a bit withdrawn. Then what can happen is that pneumonia sets in."

"Pneumonia?" Jenny asked.

"Yes, it comes on if someone is so weak that they can't fight infection. You find that, ever so gradually, their breathing becomes shallow and slightly faster and then the concentration of oxygen in the bloodstream goes down and that makes them blissfully unaware of what is happening to them."

"Thank you for explaining it to me, Sally. You sort of feel alone with it all and it's great that we have you to help us out and decide on the best drug and such like and answer all these silly questions."

"They're not silly questions at all. You can ask anything you want. Anything at all. Fire away."

"Are you superstitious at all?" asked Jenny.

"Well," said Sally. "I'm not sure about that one to be honest. I probably could be."

"Have you heard of the death knock?"

"The death knock?" asked Sally.

"Well, my grandmother in Ireland said that where she grew up in County Kerry there was a local superstition that if someone in the house was going to die then you'd hear this mystery knock. Three knocks on the front door of the house. Always at night. And if it happened three nights in a row then before midnight on the day after the third lot of knocks the person would die."

"So that's three knocks on the front door for three nights in a row and, if that happens, then after the third night the person will die?" asked Sally.

"Yes, that's it apparently. Three nights. The dying person never gets to hear them on the fourth night. Never. Three knocks each on three nights then that's it," said Jenny.

Two days later Joe's pain got worse. Jenny asked Johnny to visit. He phoned Sally from the Health Centre and arranged to meet with her at the Bradford's house at twelve thirty. It was now only four weeks from Christmas and Joe looked very failed. It was as though the cancer in his gullet was taking his whole body over and that not even one bodily system had remained unaffected. On top of all this, he looked nervy and agitated. They both felt sorry for him and Johnny also, according to both Jenny and Sally, appeared visibly upset.

The four of them discussed the various options available. It was decided between them to try Joe on a syringe driver. Sally O'Donnell explained to Joe and Jenny what it involved.

"It's a device which slowly injects painkilling medication through a tiny needle just under the skin, just to the side of the tummy button."

Joe nodded in agreement. Sally went on to explain that the advantage of these was firstly that they were safe and secondly the painkiller doesn't wear off in the middle of the night, since it is slowly injected throughout the 24-hour period.

"What I think we'll do, Joe, is to start you on 30mg of diamorphine per day, plus some midazolam, which is a mild sedative and then we'll see how you are tomorrow," explained Sally.

She reassured them that this dosage should help and that the strength could be changed higher or lower if required, and then she excused herself as there were more home visits to do and she said that she would call again the following day.

Johnny had a word with Joe and then he made the standard excuse that doctors make if they want to talk about the patient out of earshot.

"I'll just go into the kitchen to count your other tablets, Joe. I'll be back in a couple of minutes or so. Can you help me please, Jenny?"

They went into the other room and quietly closed the door.

"These should settle Joe down, I think," said Johnny. "They should make him fairly pain free and more settled mentally. How are you coping with it all, Jenny?" he asked.

"I'm not so bad, all things considered. We sleep in separate rooms—Joe himself suggested it—'cos he can get a bit restless and he doesn't want to keep me awake. I still wake the odd time, though." She paused for a second. "Can I ask you, Doctor? You don't look one hundred percent yourself. I shouldn't be allowed to ask you this really, Doctor, but I'm going to anyway. Are you all right yourself?"

"Thanks for asking, Jenny," Johnny replied. "I really do appreciate it. Nobody ever asks doctors if we are all right. Never." He paused and his eyes reddened slightly. "I'm an emotional person, Jenny. Whether or not that's a good thing in a doctor I'm not totally sure, to be honest. Anyway I'm upset about Joe and I'm upset about this GMC business. Two things really."

"Are you sleeping at night?" Jenny Bradford asked.

She suddenly realised that there was a bit of role reversal going on here and she promised to herself that she would shut up if Johnny didn't seem to want to talk about it.

"More or less, Jenny. Thanks for asking. If I don't go to the pub then I take those over-the-counter tablets that you can get at Patel's Pharmacy. They're on the shelf next to those ones that make you shit and lose weight. At least I'm not troubled in that department. The girl always asks if I'm taking anything else and then says not to take them long term, then it's 5 pounds 57 pence a packet and then she says 'Do you have a Patel's Preference Card?' and I pretend that I have and that I've left it at home and then she says 'I'll validate your receipt Dr Cash' and I say thank you and so, yes, I'm sleeping okay Jenny, thanks."

"We'd be stuck without you, Doctor, to be sure. Thank you for everything you and Sally O'Donnell are doing. I'm sure I'm not allowed to ask this one either but how is the GMC business going?"

"Don't tell a soul, Jenny. You've got to promise me that you won't tell anybody. Honestly. There's going to be a hearing. Twenty third of December. Two days. Just what you want, isn't it." He paused for a minute, almost lost for words. "You have to promise me that you won't tell Joe. He's got enough on his plate without worrying about me."

"I won't tell him, Doctor, I promise," said Jenny.

So Johnny wrote out prescriptions for Diamorphine and Midazolam and sterile water for injection and gave the prescriptions to Jenny. They went back into Joe's room.

"Sorry that took so long, Joe. I've done these prescriptions and Jenny will get them from the chemist and I'll ask the District Nurse to come over later and set the syringe driver up. Kirsty Craig. Lovely girl and a good nurse too. Her mum and dad have the Railway and I think she still lives there with them. It doesn't get much better than that, Joe. Living in a pub. Cuts down on taxi fares."

"That's great, Johnny," said Joe. "How are you, by the way?"

"Working too hard but apart from that no other grumbles to be honest."

"Nice to hear it," said Joe. "And thanks for everything you are doing."

"Anytime."

Johnny left and Jenny went to the Pharmacy and two hours later Kirsty Craig, resplendent in blue, arrived and painstakingly explained all about the syringe driver and what it does.

"There's a battery in it which slowly empties the syringe over a 24-hour period and then we top it up again tomorrow."

And so she opened the ampoules, mixed the dry powdered diamorphine with the sterile water and then mixed that with the midazolam and she then carefully put all the ampoules in the sharps box and then made meticulous notes on a large blue card. She started the syringe driver going.

"You'll feel the benefit after a couple of hours or so and then you should feel comfortable all day and all night, Mr Bradford," Kirsty said.

She packed up her belongings and promised to return the following day.

"Thanks for everything," said Joe.

After two hours he felt the pain diminish and shortly after that a lovely feeling of relaxation came over him. That night he slept better than he had done for a while. As promised, all three health professionals visited him again the following day and he told them how much better he was feeling. And he was very grateful to them all.

On December 2nd Johnny got up even earlier than usual for the 45-mile drive to Sheffield. He put four hours on the parking ticket, just in case the meeting was even longer than he feared.

Charles Taylor introduced Andrew Henriques.

"I have instructed Mr Henriques to represent you at the Hearing, Dr Cash. Andrew is a very safe pair of hands, believe you me."

Johnny knew that people shouldn't always go by first impressions but first impressions of Mr Henriques were highly favourable indeed. If a television drama series wanted an actor from central casting to play a wise distinguished and successful barrister then Andrew Henriques was your man, about ten years older than Johnny or Charles Taylor with elegant thinning grey hair and a wise, kindly face. The only thing which didn't fit was the fact that he was dressed the way a deputy head teacher from a large comprehensive school would dress if he were out shopping on a Saturday afternoon in autumn—cord trousers and a Harris tweed jacket.

"Forgive my apparent lack of sartorial elegance, Dr Cash. I save my five hundred guinea suits for the enemy to look at. Power dressing and all that. I bloody well hate it, to be honest. Feel much more comfortable as I am. As for those bloody wigs, well they keep the heat inside your head and that's all they are good for."

Johnny was impressed by Mr Henriques' intelligent but relaxed manner.

"Dr Cash, I've been reading through all the papers relating to these two slight difficulties you have with the General Medical Council. I think I understand most of it. What I don't understand is why Mr and Mrs Hillman have put in a complaint about you. It doesn't add up to me. You saved that little girl's life, didn't you? That's how it looks to me."

"Yes, that's how it looks to me," Johnny said. "I saw Orla the night before and I examined her thoroughly and I couldn't find much wrong with her."

"Mr Hillman says that the examination was cursory and brief and hurried," said Mr Henriques.

"I don't know how he would know because he wasn't there," said Johnny.

"Is it true with meningitis that at the very start of the condition that it's completely undetectable?"

"Absolutely," said Johnny. "It's scary, but it's true."

"And then the following morning would it be fair to say that you were brilliant?"

"I wouldn't say brilliant but I did my job very efficiently, shall we say?"

"I agree, Dr Cash." Mr Henriques paused for a minute. He then continued, "Have you ever done anything else which might have upset him?"

"Nothing I can think of. Nothing at all. Mind you, he is known to be an intimidating character. Upsets people at the drop of a hat. I have to say that I don't like him. There are not many patients I would say that about. Very few, in fact, but he's not my favourite person. A wife beater, I would say."

"Thank you for the warning," said Mr Henriques.

He looked through the papers again.

"Now tell me about those morphine ampoules. Have you any idea where they came from?"

"None at all. I'm aware of the strict regulations about storage. I haven't a clue to be honest."

"Does anybody else have access to your house?"

"I have a cleaning lady, Judy Carter. She cleans at the Health Centre and she cleans my place every couple of weeks. She's the most honest person you could ever meet, anywhere. And she's a good singer as well, for what it's worth."

"Is there any possibility that she could have found the injections on your desk at work and taken them home for your safe keeping?"

"No. Never."

"How can you be so sure, Dr Cash?"

"I never leave morphine ampoules out at work, ever. When they arrive they are logged into the Controlled Drugs Register and immediately placed inside a locked cupboard inside another locked cupboard. Like Fort Knox but even safer."

Mr Henriques smiled.

"Just testing you, Dr Cash. I knew that that was what you would say. I might have to question you like that in Manchester. Don't worry, I will steer you a bit but it can get, shall we say, a bit nerve wracking on the witness stand."

"I'm sure," said Johnny, with a nervous smile.

"Now, as for the other side," Mr Henriques went on, "the General Medical Council have appointed Mr Morton Gould to present their side of things. He's an old warhorse. In his early sixties, with a razor sharp intellect." He paused. "The most notable thing about him is that he hates to lose a case. Ever. He would sulk for weeks. He must have oriental blood in him, even though there's none visible. Something about losing face. He would take defeat personally. Having said that, I'll be ready for him. Just you watch."

"Thank you. I'm sure you will, Mr Henriques," said Johnny.

"Someone once told me that Mr Gould would sell his granny for a shilling, and having faced him in court, I'm sure they're right. But we'll be ready for him, Dr Cash. It will be a nice lead up to Christmas for us all." He smiled. "Is there anything else you wish to ask me, Dr Cash?"

"Well," replied Johnny. "What is the worst outcome that we could be looking at here, Mr Henriques?"

He paused to think for a few seconds.

"The GMC are a frightened beast, Dr Cash. I'm sure that you are aware of what that means. What you find is that frightened beasts can behave in an unpredictable way. To answer your question, the worst that could happen is that you are fired, struck off. Career finished. Get a job as a taxi driver. That sort of thing. More likely though is either a suspension or a written warning which would stay on your file for five years. Something like that."

"But I haven't done anything wrong," said Johnny.

"I know that. Charles Taylor here knows that. You know that. All we have to do is to convince our learned friends in Manchester that that is the case and I promise you that I will do my damndest to try to convince them of that fact, Dr Cash."

"Thank you, Mr Henriques," said Johnny.

"Any time Dr Cash." Mr Henriques paused for a second. "One more question, Dr Cash. Judy Carter. Is she the Judy Carter in Nashville Express?"

"Yes. I didn't think you'd have heard of her," said Johnny.

"I'm waiting for them to release their first album, Dr Cash, and I'll be the first one in HMV to buy a copy. I only have one country album in my vast collection—'Hank Turner, the Gas Station Hero.' Lovely man. Shame what happened to him. He stood for what I stand for, Dr Cash. He never forgot the people who knew him when he was starting out, when he was poor."

"I bet that you were never poor, Mr Henriques," said Johnny.

"I'll give you poor. My mother couldn't even afford to breast-feed me. That's how poor I was, Dr Cash."

Mr Henriques put on his hat and coat, shook hands with them both and got ready to leave.

"23rd December. Nine o'clock. I'm looking forward to it," he said.

With that he was gone.

Chapter 26

AS DECEMBER ROLLED ON stutteringly in the direction of Christmas, Valley Health Centre was having one of its busiest Decembers on record. As well as having to see to the usual three thousand unwell elderly patients who attended every month of the year, year in, year out, there were the last of the influenza vaccinations to do. Every year they administered over a thousand of these, and in this particular year it didn't, for once, seem to make an enormous difference as a type of flu seemed to be sweeping the valley. Like the Vikings a thousand years earlier, it had arrived from Norway and Sweden. Being Scandinavian, at least it was an honest and reliable type of flu, in that it struck very much to the rulebook and went away after about a week. The other Scandinavian habit of this flu was its egalitarianism. It affected young and old, rich and poor, beautiful and plain people without favouritism. The only difference was that the old and the poor seemed, unsurprisingly, to take longer to get better.

Susan collared Johnny at quarter to eight one morning.

"We have allocated 105 appointments to be available today and by quarter to nine they'll all have gone. Emma's feeling the heat a little bit again. That Mr Cameron has been laying the law down to her and Clive Hillman was complaining about his prescription not being ready yet again. She'll be in tears again at this rate."

So Johnny agreed to see extra patients after six o'clock that evening. During the course of the day he came to the conclusion that anyone who could return your telephone call in less than 12 hours was a bit underemployed.

"It's a lonely feeling," he told Susan later, "Knowing that from eight in the morning till eight at night you're going to be so busy that you'd happily pay another person a tenner to go and shit for you 'cos you didn't have the time to do it yourself."

He then thought that if GPs were airline pilots then the job description would go something like this (in fact he wrote it on a piece of paper at ten o'clock that night at the end of the repeat of 'Midsummer Murders'):

What pilots would do if they were like GPs:

1. Study the flight plan to Glasgow
2. Check the plane over
3. Take off and fly in direction of destination
4. Fill in the forms for revalidation later in the year
5. Serve the meals
6. Talk to air traffic control
7. Discuss with an obnoxious passenger, who had looked things up on the internet, why you were flying at 32,000ft and not at 31,500ft and explain why in detail
8. Clear away the trays
9. Fix a faulty speedometer
10. Take a call from head office saying you're not working fast enough or well enough
11. Train a junior pilot and correct their mistakes
12. Land in Glasgow
13. Prepare to fly back in three hours
14. Take a call asking if you can "just" fit in an extra flight to Aberdeen and back in the three hours
15. Fly back home as planned
16. Do the same again
17. Do two hours home study and go to bed at midnight
18. Get up at six to do the same again next day

To finish off the note he wrote: I am not being disrespectful to airline pilots; far from it, in fact.

The other thing on Johnny's mind was what his two partners at the practice, Patrick and Angela, would say. He called a half hour meeting at seven the following night. His partners were very kind to him. He loved them dearly and he acknowledged in his own mind that a medical partnership is a bit like a marriage and that the main difference is that you see more of each other and, believe it or not, there is more that can go wrong. They all gathered in the little sitting room over a cup of tea.

"I'll need the 23rd and 24th off, I'm afraid," said Johnny.

"I'll book it off also," said Patrick. "I'll come and give you moral support."

"I appreciate it, Patrick, honestly, but it will be chaos here coming up to Christmas."

"I'll organise a locum if I can. Leave it with me."

Johnny was touched by his kindness.

"The other thing, of course," said Johnny, "is what if they don't allow me back."

"I don't think that's terribly likely, is it?" asked Angela.

"Not necessarily likely at all, to be honest," said Johnny, "but they do have an air of unpredictability about them. You know that as well as I do."

"Point taken," said Patrick, nodding in agreement.

"The other thing about all this and it is the part of it that grieves me more than any of the rest of it, is the fact that I might not be able to keep my promise to Joe Bradford. You know me. I would never in a million years make a promise to anyone that I couldn't keep and I promised, I promised that poor man that I would look after him until the very end of his life. I promised him that and now it looks possible that I'll have to go back on my word. I would do anything for that man. Anything at all. I would lay my life on the line for him twice over if necessary because 38 years ago he did exactly the same for me." Johnny started to become tearful. "And now I'm possibly going to break my promise, and it grieves me, it grieves me deep down inside." He stopped talking.

"We could take over his care, Johnny," said Angela, looking concerned. "Only if you want us to, that is."

"I know you could and you'd probably do it a bit better than I would but I promised him, Angela, I promised him. I promised that I would look after him to the end. It's as simple as that."

"Johnny, you're being too pessimistic. It won't end up like that," said Patrick. "What I don't want to see, Johnny, is you getting burnout over all this. Burned out doctors are a risk to themselves and I'm not going to allow that to happen. We think too much of you. I've heard of doctors, not so far from here, getting burned out and then it's a slippery slope towards too much booze, self-prescribing sedatives and then it gets very, very messy. Very messy. We're not going to let you get anywhere near that point, Johnny, ever."

"It will work out, Johnny," said Angela, "and we are here for you. We're here for you and we're here for Joe Bradford and we're here for whoever needs us. It is what the job is all about and we will never, if you need us, let you down. Ever."

The next morning both Patrick and Angela put their heads round Johnny's door just before eight o'clock and checked that he was feeling all right. He was.

The day was busier than ever. The preparations for the Christmas Eve party were in full swing. The format would be similar to last year: the Steamer, with its big function room, but with a different comedian and a different band. As in the previous year, there were strong rumours that Judy and Johnny would sing together on stage. It had become a bit of a high point of the night. Johnny looked back and, after racking his brains, he still could not recollect how it had ever started. They had sung together for seven or eight years now, and Nashville Express had made it a policy not to accept Christmas Eve bookings as a result. But who had first asked them to do it remained a mystery.

Joe Bradford became weaker and by mid-December his dose of morphine in the syringe driver had gone up eightfold; however, he tolerated it well and was not in any significant amount of pain. Johnny and Sally were, separately, visiting him every two or three days.

Jenny lay with him on top of his bed at bedtime one night. For a second or two Joe started sobbing and then stopped again. Jenny dried his eyes for him.

"Do you think I'll see Christmas, Jenny?" he asked, trying to hold back the tears.

"Sure you will, Joe, sure you will," she said.

"Do you remember last Christmas? Slipping in the snow?"

"I do. We'd had a lovely couple of drinks. We've had some good times together, Joe Bradford. Some good times together."

One minute or two later, Joe settled down for the night and slept right through.

Johnny came to visit the next day, after morning surgery.

"How are you, my old friend?" he asked.

"Not so bad, Johnny. Not so bad, thanks to you." He paused for a second. "Johnny, there is a question I have to ask you. I hope you don't mind."

"Not at all, Joe," Johnny replied. "Ask me anything you want. The right dose of morphine, the length of the second longest river in Uzbekistan, anything at all, in fact. Ask away."

"Johnny, this is serious." Joe went on, "I'm worried about you, Johnny. You've not looked yourself this last couple of weeks. Every time you come to see me you look more worried. What is it, Johnny? You can tell me. You know that."

"I'm in trouble, Joe, big, big trouble. About as big as you can get without murdering somebody, I'd say."

"What's happened?" asked Joe.

And so Johnny took a couple of minutes to recount that long, slightly sorry tale. He then went on.

"I've done nothing wrong, Joe. Nothing wrong. I know that for a fact. But whether I can convince the G.M.C. of that, I'm not so sure at all."

"What could they do to you?" Joe asked.

"They could fire me, Joe. It's as simple as that. By New Year's Eve I could be delivering pizzas or driving a taxi, washing puke off the back seat."

"It won't come to that, Johnny."

"You don't know them," said Johnny.

"Johnny, you are going to fight your way through this, Johnny. I know you will. Now cheer up. Doctor's orders and all that."

"Thanks Joe. Thank you."

Johnny wrote some prescriptions and promised to come again in two days.

That night Joe slept well but Johnny found out half an hour before bedtime and long after the pharmacy had closed that he had none of his over-the-counter sedative tablets. He went to bed at eleven thirty and found that he could not sleep. During the four hours before he managed to get to sleep he went halfway to hell and back and all his worries crossed his mind and became magnified and tortured him as he lay awake. When he finally drifted off to sleep he had a vivid dream about driving taxis and customers being rude to him and running off without paying. At six thirty he got out of bed wondering if he would actually get through the day.

That day at work, things went from bad to worse. Johnny's last patient that night, at twenty to seven, was Mr Cameron.

"It's time you lot started earning your money, I think, Doctor. You just sit there and write prescriptions all day. I could do that."

Johnny didn't think that he had the strength to rise to the bait.

"Mr Cameron, in your working life, were you ever able to delegate your work to someone else?" Johnny asked.

"Of course, Doctor. I could say to one of the juniors 'do this', 'do that' and they would do it."

"And what time did you finish at night, Mr Cameron?"

"Always home for five thirty, Doctor. Tea ready on the table."

"Mr Cameron. How good are you at telling the time?"

"I don't know what you mean, Doctor."

"Mr Cameron, I trained for nine years to do this. It might not look much to you, Mr Cameron, but I'm not allowed to delegate my work and I'm not allowed to make mistakes and if I do make mistakes then the fires of hell will consume me. Mr Cameron, it's ten minutes to seven. Now tell me what you want from me, Mr Cameron."

They went through a list of five ailments and at exactly four minutes past seven Mr Cameron left.

When Johnny came out of his room, Susan congratulated him for dispatching Mr Cameron home.

"I would just like him to emigrate, Susan. Dunedin, South island of New Zealand. That is as far away as you can get from here, Susan. I would be happy with that."

Johnny went to Patel's pharmacy and got his over-the-counter sedatives and then when he got home he did something unusual. He was not a home drinker and never had been. The good news, though, was that he had had two gifts from patients that day, Christmas gifts nearly a week early. One was a small bottle of Teacher's whisky and the other was a full size bottle of anCnoc, single highland malt, established 1894, 12 years old. Both bottles looked lovely.

Johnny had one drink of the Teacher's and then another and then another and then another and then he realised that the bottle was empty and that he felt drunk. And then the peril of his situation hit him, like an express train. He felt terrible and didn't know what to do or where to turn.

At that point Kate rang to check that Johnny was going to the quiz the following night. On hearing her kind, friendly American voice he broke down in tears.

"Johnny, what on earth is the matter?" she asked.

"I can't tell you, Kate. I'm in some sort of trouble, Kate. It's terrible."

"Ten minutes. I'll be there."

She put the phone down.

The doorbell rang. Johnny let Kate in. They sat down together on his settee.

"I've never seen you like this, Johnny. What's the matter? You'd better get me a drink first. I'll get a taxi home if necessary."

They opened the bottle of expensive malt and Kate poured a drink for both of them and then Johnny went through the whole story from start to finish. Two complaints and he could lose his job completely and forever. What is more, he still felt that he had done nothing wrong.

"The whole fucking thing is a charade, Kate. I've done nothing wrong."

"It doesn't seem right, Johnny. It doesn't."

Johnny became more and more distraught as the whisky took hold of him.

"Kate, for years I have had a constant need, day or night, in sickness and in health, whether fresh or weary, to work with precision. And, as God is my judge, that's what I've done, Kate. You look at every patient from every angle and you live with the thought that there is on every occasion an accusing barrister looking over your shoulder and you say to yourself, is this drug right, or is another drug right, or will they clash or should I admit the patient to the hospital? Christ knows, Kate, we do that dozens of times every day and then this happens."

She snuggled slightly closer to him on the couch.

"Johnny, it will work out. It always does, Johnny, you know that."

"Kate," he paused and wiped his eyes, "without my job I would be nothing. It's all I do. It's what I am. Without it I might as well be dead."

She interrupted him.

"Don't even think of talking like that, Dr Cash. I will not hear of it. Ever."

"Kate, every hour there is a train from here to Leeds and one to Manchester and one to Preston. And in the other direction. Eighteen hours a day. That's a hundred trains a day, Kate. It would be so easy."

He was really drunk now and there was no consoling him.

"When it's raining in January, Kate, and I have no job and no future and there are a hundred trains a day, it would be so easy. The only person I would feel for would be the train driver, Kate. The only person. Joe Bradford is dying, Kate, but I feel that I'm dying faster than he is."

"Jesus, Johnny, don't talk like that. Please."

"Okay then Kate. I know that you and my friends will see that I'm all right."

"Everyone will see that you're all right. You can be sure of that."

"Thank you, Kate." He paused for a moment. "You know, Kate, my namesake, Johnny Cash, the man in black, had a simple philosophy in life. You know what it was, Kate? What he said was never think you're better than the next man, 'cos you're not, and always do your best, whatever you do. That man was so humble that when he appeared on stage he said, 'Hello, I'm Johnny Cash and thank you for coming to see me tonight.' Thank you for coming to see me tonight." He paused for a few seconds. "Thank you, Kate, for coming to see me tonight. You never think that you're better than the next person, do you, Kate? And you put your heart and soul into things and do your best, don't you Kate?"

"Just like you do, Johnny. We're all in this together and we'll get through it together. You can bet your bottom dollar on that one, Johnny Cash."

"Kate, put me to bed will you? I've had too much to drink, Kate. Put me to bed, Kate."

And so, ever so gently, Kate led him by hand into the bedroom, slipped his shoes off his feet, got him to lie down on the bed and covered him with the duvet. She then dozed for an hour on the other side of the bed on top of the duvet, mainly to see that he was all right. She then woke up about one o'clock and phoned for a taxi to take her the two miles home. She walked back at six in the morning to recover her car and at seven she phoned Johnny.

A bleary voice answered at the other end—"Hello" or something like that.

"Johnny, it's Kate. Just wondering how you are."

"Thanks Kate. I feel quite a lot better. And thank you for coming to see me last night, Kate: it meant a lot. Honestly."

"Anytime Johnny."

"How did you get home, Kate?"

"I dozed until one o'clock then I got a taxi and walked back for my car this morning."

"You're a star. You know that."

"Johnny, if you need me again, you call me, you understand?"

"I will, Kate, thank you."

"Not long to Christmas."

"You're right Kate. In fact, you're always right."

Johnny had the worse hangover of the two of them but he got through the day and at the quiz that night pretended that he had the gastric variety of the Scandinavian flu that was doing the rounds. He stuck to orange juice and at the end of the night, he realised that on a cost per pint basis, it was more expensive than beer.

To add insult to injury they lost the Christmas quiz on the tiebreak question. Whoever got the answer to the following question correct the soonest would win the quiz.

The question was, "Name a reference to beer in a Christmas carol." Johnny's team didn't know. The teachers got it after half a minute's deliberation.

Johnny got home sober and switched on the radio while he had some supper. It was playing carols from Kings College, Cambridge, and at the moment he switched the radio on out came the words, "mild he lays his glory by."

Chapter 27

DECEMBER 21st BROUGHT A LIGHT SNOWFALL on the higher hills above the valley. At the lower levels in the town of Valley Mills, the precipitation was falling as a grey cold drizzly rain.

The Health Centre was extra busy that morning and after a long surgery and with the prospect of an equally long one in the afternoon, Johnny set out on his house calls at just after midday. He had six calls to make. One was to a lady of 99 in a nursing home who sounded as though she was developing a respiratory infection; one was to a 23-year-old schizophrenic man who was hearing more voices than usual; one was to a 97-year old man who lived alone and who had "gone off his legs" as the neighbour put it; one was to see an 88-year-old lady who had come home from hospital the day before having suffered a heart attack (she was also diabetic and had long standing leg ulcers); the fifth patient was at Buckden's Funeral Service Rooms of Repose (in Calder Street, next door to Valley Working Men's Fruiterers—the deceased was one of Aubrey Kendall's patients and it had become the law that a person had to be assessed in private by an independent doctor before the Certificate could be issued [Noel Buckden greeted Johnny with his usual phrase 'it will soon be standing room only in here doctor, if we get any busier']); and the sixth patient was Joe. As on most days, Johnny wondered if he would be back by five to three to start again in the afternoon. He reckoned that he could eat his chicken sandwich with Noel while they turned Mrs McGann over to look for bullet wounds etc.; at 102-years-old it would not be a very likely possibility but the form said that you had to perform a thorough examination and interview the family. He wondered why deceased centenarians could not simply be allowed to rest in peace before the funeral.

Johnny made it to Joe Bradford's by two fifteen. Joe was stable and he was on a large dose of diamorphine by means of the syringe driver.

"He's comfortable, Doctor. And rested, also," said Jenny.

Johnny stayed for ten minutes and checked Joe over. There were no signs of infection anywhere. The dose of diamorphine could stay the same and Johnny said that instead of leaving it two days until 23rd he would come after work on 22nd for reasons that maybe only thirty people in the entire valley knew: Johnny was aware that if the Hearing went badly for him then at least 3 million readers of the *Daily Mail* would see his picture splashed all over the newspaper on 27th December, competing for space with the stories from premiership football matches—held on Boxing Day.

The following day was even busier. Patrick had kindly arranged a locum doctor to cover for the two days of the Hearing. Dr Mistry telephoned at lunchtime to confirm the arrangement and promised to be there by twenty minutes to eight in the morning.

Johnny was preparing to leave at six thirty when Susan and young Emma knocked on his consulting room door.

"Johnny, we simply want to wish you well for the next two days. You know that we will be thinking about you," said Susan.

"Thank you ladies. You are much kinder to me than I really deserve," Johnny said.

"Dr Cash, you must let us know here as soon as you know something," said Emma.

"I promise, Emma. As soon as I know what's going on I will let you know straightaway."

Susan bent over and looked him straight in the eye.

"You are more than a match for them, Johnny. You know that."

With that they left. Johnny tidied his desk, just in case, had a long slow fond look at his certificates on the wall, thought about where he would hang them in his taxi if taxi driving was going to be his next job (next to the meter, he thought), switched off the light and set off to call in and see Joe and Jenny.

Jenny stopped him in the hallway of the house.

"How is Joe?" asked Johnny.

"He's a bit worse, Doctor, to be honest. Weaker, you know."

Jenny Bradford paused for a minute and then she hesitantly started speaking again.

"Doctor, I'm a bit superstitious and I heard about an old belief from the west of Ireland that states that if you get three mystery knocks on the door in the night and if there is a dying person in the house then if you hear it three nights running then the sick person will die after the third night. They never live long enough to hear it the fourth time. The death knock, they call it."

"I must be truthful Jenny but I've never heard of it before, ever," said Johnny.

"Well, Doctor," she said, "I heard it last night. I woke about half past three and I was lying awake and then it happened. Three clear knocks. I went downstairs and opened the front door but there was no-one there. Not a living soul, Doctor."

"Does that mean…" Johnny tried to say.

"It means, Doctor," Jenny interrupted, "that if it happens in the middle of the night tonight and tomorrow night then Joe will pass away on Christmas Eve. It means that he will die before Christmas."

"Well, Jenny, with his condition and all that, I'm afraid to have to say that it is possible, Jenny. It could well happen."

"Thank you for being so open and helpful, Doctor. And I honestly mean that," said Jenny.

"Thank you, Jenny."

"Can I ask, Doctor, but how do you think this complaint thing will go? I suppose it's hard to tell really."

"Well, I have to be in Manchester at nine in the morning and it will run for tomorrow and the 24th, Christmas Eve. I'm staying in a hotel tomorrow night, and I promise to keep in regular touch by telephone. Beyond that, Jenny, we can only pray."

Jenny paused for a minute.

"Thanks for everything you've done for us, Doctor. You've been well…" Suddenly she became lost for words and slightly tearful. "Well, you know what I mean."

"Thank you, Jenny," said Johnny. "I'd better go and have a word with Joe."

He went upstairs and had a long chat with Joe Bradford, asking about his symptoms and about how he was sleeping. After about fifteen minutes Jenny came in with a whisky bottle and two glasses.

"Joe was wondering if you'd have a Christmas drink with him tonight, Doctor."

She put the bottle and the two glasses down. Johnny did a quick mental calculation. He didn't usually drink alcohol with patients but this was different, very different and there was a big possibility that this would be the last time that he would see his long time friend and childhood rescuer alive. Furthermore he was only driving about a mile home.

"I'll have a small one, Jenny, please," said the Doctor.

"Same for me, love," said Joe, looking a bit frail.

It transpired then that Johnny stayed for three quarters of an hour, sipping slowly at the neat whisky.

"We had some good times," said Joe. He had to expend a lot of effort even just to speak a little.

"Without you I'd not be here today, Joe. I haven't forgotten that and I never will, Joe, ever. I'll never ever forget what you did for me."

"It was a lovely holiday, Johnny."

Joe became more and more happily contented, as the morphine and the whisky started working together. And so they talked endlessly about past times that they spent together. After about half an hour, Johnny realised that he had better get going to pack his things for the early start in the morning.

"I'll be back to see you Christmas Eve, Joe," said Johnny. "As soon as Manchester is sorted out I'll be straight here."

Johnny bent over and hugged Joe in the bed, and then, too upset to speak, wiped his eyes, gave him a little wave and, holding back his tears, left the room and went downstairs.

Jenny stopped him at the bottom of the stairs.

"Thanks again for everything, Doctor." She could see that Johnny was almost too upset to speak. "I hope that it goes well for you."

"Thank you, Jenny. By the way, you married a lovely man."

"Thank you." She paused for a couple of seconds. "Joe knew," she went on, "that something was worrying you. He couldn't work out what it was though. But he knew. He could tell there was something wrong, and I didn't say a word to him about it. Not a word, Doctor. Just as you requested."

"You're great, Jenny, and you've looked after Joe very well. He wanted to stay at home and you allowed him to do that."

"It's the least I could do, Doctor. The least I could do. I got into a routine these last few weeks. The strangest thing though is that he didn't want to talk about it. Hardly at all. He spoke up a bit when we were in America but since then he's hardly wanted to talk. He just kept his thoughts to himself."

"We're all different, Jenny. Some people just think things and keep turning the thoughts over in their minds. We all cope with things in different ways."

"You must see it all in your job, Doctor. All the time."

"It's a strange job, Jenny. We do everything we can for our patients. Everything we can and we even become quite fond of some of them. And then they go and die on us, Jenny."

At this point Johnny became tearful again. He dried his eyes.

"I'm sorry about this, Jenny. I'll have to go. I'll keep in touch from Manchester by phone."

"Thank you, Doctor," she said.

And with that he was gone.

Johnny went home and started gathering his belongings together for his 36 hours away from home. In a neat pile he put his official documents for the case, best suit, shirt and tie, a change of suit, shirt and tie, clean undies and socks, toothbrush and toothpaste, razor, blood pressure pills, cholesterol pills, over-the-counter mild sleeping pills and cinema times for central Manchester for the evening. He would probably go and see 'Terminator VI: Fightback.' It was the latest movie in the franchise and the role of the hero was played by a new actor who had recently been the Labour Mayor of Stockport. He fancied the Director's Cut which was to be screened at 8.45pm. Surely the first day of the Hearing would be over by then.

Johnny settled down to watch the Ten o'clock News. At five past he got a text from Kate saying 'Good luck. Everyone thinking about you. Kate x' and at ten past ten he got a call from Rosaleen, Patrick's wife.

"Johnny. I'll pick you up at seven o'clock and run you both to the station. Patrick's feeling a bit fluey but he's just had a paracetamol and he's gone to bed. Should be okay in the morning."

Johnny's alarm was always set for 6.30. He was in a deep sleep, having a dream about hiking the Appalachian Trail with Kate (the mountains were higher than you could believe and he kept falling a long way behind Kate's beautiful backside) when the phone woke him at 6.15.

"Johnny. It's Rosaleen. Sorry to ring so early. It's Patrick. He's got so much worse in the night. It's this flu. He's shaking so much that he can't get out of bed. He's so sorry, Johnny, but he'll not be able to come with you. He's mortified."

"Rosaleen. Don't worry. The important thing is that he offered to come and give me some support. And I appreciate that, Rosaleen. Tell Patrick that I hope he feels a bit better. Paracetamol. Every four hours. Fluids."

"Thanks Johnny. I'll tell him and I hope it goes well, Johnny. I hope you're okay."

"Thanks Rosaleen. And all the best for Christmas."

Johnny got dressed, straightened his tie, brushed his hair, gathered his belongings and set off to walk to the station to catch the 7.27 train to Manchester. The train was on time and became full after stopping in Rochdale.

Five minutes to nine, Johnny walked into the elegant marbled hallway of the General Medical Council and reported to reception.

"Dr Daniel John Cash, GMC number 1742590."

"Thank you Dr Cash. If you take the elevator to the 7th floor and follow the signs."

"Thank you," said Johnny.

He pressed button number 7 in the lift. The next 36 hours would either be bad, very bad or very, very bad.

Chapter 28

JOHNNY TOOK THE LIFT up to the seventh floor reception and presented himself to the young lady on the desk. She was friendly and polite but retained a slight air of formality.

"Has anyone come with you, Dr Cash?" she asked.

"No, Mam," Johnny replied. "All on my lonesome."

"Fine, Dr Cash," she said. "I bet you're feeling nervous about it all."

"I am indeed, very nervous," Johnny said.

"Well, Dr Cash, the timetable says that God willing we should have it all wrapped up by Christmas. If you take a seat then someone will show you in, in the next few minutes. It will be Hearing Room number 7."

"Jesus," Johnny thought, "Christmas starts in 39 hours' time."

It was too close for comfort. Then he thought about Joe Bradford for a minute or two. Then it dawned on him that the General Medical Council must be like a suburban multiplex cinema. All that was missing was posters on the wall advertising forthcoming attractions.

He looked at the eight different doors into the eight Hearing Rooms and guessed that you could have: 1. Sexual relations with a patient, 2. Self prescribing of opiates, 3. Failure to conduct a thorough clinical examination on a patient, 4. Brawling at a football match, say Everton vs Manchester City, 5. Failure to visit a sick patient, 6. Driving a motor vehicle whilst intoxicated, 7. (his own) and 8. Misuse of a practice computer for personal gain.

After about five minutes a man in a suit called Johnny into room number 7 and advised him where to sit. There was a table in the shape of a horseshoe around which were seated six other people. At the end of the room there was a small public gallery which would hold about a dozen people.

The G.M.C. Legal Advisor introduced everyone to Johnny.

"Before we start, Dr Cash, I would like to introduce the five other people in the room. Firstly we have our two panel members, one medical and one lay. This is Professor Lennox Gillespie, Professor of Surgery at the University of Aberdeen, and this is Mrs Sylvia Rahman, non-executive director of Yorkshire Solutions PLC. Next we have our stenographer, Miss Julie Wolstenholme. I am Philip Watson and I am a lawyer. My purpose is to give legal advice to the Panel Members. Finally we have Mr Morton Gould who is presenting the case against you on behalf of the General Medical Council and then we have Mr Andrew Henriques who is acting for your good self. Do you have any questions at this stage, Dr Cash? We will start the formal proceedings shortly."

Johnny felt a bit overpowered by it all.

"No Sir," he replied in a quiet voice.

There was about ten seconds' worth of silence whilst people shuffled papers and then, slowly and deliberately, Mr Morton Gould shuffled to his feet.

"Dr Cash, before we start, would you like a glass of water or anything?"

"No Sir, I'm okay, thank you," Johnny replied.

He actually felt about a million miles away from being okay but he didn't wish to admit it at this early stage.

Morton Gould continued: "This is a Fitness to Practise Hearing, Dr Cash. The purpose of this hearing is to ascertain whether or not you are fit to work as a doctor in the future."

"I understand," said Johnny.

"I will list the two charges against you shortly, Dr Cash, but before that I wish to briefly describe to the Court what Fitness to Practice means."

"But you do not have a definition of Fitness to Practise, Mr Gould," Johnny blurted out. "No one has ever come out with a watertight definition."

At this point Andrew Henriques stood up.

"Dr Cash, you will have plenty of time to comment later, when the time is right."

He sat down again. Morton Gould went on at length.

"To practice safely, doctors must be skilled in what they do. We cannot have doctors who pretend to be competent and who are, in fact, not competent. They must maintain effective therapeutic relationships with patients and respect their autonomy. Doctors must act responsibly if they or a colleague falls ill and as a result of this illness their performance suffers."

The whole court listened in absolute silence.

Mr Gould continued, "Doctors have a respected position in society and their work gives them privileged access to patients, some of whom can be vulnerable. A doctor who shows that he or she cannot justify the trust placed in him or her should not continue in unrestricted practice. The public of the United Kingdom of Great Britain and Northern Ireland is entitled to expect that their doctor is a fit and proper person."

Johnny wondered how long this introduction would go on. Mr Gould continued talking.

"Doctors of the United Kingdom must provide good standards of clinical practice; they must keep up to date, maintain their wide range of skills and constantly audit their performance. They must work well with their professional colleagues. Furthermore, if they have teaching responsibilities then they must teach colleagues in a professional and effective manner. Doctors must also be honest and trustworthy and they must not allow their own health to endanger patients.

"A question of impaired fitness to practice is likely to arise," Mr Gould continued, "if a doctor's performance has harmed patients or put patients at risk of harm or if they have shown reckless disregard of clinical responsibilities towards patients or if they have violated a patient's trust or if they behave dishonestly, fraudulently or in a way designed to mislead or harm others."

Mr Gould paused briefly and then continued in his overpowering and pompous way: "Is there anyone in the room who is not aware of what being Fit to Practice means?"

Everyone shook their heads, much to Johnny's relief.

"I will, therefore, now list the two charges. Dr Daniel John Cash, you are a General Practitioner working at the Valley Health Centre in the town of Valley Mills in West Yorkshire in England."

Johnny nodded in agreement.

"Dr Daniel John Cash, you are present here today, the 23rd of December 2013 at a Fitness to Practice Hearing of the General Medical Council in Manchester, England.

"It is alleged that, firstly, in September 2012, you wilfully misdiagnosed the condition of your patient, Orla Hillman, a little girl aged two, who was suffering from meningococcal meningitis. Secondly, it is alleged that you recklessly kept ampoules of diamorphine in your dwelling house and that these ampoules were not kept in a locked cupboard inside another locked cupboard according to the regulations and that there was no proper record of those ampoules of diamorphine. In fact, there was no record at all. These are both serious allegations and they both bring into question the ability of Dr Daniel John Cash to continue his career as a doctor. These are the two charges against you. Do you have anything to say at all, Dr Cash, at this stage?"

"I intend to vigorously defend myself against these charges. In fact, in my professional opinion, it is nothing more than a bloody witch-hunt. Nothing more," said Johnny.

At this point both Morton Gould and Andrew Henriques started to speak simultaneously. Their jumbled comments were as follows: Mr Gould said, "Dr Cash will be reminded that this is a Court and that maybe he should respect the Court by means of a measured use of language. Expletives are not acceptable." Mr Henriques said, "Dr Cash, I understand your frustration but I will encourage you when and if there is a time in the proceedings for you to give your opinion. For the time being we should stick to the facts."

Johnny apologised to them both.

After a short break Morton Gould went on to describe Johnny's two consultations with Orla, namely the last appointment in the afternoon surgery and then returning as an emergency the following morning, following which she was rushed to the hospital.

He went on, "I now wish to call my two witnesses, Orla's mother and father, Mr Clive Hillman and Mrs Karen Hillman."

The court usher left the room and returned shortly afterwards with Clive and Karen; he showed them where to sit. As they were taking their seats Clive lifted his arm and pointed straight towards Johnny and very calmly said, "Before we proceed any further, I want it on record for the Court that this is the Doctor who nearly killed my little girl."

Nobody responded to this accusing jibe.

Morton Gould got up to speak again.

"Mr Hillman has told me that his wife has said she is too nervous to speak in Court and that he is to speak on her behalf."

Karen said nothing and simply looked ahead, staring at the floor in the middle of the room.

"Mr Hillman, I would like you to know that you can take as long as you need to answer these questions and I apologise in advance if it is an ordeal for you. Mr Hillman, can you please describe Orla's condition when she was brought to see Dr Cash on the first of these two occasions?"

Clive Hillman started. He looked threatening; his five hundred guinea suit showed he meant business and he went on to speak in what Johnny thought was a cold and callous way. Karen kept absolutely silent.

"When my wife brought Orla to see Dr Cash, it was obvious that Orla was in an advanced state of a serious illness and it was even more obvious that she should be in hospital immediately."

Johnny said nothing but he was unimpressed: he felt that only arrogant people used the word immediately in everyday speech because, according to the strictest definition of the word, by the time they have spoken it immediately is gone; he reckoned that people who use it are a bit thick also. If only he could convince the Court of this fact.

"Can you describe Orla's condition, please, Mr Hillman?" he went on.

"Well, she was unwell from about five o'clock onwards. Feverish, floppy, unresponsive. And Dr Cash said that it was nothing very much. That's what he said."

"And what was Orla's condition like during the course of the evening?"

"She was worse," said Mr Hillman. "She was very unwell. If Dr Cash hadn't said that she wasn't unwell then we would have sought medical attention again during the course of the evening. It's all his fault."

He pointed at Johnny again.

"And then, you allege that Dr Cash slowly and belatedly realised next morning the true nature of Orla's condition and that if he had only done so some fourteen hours earlier then Orla's condition would not have been so critical?"

"That's exactly what I allege, Mr Gould," said Clive Hillman.

"And it is because of his negligent delay in making a diagnosis that your daughter Orla nearly died?"

"That is correct, Mr Gould. Dr Cash is not fit to be a doctor and he should be disbarred immediately."

"Thank you, Mr Hillman, for being so helpful giving your evidence. My learned friend here wishes to speak to you in due course. Please do not let him intimidate you in any way. Mr Henriques is here to defend the status quo and to allow the cosy medical establishment to continue in its self-serving way, where its main priority is, dare I say, to look after itself."

Mr Gould sat down.

Andrew Henriques got to his feet and started to speak.

"Mr Gould; thank you for taking us through the case for the General Medical Council vs Dr Daniel John Cash with respect to the first of the two charges. As you are all aware we will deal with the evidence concerning the second of the two charges as soon as we have dealt with the case of Orla and her unfortunate illness. First, I would like, if I may, to ask if Mr Hillman could update me about Orla's condition. How has your little girl been recently, Mr Hillman?"

"She has made a full recovery, Mr Henriques, but it was touch and go for quite a while."

"Thank you for updating us, Mr Hillman. I now wish to address Dr Cash. Dr Cash, how long have you been a General Practitioner, may I ask?"

"Approximately 16 years, Sir," Johnny replied.

"And would you say that you are highly experienced at your job, Dr Cash?"

"If you call working twelve hours a day for 16 years, following on from 9 years training as being experienced, then I have to say that I am. Very experienced, I would say."

"Thank you, Dr Cash. Now I want to get on to the subject of meningococcal disease. Can you tell us a bit of what you know about the condition and how it is treated?"

"Certainly, Mr Henriques. I am aiming these comments about meningococcal disease at everyone in the room including non-medical people so I will try to avoid flowery language if that is agreeable," Johnny said.

There were gentle nods of agreement all round.

"Carry on, Dr Cash. In your own time," said Mrs Rahman.

"Thank you," said Johnny. "I will start by saying that meningococcal disease is a rare infection but, at the same time, it is the commonest infectious cause of death in children in westernised countries. It is hard to diagnose in the earliest stages because there is nothing really to go on at the beginning. The classic signs and symptoms of a rash which doesn't blanche, a stiff neck and sensitivity to light are often a much later development. When the condition is suspected or recognised, it is essential to admit the person to hospital. It is very helpful also to administer an injection of penicillin at a dose appropriate to the age and the size of the person."

"Thank you, Dr Cash," said Mr Henriques. "Can you tell us about what happens when the person arrives at hospital, after you have administered the penicillin?"

"Well," said Johnny, "they are treated intensively with intravenous antibiotics. They are usually very, very ill for a few days and sadly a significant percentage of people with this condition die in the first few days of the illness."

"Thank you, Dr Cash. I now want to go back to the earlier part of the illness if I may," Mr Henriques continued. "Would you say that it is a hard condition or an easy condition to diagnose in the early stages?"

"It is a hard condition to diagnose," said Johnny.

"And why would you say that that is the case, exactly?"

"Because when it starts it looks like and sounds like a lot of other conditions, conditions which are much less serious."

"What do you mean, looks like and sounds like, Dr Cash?"

"Well the symptoms are often the same as, let us say, a throat infection or something like that."

"Are there any differences at all in the early stages?" said Mr Henriques.

"None at all, unfortunately," said Johnny.

"Fine, Dr Cash. For the benefit of the non-medical people in the room, and that includes myself and my learned friend Mr Gould here, can you explain the processes by which a doctor diagnoses an illness. Just tell us in general terms what you do."

"Well," said Johnny, "we use what we call hypothetico-deductive reasoning."

"Hypothetico-deductive reasoning? Maybe you should explain it to us, for our benefit," said Mr Henriques.

"What we do is, when we are trying to diagnose a condition, we gather in as much information as we can, and we ask questions to test our ideas; we do it almost without thinking," said Johnny.

"Almost without thinking?"

"If you have been doing it a long time, like I have. Let me quote one example. Say you have a lady in her early thirties with a swollen abdomen and a discomfort. You might think that she is suffering from one of several things, such as, irritable bowel syndrome, fluid retention, a large cyst in her abdomen or indeed that she may be pregnant. Then, if you look in her notes and find that she has had a hysterectomy then you can rule out pregnancy, so you then ask questions relevant to the remaining possibilities."

"Can we say then, Dr Cash, that it is not an exact science?" asked Mr Henriques.

"It is not an exact science," said Johnny, "but it is the best that we have got and, thank God, it works well most of the time."

"Why do you not do every test on every patient that comes through your door?"

"There are several good reasons why. One is the immense cost. One is the inconvenience to the patient. And one is the fact that people would die."

"People would die?" asked Mr Henriques.

"Yes, people would die. If you wait for the results of every test then people would die. You have to be cleverer than that," said Johnny.

"Give me an example of being cleverer than that."

"Well, say you have a lady in front of you who is in a state of collapse and who says she might just be pregnant; well, you don't think to yourself 'let's do a few tests for ectopic pregnancy and see what comes up.'"

"Why is that, exactly?" asked Mr Henriques.

"Well, that lady could die from internal blood loss within an hour, so you ring for a 999 ambulance, phone the hospital, ask them to have blood transfusions and an operating theatre ready, get her in and say a little prayer. We don't have the luxury of tests in a situation like that."

"You said that you might say a little prayer," said Mr Henriques. "Do you mind if I ask if you are a religious man, Dr Cash?"

"I am at a time like that," said Johnny, and a very gentle laugh went round the room.

"Thank you for that, Dr Cash. So what you are saying is that many diagnoses are made using vast experience, just as much as ordering tests?"

"I think that vast experience counts for a lot," said Johnny.

Mr Henriques then took Johnny through what he did with Orla during the two consultations, which were about fourteen hours apart. Johnny explained in detail what he did on both occasions and why. He answered Mr Henriques' questions for over half an hour and Mr Henriques thanked him for answering in such detail.

"One more question, Dr Cash. How many patients do you see on an average busy day, may I ask?"

"Between thirty five and forty and sometimes more."

"Thank you, Dr Cash. I have no further questions for you at this stage."

The chairman suddenly came to life and started speaking.

"I think that, maybe, we should break for forty-five minutes for lunch and then reconvene about one thirty," said Professor Gillespie.

Johnny wasn't particularly religious but when the lunch break was announced he said a short silent prayer which went something like 'Thank you God for letting me survive the first morning of my hearing' and then he went to Starbucks and ordered the largest latte he could find, and a chicken sandwich, and he was glad on this occasion not to have to eat it at the Funeral Parlour whilst lifting up Mrs McGann's right leg.

The Hearing resumed at 1.35. It was the turn of Morton Gould, acting on behalf of the General Medical Council, to question Johnny.

He cleared his elegant throat and addressed the Court.

"I intend to demonstrate to the Court how the reckless and slapdash behaviour of Dr Daniel John Cash nearly cost Orla Hillman, a helpless two-year-old girl, her life. I will show how this negligent doctor nearly terminated this little girl's life at the age of two and how he nearly deprived a frail and vulnerable toddler of the chance of another eighty or ninety years of life. I will first address Dr Cash."

"Dr Cash, I take it that you did examine Orla on the first occasion at the end of a very busy day?"

"That is correct," replied Johnny.

"Can I ask you, Dr Cash, if you yourself were tired from overwork by this time of day?"

"Not at all," replied Johnny. "Doctors are well used to working a twelve-hour day and I had only worked ten hours by this time."

"Ten hours, Dr Cash. Is that not a long time?" said Mr Gould.

"I am well used to it, Mr Gould."

"Can I ask how you found Orla's condition to be?"

"I examined her very thoroughly and found evidence of a slight infection in her ears but no definitive sign of anything else."

"No definitive sign of anything else, Dr Cash? We have since learned that Orla Hillman was suffering from an advanced state of meningococcal disease. She, by the sound of things, was very ill. Can I ask you to reconsider your answer, Dr Cash?"

"I will reconsider it but I will not change my answer. She had no sign whatever of meningococcal disease at that time."

"Dr Cash, when you saw this little girl early the next morning you finally made your diagnosis, after a delay of fourteen hours, a delay which nearly cost her her life. How do you respond to that, Dr Cash?"

"Mr Gould, there is a time for any patient with any established medical condition that they did not have that condition. Gallstones, for example. For every person with gallstones, there was a time for that patient when they did not have gallstones, and it is the same with meningococcal disease. It can come on out of nowhere in a matter of hours," said Johnny.

"Mr Hillman's statement says that Orla definitely had that condition when you saw her the first time," said Mr Gould.

"I do not agree, Sir," said Johnny. "I do not agree."

"Thank you, Dr Cash. I wish now to question Mr Hillman, Orla's father.

"Thank you for taking the time from your busy schedule to allow yourself to be questioned, Mr Hillman. I am sure that your evidence will be helpful."

Clive nodded in agreement.

"Will you please describe Orla's condition when she was brought home after seeing Dr Cash on the first occasion?"

"She was very unwell, Mr Gould," said Clive. "Very unwell. If Dr Cash hadn't reassured us then I would have taken her to the hospital in the evening."

"What was she like for the rest of the evening?" asked Mr Gould.

"She went worse; she had a high fever and she was delirious."

"How sure are you about this, Mr Hillman?"

"Very sure. Absolutely sure, in fact," said Clive.

"How many times during the course of the evening did you check on her?" asked Mr Gould.

"About ten times an hour, all evening."

Suddenly Karen Hillman stood up and interrupted them.

"I cannot sit here and listen to all this nonsense," she said. "My husband was out of the house all evening."

A hush descended over the courtroom.

"Mrs Hillman will have an opportunity to speak out soon," said Mr Gould.

"Mr Gould. My husband was out of the house all evening. There is no way that he would have known anything about Orla's condition. No way at all."

"Fine, Mrs Hillman. You are obviously keen to make your point known," said Mr Gould. "Please tell everyone here why, in your opinion, there was no way that your husband would have known what was going on with regard to Orla's condition, taking into account, of course, that your husband said that you were too nervous to speak in Court."

"I will tell you why I felt I was too nervous to speak in Court."

"And why is that, Mrs Hillman, may I ask?" said Mr Gould.

Both Mr and Mrs Hillman looked red in the face.

"I was nervous because, because," she said hesitantly, "my husband said that if I told the Court the truth then he would, to use his exact words, 'fucking well kill me.'"

The courtroom was stunned into silence.

Mr Gould continued, slowly and deliberately.

"Tell me what your version of the truth is, Mrs Hillman."

She hesitated for a few seconds.

"My husband was out of the house all evening from half past five until midnight. At a Sportsman's Dinner or some such thing. Where men with no money spend silly amounts on equally obnoxious friends." She paused. "That's it. I've said it now. Orla was fine all evening when I was playing with her and Clive came home in a minibus taxi. Nearly fell out of it, he did. He staggered up the stairs and fell into bed in a drunken stupor. He is doing this as part of some vendetta against Dr Cash. God only knows why. That doctor saved Orla's life. He spotted her condition within seconds the following morning and gave her some penicillin by injection and got her straight into hospital. That's the truthful version of what happened. I swear to God that it is."

Morton Gould indicated that he had no more questions.

Andrew Henriques got to his feet, shuffled his papers and asked Karen Hillman about two more things.

"Mrs Hillman, when did you notice a change in Orla's condition?"

"At quarter past seven in the morning, Sir. She just didn't look right. It's quarter past seven when I first became worried."

"Thank you, Mrs Hillman. Just one last question, Mrs Hillman. I want you to take your time before answering this one. Take as long as you want. Mrs Hillman; you said that your husband threatened to, to use your own words Mrs Hillman, he threatened to fucking well kill you. Mrs Hillman, has your husband, Clive Hillman, ever deliberately physically harmed you? Take your time before answering, Mrs Hillman."

Karen paused for a couple of seconds.

"Yes," she said.

"How often has your husband physically harmed you, Mrs Hillman?"

"He beats me two or three times every month, Mr Henriques, without fail. It's as regular as clockwork."

There was silence for about ten seconds.

"I have no further questions, Mrs Hillman. Thank you for being so gracious and for being so open and honest in front of the Court."

Mr Henriques sat down.

The panel members whispered into each others' ears briefly.

"That concludes the business for today. Thank you everybody. We shall meet again at nine o'clock in the morning. Nine o'clock sharp," said Professor Gillespie.

It was five o'clock. Never had a day for Johnny gone so quickly. He felt that he had been running high on nervous adrenaline.

Mr Henriques was waiting for him in the lobby of the General Medical Council building.

"Dr Cash, what did you think about your first day in court?" he asked in a friendly fashion.

"Well, Karen Hillman's testimony would fit with what really happened. I am just worried that Clive will beat the shit out of her tonight, to be honest."

"Dr Cash, there is a phrase which says, 'If you live by the sword then you will die by the sword.' Dr Cash, one of the Hillmans will destroy the other. They are those sort of people and I say that despite Karen speaking out in Court. The only six things we don't know about this particular bit of destruction are namely what, where, when, how, why and who. To quote Rudyard Kipling, 'A man marries a woman like her and expects her to behave like Mother Teresa of Calcutta.'" He paused. "Dr Cash, you saved Orla's life. As for the parents, I wouldn't give a tinker's shite for either of them. See you in the morning, Dr Cash. Nine o'clock. Sharp."

Johnny went back to his hotel to freshen up, and watch the six o'clock news. The siege of Harrogate had entered its fourth day. Some wealthy local retired people had kidnapped the head of the Inland Revenue in Yorkshire and were threatening to amputate his fingers one by one if income tax and inheritance tax were not reduced by ten per cent. They had set up a video link to relay the proceedings to the outside world, and it was being shown live on breakfast television in California at that very minute. The man, Mr Aidan O'Rourke, was being held in a basement and was wearing a headband straight out of The Deer Hunter and was speaking to the camera.

"It is not morally right for governments to tax their citizens at over sixty per cent so that governments can spend their citizens' money like sailors on shore leave and I apologise unreservedly."

The Police had the place surrounded. One of the pensioners was ex-army and he told them (by special phone link) that the Honda Civic in the driveway had been rigged to explode if anyone came near (it was subsequently found not to be so).

The other story was that a local footballer, called Mr Gadd, had had sex with a girl in the toilets of a nightclub. They had started having sex at two minutes to midnight until one minute past, according to all the witnesses. The girl had then gone to the police the next day saying that she had only become sixteen at midnight. The Sun ran the headline the following day which said, 'Two out of three, that's bad, Gadd.'

Johnny got the bus two miles past the University to visit the Taj Mahal Restaurant in the Curry Mile in Rusholme and ordered a lamb tikka madras and mushroom pilau rice.

"Any side dishes, bhindi baji, Bombay potatoes, peshwari nan, pint of Cobra, anything like that, Sir?" asked the young waiter.

"No, I'm okay, honestly. Thank you."

Johnny reflected on how there was hardly any setting in life where they didn't want to try to sell you more than you really want to buy; from supersizing burgers to stuff you spray on your shoes, to premium economy seats on airplanes to luxury cinema seats with free use of a telescope; they always want some more of your f*****g money. The only place where this doesn't apply was sex within marriage. He had yet to hear a story from any of his married friends in the pub where they were starting to have sex with their wives when she suddenly started saying, 'Are you sure you don't want me to turn over or feel hungry or dress from head to toe like a lifeboat woman?' or whatever. It simply never ever happened.

The meal was delicious and Johnny felt a little better by the end of it.

Outside the restaurant he found a bright spot near a shop window and telephoned Jenny Bradford, to check on Joe's condition.

"He's worse, Doctor. Thank you for ringing, by the way. It is good of you. Sally O'Donnell had to increase the dose in the syringe driver today and Joe is comfortable but he is so much weaker," said Jenny.

"I'm sorry to hear that, Jenny. Honestly I am. I will phone you again in the morning before the case starts, Jenny. And, God willing, I'll be there to see you both by this time tomorrow, Christmas Eve."

"Thank you, Doctor. Can I tell you one more thing?"

"Of course," said Johnny.

"Well. You know that thing about the three knocks on the door? Well. It happened again last night. Three knocks. As clear as anything. Well, if it happens again tonight, Doctor, it means that Joe will die sometime tomorrow, before midnight."

"Oh Jenny, I'm so sorry. That's terrible," said Johnny.

"Thank you, Doctor. I hope you didn't mind me telling you. As though you haven't got enough on your mind at the minute."

"Not at all, Jenny. Anyway, keep your fingers crossed and I'll be there by this time tomorrow and I'll phone you at breakfast time in the morning. And give Joe my love, won't you Jenny? Don't forget, give Joe my love."

"I'll not forget, Doctor, honestly."

"Thank you, Jenny. You have been brilliant."

"And so have you, Doctor. Whatever you do, Doctor, don't worry about me. You have given me fair warning about what is going to happen and it's as though I'm ready for it, to be honest. It's as though I'm prepared for it."

"Have the children been to visit, Jenny?" asked Johnny.

"They're here now, Doctor."

"Okay Jenny. I'll ring in the morning, about eight."

"Okay, Doctor."

Johnny felt too upset to get any enjoyment out of watching a film at the cinema so instead he did what he had never done before, that is, went into a pub alone for the purpose of having a drink. He always worried about people who drank alcohol alone and now, here he was doing that very thing.

He had four pints of beer, on top of the large bottle of Amritsar Golden Ale in the curry house and, during the next two hours, he thought about lots of things which included, in totally random order: how Jenny Bradford would get used to being a widow; how she had never once batted an eyelid during the whole fourteen months and had never ever shown any hesitation in helping Joe during his illness. Then he wondered how he would do as a taxi driver if his career were terminated tomorrow, wiping puke off the back seat at half two in the morning; how his friends and colleagues had supported him; the incident on the rug with Kate, trying to decide which of them had started it and which of them had tried to stop it; and how he loved being a doctor really despite the pressure; and Joe Bradford carrying him above the waves when his appendix nearly burst when he was five; then Mr Cameron making young Emma cry and finally, he wondered what he would sing with Judy on stage at the party the following evening, Christmas Eve.

Then he did another thing he had never ever done before in public. He sat in the corner of the pub and tears started to roll ever so gently down his cheeks. He tried to dry them but they just kept coming. This happened about half way through the fourth pint of the evening.

A man of about sixty, who had been drinking in a group of five men, came over to sit next to Johnny.

"Are you all right, son? We're all getting a bit worried about you. I hope you don't mind me asking?"

He was a Scottish man with red hair.

"I'm all right, honestly," said Johnny, "but I appreciate you asking me. I really do. Thank you."

"It's always one of three things. Work, women or money. Always one of those three. Now which of them is it, son?" asked the Scottish man.

"It's all three, I'm afraid."

"All three? Jesus. That must be bad."

"It is. Tomorrow I might lose my job and if I lose my job I lose my home. I have no wife and no children. And I spent a couple of evenings with an American girl—lovely she is—but I messed that up big time."

Johnny's tears started slowly flowing again and he wiped his eyes.

"What work do you do, son, if you don't mind me asking?"

"A doctor. G.P. in West Yorkshire."

"You're a nice, decent man but you don't look like a doctor tonight, sitting in a pub miles from home crying your eyes out."

"I never know what a doctor's supposed to look like," said Johnny, cheering up a bit.

"Well, where I come from, a doctor looks, well, like a doctor."

"Dr Finlay's Casebook? Big house? Janet the housekeeper? Well, it's not like that any more, honestly."

"I'll tell you a story, Doctor; then, when I've told you this, you're going to sup up and go and sleep it off somewhere."

"Okay," said Johnny.

"Doctor, I moved here from Scotland thirty years ago. From outside of Glasgow. I worked on the sites. Some big ones. Hospitals. Motorways. That sort of stuff. And then I met my wife. English she was. Got married 28 years ago. Then we had two bairns. Alasdair just emigrated to Canada two years ago. Annie would have been twenty-seven last week. Would have been. July 2005 she was in London. Eighteen. Down there for a job interview. Something in banking. The evening of 6th July we took her to Piccadilly station to get the train, said we'd pick her up again at Piccadilly station on the Friday evening, the 8th. After that we never saw her again. At dinnertime on the Thursday, there was something on the radio about a power surge on the London underground and then the news got steadily worse all day. We never saw our Annie again. July the 7th. I'll never forget it. Then last year my wife got breast cancer. A tiny lump. But the doctors think she'll be okay. You doctors are a good crowd of people."

"Thank you," said Johnny. "Do you mind me asking? Do you ever get bitter?"

"Not now, Doctor, not now. I did at the beginning. I thought my world had come to an end. Completely to an end. I wanted to murder the bastards that did it but then I thought no, what good would it do? What good would it do indeed? It would do no good at all. That's how much good it would do. An eye for an eye, that's what people said at the start. An eye for an eye. And then I thought, right, we'll have the whole world blind at this rate."

"You're right," said Johnny.

"Doctor, do you know who helped me the most? It was people who sat and quietly talked and listened and said to me, 'Mate, you're not alone with this, you know.' It was people like that who helped. The Indian man who has the newsagents. He wouldn't let me out of the shop without asking me if I was okay. And my workmates. That sort of thing. It helped a lot. What you find, Doctor, is that it's the spirit and the actions of the good people that comes out on top in the end; those other folks, the not so good ones, they give us a decent run for our money at times but it's the good folks who will triumph. You can bet your bottom dollar on that one, Doctor. The specialist who is treating my wife for her breast cancer. He says she'll be cured. You do a good job, you people. And do you know why you all do a good job? It's because it's a partnership with the patient. We feel that we're all in it together, pulling in the same direction. That's what it's all about, Doctor. If one person has a problem it should be everybody's job to sort it out. That's what I think."

"Thank you," said Johnny. "Can I ask you, Sir, what is your name?"

"Duncan," said the Scottish man.

"Duncan, you've been very kind to me tonight, Duncan, and I will always remember it; thank you," said Johnny.

"Doctor, you are a good man and you will do well tomorrow. Whatever the outcome, Doctor, it will work out, I promise you."

"Thank you, Duncan."

"Now Doctor, you go back to your hotel and don't go to the bar and go straight up to your room and go to sleep. That's what you should do, Doctor."

Johnny decided to have just one more drink before he took the Scottish man's advice. He reckoned that it would settle his nerves and help him get to sleep. He asked the barman for a double whisky.

"Are you sure, Sir? You're looking just a little wobbly, if I may say."

"I'll be okay. Just the one, then."

"Okay Sir. That'll be four pounds twenty please. Then that's it, Sir."

"You're right, my friend. Thank you."

Johnny slowly sipped his double whisky at the bar. Half way through it the kind Scotsman came over to have another word.

"Doc, it's none of my business. None of my business at all, you understand, but when you've had this one you're going back to your hotel to sleep it off. We're worried about you, Doc. You've had enough for one night, Doc. Honestly."

Johnny smiled and grabbed the man's hand to shake it.

"Thank you, Duncan. You're right and I'm going to take your advice."

"Fine, Doc. Happy Christmas to you."

So Johnny slowly sipped his drink and in the next two minutes he changed his plans. His life had now come to an end. He would not be able to continue working as a doctor and his level of functioning had reduced to being advised by two kind and well meaning strangers, the red haired Scottish man and the barman. This is what it had come down to and he decided here and now that he was going to end it all. It was time to do something about it.

He supped up and stumbled out of the pub. It was just after eleven o'clock and a fine, cold drizzle was falling slowly from the dark Manchester sky. He walked about 50 yards to the junction where Great

Western Street came out on to Oxford Road and straightaway he could see a taxi. He flagged it down.

"Where to, mate?" asked the driver.

"Railway Road, please. Just near the crossing."

"Sure, mate."

The journey took about five minutes.

"That's five quid please, mate," said the taxi driver.

"Here's twenty, my friend. You can keep the change."

"I can't, mate. It's too much."

"Go on. It's nearly Christmas."

"Are you sure?"

"Buy your wife a drink and some chocolates."

"Cheers mate; have a good one."

"And the same to you, my friend."

The taxi pulled away. Johnny looked round. The railway crossing on this suburban street was about a hundred yards away. He knew that there was a train every twenty minutes in each direction till about midnight. That would mean an average wait of about ten minutes. He reckoned that there was about an even chance that in ten or eleven minutes or so his many problems would be over. The pleasures of life had retreated so far into the background of his consciousness that all he could see ahead was disgrace, humiliation and ruin. He had drunk a lot of beer that evening but, at the same time, he was sober enough to realise that his career would end tomorrow. Everything he had worked hard for would come crashing to an end. Everything. He had done the sums and he had worked out that carrying on was not a worthwhile option.

Johnny walked in the direction of the crossing. He could see that the station was just down a short path to the left. At this point the gates came down and the red lights flashed, stopping traffic. On both sides were modern houses built in the nineteen seventies. Inside them people would be watching late night TV, wrapping presents or going to bed. Some of the houses shone bright with Christmas lights.

A train left the station and picked up speed travelling from left to right. As it went over the crossing, Johnny could see that there were about 20 passengers on board. It looked warm and inviting.

The gates went up and Johnny walked towards the track. No one could see him. The next train would, no doubt, be travelling from right to left. He looked down the track to the right. The two lines each divided, making four lines altogether, about twenty yards down the track. He wanted to die out of sight of the road. It would not be fair on people driving or walking past it; it would cause them terrible undeserved distress which would be even worse for them so close to Christmas.

Kind and considerate to the end, Johnny therefore walked about thirty yards down the track. There was just enough light from the streetlights to see that, of the two inbound lines, one was clean and shiny and polished and the other was slightly rusty and not so frequently used. He checked his watch. The inbound train would be along within eight minutes.

Johnny then did a final calculation. The future problems in his life outweighed the good bits by a ratio of about a hundred to one and there was no chance of it ever getting any better. Ever.

He checked his pockets, simply to remind himself as to what they would find. Wallet containing about eighty pounds; one debit card; two credit cards; one Boots Advantage card; one Tesco club card; West Yorkshire library card; Drivers Licence. Loose change in trouser pocket. Hotel room key in other pocket. Hair a bit damp. Nothing more to check really. Bladder a bit full.

Dr Daniel John Cash, middle-aged family doctor with a previously unblemished record and highly popular with his patients, chose his spot and lay down across the brighter of the two railway lines. It was difficult.

The line was a continuously welded steel rail with a gauge of four feet and eight and a half inches resting on timber sleepers on a crushed stone ballast bed. Johnny got down and lay on his side with his back to the direction the train would come from. One rail made a perfect fit with the right side of his neck; he wished that he had brought a small pillow from the hotel room just for his head. The other rail came just above his ankles. They would find his body in four distinct sections after the train stopped. Two feet (with ankles), one torso with shortened legs attached. Etc.

Vehicles kept driving over the level crossing and he could see three people standing on the in-bound platform waiting for the next train. He felt like running over and telling them to phone home to say that they would be late home that night or maybe to club together and get a taxi.

Johnny waited and, at first, nothing happened. Then, all of a sudden, with that feeling that you can only get after a night in the pub, he went from having a comfortable bladder to bursting for a pee in about ten seconds. For a minute he thought that he could hang on as the train would surely be along shortly but after a minute was up, he was so desperate to go that he thought, well fuck it I'd better do what nature intended.

He got up slowly from the railway track, turned his cold and stiff body towards the bushes at the side, lowered his zip and poured forth in the direction of the back garden of a house. Inside there was a lady clearly visible (about seventy) in the kitchen. She reached into a cupboard and removed a large packet of cornflakes followed by a bowl from the next cupboard.

It seemed to take an eternity to empty his bladder. He wiped his hands on the wet grass beside the track, dried them on his jacket and, for the second time that night, lay on the railway line.

Johnny wondered if he had left any work undone from the day before and he thought about Kate and wondered what she would say when she found out on Christmas Eve that he was dead. He felt bad about the timing but he knew that, one day, she would understand and, hopefully, forgive him.

And then it started. You could feel it before you could hear it. The cold, hard rails started to vibrate. At first, it was almost imperceptible but then it became more forceful and then you could hear the low-pitched sound of the train. The red lights flashed and the crossing gates went down. The noise got louder, the line shook more and more and the noise became deafening. Johnny thought that this must surely be what it is like entering hell.

The train got closer and closer and, finally, Johnny knew that his life would soon be over. For the first time in weeks he actually felt calm and relaxed.

Chapter 29

JOHNNY CLOSED HIS EYES and braced himself and had one last look at the people waiting on the platform.

The vibration and the deafening noise were more than he could take and he was comforted by the fact that in two more seconds he would be dead.

He counted one, two etc., and then realised that he was still counting and that he had got up to ten and then twenty. He opened his eyes and saw a freight train passing about six inches away from the top of his head. It was doing about thirty miles an hour and then the driver applied the brakes. A few feet nearer to the crossing the two lines joined and Johnny realised that he had escaped death by six inches in one direction and about ten feet in the other. The train had been travelling on the less frequently used track and it had missed him by a hair's breadth.

The goods train stopped and less than two minutes later the driver came running down the side of the track waving a flashlight. He shone it in Johnny's frightened face.

"Jesus, Mary and Joseph! That was a close one." The driver himself looked shocked. "Give me your hand. I want to shake it."

"Why do you want to shake it?" asked Johnny, trembling.

"You're the sixth person who has done this in front of my train over the past 25 years and you're the first one who has been able to answer me back. That's why I want to shake your hand." He paused. "I'm Paddy Kelly. Kelly, the boy from Killane. Been in England 25 years. What's your name, son?"

"Johnny. Johnny Cash. Yorkshireman. And I can sing a bit. Not as good as the man in black but I try. Honestly."

Paddy the engine driver helped Johnny the doctor to his feet.

"You scared me there, Johnny. Really scared me."

"I'm sorry."

"Don't apologise. I'm just glad that we're having this conversation."

"So am I, Paddy. So am I."

Paddy got his mobile phone out and made two calls, firstly to the signalman and then 999 for an ambulance.

"I've got a man called Johnny Cash here and I need an ambulance. He needs checking over at the hospital. As soon as you can, mate, if you will."

"Tell them I'm a doctor as well," shouted Johnny.

"Jesus, mate. What are you going to tell me next?"

"It's true."

"Okay." Paddy paused and then spoke again into his mobile. "He's a doctor. A bit drunk. Just found him having a sleep on the tracks here. Seems to be all right otherwise. Thanks."

He put his phone away. They both sat on the rail nearest to the fence.

"The passenger train that would have been on the line you were laid on was held up by a mechanical fault. They let me through first instead. A close call, Johnny. A close call."

"You're right there, Paddy."

"I have two daughters who are doctors, Johnny. One is a Psychiatrist and the other a Pathologist. So the Kelly family are world experts on railway suicides. We could write a book about it. Johnny—promise me one thing."

"What's that, Paddy?"

"If you get like this again, Johnny, go and get help. Get help at an early stage. People worry that others will think less of them. That's what they think, Doctor. They are afraid that people will think less of them. Well, in God's name that has to be better than gathering round their graveside the first week in January, with flakes of snow coming out of a grey sky and everybody wondering what they could have done differently."

"You're right, Paddy. You're a smart man, you know. A smart man."

"Doctor, I went on Millionaire last year. Won two hundred and fifty thousand. That's how smart I am, Doctor. Two hundred and fifty thousand quid. But I like driving goods trains, sure I do. I took Mary and Caroline and Siobhan to Barbados. Five star hotel. Brilliant it was. Two weeks. Cost us ten grand. Ten grand. Finest place you could ever visit but after eight or nine days I couldn't wait to get back to driving these feckin' trains. There's two hundred and forty thousand left in the bank."

A minute later the ambulance pulled up on the crossing and the paramedics walked down the trackside looking for Johnny.

"I don't think he's so bad, lads, to be honest," said Paddy, "but he needs a cup of strong coffee and an early out-patient appointment in the next ten days, I'd say."

Johnny shook Paddy's hand.

"Thank you, Paddy. Thank you."

"Don't forget what I said, Doctor. Don't bottle it up. And have a good Christmas. And don't drink too much. Guinness is all right, you know but stay off the shorts."

With that they got into the ambulance and headed off to the hospital.

The emergency room was full of people who had consumed too much pre-Christmas cheer but they managed to see Johnny within two hours and the doctor interviewed him at length. Dr Singh wanted to admit him but Johnny managed to convince him that he was okay and by three o'clock he had sobered up enough to be allowed to go back to his hotel in a taxi.

Johnny was in bed by four o'clock; he had set his alarm for seven but after a fitful sort of sleep he was awake a full fifteen minutes before the alarm went off. He showered and had breakfast—a sort of condemned man's type of breakfast. It was included in the price of the room and a long day was ahead, so he had cereals and fruit followed by the biggest cooked breakfast he could fit on his plate, with toast and proper butter and one of those little things with marmite in it. The nice young Latvian waitress asked him whether he preferred tea or coffee.

He said, "Coffee, please, and as much as you can bring me without losing your job."

"Bad day coming up?" she asked, smiling.

"Bad day already," said Johnny.

"You will feel better with some coffee inside you, Sir," she said.

And so Johnny took two paracetamol with codeine tablets to, hopefully, ease his headache and then his blood pressure pill washed down by a fifth cup of coffee.

The hotel dining room was full of Christmas decorations and the menu for Christmas day lunch was up on the wall, saying early booking essential. The cost per head was the same price as a last-minute holiday somewhere booked online outside of school holiday times.

At eight o'clock Johnny phoned Jenny Bradford, as promised.

"Hi Jenny, it's Johnny here, Dr Cash. I was just wondering how things were with Joe?"

It was a time-honoured phrase he used; rather than asking how the person is, just in case he or she had died in the night.

"Doctor, I'm afraid… I'm afraid he's much worse, Doctor. Sorry to have to tell you that."

Johnny breathed a silent sigh of relief; at least there was a chance, even if it was only a slender chance, that he would be able to keep his promise and see Joe Bradford to the end of his illness. He reckoned that his chance of being with Joe when he died was, maybe, ten per cent; he certainly didn't put it any higher than that.

"Is he in any pain, Jenny?"

"No, thank God, but he's become a bit delirious in the night and his breathing has become a bit faster and a bit shallow. I don't like the look of him at all, Doctor."

"Have you slept much, Jenny?"

"A couple of hours, maybe. That's all."

"Right Jenny, obviously Joe is deteriorating but the most important thing is that he's not in pain. So Jenny, God willing, if things go well today, then I'll be there at your house by early evening. I'll come as soon as the case finishes. It'll take about an hour or so from Manchester. God willing, of course."

"Thank you, Doctor. Oh, there's one thing I forgot to mention. You know that thing about the three knocks on the door, in the night, for three nights running?"

"Yes, Jenny."

"Well Doctor, it happened again last night, about two o'clock this morning. I heard it as clearly as anything, Doctor, and you know what that means. It means that it will happen today, before midnight."

She couldn't bring herself to say the exact words that Joe would die.

"I'm so sorry, Jenny. I'm so sorry." He couldn't think of anything further to say at this point, except, "There should be a recess around half twelve or one. I'll phone you then."

"Thank you, Doctor."

"Look after yourself, Jenny."

Johnny and Andrew Henriques and the others started gathering about five minutes to nine and exactly at nine o'clock the second day of the Hearing started. Johnny thought to himself that there must be a much better way of spending Christmas Eve than this.

Lennox Gillespie started off.

"Today we hear the second of the two charges against you, Dr Cash. That is that you had in your possession four ampoules of diamorphine, diamorphine which you could not account for, had no record of and which was not stored in a locked container inside another locked container. Dr Cash, do you intend to defend yourself against these charges?"

"I do, I do," said Johnny.

"Dr Cash, why did you say 'I do' twice?" asked Professor Gillespie.

"Well, you said diamorphine twice, Professor," said Johnny.

"Dr Cash, please don't split hairs."

"I won't, Professor Gillespie. I certainly won't split hairs. As we all know, splitting hairs is the job of the General Medical Council."

Andrew Henriques rose quickly to his feet.

"Doctor Cash, if you don't mind. That comment was uncalled for."

"I apologise unreservedly to the Court," said Johnny.

Morton Gould got to his feet.

"Dr Cash. The one thing that I can thank you for in this sorry mess, this big hole that you have dug for yourself, is that you have not denied that the evidence was in your house. You have admitted that these four ampoules of diamorphine, diamorphine which could kill if it got into the wrong hands, were in a carrier bag in the bedroom of your dwelling house. Do you still admit that, Dr Cash?"

"I do, Sir. However, at the same time, if these ampoules of diamorphine, diamorphine which is a safe drug when used properly, were to be forensically examined, then no trace of my fingerprints would be found."

"And how do you know that for certain, Dr Cash?"

"Because I never touched them. Ever."

"You never touched them?"

"No, Sir, I never ever touched them."

"So how, pray, did they happen to be in a supermarket carrier bag in the corner of your bedroom, mixed up with various half used courses of antibiotics and suppositories, along with a supermarket receipt dated Thursday 25th June 2009 timed 8.08pm stating that you purchased 24 cans of Norseman Lager, one bottle of Jacob's Creek wine, a bag of cashew nuts and, I am ashamed on your behalf to say, a magazine entitled *Readers Wives 40-49* costing five pounds and ninety nine pence. *Readers Wives 40-49*. Can you explain why you bought that magazine, Dr Cash. Please, pray, tell the Court."

"I thought that your wife's photograph might be in it, Sir. Maybe she could have lied about her age, Sir."

Even Professor Gillespie started to smile but then he promptly looked serious when he realised that other people were watching him. Morton Gould turned redder and redder in the face.

"Dr Cash, that comment was totally uncalled for," said Mr Gould.

"I am sorry, Sir, but what I bought on that date is absolutely no business of the General Medical Council, and because it is no business of the General Medical Council, then you had no right to mention it, Sir, in my humble opinion."

Andrew Henriques stood up.

"Dr Cash, I feel I that I must advise you in the strongest terms to mind what you are saying."

"I am sorry, Sir. I apologise."

Mr Gould continued.

"Dr Cash, I want to ask you several things about controlled drugs. The rules. That sort of thing, Dr Cash. Dr Cash, tell me what is the title of the set of rules which cover this area."

"They are called the Controlled Drugs (supervision of management and use) Regulations 2006," said Johnny. "These cover the receipt, supply and stock holding of controlled drugs. Records have to be strictly maintained. Separate records should be kept for each drug and different doses of controlled drugs. When morphine and diamorphine are stocked, it is essential to record the date on which the supply was received, the name and address of the pharmacy from which the drug was obtained and the quantity of the drug received. If such a drug is obtained on a prescription then the identity of the person who collects the drug has to be recorded. Stocks of these drugs should be kept in a doubly locked container."

"Thank you, Dr Cash. May I ask you what you would describe as a reasonable minimum quantity?" asked Mr Gould.

"There's no absolute definition, Mr Gould," said Johnny. "I suppose that we would have to ask the man on the Clapham omnibus what he would think."

"The man on the Clapham omnibus?"

"Yes. This mythical man is thought to be the arbiter of common sense, of reasonableness. Let us say, maybe, 5 to 10 ampoules. Certainly no more than that."

"Thank you, Dr Cash. Can I now ask you about destruction of controlled drugs? Let us say drugs which are not required. What do you know about the rules about this, Dr Cash?"

"Well, Mr Gould, a doctor or a nurse may destroy controlled drugs returned to him or her by a patient. This should, if at all possible, be witnessed. Liquid formulations should be mixed into cat litter. Tablets should be crushed and placed into a small quantity of hot, soapy water. Ampoules should be crushed with a pestle inside an empty plastic container. As soon as the ampoules are seen to be properly broken, they should then be mixed into hot soapy water and then cat litter. Houdini would never even get out of that mess."

"Finally, Dr Cash," Mr Gould went on, "Can I ask you about drugs which a G.P. may carry in his or her medical bag? What are the rules about these?"

"Well," said Johnny, "the bag must be lockable and keys must be kept separate and the bag must be in the doctor's possession. They must not even be kept in a locked car overnight. Sixty four years ago, in the case of Rag vs Wyles, the judge ruled that a locked car was not held to be safe custody for a doctor's bag."

Mr Gould looked astonished. Now the doctor was quoting legal judgements. Impressive, but he had to even the score as far as the *Readers Wives* jibe was concerned.

"Dr Cash, do you admit that you broke the rules by having some ampoules of diamorphine in your house in a supermarket carrier bag?"

"I do," said Johnny, "but as God is my judge, I cannot explain it. I have no idea who put them there. I am sorry, Mr Gould, but I have nothing further to add. I know all the rules but I seem to have inadvertently broken them."

"I have no further questions. Thank you, Dr Cash. Oh, just one more thing, Dr Cash. Your choice of reading matter. Stick to medical journals in future, Dr Cash."

Andrew Henriques got to his feet.

"Dr Cash, have you any idea where the ampoules of diamorphine came from?"

"Not at all, Sir," said Johnny. "I am being honest when I say that I have no idea. I am sorry."

"Dr Cash. How would you say you stand as a G.P? As a G.P. in Valley Mills?"

"I feel that I am respected. I have a traditional approach to the job and I provide, what I feel is, holistic family doctoring. I have done it for many years. I work long hours and I love the job. It is my life, to be honest."

"Thank you, Dr Cash. I have, for the Hearing, several letters from grateful patients which I would like to leave for the Panel to consider. Even more importantly, I have letters from four other doctors. One from Dr Moore and one from Dr Townsend. These two doctors are partners in Dr Cash's practice. I also have a letter from Dr Fiona Graham, who is now an established G.P. in Glasgow. Dr Graham was trained as a G.P. by Dr Cash. Finally, I have a letter from Dr Hussein, who is in charge of training young general practitioners in West Yorkshire. I have to say that all these letters and references are highly complementary. Dr Cash is a fine doctor and I wish to argue the fact that there is no proof whatever that Dr Cash has done anything wrong. No evidence whatever."

Mr Henriques sat down.

Professor Gillespie took over.

"We will have a break for thirty minutes while we consider our possible responses to the evidence placed before us. We meet again at eleven forty five."

Mr Henriques had a go at Johnny in the lobby.

"Jesus, Dr Cash, my job is hard enough without you deliberately aggravating our learned friend. *Readers Wives 40-49*. I ask you."

"I'm sorry. I was foolish."

"Don't worry about it any more, Dr Cash. It's done now. One more question, Dr Cash. Which supermarket do you say you bought it from?"

"Robinson's. Valley Mills. In the aisle between the canned soup and the soft drinks, I think." Johnny paused. "How do you think I've done, Mr Henriques?"

"It's hard to say, Dr Cash. These things do have a large air of unpredictability about them. The GMC is a frightened beast. I think you know what I mean by that. You were brilliant on the stand, notwithstanding your little outbursts."

"Thank you," said Johnny.

"When you make your statement in front of the panel simply do your best. Speak from the heart; that's what they want to hear. Just speak from the heart."

They had a cup of coffee. Johnny then went to phone Jenny Bradford.

"Hi Jenny, it's me again. I'm just wondering…"

"He's much worse, Doctor. Worse since we spoke earlier. I don't think he'll see the afternoon out."

"I'm devastated, Jenny. God willing though, I'll be along later. God willing, Jenny."

Johnny looked round to see Mr Henriques beckoning him to come back into the Hearing room.

"I'll have to go, Jenny. They're calling us back in."

"Okay, Doctor. Thank you again."

"Don't forget, Jenny. Give Joe my l…"

At that point the battery on Johnny's phone went dead.

They all went back in. Sylvia Rahman addressed the room.

"Dr Cash, we have considered the evidence that has been put before us. We have read the many letters and references which have been provided on your behalf. What we would like you to do is to tell us, in your own words, what you think has happened here and please also feel free to tell us anything which has not been mentioned here, either yesterday or today, which you feel may be relevant in helping us to come to a decision."

Johnny nervously got to his feet.

"I am grateful to the panel for listening to the arguments put forward by Mr Gould and by Mr Henriques. These two learned gentlemen have described what has happened, with regard to these two complaints."

Johnny continued, "The situation with regard to Orla is a nightmare for all parents and all doctors. It is a nightmare for parents because they are in a situation where they have a young child, a son or a daughter, who may die. And die they sometimes do, despite the best medical attention in the world. The same condition is a nightmare for doctors because at the very beginning of the illness there is nothing to go on, nothing to diagnose."

"Nothing to diagnose?" interjected Sheila Rahman.

"No, Mam, absolutely nothing at all. There are absolutely no features at the start of the illness which would make you say that this person is suffering from meningococcal disease. It is not as though they come in with a big letter M stamped on their forehead. A busy G.P. may see two thousand poorly children every year. And let us say that you have one child with this condition every five years. That is one person in ten thousand. One in ten thousand." Johnny paused for a minute. "I don't blame Mr Hillman for wanting to complain against me. I don't blame him at all. All I am saying is that from our side of the desk it's not as easy. Nine years training and it's still not easy. It's not easy at all, in fact."

"Thank you, Dr Cash," said Professor Gillespie. "Dr Cash, do you have anything else you wish to say to the Court before Mrs Rahman and I withdraw to make our decision? Briefly, of course, Dr Cash. Time is getting on, you know."

"Thank you, Professor Gillespie," said Johnny. "I would like to make just one more point in front of the Court, if I may."

"Please go on, Dr Cash," said Prof Gillespie, "but please if possible, keep it fairly brief."

"Thank you. What I would like to say to everybody," said Johnny, "is that since I turned eighteen and went to University, I have lived and breathed our National Health Service and the reason that I have done that is that I believe in what it does, and I believe in what it stands for, the health of the people of this great country of ours, healthcare which is available for sick people even if they cannot afford to pay for it. The 5th of July 1948, the day our National Health Service started, was a big event in the history of our country, an event which changed the lives of generations of men, women and children. Our health service was born in the ninth of nine consecutive years of great sacrifice and austerity born by the people of this country, a year which followed a winter of bitter cold and shortages of basic items such as, bread, meat and potatoes. I am proud to work in an organisation which now, 65 years later, is still based on the same principles put in place by the founding fathers. Since then, there has never been a time when a family with a sick child or an ill grandparent had to make a terrible choice, a choice between medicine or food." Johnny spoke more slowly. "Medicine or food? Just think of that. The reason I believe in what I do is that the people of this country have a right to have healthcare which is amongst the best available without having to make that awful choice."

Johnny paused for a drink of water.

"Dr Cash, please continue but please make it as brief as you can. Time is getting on you know," said Prof Gillespie.

"Thank you, Sir," Johnny continued. "This business of the morphine injections; I swear to God that I have no idea how they found their way into my house and I wish that I had asked the police to examine them for evidence of my fingerprints because they would have found none. None at all." He paused. "I just want to make one more point before you decide whatever sanction to apply to me."

"Dr Cash, please. Please do hurry," said Mrs Rahman, impatiently.

"What I want to say is that I have performed my duty to the people of Valley Mills for over fifteen years now, fifteen years I have enjoyed and fifteen years that I would never have swapped for anything. As God is my judge, I have never, ever run away from a difficult complex patient. I have always done my best and I have never, ever said to a patient, 'Go away, don't bother me, I can't help.' Never. When it's time to stand and be counted, I will be able to hold my head up and look anyone in the eye and say, 'Well, I'm not a professor or a Nobel Prize winner or anything fancy like that, but when my patients needed me I was there for them.'"

Johnny wiped away a tear.

"My friend, Joe Bradford, is this minute lying in his bed at home dying of cancer of the gullet and because I am here today I am in dereliction of my duty to that poor man. I promised him a year ago that I would be there with him and I have had to break my promise, just so that the authorities can be seen to be keeping a close watchful eye on the likes of me and other doctors and punishing us and getting our pictures in the newspaper if we have done something which the people in ivory towers don't like."

"Dr Cash, this is sounding as though it is becoming personal," said Prof Gillespie.

"Personal, I will give you personal, Professor Gillespie. It is personal for the families of doctors who kill themselves when they are subjected to malicious complaints, complaints from which there is precious little protection."

"Dr Cash, please finish off this little tirade of yours," said Professor Gillespie, looking annoyed.

"Professor Gillespie, my tirade has not even started," said Johnny.

"Dr Cash, if you do not shut up, I will call security and have you forcibly removed," said Professor Gillespie.

Johnny spoke quietly this time.

"Professor Gillespie, the newspaper article usually goes something like this: 'Dr Smith, a caring and respected family doctor, killed himself because he could not live with the stress of a complaint by a patient, a complaint which was later thrown out because it was unfounded. The driver of the train saw the doctor run out and lie on the track but there was nothing he could do. Three months later the coroner recorded that Dr Smith committed suicide.' Professor Gillespie, nobody looks after us when we are complained against. There is no system. Professor Gillespie, thank you for listening. That is my last word on the matter."

For a few long seconds, the Court remained silent. Everyone wondered who would speak next.

Professor Gillespie broke the silence.

"The Panel will now withdraw. Ladies and gentlemen, we shall reassemble in twenty minutes. Thank you."

Johnny felt unable to speak to anyone. He stretched his legs out in the street for five minutes. People were busily getting ready for Christmas; it would be Christmas day in less than ten hours and Johnny wondered how he would be spending it. After a few minutes he went back inside and nervously took his seat.

Professor Gillespie and Sylvia Rahman came back in and the professor started to deliver his verdict. His tone was businesslike and not particularly friendly.

"Dr Cash, we have listened to the arguments from both sides with regard to the two charges against you, namely that of misdiagnosing Orla Hillman and that of the unauthorised possession of four ampoules of diamorphine. The determination of the panel is as follows:

"We find that with regard to Orla Hillman, there is no case to answer. With regard to the ampoules of diamorphine, we find the case proven."

Johnny's face became ashen.

"Dr Cash, we also have been doing research by means of our contacts in and around Valley Mills and the surrounding district. We have heard that you are prone to use bad language, that you frequent public houses and have been spotted playing in a beat group in lower class establishments. Dr Cash, we feel that this sort of behaviour is not compatible with being a respected and trusted family doctor."

"A beat group," Johnny thought. "That was surely a term which disappeared fifty years ago."

"Dr Cash, in considering the matter of sanction, the Panel has borne in mind submissions made by Mr Gould and Mr Henriques. The panel has noted the GMC's Indicative Sanctions Guidance which states that the Panel must have the public interest at heart. The public interest can be defined as having three related but distinct strands, namely the protection of patients, the maintenance of public confidence in the profession and the declaring and upholding of proper standards of professional behaviour and conduct.

"Dr Cash, the reputation of the profession is more important than the fortunes of any individual member. Membership of a profession brings many benefits but that is part of the price.

"Dr Cash, a family doctor who worked not ten miles away from where we are now caused a lot of harm to many patients by means of inappropriate use of controlled drugs, such as morphine and diamorphine. For this reason, Dr Cash, and so as to send a clear message that we will not tolerate this sort of behaviour, we have decided to suspend your registration with immediate effect. Dr Daniel John Cash, the panel has decreed that you must carry out no work as a doctor for a period of six months from today. You may resume work on the 24th of June 2014. That concludes the Hearing. A merry Christmas to you all."

For at least the third time in less than 24 hours, the tears welled up in Johnny's eyes. The panel members rose to leave the room. Andrew Henriques came over to offer sympathy to Johnny. At this point, an usher entered the room.

"Can I speak to whoever is representing Dr Cash, please?" he said.

Mr Henriques raised his hand like an obedient schoolboy.

"Mr Henriques, I have a young lady outside who says that she may be a material witness."

Mr Henriques looked puzzled.

"Could everyone just hold on for one minute, please?"

Everyone sat down again and Mr Henriques followed the usher out of the room.

"Mr Henriques, this is Judy Carter. She says that she may be able to help Dr Cash," said the usher.

"Miss Carter. Thank you. I have heard a lot about you, Miss Carter," said Mr Henriques.

"Really?" said Judy

"Dr Cash says that you are gorgeous," he joked, "and he says that you are a brilliant singer."

"Thank you, Sir," said Judy.

"Now tell me what you have got for us, Miss Carter."

"I know who planted the drugs in Dr Cash's house."

"Honestly?"

"Yes, honestly," said Judy.

"Right," said Mr Henriques.

Mr Henriques went back into the room.

"I request a thirty minute adjournment. I have some important evidence to present."

"Mr Henriques, we are finished. The case is over," said Professor Gillespie.

Mr Henriques looked annoyed.

"It is Christmas, for Christ's sake. What the hell is the matter with you people?"

Mr Gould joined in.

"I have to get the next train back to London to be with my family."

Mr Henriques was by now blazing mad.

"To be with your family. Dr Cash doesn't even have a family. When you lot come to meet your maker and he asks you what you said to Dr Cash on Christmas Eve, 2013 and you tell your maker that you deliberately let Dr Cash down and ignored his cries for help and your maker then says, 'I don't really want your type of person in here,' then what will you say then? Look at him, for God's sake. This man has never harmed a living soul in his entire life and now you are turning your backs on him because you are hurrying home to your families; well I am ashamed of you. That's what I am. Ashamed of you. Ashamed of you both, in fact."

The two Panel members looked at each other and nodded.

"Thirty minutes," said Mrs Rahman.

"Thirty minutes," replied Mr Henriques.

He pointed to the door.

"Johnny, out here. Pronto."

The three of them huddled together on a seat in the corner.

"We have twenty nine and a half minutes," said Mr Henriques. "What have you got for us, Judy?"

"Well," she said, "I was hoovering Dr Cash's place yesterday and I moved the bed and there was an empty packet just under the bed. A packet of diamorphine ampoules. Five ampoules but there's just the packet. Nothing inside. And there's a patient's name on the outside of the packet. Percy Potts."

"Percy Potts?" said Mr Henriques.

"Yes. He's Martin Roberts' uncle and I heard through the grapevine that Mr Potts had cancer last year and that he was on one of those syringe driver thingys."

"That's right," said Johnny.

"Well, last year I was cleaning at your place and Martin Roberts banged on the front door and asked if the doctor was in because he had an old man with him and the man was unwell and he had found this man in the street and he wondered if the doctor was there and he asked if he could bring him in for a drink of water. So I said come and sit in the lounge and I went through to the back kitchen and got the man a drink of water. I remember it well. I had Hank Turner playing, really loud."

"Who was the old man?" asked Johnny.

"I don't know," said Judy. "I've never seen him before or since."

"Have you brought the packet with you, Miss Carter?" asked Mr Henriques.

"It's here, in my pocket," said Judy.

"Thank you," said Mr Henriques. "I'll just look to see if the batch numbers match each other."

He looked through his extensive folder of notes.

"Miss Carter, you are a genius as well as a good singer. They match! The number on the ampoules and on the packet is the same. They are both 2EZ491B." He paused. "Dr Cash and Judy Carter, we are half way there. If only we could get hold of Martin Roberts, I wonder how we could do that?"

"He's sitting in a pub one hundred yards away from here, as we speak."

"A hundred yards away? How do you know?" asked Johnny.

"I've seen him. He's in there now."

"Where?" asked both Mr Henriques and Johnny simultaneously.

"The Light Dragoon," said Judy.

"The Light Dragoon?" asked Johnny.

"It's a pub. Just round the corner."

"And he's there now?" asked Mr Henriques.

"Yes, well I hope he's still in there now. I walked past about five minutes ago and you could see him through the window."

"How come he's in there now?" asked Johnny.

"Well, one night in the Railway, in Valley Mills, he was as drunk as a lord and obnoxious with it. Kept saying that he wanted Johnny's number to thank him for looking after his uncle, Percy. So I got his mobile number from him. Told him Johnny would ring him. Then he kept saying that he was looking up an old flame, Belinda Blackburn, who works in London. He said he'd not seen her or spoken to her for years."

"So how did you get him to come to Manchester?" asked Mr Henriques.

"Well, last night, I got my friend in London to phone him from a phone box and she pretended to be Belinda Blackburn. She then said that she was coming up from London to Manchester, just for one day, on business and that she would be in the lounge of the Light Dragoon at three o'clock."

"Fantastic, Judy," said Johnny, looking at his watch. "Jesus, it's ten past. Let's get going."

With that the three of them went out on to the street and, as quickly as possible, ran round the corner. The Light Dragoon was twenty-five yards away. All three of them looked through the window and there he was, Martin Roberts, wearing a suit and a shirt and tie.

The three of them burst in through the door and Johnny made eye contact with Martin Roberts. Martin froze in his seat. He went pale and started sweating. The other drinkers stopped talking, anxious to see what would happen next.

Johnny bent over and grabbed Martin Roberts by his tie and hauled him out of his seat.

"You're coming with me, you fucking little piece of shit."

"But I'm waiting for Belinda Blackburn," said Martin.

"You've been set up," said Johnny.

At this point, the landlord raced round from behind the bar.

"Gentlemen, and you madam, if you don't mind," he said.

"It's okay. I'm a doctor," said Johnny.

They hauled Martin Roberts by his tie into the General Medical Council building and into the lobby outside the Hearing Room.

Mr Henriques paused for a second or two to think.

"Judy, how will you do in the witness box?" he asked.

"Fine, Sir. I'm sure I'll be fine. Honestly."

"Right then, you're on first. And don't let on that this little toad is here until you have to. Okay?"

"Fine," said Judy.

Mr Henriques walked Martin Roberts over to the usher.

"What can I do for you, Mr Henriques?" the usher asked.

"This man here. Martin Roberts. If he moves, breathes, speaks or shits in his pants, then shoot him. You understand?"

"Yes, Sir. We've not had anything this exciting since the five-in-a-bed case. 1997, I think it was."

They went back in and Mr Henriques addressed the Court.

"Ladies and gentlemen, I have a new witness who will explain how the ampoules of diamorphine were planted in Dr Cash's dwelling house, planted maliciously by a man called Martin Roberts."

Mr Henriques then described the chain of events about Martin Roberts and the old man pretending to be ill and then Judy finding the outside of the packet and the serial numbers matching.

Mr Morton Gould then got to his feet.

"Miss Carter, can you please describe yourself?"

"What do you mean, Sir? I don't understand."

"You don't understand what, may I ask?"

"I don't understand your question, Sir."

"Miss Carter, will you please describe yourself?"

At this point, Judy suddenly realised who this man was. He was, of course, the man who had defended Keith Saville, the boy who had raped her and made her pregnant.

"Of course, Sir. Would you like my height, my weight or the size of my tits, Mr Gould? If you really want me to describe myself then I will, Sir."

"Miss Carter, please refrain from being flippant with me. What I meant was what sort of work do you do?"

"I am a cleaner, Sir. At Valley Mills Health Centre and also occasionally at Dr Cash's house."

"A cleaner, eh, Miss Carter. Do you mind me asking what sort of University degree do you need to be a cleaner, may I ask?"

"None at all, Sir. Being a bright man like you purport to be, I thought you would have known that, Sir."

"Thank you for that bit of insight, Miss Carter. Now, Miss Carter, I want to ask you about the time you say that Martin Roberts called at Dr Cash's dwelling house. Can I put it to you that you are making this whole thing up and that your recall may not be, shall we say, very astute? After all, you are, as you just admitted, a lady with no formal qualifications. I put it to you that your recall of the events may not be as clear as the recall of a more intelligent person. What would you say to that one, Miss Carter?"

"Mr Gould, how intelligent would you say that you, yourself, are, if I may ask?" said Judy.

"I would say that I am very intelligent, Miss Carter."

"And how would you describe your recall, Mr Gould?"

"Miss Carter, will you please tell me where this is leading?"

"I will not, Mr Gould. I simply want you to answer my question about your powers of recall. That is, if you understand my question, Mr Gould."

"You impertinent little so and so," said Mr Gould.

"Just answer the question for me, Mr Gould. I would say that it is simple enough, to be honest."

"Miss Carter, I will answer your question but first please do not underestimate me, you understand? My powers of recall are excellent, Miss Carter, but I don't understand how relevant all this is."

"Don't understand how relevant, eh? Don't understand how relevant." Judy paused. "Let me test your recall, Mr Gould. Mr Gould, can you remember where you were on June 15th 1999?"

"I do not see the relevance of your question, Miss Carter."

"It is a simple question, Mr Gould. You say that my recall is not very good because I am stupid. That is what you infer, is it not?"

"No," said Mr Gould.

"Well, that is what you led me to believe, that you are smart and I am stupid. Is that not the case, Mr Gould?"

"Not at all, Miss Carter."

"Thank you, Mr Gould. Now where were you on June 15th 1999?"

"I have to say that I don't know, Miss Carter."

"You don't know?"

"No, I don't, Miss Carter."

"Do you remember a boy called Keith Saville, Mr Gould?"

"Not off the top of my head, Miss Carter."

"Let me refresh your memory then, Mr Gould. Keith Saville was a rapist who made a young girl pregnant. Do you remember him now, Mr Gould?"

"A little, Miss Carter."

"You defended Keith Saville and you said that that young girl led Keith Saville on and encouraged him to rape her. That's what you said, Mr Gould."

"And how do you know all this, Miss Carter?"

"Well, I was that young girl, Mr Gould. I was that young girl. And you were awful to me, Mr Gould."

The Court fell silent. It was then Mr Gould's chance to speak again. He looked subdued.

"Miss Carter, how are you so sure that Martin Roberts planted that diamorphine in Dr Cash's house? For all we know, you could be making all this up simply to protect your boss."

"Because Mr Roberts told me that he did, Sir."

"And where, pray, do you think that Martin Roberts is now, late afternoon on Christmas Eve, Miss Carter. I would love to speak to him so that I can show this story of yours up to be a tissue of lies from start to finish. Where is he now, Miss Carter?"

"He is out there, sitting in the lobby, Mr Gould. I can have him in here in less than sixty seconds, Mr Gould."

"I have no further questions, Miss Carter."

Mr Gould looked dejected.

Mr Henriques left the room and, thirty seconds later, returned with Martin Roberts. Mr Roberts took the witness stand. Mr Henriques started the questioning.

"Mr Roberts, did you, in 2012, secretly plant some ampoules of diamorphine in Dr Cash's dwelling house?"

"I did, Sir, I am ashamed to say."

"Mr Roberts, your actions have caused immense distress to poor Dr Cash here."

Mr Henriques half turned towards Johnny.

"Dr Cash has gone through hell for the last twelve months. Mr Roberts, you cannot even begin to imagine the pressures which befall a doctor under investigation."

He turned back towards Martin Roberts.

"Mr Roberts, I would like you, for the benefit of this Hearing in general and for the benefit of Dr Cash in particular, to describe what you did and why you did it. I want a proper explanation, Mr Roberts."

Martin Roberts started to speak. Johnny listened for a hint of contrition in his voice but could not really find one.

"The four ampoules of diamorphine belonged to my Uncle Percy. Percy Potts. He died of cancer last year. Dr Cash and his team looked after him at home and he died peacefully and I will always be grateful for that. The district nurse was loading Uncle Percy's syringe driver daily. When Uncle Percy died, half way through an episode of 'Coronation Street', there were four ampoules left over. The district nurse was just about to destroy them—mix them into some cat litter, I think—I was to be the official witness—when her emergency bleep went off. Someone somewhere was in distress. The nurse asked me to destroy the ampoules and I promised that I would."

"Go on, Mr Roberts," said Mr Henriques.

Everyone watched him intently.

"I thought I was being smart. I just held on to them."

"You are aware that that is illegal, Mr Roberts?" said Professor Gillespie.

"Yes, Sir. I am sorry."

"The Police might extend their enquiry in your direction, Mr Roberts. I will take it upon myself to recommend that they do just that," said Professor Gillespie.

Martin Roberts continued, "One night in the Railway, a pub in Valley Mills, I was talking to Clive Hillman. Clive told me that Dr Cash here had misdiagnosed his daughter, Orla. That she had nearly died due to his gross negligence. Two years old, she was. Then I told Mr Hillman that I had seen something embarrassing in his medical notes."

"How, pray, did you manage to do that, Mr Roberts?" asked Mr Henriques.

"It was last year. I was in to see Dr Cash. Clive had had the appointment before mine. When it was my turn Dr Cash called me in and he beckoned me to sit down. Anyway, at that exact minute, an old lady collapsed in the reception. They called for Dr Cash and he went dashing out. Whilst I was in his room alone, I noticed that Clive Hillman's notes were still on Dr Cash's computer screen. Something about impotence. A prescription for some Dykohard tablets, I think."

Mr Henriques interrupted.

"Could this be true, Dr Cash?"

"I think so, Sir. It all happened so quickly. I thought that the old lady might die if I didn't see to her straight away."

"Fair enough, Dr Cash. That really shouldn't happen but I am sure that we can understand it in the circumstances."

He paused for a second time.

"Mr Roberts, please continue your narrative."

"Anyway, I told Clive Hillman what I had seen and he was livid. Beyond livid, if you ask me. I have never seen anyone as mad, ever. He was ready to boil over. So we hatched our little plan."

"What happened then, Mr Roberts?" asked Mr Henriques.

"Well, Clive Hillman wanted retribution. I told him that I may be able to help. I told him that I had the injections of morphine and we decided that I would plant them in his house. I knew which day Judy Carter here did his cleaning so I bribed an old man to pretend to be ill. Twenty quid I gave him. We turned up at the doctor's front door when we knew that Judy would be there and we hoodwinked her into getting the old man a drink of water. While she was in the kitchen I put the ampoules in the carrier bag in Dr Cash's bedroom. She didn't hear me because she had some music playing really loud. 'Hank Turner, the Gas Station Hero', I think it was. I quickly took the ampoules out of the packet but forgot the packet itself. I asked Judy not to say we had been because it would be like taking advantage."

"Taking advantage? For God's sake, Mr Roberts," said Mr Henriques.

"Anyway, Clive Hillman then contacted the Police and told them that Dr Cash was selling left-over morphine from his house."

"And why would Mr Hillman want to do all this, Mr Roberts? What was his motivation?" asked Mr Henriques.

"He felt that if he couldn't get Dr Cash one way then he would get him the other. 'One way or the other, we'll get him.' That's what Clive Hillman said."

"Is there anything of this story left to tell, Mr Roberts?" asked Mr Henriques.

"Not very much, really."

"Mr Roberts, what was your own personal motivation in this case? What drove you to do it?"

"Two things," said Martin Roberts. "The first one was money. Clive really knows how to motivate a person. He said that if Dr Cash simply received a warning from the General Medical Council then he would give me one hundred pounds. Cash. Sorry about that, Dr Cash. In notes, I meant. One hundred pounds in notes. Then he said that if Dr Cash got suspended then I would get one thousand pounds, and then he said that if Dr Cash got struck off the medical register permanently, forever, then I would get ten thousand pounds."

"Ten thousand pounds?" asked Mr Henriques.

"Ten thousand pounds, Sir; that is correct. A lot of money."

"And what was the other one, Mr Roberts? What was the second thing that motivated you, apart from money?"

"A few years ago Dr Cash and I had a disagreement."

"A disagreement? About what?"

"We fell out over a girl. We both wanted to take her out. Anyway, she preferred Dr Cash over me."

"I'm not surprised, Mr Roberts, to be honest," said Mr Henriques.

"Nice girl she was," said Martin Roberts. "Belinda Blackburn she was called. I was very cut up about it. Anyway, it didn't make a massive difference in the long run because a few months later she moved to London. She was lovely, mind you."

Mr Henriques sat down. It was now Professor Gillespie's chance to speak.

"Mr Roberts, I am sure that you will be pleased to learn that you are not going to make a red cent out of this little debacle. Furthermore, I feel that it is much more likely than not that you will receive a visit from the police early in the New Year."

He stopped for a drink of water and then resumed.

"Dr Cash, do you ever watch Cowboy films, westerns?"

Johnny looked puzzled.

"I do, Sir. I love them. My favourite is 'High Noon' where Gary Cooper deals with the baddies. It has everything—love, greed, betrayal. A bit like here, Sir, but the mortality rate is different."

"Well, Dr Cash," said Professor Gillespie, "I am going to be a bit like one of those sheriffs in a cowboy film, you know, where someone has done something wrong but it's not quite bad enough to put them in jail for it."

"Yes, Sir," said Johnny.

"Dr Cash, we don't want to see you round these parts again. Ever, Dr Cash. Dr Cash, all charges brought against you by the General Medical Council have been dealt with. You have no case to answer for either of these charges and you are free to leave this building without any official stain on your character. However, Dr Cash, I have to say that I have a niggling uneasy feeling about you. I worry about what you get up to. Therefore, Dr Cash, I want you to pretend that I am a sheriff in a Western." He paused for a second. "Dr Cash, I don't ever want to see you round this neck of the woods again, ever. Dr Cash, we are running you out of town. Don't ever get yourself reported to the General Medical Council again, Dr Cash, because the penalties are likely to be severe. Do you understand me?"

"Thank you, Sir. I do," Johnny said.

"That concludes the Hearing," said Professor Gillespie. "Merry Christmas, everybody."

That was it. Finished.

Johnny looked at his watch. It was five o'clock. He shook Mr Henriques' hand and thanked him.

"You don't need to thank me, Dr Cash," said Mr Henriques. "It's Judy Carter here who did all the real work. You were great, Miss Carter."

"Thank you, Sir," said Judy.

Johnny and Judy put their coats on and set off to leave.

"You were brilliant, just brilliant," said Johnny.

On the way out they passed Martin Roberts standing in the lobby. Johnny went over to whisper in his ear.

"I'll sort you out later, twat face," he said.

"Threatening patients now, are we?" said Martin. "I could just report you to the GMC, you know. In fact, to save the price of a stamp, I could do it right now."

"Martin, it wasn't a threat. Believe me," said Johnny.

Johnny and Judy set off to find Judy's car. It was dark and a fine drizzle was falling and the Christmas Eve traffic was leaving Manchester very slowly. Cars were filled with people driving home from work or with families doing last minute Christmas shopping.

Judy's car was a 10-year-old Peugeot 205, painted bright purple with racing stripes and alloy wheels; she had parked it three streets away in a small car park. They got in and headed off in the direction of Valley Mills, a drive that would normally take about an hour and twenty minutes. Christmas Eve traffic would add at least a few more minutes to the journey. The Peugeot rattled along the busy roads.

"Judy, I can never thank you enough for what you did today," said Johnny. "I was sure I was going to be suspended… in fact I was, for six months, just before you arrived. You're an absolute star. Thank you again."

"It was as close as that, eh? Well, you know, Johnny, there were two people looking after you today, him or her up there and me down here."

Johnny then asked Judy if he could borrow her phone to call Jenny Bradford.

"Joe Bradford is dying, poor man," said Johnny. "I promised his wife that I'd visit today if I was acquitted. If he's still alive, that is."

"He's as poorly as that, do you think?"

"Yes, I'm sure. At breakfast time today his wife said that he wouldn't last the day out."

"I think I've only enough credit in my phone for about half a minute, Johnny. Sorry about that. It's pay-as-you-go and I forgot to top it up yesterday. Try it anyway."

Johnny dialled the number. Whatever Jenny Bradford was going to tell him he was dreading it.

"Jenny. It's Dr Cash. I was just wondering…"

"He's bad, Doctor, real bad. Sally O'Donnell has just been and she says he'll only last another hour… I hope you don't mind me asking, Doctor, but how did you get on?"

"Thanks for asking, Jenny. I've been…"

And at that point Judy Carter's phone went dead. Completely silent.

"You're right about the phone, Judy. Thank you anyway."

"How is Joe Bradford doing?"

"He's bad, Judy. Hopefully we'll be there in an hour, I promised him, you know."

"We'll do our best."

They drove on and headed out into the hilly country outside of Manchester. The fine drizzle turned into small snowflakes.

"You can drop me off at Joe Bradford's and then, God willing, I'll see you later at the party. Do you still feel up to going, Judy?"

"Yes. It's important that we do. Firstly, you have something to celebrate and secondly, we promised that we would entertain the troops. We'll manage one song, Johnny, at the very least."

"Judy, what the hell would I do without you? I think we could have a change. What about Rodgers and Hammerstein? What would you say?"

"Kind of apt, I think, Johnny."

"I just hope that we make it to Joe's house in time."

With that they headed northwards into the dark night, the ancient windscreen wipers deflecting the snowflakes.

Joe Bradford was already in the last hour of his life on this earth. The two children were downstairs and Jenny sat at the bedside, holding his hand. He was slightly delirious but not in pain. He was pale and breathless and perspiring.

"Do you think Johnny will be allowed to come and see me, Jenny? Did he get acquitted?"

"I hope so, Joe. You know that he promised you."

"But they might have fired him or suspended him. You know what those people are like."

"He'll be here, Joe. Just you wait and see."

"But he might not, Jenny. They might have stopped him."

At this point Joe Bradford started crying.

"I just want to see him, Jenny. I just want to see him. Just once more. That's all I ask." He paused for a minute, "Jenny, I just want to tell you how much I love you. I always have and I always will. Always."

"Joe Bradford, you are such a charmer. I have always loved you, too, and I will love you for the rest of my days."

Joe dozed for a couple of minutes and then opened his eyes again.

"How long was I asleep?" he asked.

"A couple of minutes, that's all."

"Are the children all right downstairs?"

"Yeh, they are fine. I just went down to see them."

"Any sign of Johnny?"

"Not yet, Joe, but he won't be long now. I'm sure of it."

Joe dozed for about five minutes and woke up again.

"I haven't got long, have I Jenny?"

"Joe, you shouldn't think like that."

"Jenny, I can feel it. I can feel my life drifting away from me."

Jenny mopped his brow and gave him a sip of water.

"Thank you, Jenny. That tasted like nectar."

He dozed for another minute and then opened his eyes again.

"Jenny, I think I just heard a car door outside. Just have a look out of the window, will you?"

Jenny parted the curtains. A purple Peugeot 205 had stopped outside the house and walking up the front path, dodging the snowflakes, was Dr Cash.

"Joe, Johnny's here. He's come to see you."

The two children opened the front door.

"Hello, Dr Cash," they said, "thank you for coming. Dad will be so pleased to see you. Mum's upstairs with him."

Johnny raced up the stairs. Jenny met him on the landing.

"Thank you for coming, Dr Cash. Joe has been asking for you all day."

"Anytime, Jenny."

"Who brought you?"

"Judy Carter."

"If she's waiting I'll get the children to get her to come in. We can't leave her out there on a night like this."

"She'll be delighted."

"How did you get on, Doctor? With the authorities, I mean?"

"Acquitted. No case to answer on either charge."

"Thank God."

"Thank God, indeed. And thank Judy Carter also. I'll tell you the whole story another time. I'd better go in and see Joe. Thanks Jenny."

Johnny went into the bedroom. Joe looked very, very frail. He was pale and sweating.

"Johnny. Thank you." He stopped to get his breath back. "How did you get on?"

"Acquitted. Not guilty. It's all over, Joe. All sorted."

"Thank God, Johnny."

"How are you, my old friend?"

"I'm okay, Johnny. I'm comfortable and my family are in the house with me. I can't ask for more, Johnny."

"It's so good to see you," Johnny said. "For a minute or two I was beginning to doubt…"

"Don't even think about it, Johnny. You mustn't. It's over and it's all behind you. You're a fine doctor, Johnny, and you are going to serve the people of this town for another twenty years. Not all of them deserve you but I guess that they are stuck with you."

He smiled and wiped away a tear at the same time.

"Dr Cash, they couldn't ask for anybody better."

"Joe Bradford, you are just an old charmer. That's what you are. An old charmer."

Jenny came back into the room. Johnny said that he would go downstairs to have a chat with the children and with Judy. They had a cup of tea together.

While the others were downstairs, Joe held Jenny's hand and told her again how much he loved her. They then just thought their own thoughts in silence. Joe kept dozing and waking again. The morphine kept him comfortable and calm. He thought about things he could remember over the last 52 years; his memories of childhood in this same house, starting school, carrying Johnny above the waves, the Bay City Rollers record, starting work, the day he met Jenny McBride and the day he married her, then the birth of their children and watching them grow up into fine adults. Nice, honest, hard-working young people.

"Jenny, will you ask Johnny to come back in? You stay as well."

Jenny went down and brought Johnny back upstairs and they sat with him, one of them on each side of the bed. The room was fairly dark and the snow was falling more heavily outside.

"Jenny, thank you for everything. If only I could find words to say what I want to say but I can't, Jenny. But you know what I want to say, don't you, Jenny?"

"I do, Joe, I do. You know I do."

"Thanks, Jenny."

He dozed for a couple of minutes and then opened his eyes again.

"Do you remember the island, Johnny?"

"I do, Joe."

"Well, I got you through that. And you got me through this." He paused for a few seconds. "I knew they'd acquit you, Johnny. I knew they would."

"Thank you, Joe."

"So we're all all right now. I'm safe and you're back in business, Johnny. And you're all right, Jenny."

She nodded.

Joe Bradford then had one last look at Johnny and then he looked deeply into his eyes and then he said, "We made it, Johnny, we made it." He then looked at Jenny. "And you, too, Jenny, we made it. Thanks for everything."

And then, in the same bedroom of the same house in which he had been born, fifty two years earlier, and just a little over one year and one month after becoming ill, and surrounded by his loving family, he closed his eyes, stopped breathing and, ever so peacefully, he died.

They went downstairs and talked about all sorts of things, the sort of things that people talk about when somebody has just died, like who should they ring first, what about the death certificate, and the syringe driver and would Noel Buckden be open on Christmas Eve.

The children shook hands with Johnny and with Judy and Johnny and Judy then said that they'd better be getting going. Jenny followed them to the front door and before they left she took Johnny's hand.

"You were brilliant, Doctor. Thank you. Just knowing that you were there made all the difference. And we knew that you would keep your promise. We knew all along." She paused for a second. "Merry Christmas. Merry Christmas to both of you."

With that, Judy and Johnny headed off through the snow. Johnny then realised that many times in his career he could recall moments when you go from a state of despair and sadness to a state of happiness, partly because that's exactly how you felt and partly because it's what the patient expected. You had to be able to go from a depressed patient to a patient who has just won a million on the lottery, to telling a patient that they have cancer and you have to be able to do things like that several times every hour.

Johnny had been genuinely, unequivocally upset about Joe Bradford's illness and his death but now it was still Christmas Eve and it was party time.

Chapter 30

"**JUDY, DROP ME AT MY HOUSE** and I'll get changed and get a taxi and I'll see you at the Steamer. About nine. And thank you."

"You're on."

Johnny phoned for a taxi for a quarter to nine and started getting changed. He was putting his clean socks on when the phone rang. It was Angela on her mobile.

"Johnny, we were just wondering…"

"Acquitted on all counts, Angela. No case to answer. Judy Carter saved the day."

"That's fantastic! And how *are* you?"

She accentuated the 'are.'

"I'm all right, thank you. How's the party?"

"Just getting going. How are you getting here?"

"Taxi."

"Brilliant. We'll see you soon."

Johnny met Judy in the car park bang on nine o'clock. Judy looked beautiful.

Inside, the band was playing 'Is this the way to Amarillo' and the party sounded as though it was in full swing.

At the end of the song, Judy and Johnny entered the room as unobtrusively as they could. As soon as they were spotted all of the Health Centre crowd rose to their feet and gave Judy and Johnny the loudest standing ovation that anyone could ever recall. This standing and clapping became infectious and the people from Valley Hauliers, on the next table, stood up and joined in. Gerry Brogan, the managing director, said to his wife that whoever these two people are, they must have done something very special.

Johnny and Judy downed a couple of drinks and shook hands with all of their party.

The band sang 'I wish it could be Christmas everyday' and at the end of the song, Susan went up to the stage and whispered in the lead guitarist's ear and he then nodded.

He went back up to the microphone.

"Ladies and gentlemen, we have two special guests here tonight and they are going to do a song for you. Just one and it's very special. Please folks, welcome Judy and Johnny.

The applause started again and it took a minute to die down. Johnny took the microphone.

"Just one song, folks, and I dedicate it to Joe Bradford, who died a couple of hours ago. And for Jenny Bradford also, I think."

Judy then took over.

"I think we also have to say that this song is for Johnny. Give him a big round of applause, everybody."

When the clapping subsided, the two singers and the band all looked at each other for a second and then they broke into 'You'll never walk alone' and it was just perfect.

Chapter 31

JOHNNY AND THE TEAM soon got back to work after Christmas. The busy period between Christmas and New Year brought lots of illness to the valley and it was difficult doing house calls; the wintry weather had made driving along some of the smaller roads difficult.

Johnny completed Joe Bradford's death certificate, saying that his friend had died from Carcinomatosis secondary to Carcinoma of the Oesophagus. He found that he missed visiting his friend and he always remembered that without Joe's brilliant help 38 years earlier things would have turned out very differently.

On 5th January 2014, Johnny received a nice letter from Jenny Bradford which read something like this:

2nd January 2014

Dear Dr Cash

I wish to thank you, very sincerely, for looking after Joe so well over the last year and a bit. We could not have got through it without the help from your wonderful team and we will always be grateful to you for the excellent care provided.

Your diagnosis was correct and whilst you were unable to cure him, you did everything within your power to help him to bear his illness with courage and fortitude and without pain. You anticipated our needs even before we were aware of them ourselves and you never showed even the slightest sign that we would be abandoned simply because Joe could not be "cured" by modern medicine. I would go so far as saying that what was provided was modern medicine at its very best and I feel privileged to have witnessed it myself. Special thanks are due to Sally O'Donnell and the other nurses. Also your reception staff who were always pleasant and always helpful and who always treated us as though we were royalty. We are ordinary folks and what we got was NHS care at its best which allowed Joe to die with great dignity in the place of his choosing, the same bedroom in the same house in which he was born. This was, surely, cradle-to-grave care provided in abundance.

I hope that you, Dr Cash, have recovered from your ordeal. I didn't say anything to Joe (you asked me not to as not to upset Joe) but he realised that something was wrong and on a couple of occasions he asked me if I knew anything but I always said no and it's just that doctors work long hours and they get anxious and tired if they care a lot about their patients. We had every confidence that the GMC would deal with your case in a sensible fashion and we knew that you would do everything in your power to keep your promise to visit Joe right through to the very end. When I told Joe, on Christmas Eve, that it was you walking up our front path through the snow to visit him, he was totally grateful for the fact that you were coming to see him again. You comforted him, yet again, and he died knowing that everything that could have been done for him was done and that it was done in a professional and, at the same time, friendly manner.

Joe didn't talk much about his illness; I think it must be the case that some people simply prefer to keep their thoughts to themselves. I wish that he had talked more than he did because I never knew fully how he felt about his illness but then I realised that non-verbal communication is just as important. I was privileged to have known him for 28 years.

I am not sure what the future holds for me but my family, friends and work colleagues have been wonderful and I am sure that I will, eventually more or less, adjust to life without Joe, although the period of adjustment will be painful.

I will never forget the help and the care given by you and your team to Joe. You are all worth your weight in gold. Please pass on my grateful thanks and may God bless you all.

Yours sincerely
Jenny (Bradford)

Johnny maintained his friendship with Kate by means of the quiz in the Railway on a Thursday evening. In the middle of January she had a big suggestion to put to him: in July, her first cousin was getting married and she had had an invitation to attend the wedding.

What is more, the invitation said Kate plus friend or partner, the wedding was in Connecticut and what would Johnny think to making a full week of it, with maybe four nights in Manhattan first? Johnny had never been to New York before and it took him all of two milliseconds to agree to go. Kate had a friend on the lower East Side who could accommodate them both.

"There is one little bonus for you, Johnny," Kate said the following Thursday Night. "You might get to meet President MacDonald. It depends on those Secret Service guys in dark glasses. I have taken the liberty of giving them your name and address and they will send you a form to fill in."

"What will it say?" asked Johnny.

"Any misdemeanours or any plans to overthrow the government?"

"What about surviving the General Medical Council?"

"Anyone who can survive them qualifies for an interview to become a CIA operative."

"I think I'll stick with what I'm doing, thanks."

Over the next few weeks, they booked flights MAN to JFK and looked forward to the trip.

Judy Carter applied to go on 'England's Got Talent'. They would be auditioning in Manchester before Easter and she felt she would be in with a chance of going on TV: Nine million viewers would do her career no harm at all.

July came around. Kate and Johnny loved New York. Kate's friend had asked how many bedrooms would be required and she said, "Well, two to start with and then I'll see if I can work on him a little bit."

So after four days of the Empire State Building and Ellis Island and Central Park they got the train up to Hartford in Connecticut. They had booked adjacent rooms in the Marriot Downtown where the wedding reception would take place. It was a lovely day and the three hundred and sixteen guests had a wonderful time. Johnny wondered how much it must all have cost but whatever it was it was worth it. The Secret Service had searched him on arrival and all the doors and exits were guarded by men and women in dark glasses.

Johnny had had about four glasses of wine and four bottles of Budweiser and was soaking up the atmosphere. He closed his eyes to listen to a particularly nice song the band was playing and, maybe, drifted off for a couple of seconds to be woken by Kate gently tapping on his shoulder.

"Johnny, someone over there wants to talk to you."

"Who, Kate?"

"Come over here and find out."

Kate then led him over to meet President MacDonald. They shook hands and President MacDonald told Johnny that Kate had said a lot about him.

"What's your first name, Dr Cash?"

It's Daniel, Mam, but everybody calls me Johnny, just like the great man himself."

"Johnny, just call me Maddy," said the President. "I don't like any of this official 'Mam' business. It's great to get a day away from official duties." She paused. "I'll tell you a story about Johnny Cash. It's a long story but I'll tell you anyway. My great grandmother came over here from Ireland—somewhere near the border, Fermanagh and Monaghan. Came over here with the clothes she stood up in. Anyway, after ten years, she bore my grandmother—Granny was born in 1919. She grew up and in 1953 she opened this small grocery store. Gloucester, Massachusetts; a fantastic town, real people lived there. Anyway, her customers knew if the great Johnny Cash was playing anywhere in the state of Massachusetts then Granny would get tickets and close the shop early. Midday at the latest. Her customers knew that if the man in black was singing then Granny would be there; they'd stock up on groceries the night before." She paused for a second or two. "Dr Cash, do you sing, by any chance?"

"Well, Mam, I do but…"

"None of this 'Mam' crap. I said just call me Maddy."

"Okay Maddy, I do sing but…"

"But my but, Johnny. I'll have a word with the band and you can do a number or two with them later."

"Okay. If I must."

"Johnny, you must. You can see how I run this great country of ours, can't you?" she smiled.

"Yes, Maddy."

"Do you know who my own favourite singer was, Johnny?"

"No, Maddy."

"Well, my own favourite singer was Hank Turner, the Gas Station Hero. Died in London a few years ago. I heard that the woman who was with him, Martha Brodie, she was my auntie's second cousin, on my Dad's side. From Newcastle, I think."

"Really. It is a small world," said Johnny.

"Johnny, you are right. It *is* a very small world. Very small. I'll tell you what I liked about Hank Turner. Two things. First, he was a brilliant musician and second, he never forgot the people who put him where he was. He never, ever forgot about the ordinary guy in the street. The man who swept his gas station forecourt meant just as much to him as the bigwigs in Nashville or the Hollywood crowd. That's what impressed me about him more than anything else he ever did."

"That's great," said Johnny.

"Now, Dr Cash, I want to talk business for thirty seconds. Is that okay?"

"Sure, Maddy. Fire away."

"Is it true that in your country if someone is sick and they need a doctor then they don't have to pay?"

"That's right, Maddy. Rich or poor, makes no difference."

"Right, Johnny. The day after Labor Day I want you in my office. Book a week's vacation and come over and tell me all you know. You'll find me easily enough. It's a big white building. Pennsylvania Avenue. Nine o'clock sharp. And bring Kate with you."

"Yes, Mam."

"Johnny, this is your final warning."

"Okay, Maddy."

"See you in September—Nine o'clock sharp."

"Yes, Maddy."

"Right. You're on stage next."

"Yes, Maddy."

The song went down very well. Seven weeks later, Johnny and Kate spent a day in the White House. The President paid for the airline tickets and asked Johnny if a fee of ten thousand dollars would be acceptable payment for his thoughts and ideas on healthcare. Maddy MacDonald knew, however, that the real struggle would be on Capitol Hill.

Johnny and Kate had three nights in Washington D.C. Kate flew to Seattle for five nights to see her family. The following week they were both back in the Railway on the Thursday night. The quiz started at twenty five past nine and their team came second. They blamed their lacklustre performance on delayed jet lag; the following week they won handsomely.

That just about wraps up this account of the lives of some of the good folks of Valley Mills, a town which will still be there in a thousand years, God willing, aided and abetted by the hard work and good nature of its citizens. So, let's find out what happened to the other people in this story.

Al Hussein got further, hard earned promotion and became Regional Director of General Practice Training.

Susan became Practice Manager and Emma settled in and became a valued member of the Health Centre team before marrying three years later and having her first baby, a beautiful eight-pounds boy called William.

Fiona Graham continued working as a G.P. in Glasgow. She enjoyed the work and was loved and respected by her patients in equal measure.

Martin Roberts was interviewed under caution by the Police with regard to the ampoules of diamorphine. At the end of the interview, the Inspector told him that he was a free man but that if they could jail a person for simply being a prick then he would get ten years with no chance of remission.

Clive Hillman's business folded leaving large debts to all and sundry. The creditors received 1.1% of what they were owed.

Karen Hillman then divorced Clive on the grounds of cruelty and within nine months of the divorce she married a builder called Roger Crellin who possessed manicured hands and a Ferrari. He bought her a BMW convertible for a wedding present and two weeks after the honeymoon beat her to within an inch of her life when she refused his advances.

Jenny Bradford continued working at Robinson's and two years after Joe's death she met Philip Hothersall, a widowed science teacher and a romance developed. Both sets of children liked both Jenny and Philip and they continued seeing each other regularly.

Judy Carter continued her daytime jobs and also kept touring at weekends with Nashville Express. Johnny advised her to apply to go on the TV show, 'England's Got Talent.' Her performances were stunning and six weeks later she made it through to the final. Her rendition of 'Don't it make my brown eyes blue' had the nation in raptures and she came first. A recording contract followed and her debut album, released three months later, was entitled 'Under a Northern Sky.' It stayed at number one for five weeks. The following year Judy embarked on a North American tour doing twenty-two concerts in four weeks. She started in Halifax, Nova Scotia and the eighth concert was on Long Island. The following day she met Dean again; she had not seen him for many years and the two of them got on well. He promised to visit her in England the following year.

Valley Health Centre continued to serve its patients with friendly professionalism and everyone who worked there felt proud to be part of a brilliant team who made a massive contribution to the health of the people of the town.

So, dear reader, next time you go to the doctor's, have a good look at the faces of the people who work there. Then have a look behind the faces. You never know; they may have a story to tell. Honestly!

CPSIA information can be obtained
at www.ICGtesting.com
Printed in the USA
BVHW030227300121
599005BV00010B/685